The Ride Along

By

Michael & William Henry

The Ride Along

Copyright 2011 by: Michael Henry and William Henry
Cover Design by: Laura Shinn
Formatted by: Laura Shinn
Author photography by: T.G. McCary
ISBN-13: 978-1466242432
ISBN-10: 1466242434

Other books available by these authors:
Three Bad Years – *A Willie Mitchell Banks Novel*
   (Michael Henry)
At Random – *A Willie Mitchell Banks Novel*
   (Michael Henry)
Veterano (William Henry)

All Rights Reserved—This book is licensed for your personal enjoyment only. No part of this publication can be reproduced or transmitted in any form or by any means, electronic, mechanical, or otherwise, without written permission from Michael Henry.

The Ride Along is a work of fiction. Names, characters, places and incidents are either used fictitiously or are products of the author's imagination. Any resemblance to actual events, locales, or persons, living or dead, is entirely coincidental.

Dedication:

To Carl and Eula, Bill and Ann. They started it all.

Acknowledgments

Thanks to Tom Murchison and David Fite, both insightful readers, for comments and suggestions. Thanks to Debby Habig for New Orleans assistance. Thanks to readers Eddie Ahrens and Bernard and Lucianne Wood for encouragement and comments. Thanks to booksellers Mary Emrick and J. Michael Kenny for their help and support.

Many thanks to my agent Bob Diforio for his hard work on my behalf.

Most of all, thanks to all the readers of the first two novels, THREE BAD YEARS and AT RANDOM for their interest in Willie Mitchell and Jake Banks, and David Dunne. It means a lot.

Blurb

Assistant U.S. Attorney Jake Banks gets re-assigned to New Orleans to follow his ex-girl friend, FBI Special Agent Kitty Douglas, working on a federal task force to stop the flood of assault weapons from the Port of New Orleans to drug cartels in Mexico. Riding in an NOPD patrol car, Jake encounters Cuban-born Ignacio Torres, a Santeria priest and sorcerer, mystical leader of Los Cuervos, a cult-like gang smuggling thousands of weapons out of the port.

Torres kills the two cops hosting Jake's ride along, but mysteriously allows Jake to walk away. Jake works with NOPD detectives and Kitty's FBI task force to locate Torres and his drug-smuggling cult, but Los Cuervos and the sorcerer become the hunters, pursuing Jake and Kitty on the gritty streets of N.O.

Kitty survives a horrendous assault by Los Cuervos, and Jake disappears. His father, Mississippi District Attorney Willie Mitchell Banks, and David Dunne, Jake's mentor and leader of the covert Domestic Operations Group (DOGs), arrive in N.O. They search the dark corners of the French Quarter to find Los Cuervos and the sorcerer Torres, but whether they can save Jake is not resolved until the thrilling final pages of THE RIDE ALONG.

To view more of Michael & William Henry's work, visit:
http://henryandhenrybooks.com

Chapter One

Jacob Pinckney Banks walked away from the cops congregated behind the rundown apartment houses on Philip Street on the river side of Magazine, four blocks north of Tchoupitoulas. He wanted to sneak a look at the taggers' work in the grimy alley between the wood-framed apartments.

His arm hurt like hell. The pain medication the medic gave him twelve hours earlier at the combat training camp in Virginia had worn off. It's the price you pay for practicing with real knives—sometimes you get cut.

Jake studied the graffiti on the dirty, deteriorating wooden siding in the alley. The symbols were freshly sprayed by the pee-wee gangster in the back seat of one of the two NOPD cruisers stopped between the apartments.

He focused on the Hispanic kid in custody so he wouldn't think about how his arm ached and itched. The pee-wee leaned his shaved head against the car window. No more than eleven or twelve, he was being used by gangsters whom the kid considered his family.

The pee-wee never had a chance.

Jake walked back through the alley toward the cops.

Dominguez waved to Jake. "Let's go, Banks."

Byrne and Dominguez were the two cops hosting Jake's first NOPD "ride along." FBI Special Agent Kitty Douglas, now assigned to the New Orleans office near the Lakefront Airport and UNO, arranged it for Jake. It was nice of Kitty because they were no longer a couple. Jake and Special Agent Kitty had been hot and heavy when they'd worked together in Jackson, Mississippi, where Jake spent his first year out of Ole Miss law school as an assistant United States attorney for the Southern District of Mississippi.

Jake could no longer stomach working for the smarmy academic Leopold Whitman, U.S. Attorney for the Southern District of Mississippi in Jackson, especially after the way Whitman treated Jake's father, District Attorney Willie Mitchell Banks.

David Dunne pulled some strings and had Jake appointed an assistant U.S. attorney for the Eastern District of Louisiana. Jake wanted New Orleans for two reasons. It was as far away as Jake felt he could be while his father was recovering from an attempt on his life. New Orleans was a six-hour drive from Sunshine, close enough for him to get home frequently to check on Willie Mitchell's progress. Also, Kitty had been transferred from Jackson to the New Orleans office, and though they had broken up, Jake couldn't seem to get her out of his mind. At times he thought Kitty might still love him, but she was so focused on her career, and her emotions were so difficult for him to fathom, he could never be sure how he stood with her.

Jake had been in New Orleans off-and-on for eight months, much of which had been spent at training camps in out-of-the-way venues around the country. The goal was to get physically stronger and faster, and to learn to fight in close quarters, and kill if necessary, with or without a weapon. When he was in town, he stayed in touch with Kitty, taking her to dinner when he could talk her into it. She was caught up in advancing up the FBI ladder and had little time for Jake or a relationship. Working long hours on operations Jake knew were dangerous, Kitty seemed determined to blaze trails in federal law enforcement, to show that women Special Agents could be every bit as tough as men—and every bit as brave.

Jake admired her for it, but was conflicted. A part of him still wanted her for his girl friend. He daydreamed about their lovemaking, visualizing her naked body, her long legs, straight dark hair, and gorgeous olive skin.

And her strength and staying power in their lovemaking—man-oh-man—she was something. He had never experienced a woman like Kitty.

Dominguez turned in his seat and grinned at Jake.

"Hey, Jake. Could you stand some groceries? There's a great little taco stand near here. They a lot better than a Lucky Dog you get in the Quarter."

Jake came back to earth. He glanced at his watch. *One a.m.* "Sure. I could eat."

"Hey, man, what happened to your arm?"

"I tore my triceps trying to lift too much."

"That's why I never touch weights," Dominguez said. "I tell my partner not to, but he don't listen to me."

Dominguez's partner ignored him. He drove out of the alley onto Philip toward the Mississippi River, then right on

Tchoupitoulas, uptown through the Irish Channel. Jake studied the crowded gang signs on the brick and cement wall separating the street from the train yard and river. From the Morial Convention Center to Audubon Park, there were scores of dilapidated wharf structures and warehouses, many of which were no longer in service. New Orleans, once the busiest port in the South, the "Gateway to South America," had long since been outpaced by Houston and Miami, and a myriad of smaller, more modern and efficient ports around the Caribbean. Jake knew it was because the old monied and political class in the city was lazy and cliquish, not interested in doing business with anyone who wasn't in Rex or Comus or the other exclusive Mardi Gras krewes. Starting in the late sixties, ambitious business men, frustrated by the slow pace and backward-looking nature of New Orleans political and business leaders, took their money and ideas elsewhere in the South, beginning a significant downturn in the city's economic status. The steady, forty-year decline of New Orleans was punctuated by Hurricane Katrina in 2005.

Dominguez made a sweeping gesture. "None of this went under water in Katrina," he said. "People who settled here long time ago knew to build next to the river where it's higher. It falls off the closer you get to the lake."

"There still a lot of Irish living in these neighborhoods?"

Dominguez punched Byrne in the arm and laughed.

"Naw, man. My people moved Byrne's people out of the Irish Channel years ago. And after Katrina, thousands of *Mexicanos* who came in town to work and rebuild the city decided to stay. Lot nicer around here now in the Irish Channel with...," Dominguez shook his finger toward his partner, "...the Irish gone."

With his eyes fixed on the street and not a hint of humor, Byrne gave Dominguez the finger.

"He really does like me," Dominguez said to Jake, "he's just putting on a show for you."

In the back seat, separated from the cops by a steel screen, Jake studied the two men. He figured Byrne for a jarhead. Crew cut and muscled, Byrne told Jake he'd joined NOPD after ten years with the Marine Corps. "Two tours in Iraq and one in Afghanistan," Byrne said.

Byrne was in his early forties and ended every sentence: "Understand?" The instructor at training camp who sliced

Jake's arm, Sergeant Lupo, did the same thing. Jake flashed back to training every time Byrne said it. Maybe it was a Marine thing. It made his arm hurt.

Dominguez was only a couple years older than Jake, maybe twenty-eight; twenty-nine at the most. Black hair and nice-looking, Dominguez was laid back and jovial.

Byrne was the opposite, stern and intense. Jake had seen him smile only twice on the ride along. Jake figured Dominguez laughed so easily because patrol duty in New Orleans had not yet darkened his disposition. Jake was sure it would.

Jake's assignment within the New Orleans United States Attorney's office was gang activity, which had picked up after the lull created by the Katrina *diaspora*. The hurricane and ensuing flood, together with the significant military presence in the city for an extended period, had driven a lot of endemic black gang members west to Houston. The indigenous New Orleans gangs had been poorly organized and were centered around housing projects like Calliope, Magnolia, Desire, and Florida. The ones that still existed by the time Katrina struck were wiped out by the hurricane and its aftermath. In the last couple of years before Jake's arrival, West Coast Hispanic gangs with Houston contingents had moved into the Crescent City. They recruited locals, but were better organized than the former local gangs. Their marching orders came from upper level management out of town, and their violence resulted from their desire to grow their business rather than from *ad hoc* personal vendettas.

Dominguez said several things about the New Orleans Hispanic gangs during the ride along that Jake knew from his research were wrong. Jake sensed Byrne knew they were wrong, too. Neither Jake nor Byrne corrected Dominguez. No reason to.

Heading west on Tchoupitoulas toward Toledano, they passed an Hispanic teenager on a bike wearing a Saints hat. Dominguez pointed to the young man and jabbed Byrne in the arm.

"There's that kid again," Dominguez said.

Byrne seemed to recognize the kid, too. He did a U-turn and gunned it back to the teen. Byrne drove up on the curb near the corner of Washington Street and stopped.

Byrne and Dominguez jumped out. Jake reached for his door handle before remembering there was none. He rapped on the glass. Dominguez rushed back and opened Jake's door.

"Sorry," the cop said. "Forgot."

Dominguez and Jake arrived next to the kid at the same time. The kid smiled broadly with his hands in the air, chewing on a plastic straw. He looked no more than twelve or thirteen to Jake.

"*Qué onda, Juanito?*" Dominguez asked.

The kid chuckled. "What's up, officers?"

"Look at you all *chignon* and shit," Dominguez said. "Nice bike, Juanito. Who'd you steal it from? You holdin'?"

"No, sir." Without prompting, Juanito laced his fingers behind his head and turned his back to the cops.

"He knows the drill," Dominguez winked and said to Jake.

Dominguez took the kid's Saints cap and gave it to his partner. Byrne checked the inside of the cap. Dominguez put one hand behind Juanito's head covering the kid's hands, and frisked him with the other. The young cop removed the kid's cell phone from his front pocket and gave it to Byrne. Dominguez gently turned the kid around.

"What're you doing on this corner?" Dominguez asked.

"Just hanging out, officer."

"Right," Byrne said. "I tell you what. We're coming back here in ten minutes, and if you're still here I'm taking you in. *Comprendez?*"

"On what charge?"

Byrne snapped. "Don't act dumb. You know it's way past curfew. Understand?"

Byrne gave Dominguez the Saints cap and phone. Dominguez put the hat on Juanito's head but kept the phone. Juanito's smile morphed into a sneer. Dominguez gave him a mini-salute and the two cops and Jake walked back to the black and white.

Jake said nothing in the back seat. He knew they kept the phone because it had the walkie-talkie feature gangs used to communicate. It was also clear to Jake that the partners had no probable cause to confiscate Juanito's phone. It was an illegal search and seizure. But there were no possible repercussions to the two cops. Juanito was not going to complain to anyone but his gang leader.

From the tiny "TM" tattoo Jake spotted under Juanito's left eye, Jake knew the kid's gang affiliation, but said nothing about it because he knew cops liked to be the sole repository of information. Knowledge was power, and the cops wanted to keep it to themselves. Jake would learn more on the ride along keeping his mouth shut, so he did.

"That kid, Juanito," Byrne said, "is a validated gang member. He's a lookout on that side of the street. When we passed him the first time he probably notified his gang to cool it." Byrne paused for a moment. "Fucking walkie-talkie phones."

"This street belongs to Juanito's gang," Dominguez said. "They run some drugs but mostly prostitution. They pimp out their little hood rats."

Jake had studied a report on the street and Juanito's gang, but did not mention it to the two cops. The report said the gang got muscled out of most of their valuable narcotics business by a bigger gang headquartered in Mid-City, just north of them; that's why they were mainly into prostitution these days.

Byrne grabbed the radio. "Unit 20 taking fifteen to eat."

The radio crackled. "Unit 20 go ahead."

"Sweet," Dominguez said. "Let's get some grub."

Byrne headed west on Tchoupitoulas again. Jake noticed Byrne eyeing him in the rear view mirror. Jake tried to ignore it. He focused on the street ahead and watched an old, red Datsun sedan dart out from behind an abandoned building on the corner of Sixth Street in front of the patrol car.

"Look out!" Jake yelled.

Byrne slammed on the brakes and cut hard to the right onto the shoulder to avoid hitting the Datsun, then jerked back left to overtake the red sedan. The move slung Jake left, then right. He felt like he was inside a washing machine. The sudden movements hurt his arm.

"Look at this fuck," Byrne said. "No lights, no plates."

"Light him up," Dominguez said.

They followed the Datsun for two short blocks, siren blaring and strobes on. "Pull that rust bucket over, you dumb fuck!" Byrne yelled. He slammed his palms on the steering wheel.

As if on cue, the Datsun turned north off Tchoupitoulas onto Eighth Street and stopped in the middle of the first block. Byrne jerked his head around at Jake. His face was crimson and his neck veins bulged. "You wait here. Understand?"

Jake watched Dominguez and Byrne approach the red Datsun. He slid over to the driver's side in the back seat to get a better view. Jake glanced at the inside of the door—no handle and no way to open the window. The impregnable steel screen was in front of him.

The cops walked closer to the sedan. Jake had a bad feeling. This was not smart. The cops did not radio their location, nor did they tell the dispatcher they were outside the cruiser. No call for backup.

Like most uptown streets in New Orleans, Eighth Street was poorly lit. There were two vacant lots on the west side of the street and an abandoned commercial building on Jake's right. The entire block seemed deserted. Jake knocked hard on the window glass but Dominguez and Byrne continued to close in on the red sedan, hands on their pistols.

The Datsun door flew open. A shirtless man with a shaved head emerged. He was covered in tattoos. As soon as he exited the Datsun he racked a tactical shotgun violently and pointed it at Byrne. It was all in one motion—and fast. The man was a blur. Byrne tried to draw his weapon.

BOOM!

Byrne's body flew backwards. The tattooed man racked the shotgun and shot Dominguez in the next split-second.

BOOM!

Dominguez spun around, blood spurting from a huge hole in his chest and back.

Both cops were down. The tattooed man walked aggressively to Byrne's body. BOOM! Right in Byrne's face. Then to Dominguez. BOOM! The young cop's head was obliterated.

The tattooed man moved incredibly fast. He had fired the four shots in less than a couple of seconds.

What now? Jake fought to control himself. He could feel his body flood with adrenaline. Everything seemed to slow down. He remembered Sergeant Lupo yelling at him in Virginia.

"You feel that, Banks? That's your adrenaline fucking you up. Don't let it take over. Hear me? You're losing it, Banks. Breathe. Control that shit. Breathe. Breathe. Understand?"

Jake concentrated on controlling his fight-or-flight response. He studied the tattooed killer.

This is happening now. What do I do?

Dominguez and Byrne were dead. No way to open the back doors or windows. Steel blocked access to the front. Impossible to reach the 870 Remington under the front seat. No cell phone and no pistol on Jake for the ride along—NOPD rules. What to do?

Jake continued to watch the tattooed man.

The killer stood with his eyes closed for a moment over each cop's body. He mumbled something over Byrne, then Dominguez. He raised his tattooed arms and hands to the sky. Saying something. He made the sign of the cross.

Praying. The crazy son of a bitch is praying.

The man threw down his hands and pointed at the bodies, now shouting, as if he were mad at the dead cops. He paced back and forth between the red Datsun sedan and the two bodies. Manic pacing. Wired to the gills.

Jake tried to study details of the man's tattoos.

He thought about hiding on the floor.

To hell with that. I'm not going to die face down quivering on the damned floor. Let him shoot me head-on.

He had a thought. Jake pulled his leather belt out of the loops and wrapped it around his knuckles. Protect his fist if he hit the man. Or, maybe grab the end and swing the buckle around to hit him in the face. Got to get out of the back seat to do that. But how? Maybe get on my back and kick the window out. Then hit him with the belt buckle.

Belt buckle versus shotgun. Brilliant.

Jake remained calm. He was actually proud of himself. He controlled his adrenaline. That part of the training worked. He was cool under fire. So what? A lot of good being cool did in this situation.

"It's amazing," he imagined the coroner would say later. "*Toxicology shows that this well-conditioned, healthy young Assistant U.S. Attorney Jacob Banks had very little adrenaline working in his blood stream at the time the shotgun pellets entered his chest and destroyed his heart. He was incredibly cool at the time of his death.*"

For the first time, the tattooed man stared into the cruiser. He started walking slowly toward Jake—then he was there, right outside the window. He tilted his head and bared his teeth while glaring at Jake. He racked the shotgun with his left hand, so fast Jake barely saw the gun move. Even with all four doors and windows closed, the racking sound was deafening. It seemed to echo inside the patrol car.

The tattooed man was two feet from the squad car. Jake sat still, watching the man's face. The man's eyes were wild—he did not blink.

A chill bolted down Jake's spine. It continued to tingle as the man's eyes focused for the first time, locking on Jake and studying him. It was as if the killer recognized Jake and was trying to place him

The man held the gun in his left hand and pointed his right index and second fingers at his eyes. He pointed the same two fingers at Jake's eyes to say, "I see you."

Jake had never seen such eyes. Intense. Piercing.

Raptor's eyes.

They bored into Jake's brain. He felt immobilized.

The killer thrust his right index finger toward Jake. He nodded as if he finally figured out how he knew Jake. Jake knew better.

Believe me, Buddy, if we had met before, I would not have forgotten.

The killer made the sign of the cross again. Backward this time. He touched his sternum, then his forehead, then his right shoulder, then his left.

Jake broke off from the man's eyes and looked down at his hands, empty except for the belt wrapped around his right knuckles. The ice in his spine had melted. He said a quick prayer.

Let's get this over with.

Jake looked up to face the man, ready to take his medicine. The tattooed man was no longer next to Jake's window. No sign of the red Datsun sedan. Jake spun around in the back seat, searching every direction. The tattooed killer was gone.

When did he leave? Why didn't he kill me?

Jake slumped in the back seat for what seemed like a long time. He sat up and looked at the bodies of Byrne and Dominguez, their blood oozing, spreading over the chalk-white marine shells on the shoulder of the narrow street. He heard sirens and turned around. Two NOPD police cruisers turned off Tchoupitoulas and barreled toward Jake with strobes flashing.

The black and whites screeched to a stop behind Jake. Four uniformed cops emerged cautiously with guns drawn.

Jake locked his fingers on top of his head and held his elbows out. He wanted to make sure they knew he was a non-combatant. He glanced through the glass to see two cops pointing their automatic pistols at his head. Jake tried to look as harmless as possible.

Don't shoot me, fellows.

Chapter Two

Willie Mitchell bolted upright, eyes wide.

"Jake," he said.

"What did you say?" Susan asked, trying to pull the sheet back over her. "Are you all right?"

It was pitch black in their bedroom, just the way he liked it. When he realized he was in his own bed he lay back on his pillow. She placed her hand lightly on his chest.

"Bad dream?"

"No. It's something about Jake."

"What?"

"I don't know. Can't remember. But it wasn't good."

"We'll check with him first thing. Don't call and wake him up now. Let him sleep."

Willie Mitchell reached over and turned the clock radio toward him. He squinted with his right eye, his good one, and moved closer to the red numbers. *One-thirty.* His left leg ached. He tried to be quiet getting out of bed, but walking into the bathroom, he heard Susan's voice.

"You need something?"

"Aleve. Go back to sleep."

In the darkness, he touched the oddly shaped Aleve bottle he kept next to his sink and water glass every night since his return from the hospital. He tapped out and swallowed two pills and returned to bed.

Willie Mitchell closed his eyes and tried to recall what it was about Jake that startled him. He adjusted his leg to get it more comfortable, but the ache remained. It was deep and generalized, from his hip to his ankle. Sometimes it throbbed. He lived with the pain every night in the eight months since he returned to Sunshine from the Jackson hospital. In the daytime the pain subsided. No one could tell him why. It seemed to him the more he moved or exercised, the better it felt. He had picked up his jogging after three months of daily therapy and was now back to his regular distance—four miles—but at a much slower pace. Eleven or twelve minute miles instead of a nine minute pace.

The therapist warned him his left leg might buckle without warning, and it had done so a couple of times, once putting Willie Mitchell on the asphalt and another time in a ditch. But the occasional tumble was worth it; he had jogged all his life and was not going to quit. Running was part of him; it made him feel almost normal.

He lay still, waiting for the Aleve to kick in, thinking about how far he had come. Willie Mitchell was in Jackson nine months before, picking a jury in a murder trial, jogging after dark around the reservoir with Jake when he got hit from behind by a car and knocked into the water. Jake pulled him from the water and kept him alive for the EMTs, who rushed him to St. Christopher's Hospital in Jackson.

The doctors said if Jake had not done chest compressions for twenty minutes while waiting on the ambulance, Willie Mitchell would have died. Jake was grazed by the car and injured his shoulder, and Willie Mitchell was grateful that in spite of being hurt, Jake was able to pull him from the water and minister to him, keep him breathing and his heart pumping. *Thank God for Jake.*

Willie Mitchell had no recollection of being hit. Everything he knew about it came from Jake, and not everything Jake told him made sense. At first, Willie Mitchell blamed his own addled brain for his confusion about the facts related by Jake. The doctors said he was in a coma in St. Christopher's for many days after the collision. But now his brain was clear, more or less, and he had been going over what Jake said happened that night. Sometimes it played over and over in his brain involuntarily.

Jackson detectives said they were still investigating the hit-and-run that almost killed Willie Mitchell, claimed the case was still open, but he knew they had no leads and had stopped looking for any. For all practical purposes, the case was closed.

He also suspected Jake knew more about what happened to David Dunne than he was letting on. Willie Mitchell had tried to find Dunne through connections he had in the FBI and in DOJ and no one seemed to know anything about Special Agent Dunne. The FBI claimed they never had an agent by that name, but he doubted they were telling him the truth. The agency might be keeping his identity a secret for a variety of reasons.

Willie Mitchell had the political stroke to get the information, but he hesitated to go that route. Mississippi Governor Jim Bob Bailey would do anything for Willie

Mitchell. So would Senator Skeeter Sumrall. Willie Mitchell's fat banker pal, Jimmy Gray, and Skeeter had been close friends since college. Jimmy had raised a ton of money all over Mississippi for Skeeter, and would raise more as needed. Jimmy knew every banker and businessman in the state—he could raise $5 million for Skeeter in twenty-four hours, just by working his cell phone. Jimmy included Willie Mitchell on every hunting and fishing outing with Skeeter, and Skeeter had grown to like and trust Willie Mitchell and depend on him for common sense advice. Skeeter told Jimmy and Willie Mitchell whenever the senator was with them that he got more out of a ten minute phone conference with the two of them than he did spending hours with the expensive business and political consultants on K Street he had on retainer.

During Willie Mitchell's recovery, Skeeter called him at least once a week, sometimes more. The senator asked Willie Mitchell if he would be interested in coming to D.C. and working with him, suggesting several positions where the senator said Willie Mitchell could do a lot more good for Mississippi and for the nation than being District Attorney for Yaloquena County.

"Not to mention a lot safer for you and your family," Skeeter added.

Willie Mitchell thanked the senator for the kind words, but told him he was fine right now being District Attorney and spending more time with Susan. As he lay in bed, waiting for his leg pain to abate, Willie Mitchell decided to stick with his plan to get the information about the hit-and-run and David Dunne from Jake, not his political contacts. He knew once he opened such an inquiry in Washington, he would not be able to control where it went. The last thing he wanted was to put David Dunne on the spot, or undermine whatever Jake was doing.

Jake knows more than he is telling.

The feeling gnawed at him—he needed to get to the bottom of it. Willie Mitchell figured enough time had passed now that he could cross-examine Jake about that night and about Dunne. He had put it off because Jake had been through a lot with his Daddy. Willie Mitchell coded when he threw an embolus after surgery on the broken bones in his left leg, and had to be shocked back to life with defibrillating paddles wielded by the young doctor on duty. Jake was in the room when his father flatlined. The nurses told Susan that Jake insisted that the young physician keep shocking Willie Mitchell until his heart started beating again. The doctor had given up, was walking out the room, and Jake forced the doctor to grab the paddles again and keep at it.

"If you don't keep shocking him, I'm going to do it myself," Jake told the doctor that night. The nurses told Susan that Willie Mitchell's heart revived on the doctor's first attempt after Jake's intervention.

Having saved his Daddy's life twice in the space of four days, Jake had become overprotective. Willie Mitchell thought that might be the reason Jake was withholding information on the hit and run and on Dunne's whereabouts. Willie Mitchell made a mental note to tell Jake that he did not have to drive up from New Orleans so often to check on him, that he was all right. He also planned to have a sit down, just Jake and him, to find out the truth about everything.

He needed to tell Scott, too, Willie Mitchell and Susan's youngest son, that there was no need to drive down from Oxford every weekend. Their lives needed to get back to normal. Willie Mitchell was going to die someday, but not anytime soon.

Nobody gets out alive.

He couldn't remember where he got that line about life, but he liked it. Flat on his back next to Susan in the darkness, it made him grin like a Cheshire cat.

Willie Mitchell resolved to tell Scott his time would be better spent in Oxford, doing what a senior in college should be doing—enjoying himself and his friends. The friends Scott made at Ole Miss would be friends for life.

Skeeter Sumrall had talked to Scott about coming to D.C. in June after graduation and working in his senate office, and if he liked it, to stay on permanently. Skeeter told Willie Mitchell if he couldn't get Willie Mitchell to come to D.C., he wanted the next best thing—one of Willie Mitchell's boys. Willie Mitchell knew Scott was getting more interested in politics and was probably going to accept the job offer.

Willie Mitchell moved his left leg slightly in an effort to reduce the ache. He thought about David Dunne again, pictured him a year ago sitting downstairs in the front parlor drinking Crown Royal. After their third drink, the two of them moved from discussing the case they were prosecuting to lighter subjects. Willie Mitchell eventually dragged out his scrapbook from the desk in the parlor and handed Dunne the old photographs of Willie Mitchell playing freshman basketball at Ole Miss. They had a big laugh at the tight-fitting trunks on the young Willie Mitchell, comparing them to the huge, loose-fitting trunks of today. Willie Mitchell remembered Dunne handling the dozen-or-so pictures.

Willie Mitchell swung his feet around and sat on the side of his bed. He fumbled in the darkness for the pad and Bic Pen he kept on his nightstand and wrote himself a note. When he woke up at night with ideas or thoughts that kept him awake, he wrote them on the pad so he would stop worrying about being able to remember in the morning. If he wrote them down, it was easier for him to get back to sleep, confident that he would not forget. Sometimes, what he read on the pad the next morning provided valuable insight into something he was working on. Sometimes, what he read was illegible, or unintelligible. Sometimes the writing made sense, but the idea was worthless. Either way, writing it down allowed him to stop rolling *"Call Robbie at C.L."* around in his brain.

He would ask his good buddy Robbie at the state crime lab in the morning how long fingerprints might last on a receptive surface. Robbie could keep a confidence. Willie Mitchell lay back down. A sharp pain shot through his left leg as he dragged it back into the king-sized bed. He suppressed a yelp and waited for it to subside.

The doctors told Willie Mitchell his leg would eventually stop aching, but it would never be as strong as before. They also said having a spleen was nice, but he really did not need it; that he could live almost a normal life without it. They explained he would need pharmaceutical help from time to time to encourage production of white blood cells and to fight infections.

The ophthalmologist told Willie Mitchell his left eye had achieved maximum recovery, that the blurred vision would be with him for a long time, maybe the rest of his life. The stronger left contact lens helped, and his right eye was dominant anyway.

Willie Mitchell did not worry too much about his painful gimpy leg, his missing spleen, and the fuzzy vision in his left eye.

What he worried about were the seizures.

Chapter Three

Brujo turned right off Rampart onto Governor Nicholls in the old red Datsun sedan stolen earlier the previous day by one of his followers. In the first block, between Rampart and Burgundy, a small man stepped from between two parked cars and extended his arm, palm toward the Datsun, the universal "stop" signal.

Brujo could barely see the man in the darkness. He pulled the Datsun to within a few inches of the man and stopped the Datsun in the middle of the turtle-backed, dirty street.

Brujo stepped from the car. He left the door open. The man hustled around the driver's side and held the door, bowing as Brujo walked past.

"Do not forget the shotgun, Felipe."

"Si, Brujo."

Felipe drove off toward the river. Another vehicle pulled away from the curb and followed Felipe. Brujo had instructed Felipe earlier to dump the car in the usual spot, twelve miles downriver from Jackson Square, on the left descending bank, just south of Meraux. The river could be accessed there from an isolated, abandoned pier with no guard rails or protective barriers. Brujo's followers had dumped many, many vehicles into the fast moving river off that wooden pier, into one of the deepest parts of the Mississippi, the river bottom being over 200 feet below the surface.

Brujo waited until the tail lights of the two vehicles disappeared when they turned left on Bourbon. Only then did he begin to walk in the darkness on Governor Nicholls toward Chartres Street.

It was after two a.m. when Brujo used his key to open the door to *La Casa de Mama Coba,* his grandmother's shop on Chartres in the most rundown block in the Quarter. The block was one shop after another, most catering to cheap tourist merchandise, others to the unique ethnic or Byzantine tastes of New Orleanians. Although an occasional tourist wandered in, almost all of Mama Coba's trade was with local customers and referrals. The stenciled sign reading *La Casa de Mama Coba* on the exterior of the storefront was small, barely noticeable.

The store did a brisk business in potions, herbs, and powders. Mama Coba's advice on the preparation of balms and her hand-made *collares,* or necklaces and amulets, made her store the most popular *botánica* in the city. She took time with every patron, suggesting spells and hexes for every purpose—curing illnesses, bringing home a wayward lover or spouse, cursing an enemy. Mama Coba was the most accomplished Santeria practitioner outside the Caribbean and Miami, where she had opened her first Santeria store and chapel. She could never be a priest because she was a woman—but that did not stop her from molding her grandson. She told others that Brujo was the most powerful Santeria high priest and sorcerer in all of North America.

Brujo walked through the shop and into the back of the building, passing Mantis, Mama Coba's assistant and Man Friday, lying on a narrow cot with his eyes closed. Mantis was tall, skeletal—his feet dangled off the end of the cot. His freakishly long hands and fingers rested on his chest. Mantis opened one eye slightly and raised a bony right index finger. Brujo acknowledged Mama Coba's assistant and walked on to the chapel.

Brujo was not sleepy—he never slept at night. Anyone who wanted to consult Brujo as a priest, or for his black magic skills, came to the chapel by appointment, from eight to ten at night, on a schedule kept by Mama Coba, who collected the fees associated with the hexes and spells Brujo provided for the clients. The remainder of most nights Brujo spent with his men in the Ninth Ward houses they used as headquarters and barracks. After their work was done, Brujo left his men and returned alone in the early morning hours to Mama Coba's, always entering his small bedroom behind the chapel while it was still dark outside. Totally nocturnal, Brujo slept all day, rising at five in time to eat dinner and receive his supplicants.

After he walked past Mantis on the cot this morning, Brujo locked the chapel door behind him. He was energized from the encounter on Tchoupitoulas, and grateful. He stood at the altar, both hands on the polished limestone slab table. It was a warm night, but the limestone was cool to the touch. He bowed and kissed the altar, thanking his saints for helping him get revenge against the two godless devils who harmed Big Demon. He lit two thick candles, one on each end of the limestone table, picked up the bronze chalice from the center of the altar and raised it above his head. He closed his eyes and began to chant.

After fifteen minutes, Brujo lowered the chalice, stared into the brown liquid, blessed it and drank. He placed the bronze cup on the altar and made the backward sign of the cross. He folded his hands in prayer, bowing his head and touching his lips with the tips of his fingers.

Brujo concentrated. He willed himself into a trance, and stayed in the same position, eyes closed, head bowed, for two hours. In his mind, with the help of the holy saints and Santa Muerte, he traveled back to the early days. Some of the events he remembered, some he learned in the lap of the only mother he ever knew—Mama Coba.

~ * ~

Brujo was born in 1971 in the city of Santiago de Cuba, Oriente province, on the extreme southeastern coast of Cuba, a stone's throw from Guantanamo Bay.

Hidalgo, Brujo's grandfather and Mama Coba's third husband, grew up with Fidel Castro. Mama Coba laughed when she told Brujo about his grandfather Hidalgo and Fidel playing together and getting into trouble as children and teens. When Fidel and Ché Guevara took to the Sierra Maestra mountains to nurture their revolution, Hidalgo smuggled rifles and Russian-made weapons to them on the backs of burros over the winding, overgrown mountain trails. Hidalgo won the confidence of the Russian advisors who mentored Fidel and Ché and continued to supply the rebels of the 26th of July Movement even after they deposed Batista on New Year's Day, 1959.

After Batista fell and Castro gained control, the Supreme Leader allowed Hidalgo to expand his gun smuggling, delivering Soviet bloc weaponry to homegrown revolutionaries in Venezuela, Panama, Nicaragua, and other Caribbean basin countries. Santos, the only child of Hidalgo and Mama Coba, accompanied his father in the mid to late-sixties on many of the weapons deliveries, after the tension surrounding the ill-fated Bay of Pigs invasion had become a faint memory.

Mama Coba told Brujo his grandfather Hidalgo would have become a rich man had not Fidel insisted on an ever-increasing percentage of the profits. Even so, Hidalgo and she made a decent living selling armaments until Hidalgo's death from pneumonia in 1969.

Their only son Santos had developed a relationship with all of his father's contacts in the family's gun smuggling enterprise, including the Supreme Leader himself. But in spite of Mama Coba's urging, Santos had no interest in continuing the gun smuggling business after Hidalgo died. Santos had spent much of his teen years helping Hidalgo, and after Hidalgo's death, Santos was intent on making up for lost time. Hidalgo had not long been in his grave when Santos began to "have some fun." He was light-skinned, with European features, and much in demand with the local ladies. Every day he drank as much local rum as his body would tolerate, and every night he sought out and slept with a different prostitute or woman of easy virtue in Santiago de Cuba. Santos ignored Mama Coba's pleas to stop his drinking and philandering. Fortified with drink, Santos made fun of her religion, ridiculing the rites of Santeria that sustained Mama Coba her entire life and made her infamous in Oriente province as a cold-blooded priestess who could cast powerful spells and exorcise demons.

Still deep in his trance standing at the altar, Brujo remembered his father from the years they lived together in Los Angeles. Brujo watched Santos fall from the heights of power because he could not control his appetites. Brujo vowed it would never happen to him.

In Los Angeles, away from the controlling influence of Mama Coba, Santos told Brujo for the first time about his real mother, and cried when he described how cruel he had been to Luna. Brujo told Santos everything was all right—it did not matter. Brujo told Santos that Mama Coba was all the mother Brujo needed.

In Santiago de Cuba, Mama Coba disdained Santos' drinking and womanizing, but she knew that Santos, with his charm and good looks, could give her what she wanted: a male child to rear from infancy to become a high priest, a *Babalawo* or sorcerer, to receive Orunmila, the Orisha of Prophecy. She would groom the child to become the most powerful High Priest in Cuba.

Mama Coba selected Luna Ortiz, a young girl she encountered after a ritual fertility mass she conducted for Luna's older sister. The Ortiz family had sufficient prestige and Spanish blood to meet the standards Mama Coba established for the mother of her child. Luna was fifteen, shy and beautiful, and a virgin. Mama Coba did not rely on the word of the Ortiz family. When she had Luna alone in her home, she led the young girl to the Santeria altar in the largest room of her house, and explained the pre-marital ritual that Santeria tradition required, going back to the Yoruban witch doctors who introduced the rites into Cuba. After lighting candles and praying over Luna's body, Mama Coba physically examined the frightened fifteen-year-old and confirmed that Luna was indeed, a virgin. She swore Luna to secrecy and assured her that every prospective bride underwent the ritual. Luna was a sheltered child, and went along with whatever Mama Coba told her—just as she did with Santos after they were married.

The wedding celebration was small but festive. After all the wedding guests departed her home, Mama Coba conducted a Santeria ceremony to bless the couple. No one else was present. Mama Coba left the young couple "to go see her sister" for a few days. Santos seduced his terrified young virgin bride in his bedroom in Mama Coba's house on their wedding night. They made love several times a day for the first six weeks of the marriage. Luna was only a child, overwhelmed by her worldly husband, in awe of his intelligence and physical prowess. He knew so many things; he was a real man. Luna was unaware of the deal Santos had made with Mama Coba. He agreed to stay with Luna until she was with child. Once Luna was pregnant, the agreement was that Santos was under no further obligation to his mother or to Luna.

Luna lived with her mother-in-law for the duration of her pregnancy, and when Luna went into labor, Mama Coba burned candles and foul-smelling powders around the terrified young girl. Mama Coba chanted and waved vulture and guinea feathers over Luna's swollen belly, imposing a powerful hex on Luna, and a blessing on the newborn.

Neighbors said later that the difficult ordeal of birth, coupled with Mama Coba's incantations over her and the infant during the process, drove Luna mad. After supervising Luna's breast feeding the infant for three months, Mama Coba snatched the infant from Luna's breast and drove the young girl from her home. Luna's family believed she was cursed and would not take her in. She died within a year on the streets of Victoria de Las Tunas not far from Santiago de Cuba, a raving, wild-eyed *prostituta*, strangled by a disgruntled customer.

Mama Coba named the boy Ignacio after the saint, and gave him her family name Torres.

Coming out of his trance at the altar in the chapel on Chartres, Brujo remembered Mama Coba chanting the ancient prayers and rites while rocking him in her arms—prayers and rituals that he still used to this day. He smiled, recalling Mama Coba whispering endearments to him as a child, calling him her sweet "*brujito.*" Her "little witch."

She told him over and over that he was the most gifted, powerful sorcerer in the world. And he believed her.

Chapter Four

As Brujo stood at his altar in the early morning hours, Jake Banks was also by himself, two miles west of Brujo's chapel, waiting in the empty interrogation room in NOPD headquarters on South Broad. He was so tired he could barely see straight. He sipped a Diet Coke and eyed two stacks of documents, each a foot high, in chairs across the room. He could tell they'd been there a long time. He glanced at his Casio watch.

Four o'clock. Out of gas. How long can they keep me? How long can I stay awake?

Detective Pizzolato's questions were repetitive and draining. Jake was exhausted when he left training camp in Virginia the day before. The miserable flight added to his fatigue. The ride along resulting in two dead cops, together with the dissipation of adrenaline when the wild-eyed killer spared him, zapped Jake of what little energy he had left. Now the fat investigator with the gravelly voice was trying to see how many ways he could ask Jake the same questions.

Pizzolato waddled back in.

"I promise you Detective Pizzolato, I've told you all I can remember. I am really, really tired."

"I know, kid. I know. Just a few more."

Pizzolato placed a NOPD form on the table and began to write on it. Jake wanted to ask the man if he needed to clear his throat. Pizzolato's voice was beyond raspy; it was phlegmy, irritating. Jake could tell Pizzolato was a New Orleans native, probably fourth generation Italian. The detective had the unique New Orleans accent. He had it bad. Jake never heard it anywhere else, either in person or in the movies or on television. He thought it was similar to the way people from the Bronx or Brooklyn talked on television--but different, and distinct. And it wasn't just the Yats, the natives of Mid-Town, St. Bernard, Algiers or Kenner. It also infected the wealthy old families uptown and in Old Metairie.

"I want to go over the description of the man one more time."

Jake stared at Pizzolato. In addition to being about fifty pounds too heavy, the detective had a pasty, pock-marked complexion under jet black hair kept in place with Brylcreem or something similar. Jake wanted to object. Instead, he answered in a monotone he hoped would convey the stupidity of the process. "Hispanic. Maybe six feet. Shaved head. Skinny build, but strong-looking. Tattooed on his chest, arms and back. Both arms almost fully sleeved with tattoos. None on his face or neck. I couldn't tell his age. Maybe forty."

Pizzolato continued writing. Jake lay his head in the crook of his good arm on the table. The Diet Coke was not getting it. Even so, Jake remembered something else. Maybe Pizzolato was on to something with the anesthetizing repetition.

"One tattoo looked kind of like wings. On his chest."

Jake heard the door open behind him and sat up. The man entering was tanned with a lot of bright white hair, maybe fifty-five. Tall, with a bushy moustache as white as the hair on his head. He leaned against the wall behind Pizzolato. Jake assumed the man was a supervising detective.

"My name's Bill Eustis, Jake," the man drawled as he shook Jake's hand. Eustis's accent had a twang; definitely not New Orleans. Jake guessed East Texas or Northwest Louisiana. "How you holding up? Pizzo wearing you out?"

"Nah," Pizzolato said. "I been easy on the boy."

"I'm really tired," Jake said. "I need some sleep."

"You've been through a lot tonight, partner. We appreciate the help you've given us so far. We're going to continue to need your assistance. We lost two good men out there and we want to get the son of a bitch that did it. Dominguez and Byrne had young families."

Pizzolato was angry. "The dirty bastard. They were both good boys. Both good Catholics."

"Could you come back in tomorrow about noon?" Eustis asked. "By then we hope to have some pictures for you to look at."

"Yes, sir. I'll be here."

Jake stood. The supervisor walked over and put his hand on Jake's shoulder. "There's news vans and reporters all over the place outside. I'll walk you out to your car. I'd appreciate your not saying anything to the press or even talking to them."

"No problem."

Jake told Pizzolato he'd see him later. Jake winced when Bill Eustis touched his left upper arm to escort him out. They walked to his silver Toyota 4Runner, somehow avoiding all the media. Jake shook the supervising detective's hand and headed home to his Warehouse District condo on the corner of Magazine and Julia that Susan and Willie Mitchell helped him buy.

Jake almost fell asleep on the ten minute drive. He unwrapped two sticks of green Extra sugarless gum and chomped on it to stay awake. There was much more traffic on Poydras than he expected this time of morning.

He parked in his spot under the building and dragged himself up the concrete stairs to his second floor apartment. Jake dropped his keys on the doormat at his front door and almost fell over when he stooped to retrieve them. Other than dropping off his luggage at seven the previous evening before the ride along, he had not been in his apartment in almost a month. He had been pushing himself to the limits of physical and mental exhaustion from dawn until dark in training camps.

He inventoried the refrigerator. Two Diet Cokes, ketchup, salsa, mustard, Jack's vanilla wafers and an almost empty jar of Jif creamy peanut butter. He put his gum in a napkin and threw it into the trash can under the sink. Jake opened the jar, grabbed a spoon from the flatware drawer, and spread the peanut butter on the flat side of a vanilla wafer. He carefully placed another cookie on the peanut butter. He leaned against the kitchen counter and devoured seven of the little crunchy sandwiches, thinking there were very few foods that did not go well with peanut butter. When the half-inch of smooth peanut butter was gone, he was disappointed his gourmet meal had ended.

He opened the refrigerator to see if there was anything else that would go with the vanilla wafers. Nothing. Just as well, because working the peanut butter off the roof of his mouth had consumed what little energy he had left. Jake looked around the empty kitchen and thought of all the errands he needed to do to make the apartment habitable again.

No food. Winn-Dixie won't be crowded. Maybe I should go now.

He walked toward the small dining room table and tripped on the carpet edge. Jake fell onto the carpet and stayed down long enough for the deep slice in his arm to stop pulsating.

Maybe not.

Jake dragged himself through the narrow, carpeted hallway and into his bedroom. He took off his clothes, being careful with his arm, brushed his teeth, took two Bayer aspirin for the pain, and fell into bed. He closed his eyes. The training camp sessions segued into the murder of Dominguez and Byrne, which replayed in his mind, over and over. While staring at the two dead cops bleeding out on the white shell shoulder of the narrow street uptown, Jake thought he heard Lupo somewhere behind him, yelling at Jake as he drifted off.

"Banks! You're being choked out. What are you gonna do? You're losing consciousness. Four seconds Banks. Three seconds. Two. The sandman's coming, Banks. He's done, Sergeant Kriss. Put him down."

~ * ~

The tornado alert siren kept blaring somewhere outside the cruiser on the deserted street. Jake's eyes were locked with the tattooed man's. He could see his face clearly now. The man's nostrils were flared, and the tip of his nose hooked. The tattoo on his chest did have wings, jet black crow's wings, and a hideous crow's face, like a gargoyle. Its tongue stuck out, and down.

But it was the man's eyes that dominated. They were sharp, intensely focused, like those of a hawk or an eagle. Maybe a crow.

Raptor's eyes.

The siren kept on, annoying Jake.

Was a tornado imminent? A hurricane?

He turned over in bed.

Oh. My ring tone.

He picked up his iPhone off the night stand, held it to his ear, kept his eyes closed.

"Hey, Banks. You up?"

"What?"

"It's almost one. We needed you here at noon."

He recognized the gravel in Pizzolato's voice. "Sorry. I overslept."

"It's important you get on down here to headquarters as soon as you can. You need me to send somebody to pick you up?"

"No. I'll be right there."

"Soon as you can."

Jake checked his phone as he walked naked into the bathroom. He turned on the shower. The phone screen said "5 Missed Calls." The first was from Kitty. The other four were from Willie Mitchell.

Jake sent his Daddy a text. *Tied up. Call you later this p.m.*

Willie Mitchell shot back. *Anything wrong?*

I saw two cops killed uptown last night. On my ride along.

Heard about cops on news. You okay?

Yes. Just a witness. Been giving info to NOPD. Call u asap.

He put the phone down on the tile counter and studied his left upper arm in the mirror. It looked better, like it was starting to heal. Jake gently rotated his left arm. It did not hurt as bad as it had the night before. He took two more Bayer.

The shower did wonders. It made him feel about seventy per cent normal. Fifteen per cent off for his arm. Another fifteen off for the fatigue, jet lag, and shock of last night.

Jake listened to local A.M. on the way to NOPD. The woman reporting from outside headquarters said she had confirmed that two New Orleans police officers had been killed after midnight in a shooting uptown off Tchoupitoulas.

Jake started to call the U.S. Attorney's office to let his supervisor know what was going on, but hit "End Call" before it started ringing. His "supervisor" was a career bureaucrat finishing his thirty years in the Eastern District of Louisiana. Jerry O'Flaherty could have cared less what Jake was doing. O'Flaherty headed the Criminal Appellate Division within the U.S. Attorney's office in New Orleans, but had not written a brief in years. He supervised other brief writers fresh out of law school. They knew their way around LexisNexis a lot better than O'Flaherty. To the great amusement of the law clerks and other assistant U.S. attorneys in the office, O'Flaherty still looked at actual law books and Shepardized critical cases the old-fashioned way.

Stopped at a light near the Superdome, Jake recalled showing up at the U.S. Attorney's office eight months earlier and reporting to O'Flaherty, who told Jake he had no idea why Washington made him Jake's supervisor, since Jake was supposed to be working gang intelligence, not appeals. Nevertheless, O'Flaherty was not going to seek clarification from Washington. He did not want to risk stirring up any kind of controversy in the waning months of his government service. He told Jake to check in every once in a while if he had a problem with something. The new Justice Department gang intelligence unit in New Orleans had been authorized and funded over a year earlier, but in the federal government's typical fashion, there was an administrative delay in deciding what minimum GS rating the head of the unit, Jake's eventual boss, was required to have. In the meantime, no one in the federal building kept up with Jake's comings and goings, so his many months of absence while attending training camps at David Dunne's behest went unnoticed. Jake did go through the motions the first time he met O'Flaherty.

"Mr. O'Flaherty, do you want me to let you know from time to time what I'm actually working on?"

"Not really."

David Dunne knew what he was doing. No one at the ugly white pre-fabricated-looking Federal Building at 501 Magazine on the corner of Poydras cared if Jake showed up or not. O'Flaherty did not want to be bothered, and never discovered that Jake had spent much of the eight months of his New Orleans employment in training camps in Virginia, Colorado, New Mexico, and Texas. No one else in the office missed Jake because he was on no one's radar except O'Flaherty, who apparently thought only about the retirement cottage his wife inherited on the beach at Waveland just west of Gulfport, less than an hour east on I-10. Jake had only known O'Flaherty for fifteen minutes, but from O'Flaherty's wistful description of the beach cottage, Jake could tell O'Flaherty longed to be there, living on the federal pension that paid him seventy per cent of his current salary with annual COLAs that would eventually put his retirement pay above $100,000 per year.

Jake arrived at NOPD headquarters and parked his 4Runner in the white shell lot at South White and Gravier. He sent a text while walking to the building. Pizzolato was waiting for him in the lobby.

"Detective Pizzolato," Jake said and shook hands.

"This is some bad shit," Pizzolato said.

Jake glanced at the detective in the elevator. Pizzolato's pocked jowls sagged more than the night before. In fact, his whole fat body seemed to sag.

Probably no sleep last night.

Pizzolato led Jake into a private office. The desk name plate said Det. Sonny Pizzolato.

"Any leads?" Jake asked.

"Maybe. We've been working all night. Nothing for sure yet. Your description helped a lot. Captain Eustis got some ideas."

"What about the car?"

"A red Datsun sedan was stolen out of Gentilly yesterday. There ain't many of those left on the road. We're pretty sure it's the car involved, but it ain't turned up yet."

Pizzolato placed a photo array of Hispanic males in front of Jake. "See if you recognize anyone out of these pictures."

Jake looked carefully at each photograph. He pointed at the fifth photograph in front of him.

"This is the guy."

"You sure?"

"Absolutely. One hundred per cent."

Pizzolato did not seem surprised. He walked out of his office. Jake studied the photo. It was a face burned into his memory. The face of the crazed man who killed Dominguez and Byrne while Jake watched. As he stared at the photograph, Jake felt anger rising in the pit of his stomach, moving into his chest. He thought about Dominguez, how nice he was to Jake on the ride along. Byrne, too, in his own jarhead way, was tolerant of Jake's intrusion into their world. The death of the two men would hit their wives, kids, and friends like a sledgehammer. Jake swore he would do everything he could to make sure the tattooed man paid a price, no matter what the legal system did—exactly why he aspired to work with David Dunne.

Jake's iPhone vibrated. It was Kitty. He smiled for the first time since the murders.

"Hey."

"I got your text. You were with the two officers that were killed?"

"Yeah."

"Are you all right?"

"I've been better. I'm at NOPD on South Broad, answering questions, trying to help."

"Maybe we could get something to eat later and you can tell me all about what happened."

"Sure. I'll be at the condo when I finish here. I'll call you."

In spite of every effort not to, Jake thought about Kitty a lot. He was glad they still talked, but hated being "a good friend."

Crap. Kitty is over our relationship. I need to get over it, too.

Pizzolato walked back into his office.

"Jake, you've been a big help. We'll take it from here. I hope we can call on you if we need something else from you."

Pizzolato extended his beefy hand. Jake didn't.

"Who's the guy?"

Pizzolato pulled in his hand.

"He bad?" Jake asked.

"Yeah."

"So, what's the next step?"

"You don't worry about that. We've got it under control. You just head home and get some rest. Go back to your legal work."

"Detective Pizzolato, I know I can help you find this guy. I want to be part of this."

"We'll be in touch."

"Okay, but I just got a text and I need to make a call to the U.S. Attorney's office. It's important. Won't take ten minutes. I'll stay right here in your office. Then you can escort me out."

"Hurry up. When I get back I'm taking you downstairs."

Pizzolato dragged his bulky frame out the door. Jake knew if he let Pizzolato push him out he might not be invited back until the investigation was over. He would have to testify at the trial if they caught the tattooed man, but Jake wanted more involvement than that. He wanted to be in on the hunt.

Jake needed Dunne's help. Right now. He dialed Dunne's number. He was used to the routine: wait for the call to transfer; once; twice; three times; then the additional delay of at least a minute. There was no telling how many exchanges around the world the phone call had been routed through, nor was there any telling where David Dunne was.

"Dunne."

"It's Jake. Got a problem."

"What?"

Jake started to tell him about the ride along and the murder of the two cops. In the background Jake heard a helicopter and someone yelling.

"I know about it," Dunne said. "I didn't know you were the guy in the back seat. Eustis didn't tell me that."

"You know Captain Eustis?"

"For years. He's a resource."

"What do you mean?"

"I'll tell you later. What problem are you having? Talk fast, I don't have much time."

Jake told him he was being squeezed out of the investigation.

"I'll call Eustis back and tell him to keep you involved."

"Thanks. How did he know to call you?"

"I got to go. I'm back stateside tomorrow. I'll call you."

Dunne ended the call but Jake kept his iPhone to his ear, occasionally saying something to give the impression to Pizzolato if he walked past the open door that he was engaged in an important phone conversation. Twenty-five minutes later, Pizzolato returned shaking his head.

"Don't know how you did it or who you know, Banks, but you got your wish."

Pizzolato curled his index finger. Jake followed him through a hallway and into a conference room. A half-dozen pissed-off detectives stared at Jake. Pizzolato motioned for him to sit. He gave the detectives a muted wave. Not one investigator acknowledged Jake.

Captain Bill Eustis, the tanned supervising detective with the white mustache who escorted Jake past the media ten hours earlier walked in and sat next to Jake. He leaned close.

"You get some sleep, Jake?"

"Yes, sir. Not enough, but it's a start."

Eustis moved even closer and spoke quietly. "Glad to have you on board. You're working with a good man."

"How did you know to call him?"

"He asked me several months ago to be on the lookout for this gangster. Gave me the same description you did. He's been of interest to Dunne for a while."

Jake nodded.

"And we made an arrest a couple of weeks ago that made me start thinking about the guy Dunne was looking for."

"So you called him after I gave you the description?"

"Right. And after I spoke to him early this morning, he e-mailed me some good intel on our suspect. Including that picture that you just picked out in that photo lineup."

Jake's iPhone vibrated. It was a text from his alleged boss, short-timer Jerry O'Flaherty.

"Your new supervisor is here and wants to see you asap."

Jake responded. *"In meeting at NOPD. Be there shortly."*

Jake watched three more angry detectives straggle in and sit in the back. Eustis stood in front of the investigators. He took off his sport coat, revealing a tan leather shoulder rig with what appeared to Jake to be a Smith & Wesson under his left arm, along with two magazines.

"All right, men," the captain said. "About two weeks ago we arrested a big Mexican named Francis Salazar in connection with the seizure of a pile of weapons at a warehouse on the Tchoupitoulas wharf. Byrne and Dominguez were the first ones at that scene, and he tried to fight his way out of the arrest, did his best to kill them."

The detectives nodded.

"Well, Salazar's been in central lockup ever since. The guy that finished what Salazar started to do, the one killed Byrne and Dominguez early this morning, is an associate of Salazar and a big time gun smuggler. I've gotten a lot of information on him today."

"Who from?" an Asian detective asked.

Eustis looked directly at Jake for a moment.

"Another law enforcement source, but that's not important," Eustis said to the Asian detective. "What's important is the man in this picture is the man Jake Banks identified as the bastard who killed Byrne and Dominguez. His legal name is Ignacio Torres. But he's known as Brujo."

Jake stared at the enlarged photograph Captain Eustis held up for his detectives to see. It was the tattooed man that could have easily killed Jake after the two cops. The chill in his spine returned briefly.

"Get a good look," Eustis said. "He's originally from Cuba, and has a criminal history in Los Angeles. He came to us from Houston—and gentlemen, *Señor* Brujo is one nasty piece of work."

Chapter Five

Jake walked into the federal building through the main entrance on Poydras. He hated enduring the scanner and metal detector protocol, but it was a GSA building, so he had no choice. Walking quickly through the public access lobby area, he rode up the elevator and exited into the foyer of the U.S. Attorney's office for the Eastern District of Louisiana. Jake swiped his access card and pushed the door open into the central reception area.

"They're waiting for you in the main conference room," the receptionist Gertrude Wilson said. Besides O'Flaherty, she was the only person in the office who had interacted with Jake. Jake had never even met Joseph "Joe Joe" Barnes, *the* U.S. Attorney. Barnes was a New Orleans politician with excellent White House connections, a three handicap at the New Orleans Country Club, and little knowledge of federal prosecution. Decked out in a linen or seersucker suit, Joe Joe lunched at Galatoire's every Friday and at least one other weekday; "lunches" that lasted until four in the afternoon. Joe Joe loved hoisting Bloody Mary's and regaling Jesuit High buddies with salty tales of Louisiana politicians, many of which featured Joe Joe somehow caught in the middle of the peccadilloes.

"Thanks, Gertie," Jake said to the receptionist as he walked past her into the large, elegant conference room featuring a Louisiana Cypress conference table, plush chairs, and thick oxblood carpet.

There were two men seated at the far end of the table. One he had never seen before; the other a man he wished he had never met.

"Mr. Whitman," Jake said. "Good to see you."

Leopold Whitman, former U.S. Attorney for the Southern District of Mississippi in Jackson, and Jake's boss his first year out of law school, gestured for Jake to join them at their end of the table. Except for the bow tie, Whitman's appearance had changed little. Short, slightly built, rimless glasses and clothing that marked him as the academic he was.

Whitman stood and shook Jake's hand—the same weak Whitman handshake Jake had become familiar with in Jackson.

Someone needs to teach the man a decent greeting.

"Meet Mr. E. Peter Romano," Whitman said to Jake and gestured to the strongly built man next to him, "your new supervisor."

Jake shook his new boss's hand.

Now, there's a good handshake.

Romano looked to be in excellent condition, with a muscular chest and shoulders, and a large head to match. He was a couple of inches taller than the diminutive Whitman, and his hair was black, receding. Romano wore a coarse black beard.

"Nice to meet you, Jake," Romano said. "I've met Willie Mitchell a couple of times at NDAA conferences where I've been on gang panels."

"Great. How long have you been in town?"

"Couple of days. This transfer was kind of abrupt."

"Where were you before?" Jake asked.

"You two can get acquainted later," Whitman interrupted. "I'm sure you'll have a lot to talk about. But I'm only here for the day, and I want to get my business done and get back to D.C."

Jake nodded and sat across the table from Whitman. Romano sat at the end of the table, Whitman on his left, Jake on his right.

"How is your father's health?" Whitman asked.

"He's getting stronger every day," Jake said. He knew Whitman's inquiry was perfunctory. Whitman didn't give a rat's ass about Willie Mitchell's recuperation. "Thanks for asking."

"First of all," Whitman said, "the fact that Mr. Romano and I are in this room at the same time, and in this city, for that matter, is entirely serendipitous."

Jake nodded at the *non sequitur*. When Whitman looked down at his manicured nails, Jake glanced at Romano, who sat stone-faced, apparently as much in the dark as Jake.

"But I wanted him to participate in this meeting because he is your supervisor, albeit recently arrived."

Whitman paused and cleared his throat. Romano waited in silence. Jake moved in his seat and a sharp pain shot through his left arm. He rotated his shoulder to work out the pain while the professor gathered his thoughts.

"Perhaps I should begin by explaining my new position. You were aware that I was promoted out of the Southern District of Mississippi six months ago?"

Jake nodded. "Yes, sir. I knew you were no longer in Jackson and had been transferred to DOJ in D.C."

"Yes. I was quite fortunate that a position opened in Washington that my superiors in the department felt uniquely suited my abilities and strengths. They all but insisted I take the position."

"Yes, sir."

"I am now the senior Assistant U.S. Attorney under the Office of Inspector General in the Department of Justice. It's a position that dovetails nicely with my interest in the events that led to your departure from Jackson, the prosecution of Adolfo Zegarra."

Jake knew this was bad news for anyone he cared about.

"Actually I requested a transfer to New Orleans after all that happened. And it was approved."

Romano moved in his chair slightly. Jake noticed his new boss appeared to be very uncomfortable, wishing he were somewhere else.

"I want to ask you a few questions about what happened in Jackson after Zegarra's plea."

"I was in the courtroom when he pleaded guilty. Judge Williams made everyone stay until you and the U.S. Marshals escorted him out of the courtroom and into the transfer wagon."

Whitman leaned forward. "When is the last time you saw or spoke to David Dunne?"

"Why?" Jake asked.

"I'll ask the questions, Mr. Banks."

Jake took a deep breath. *Once an asshole, always an asshole.*

"You and your father became fast friends with David Dunne in Sunshine during the prosecution, did you not?"

"Yes, sir. We did. He's a great guy. Is he in some kind of trouble?"

"We shall see. Let's proceed. I'll ask you again. When is the last time you saw or spoke to David Dunne?"

"You know, Mr. Whitman, the last few convictions DOJ has won against state or federal officials have been against targets or witnesses who gave voluntary statements to investigators, and later were acquitted of the underlying offense, but convicted of lying to federal investigators. What they call 'process' crimes."

Romano nodded in agreement.

"What's your point, Mr. Banks?" Whitman said.

"My point is if you are not going to tell me why you are asking me these questions, then I have to assume that answering them, no matter what I say, might turn out to be not in my best interest." He tapped his index finger into his own chest. "Am I a target of your investigation or just a witness?"

"You don't get to ask questions."

"Well, let's back up. Would you like to bring in a court reporter, swear me in, and let's record everything?"

"That's not necessary. I'll have my memory and my notes of your responses. And, Mr. Romano is a witness."

"Wait a minute," Romano said.

"Hold on Mr. Romano," Whitman said. "Just keep your seat."

"How about if I record it myself?" Jake asked.

"No. You cannot."

"Well, I can't answer and take notes at the same time, Mr. Whitman. What if I take the fifth?"

"You are an employee of the federal government. If you invoke your Fifth Amendment privilege in connection with this OIG investigation, agency regulations require that you be suspended from your position, without pay."

"Okay. How about if I ask for an attorney to be present while you question me?"

"Automatic suspension."

Jake looked over at Romano, who appeared to be appalled by the entire proceeding.

"I think I understand the ground rules," Jake said. "Ask away."

Whitman smiled.

"Mr. Banks, when is the last time you saw or spoke to David Dunne?"

Jake sat silent.

"Answer my question."

Jake said nothing. His new supervisor for gang activity, E. Peter Romano, squirmed again.

"One last chance to answer, Mr. Banks," Whitman said.

Jake sat silent, doing his best to have a look on his face that did not display any emotion of any kind. He wasn't trying to be difficult or belligerent—he just was not going to say a word.

Whitman stood and pointed at Jake.

"This doesn't end here, Mr. Banks. You're in deep trouble."

Leopold Whitman stormed from the room.

Jake turned to his new boss. "So, where were you working before they transferred you down here?"

Chapter Six

David Dunne's favorite thing about landing after dark in Los Angeles was watching the orange lights of the city grid stretch forever. This night was no different.

The six-seat VLJ Cessna Citation Mustang descended quietly in its landing pattern and touched down at the Santa Monica Municipal Airport at 9:45. Dunne was the only passenger. The pilot taxied to General Aviation while the co-pilot flipped switches on the instrument panel and made notes on a clipboard.

When the jet stopped, Dunne waited for the co-pilot to open the door. As soon as steps were available, Dunne walked out of the jet onto the tarmac without speaking to either pilot. He did not know their names and had never seen them before. They would refuel, file a new flight plan for Bangor, Maine with a two-hour layover in New Orleans, then wait in the pilot's lounge while he transacted his business. After the flight from the Lakefront Airport in New Orleans to Maine sometime around dawn, Dunne would never see the two pilots again. That was the discipline.

Dressed in black utility pants, a dark gray long-sleeved knit shirt, and a lightweight black jacket, Dunne walked through the General Aviation lobby. He carried a soft leather briefcase and a black duffle bag slung across his back. He walked into the rental car lot and opened the door to a black Ford Explorer, tossing the duffel on the back seat and the black briefcase onto the passenger seat. Dunne opened the console between the front seats and glanced at the paperwork long enough to confirm it was the right black Explorer. Under the paperwork, he saw a Schlage door key, exactly where it was supposed to be. He started the vehicle and drove off into the darkness.

Heading east on the 10, he lowered the front windows to enjoy the cool, dry Southern California air. In his line of work, Dunne had spent a lot of time in L.A. and knew his way around. He felt his phone vibrate in his pocket and answered it as he exited the 10 onto Fairfax.

"Dunne."

He listened for several minutes. "Got it," Dunne said. "Glad to know I won't need all this crap I brought. I'll contact you when I get back to the jet. Let you know how it went."

He turned west onto a side street south of Pico Boulevard and slowed the Explorer as he entered the city's Little Ethiopia district. Past the intersection of Saturn and South Point View, he glanced in his rear view mirror. Driving slowly, he studied the numbers on the houses and buildings. He stopped when he saw 8935 South Point View in plastic letters on a small, dingy apartment building with a stucco exterior that needed cleaning years ago. Dunne pulled to the curb and waited for a moment, scanning the neighborhood. There was very little traffic and few pedestrians.

Perfect conditions.

Dunne opened his black leather briefcase and pulled out a pad. He looked at his watch and wrote for a moment. Reaching behind him, he unzipped a side compartment on the duffel bag and pulled out a black knit cap and gloves. From the briefcase he retrieved a Walther .22. Dunne attached a suppressor from the briefcase and chambered a round. He retrieved the Schlage key from the console and stuck it in his left jacket pocket. He did a final scan of the neighborhood before jamming the .22 into his right jacket pocket, the interior of which had been removed to accommodate the gun. Dunne exited the Explorer, keeping his right hand in his jacket.

Climbing the short flight of stairs to the main entrance, Dunne spied a big gray cat next to the entrance. The cat stared at Dunne, but never moved. "Be right out," he whispered to the cat.

Dunne keyed in the entrance code at the box by the front door, and pushed the door open when it clicked. He walked through the foyer into the dimly lit central courtyard, past a swimming pool half-filled with water that looked black in the darkness. The arms and backrest of an aluminum lawn chair jutted out of the dark water in the shallow end of the pool. He saw no one in the courtyard. Everything was quiet.

Dunne walked two flights up the back stairs, onto a walkway overlooking the courtyard, and stopped at apartment number eighteen. After a final scan of his surroundings, he removed the .22 from his jacket, gently slipped the Schlage into the lock and turned it. He pushed the door open with his forearm and walked in the front room.

No one was in the room, but whoever used it last was a real pig. Dunne shook his head at the sight—fast food cups, boxes, and bags were everywhere. Pizza crusts littered the floor. A half-eaten bean burrito on a Taco Bell wrapper rested on the coffee table next to an ash tray filled with cigarette butts. Two dozen empty beer bottles stood at attention on a dinette table outside the small kitchen.

He walked past the closed bathroom door and stopped. Light escaped from under the door, and Dunne could hear the fan running. He continued down the hall, through an open door into the only bedroom. In the light thrown by a small lamp on the night stand between two single beds, a very thin East African lay on the bed, eyes closed. Dunne noticed two red suitcases by the door. He walked quietly and stopped next to the bed, then tapped the man on the forehead with the suppressor.

The man's eyes became wide as saucers when he saw Dunne. His scream would have been heard in the bathroom had not Dunne covered the man's mouth with his gloved left hand.

Dunne pointed the .22 between the man's eyes and shushed him. While the gaunt East African calmed down, Dunne studied his features—close cut hair, high cheekbones, golden skin.

"You Somali, too?" Dunne whispered.

The man nodded quickly. Dunne gestured to the suitcases.

"You and Hasan about to leave?"

The man nodded.

Dunne placed the suppressor higher, in the center of the man's forehead. "I heard Hasan made bail. You promise you and he will never come back to the United States?"

The man nodded his assent as vigorously as he could with Dunne's hand firmly on his mouth.

"Hasan in the bathroom?"

The man nodded yes and Dunne squeezed off a quick round through the man's forehead.

PHTTT!

"Just in case you change your mind," Dunne said as he picked up the brass casing and looked closely at the man to decide if he needed to shoot him through the head again.

Nope. He won't be coming back to the U.S.

Dunne walked to the bathroom door and listened. Over the fan he heard groaning. Dunne studied the hollow core door for a moment and tried the knob. Locked. He backed up against the wall, raised his leg and kicked the flimsy door next to the knob.

The door shattered and Dunne burst through. Hasan was relaxed against the back of the toilet, eyes closed, his pants around his ankles. He gripped a tattered Hustler magazine in his left hand and his right rested in his groin.

Hasan jumped and raised the Hustler. Dunne shot through the magazine into Hasan's chest. *PHTTT*. Hasan wilted back against the toilet. Dunne placed the suppressor against Hasan's temple and shot one more time. *PHTTT*.

Dunne ripped open the Velcro belt on the tattered portfolio next to Hasan's feet on the filthy bathroom floor. He scanned the passports and plane tickets, then fanned the thick stack of $100 bills.

"You won't be needing these," Dunne said to Hasan. He stuffed the tickets, money and passports into his jacket pocket and walked through the messy apartment quietly overturning furniture and opening what few drawers there were in the sparsely appointed pig sty.

Dunne dropped a couple of bills in the front room, stepped out the apartment door and locked it. He scanned the complex, walked down the two flights of stairs, then past the nasty-looking swimming pool and out the front door. The same gray cat stared at Dunne, but never moved.

"Take it easy," Dunne said to the cat.

~ * ~

Dunne lowered the windows and enjoyed the crisp night air on his way back to the Santa Monica airport. He ripped the identification pages from the passports, crumpled them and tossed them into a trash receptacle at an empty intersection. Ten minutes later, he did the same with the plane tickets. Nearing the airport, Dunne pulled into an abandoned convenience store parking lot, rolled down the passenger window and tossed the wad of money to three startled homeless men leaning against the dumpster.

"Merry Christmas," he called out to the men as he drove off. He thought about Hasan. The Somali terrorist had been personally responsible for the death of the entire crew of a Conoco Phillips oil tanker captured in the Gulf of Aden a year ago. The U.S. Attorney in Los Angeles had good intelligence on Hasan's plan to introduce Somali-style piracy and kidnapping along the west coast of Baja California, but the newly-appointed federal district judge would not allow the testimony about the Somali's new enterprise. The judge threw out the proffered testimony at Hasan's bail hearing, saying it was "rank hearsay."

Dunne was told by his handler that the assistant U.S. attorney did his best to have Hasan held in federal lockup pending an expedited appeal, but the federal judge was very concerned about violating the defendant's rights, and would not agree to let the federal prosecutors hold Hasan for ICE.

Dunne parked the Explorer near the General Aviation lobby and walked through to the Cessna jet. The engines were warm and the pilots began to taxi as soon as Dunne took his seat and the door closed.

The Cessna lifted off over the Pacific and banked south, then east on its way to New Orleans. Dunne lowered the window shade, leaned his head back, and closed his eyes. He thought about the morning of September 11, 2001, when he died after American Airlines flight 77 crashed into the Pentagon at 9:37 a.m. Dunne felt at peace, and thanked God for the privilege of defending the United States.

"Justice delayed is justice denied," he muttered.

Chapter Seven

Jake sat in his silver 4Runner on Dauphine, waiting for the Cyndi Lauper look-a-like to move her bicycle so he could park. Parking spaces in the Faubourg Marigny district were scarce, and on the rare occasions when one appeared, it had a limited shelf life. Although the spot was a block and a half from Kitty's apartment, Jake felt lucky, grateful to the parking gods who controlled such things.

Jake tried to make the shortest, most polite honk possible, but the orange and pink-haired woman flipped Jake the bird when he lightly tapped the 4Runner horn. It seemed she had fallen into a trance staring at the lock securing her rusty, wide-tired Schwinn to the wrought iron post anchored in the cracked sidewalk next to the asphalt. Like every street in Marigny, Dauphine badly needed an overlay.

Why would Cyndi the daydreamer park her Schwinn in the gutter and take up most of a parking place when it would have been easier to secure it to the concrete bench in front of her run-down apartment? Why would Cyndi wear a pink chiffon dress that sticks out like a tutu? And most important, why would Special Agent Kitty Douglas live in Marigny?

Gentrification produced some very cool rehabilitated single-story Creole cottages and shotguns in Marigny. The corner stores that had been converted into residences were unique. But Jake was not a Marigny-type guy. Kitty was no bohemian, either, and Jake knew from his visits and from talking to her about the district, she thought the small houses and apartments, and the crooked, narrow streets were hip, but admitted life in the district was problematic. There were terrific, tiny restaurants, coffee houses and clubs on and around Frenchman Street, but every venue was so small and the tables so jam-packed, a private conversation was almost impossible. Invariably an elbow or chair from a ponytailed forty-five-year old wearing a tie-dyed tee shirt at an adjacent table would accidentally crash into Jake's ribs or slam into Kitty's chair.

Kitty's apartment was only a couple of blocks from the few majestic live oaks on Esplanade Avenue that survived Katrina. Esplanade was the northeastern boundary of the French Quarter, and on the occasions when Kitty would deign to see Jake, they would stroll across Esplanade and through the dimly lit back of the Quarter toward Canal. If they wanted to eyeball raucous college-aged drunks or freaks, they walked on Bourbon. If they wanted to saunter among more civilized tourists or locals, they walked southward on Royal, the best walking street in the Quarter. Jake enjoyed window shopping on the West side of Royal, where one antique store followed another. Kitty had no interest in antiques or furniture in general, as evidenced by her Spartan apartment on Dauphine. Except for the BMW, there was nothing in Kitty's apartment—and in her life—that wasn't utilitarian.

On their strolls, whether they took Bourbon or Royal through the Quarter, stayed in Marigny, or ventured across North Rampart into the seedy Treme district to watch ubiquitous film crews working around Congo Square or what was left of Storyville, Jake was always armed. He usually wore a sport coat to conceal his Sig Sauer P229 .40 caliber automatic in a holster on his belt in the small of his back. On duty or off, Kitty carried her Glock, well-concealed. They wanted no trouble, but like Jake always said:

You never know.

He stopped in front of Kitty's apartment, which enjoyed a rare and coveted feature in Marigny: off-street parking for two vehicles on a parking pad of old brick. Jake knew the parking spots had to have been added before the Marigny Historic District Association began the strict enforcement of the architectural rules limiting exterior improvements to those consistent with the historic period when the homes were built. The rules would have certainly excluded construction of off-street parking spaces immediately in front of the historic homes.

Kitty's 1996 E36 BMW convertible occupied her one-half of the parking pad in front of her rose-hued wood-frame cottage. Jake enjoyed driving the perfectly engineered BMW classic when they were going together in Jackson, but since relocating to New Orleans, he had been in the car only once. Kitty did not move it unless she absolutely had to. There were times when access to her parking spot was blocked by cars parked on the street, and times when someone actually parked in her place. She told Jake she hoped whoever did it was drunk, that surely no sober driver would intentionally park in her spot. Jake told her she was giving the human race too much credit.

Jake walked past Kitty's BMW onto the brick path running down the side of the small house to her apartment entrance in an alcove midway along the length of the structure. He rapped on the door and waited. She told Jake her landlord was a sixty-year-old real estate attorney who bought the place for a song and renovated it twenty-five years earlier, before Marigny became trendy. He divided it into two one-bedroom apartments and added the parking pads. Kitty's was the back half of the house. The front apartment tenant was a single woman in her forties, a pharmaceutical rep who Kitty said was on the road most of the time, except every other weekend. Kitty had been working every weekend, and had seen the woman only a half-dozen times in the eight months Kitty had been in the city. Kitty said she and the pharmaceutical rep agreed in one of their few conversations that the lawyer was an old lecher. Kitty told the rep it didn't bother her—she could take care of herself.

She cracked the door slightly and left it for Jake to push open. He stepped inside as Kitty walked barefoot away from him toward her bedroom, wearing hip-hugging black panties and a black bra. Though he saw only the back of her, Jake felt his emotions stir. Her olive skin was flawless, and her long brunette hair swung from side to side across the middle of her back as she disappeared into her bedroom, leaving the door open. Jake moved his left arm in a circular motion. The cut felt better.

"I thought you would be here sooner," she said. "It's almost dark."

"Got tied up."

He felt like a voyeur watching her comb her hair through the open door, but he couldn't help it. Their relationship when they were a couple was extremely physical—there was a lot of sex. Jake missed those days. Watching her dress made him sad, but apparently being half-dressed in front of Jake was no big deal to Kitty. At least that was how she acted.

Get over it, knucklehead.

The rational part of him agreed with Kitty that there was no future in their relationship, that she would never be the kind of traditional wife and mother he grew up around. She wanted to climb the career ladder in the FBI, and was willing to relocate anywhere, at the drop of a hat. In spite of his protests, Jake knew she was probably right about their future as a couple. He had been away at training camps during much of his New Orleans tenure, and now with E. Peter Romano actually supervising him, he would start working on gang activity, earning his government pay for a change. Given their circumstances, he did not know how it would be possible to resurrect their relationship, even if Kitty were willing.

"Ready?" she asked.

He held open the door as she exited. "Got your key?"

"Yep," she said and walked ahead of him toward the street on the narrow brick walkway. Jake inhaled the vapors that trailed behind her. He savored her natural animal scent blended with the fresh, delicate aroma of Light Blue, the Dolce & Gabanna cologne she always wore. The fragrance resurrected vivid scenes and memories from their past together—along with a strong sense of loss.

"You look pretty," he said. "Looks like working all the time agrees with you."

What leaky, pathetic bull shit, Banks. Get a grip.

"Thanks," she said. "I'm hungry."

Walking up Royal Street on the way to Beaufort's, they made a striking couple. Kitty was 5'8" with broad shoulders and a terrific figure. She moved with athleticism and grace, looking every bit the first-team All PAC-10 soccer player she had been at Washington State. To a stranger, Kitty could easily pass for Mediterranean. Jake was six inches taller and at 170 pounds, lean and hard. More handsome than Willie Mitchell, Jake had the look of a man's man, and the confident stride of a guy who knew how to handle any kind of situation that came his way. More than a few tourists stopped and turned to watch the good-looking young couple pass.

Jake ordered a Stella on draft and Kitty an Abita Amber when they were seated at the original Beaufort's on the corner of Chartres and Toulouse, across the street from the backside of a massive white stone edifice. The big building was originally the United States District Court at 400 Royal Street, with no parking *whatsoever* for lawyers, litigants, jurors and witnesses. Now it was the Supreme Court of

Louisiana at 400 Royal Street. After many millions spent on renovation, there was still no parking *whatsoever* for anyone except the seven justices, who provided themselves private spaces under the building at tremendous public expense, or so Jake read in the *Times-Picayune*.

Every member of the bar knew Louisiana trial lawyers were by far the biggest political contributors to the seven elected justices. The same trial lawyers or their designees dominated the Louisiana legislature, and controlled many of the firms who lobbied the Louisiana House and Senate. So, when the seven justices asked the legislature for tens of millions to renovate the handsome building inconveniently located in the center of the Quarter, the trial lawyers' only question was: "Begging Your Honors' pardon, but are you certain that's enough?" The plaintiff's bar wanted to make sure the justices were in comfortable surroundings when they considered the appeals of the multi-million dollar jury verdicts in favor of the same trial lawyers who were the justice's biggest contributors.

"Let us have a few minutes," Jake told the waitress when she asked for their order.

"The sandwiches here are so big," Kitty said. "You want to split a muffaletta?"

"I was thinking more along the lines of a fried oyster and shrimp po-boy with lots of tartar sauce. I'll split that and a Beaufort's salad with you, if that's okay."

"That sounds good," she said and took a sip of her Abita. "Is Willie Mitchell still improving?"

"Getting better every day. I talked to him a couple of times this afternoon. Told him what happened. He's coming along fine."

"And Susan?"

"Really happy lately. She's stepped up to the plate since Daddy got hurt. While he was laid up she had to do some things he's always done for her, and she seems more decisive now, more independent. If there's a silver lining to all this...."

"Be sure to tell them hello for me. Now, tell me about last night."

"First let me tell you who put me on the hot seat this afternoon, wanting to know what I knew about David Dunne."

"At NOPD?"

"No. At my office. In front of my new supervisor."

She thought for a moment.

"Leopold Whitman. He's using his OIG position for revenge."

"You got it. He's such a little prick."

"What did he ask you?"

"When's the last time I saw or talked to David Dunne."

"What did you say?"

"Nothing. I wouldn't answer his questions."

"That's going to create some problems for you. When is the last time you talked to Dunne?"

"I don't know exactly, but do you want to hear about what happened on Tchoupitoulas or not?"

"Yes. I do."

He told her about the murder of the two cops and his confrontation with the killer. Kitty bombarded him with questions as he told the story. When Jake described the killer's appearance, Kitty grew quiet. Jake said he "was a Cuban named Ignacio Torres. He goes by Brujo." Kitty's jaw dropped. When Jake said he had no idea why Brujo did not kill him, Jake thought he saw tears in her eyes.

Maybe she does care about me after all.

Kitty caught herself, picked up her menu, held it in front of her face as if she were studying it. After a moment, she put the menu on the table. Jake watched her closely. She knew something.

"You know about this guy Brujo?" he asked her.

She nodded. "Some."

"Bull," Jake said. "I give you all this information about last night and all of a sudden you dummy up?"

The waitress reappeared at the table.

"We'll split an oyster and shrimp po-boy and the big salad," Kitty said pointing to the pictures on the menu. "And he wants extra tartar sauce. Could you put that on the side?"

The waitress hurried off, and Jake leaned forward, elbows on the table. "What do you know about Brujo?"

"I can't say."

"Why not?"

She shrugged.

"You've got an investigation going on Brujo, don't you?"

Kitty took a big swig of her Abita and wiped the foam off her lip. She leaned forward and spoke quietly.

"We've been working with ATF for a few months on guns moving through the Port of New Orleans to Latin America. We were in on a seizure two weeks ago in a warehouse on the river where one of Brujo's men was arrested by NOPD. Big Demon Salazar. He's in OPP."

"Eustis talked about Salazar in today's briefing. Is he talking?"

"No way," she said. "Brujo apparently runs a tight ship."

"NOPD says he's bad."

"Brujo is Spanish for witch," she said. "From what I've learned about, I can say this: you are very lucky to be alive."

Chapter Eight

An hour earlier, only four blocks from Café Beaufort's, Brujo awakened in his small bedroom adjacent to the chapel. He sat on the edge of his bed. His dreams had been vivid. The holy saints were taking him through his past, in his trance at the altar and now in his dreams. He tried to think of a reason why they would lead him on this path. Perhaps the appearance of The Other on Tchoupitoulas when Brujo punished the two cops.

In the dreams, he was a little boy at Mama Coba's side while she performed her Santeria and black magic rituals. He loved watching Mama Coba—he loved being with her. As he grew older, he began to assist her, holding the candles and hand-knitted avatars in purification and exorcism ceremonies. As his coordination developed, Ignacio proved adept at killing the goats and chickens that Mama Coba used in her rites. In some services, she mixed the animal blood and a crude white paint to decorate the bodies of the dancers and communicants. She always painted Ignacio's body first.

In his dream, Mama Coba snapped at a villager who asked her about her "voodoo" powers. "No voodoo," she said. She insisted that her Santeria came from the faith of her Roman Catholic forebears in Spain, "improved" with the rituals that emerged from the Yoruban and central African cultures imported into the Caribbean via the slaves from Central Africa countries, including the Congo, Nigeria, Cameroon, and Gabon.

As Ignacio matured, he became more than an assistant. His participation in the rituals grew, and Mama Coba's followers came to invoke both Ignacio and Mama Coba in their prayers. He remembered the first time Mama Coba's followers asked him to cast a spell by himself. It made Mama Coba proud that her precocious *brujito* inherited her power to cast spells and tell the future. In some of the rituals, she tossed dried chicken feet and bones on the floor before him. Ignacio would study the bones and whisper to his Mama Coba, who would "interpret" his vision for their followers. Her impoverished believers in Santiago de Cuba paid Mama Coba in produce, livestock, or a portion of their ration of sugar or flour doled out by the government.

By the late seventies, Mama Coba realized the Cuban economy would continue to deteriorate and the Supreme Leader's revolution would never result in prosperity for her family or the nation of Cuba. Castro had stolen from Mama Coba and Hidalgo when they were in the arms business, and now he was stealing the future from Ignacio and Mama Coba. She decided it was time to leave the island. Ignacio remembered her explaining why they had to leave the island.

"Wherever you go," Brujo remembered telling her, "that's where I want to be." He recalled Mama Coba hugging him tightly after he said it.

Whether it was luck or the intervention of her Santerian saints that brought the inept peanut farmer Jimmy Carter to the White House, he was a godsend to Mama Coba and her ten-year-old *brujito*. She gathered what clothes, money, and holy relics she could and bribed an official at a Cuban mental asylum to include her and Ignacio in the Mariel Boatlift in 1980. Reluctantly, she also included her wayward son Santos in the passage after he promised to mend his ways and help her and Ignacio become successful in the United States. Mama Coba knew Santos could be charming and manipulative, and remembered that when Santos was a teenager he was of great help to her dead husband Hidalgo in his gun smuggling businesses.

Mama Coba and her "sons" were granted political asylum by Jimmy Carter's State Department and settled in a rundown two-story rental on 54th Street in Miami. Mama Coba opened her first Santeria shop on the first floor of the building. They lived in the apartment above.

For the first time in his life, ten-year-old Ignacio spent a lot of time with his natural father. They grew close, which pleased Mama Coba. It seemed to her Santos had matured. He helped Mama Coba in the shop, and developed sources in the islands for the herbs and oils to make her secret balms and powders. In his spare time, Santos hung out in local night clubs and came to know many of the up-and-coming cocaine distributors in Miami. He learned the trade, but being Cuban, he lacked the connections in South and Central America to climb to the top of the business in Florida. Santos also knew that many of the suppliers in South America did not trust Cubans.

After two years in Miami, Santos told Mama Coba he was moving to Los Angeles to go into business with his cousin Jaime Lopez. Jaime's father was Hidalgo's brother. They left Cuba before Batista fell. Jaime had called Santos in Miami many times to let him know how well he was doing in Los Angeles. He urged Santos to join him. Jaime mailed Santos photographs of him leaning on fancy cars with beautiful women in front of the Hollywood sign and other landmarks. To Santos, L.A. seemed a perfect opportunity.

    Sitting on the side of his bed in his tiny bedroom in the back of the building on Chartres, Ignacio recalled that most fateful day of his life in Miami. Ignacio was with Santos when he said he was moving to L.A. Ignacio told Mama Coba, "I am going, too."

    Ignacio was mature for his age, and she gave him her blessing, even though she knew Jaime was doing something illegal. Jaime's father and her late husband Hidalgo always made their money outside the law in Cuba, and she knew Jaime and Santos would continue the family tradition. Mama Coba had no problem with that.

    "As long as you are steadfast in his faith," she said, "I know no harm will come to you. You must promise me you will eventually come back and work with me in my church, casting spells."

    Brujo remembered his heart swelled with joy when she gave her permission. For their journey, Mama Coba gave them all the cash she had saved. Santos and Ignacio went to the Greyhound station and bought a ticket. While they waited for the bus, Ignacio watched Santos bump into and pickpocket an old man. Santos sat down next to Ignacio and counted the money he had removed from the wallet before throwing it into a trash can outside the bus station.

    "In case we need extra money for the trip," Santos said.

    Santos put his arm around his son's shoulders.

    "I am proud you are my son, Ignacio. You are brave, and you have learned sorcery and the black arts better than Mama Coba. To honor your skills, from now on, I will call you Brujo. My sorcerer."

    "We will become famous," he said with pride. "I have seen it in many visions. The world will come to know us."

Chapter Nine

"Come on, crip," Jimmy Gray said to Willie Mitchell. "Let's go."

Willie Mitchell had finished his four-mile run at the fat banker's driveway and was cooling down, catching his breath waiting for Jimmy Gray to come out of the house to begin their fifteen-minute walk around the neighborhoods of downtown Sunshine. Jimmy was Willie Mitchell's best friend and closest confidant, and always had been. Their late fathers had started the Bank of Sunshine, one of the most profitable agricultural lending institutions in the Mississippi Delta, with Jimmy's daddy raising the capital and Monroe Banks in charge of operations. Jimmy Gray owned or controlled a majority of the stock in the company, and Willie Mitchell was the second-largest shareholder. While Willie Mitchell had been District Attorney in Yaloquena County since they were in their early thirties, Jimmy's shrewd management and timely acquisitions of other, smaller banks, had grown the bank exponentially since the deaths of their fathers, substantially increasing the value of their shares of stock.

Except for Willie Mitchell, the 300-plus pound banker was the smartest man in town. Willie Mitchell looked forward to their morning walks three days a week, in part to see what Jimmy Gray would wear.

"Nice outfit," Willie Mitchell said.

Jimmy Gray wore a wife-beater and tattered tennis shorts that seemed ready to burst at the seams. The pockets stuck out like ears on an elephant. Under the shorts, some sort of lycra or other petroleum-based material encased the banker's gigantic thighs down to his knees.

"Those some Under Armor tights?"

"Naw," Jimmy said. "Under Armor's just for skinny guys. Martha took me to the Large Ladies outlet store in Jackson. These are what they call Spanx."

Willie Mitchell laughed. "I don't believe I'da told that. I guess they make Spanx for men now."

"Yeah, they do. But, they didn't have my size in the men's."

"Damn. But don't worry, your secret's safe with me. If anybody asks I'll just tell them you're wearing panty hose."

"Well, shit, I had to do something. I was going through a tub of Vaseline a week trying to keep my thighs from rubbing raw on these walks. If these Spanx don't catch fire down there they'll work better than the petroleum grease."

"Jelly. You still at three-ten?"

"Three-twelve this morning."

"Jesus, Jimmy. You're going to keel over dead one of these days."

"I eat like a bird, Goddammit. I can't lose weight no matter what. All this exercise and I'm fatter than when we started a year ago."

Willie Mitchell rolled his eyes.

"What?" the banker said.

"I'm trying to think about what kind of bird eats like you. Maybe an emu; maybe an ostrich. Maybe Rodan from the Godzilla movies."

"Rodan wasn't a bird. He was like a pterodactyl. But you're right, he was a big eater."

"Anyway, you're only walking three days a week. At fifteen to twenty minutes each day, it works out to less than an hour of exercise. For the whole week."

Jimmy shrugged. Willie Mitchell tweaked Jimmy's substantial left breast through the wife beater. "Nice tits."

"Fuck you, let's go," Jimmy said. "You scrawny-assed, gimpy-legged, half-blind, brain-seizing cripple."

Willie Mitchell laughed and set his watch. "We're off," he said as they started out the driveway. In the street thirty seconds later Jimmy began to breathe loudly. The District Attorney glanced at the banker and saw what looked like glazed sugar on his cheek.

"How much did you weigh when we started walking three days a week?"

"You know how much. Three-oh-five."

"I know. I just wanted to remind you. What did you eat this morning?"

"Nothing. Just some coffee."

"How'd you get doughnut sugar on your face?"

Jimmy reached up and knocked it off his cheek. "That ain't doughnut sugar."

"Sure looks like it."

"Cinnabon. Martha found a recipe online for Cinnabon cinnamon rolls. You know, like at the airport. There was one leftover in the fridge. I nuked it for thirty-five seconds. You talk about good."

"You cannot lose weight eating fattening crap like that, no matter how good it tastes."

"I have a low metabolism. Just like my daddy."

"Name the very overweight actor who made several successful movies in the 1980s and died at age forty-four."

"That's easy. John Goodman."

"Wrong. You owe me two bits."

"I'm right. He was in Spaceballs and Planes, Trains…,"

"Nope. John Candy. John Goodman's still very much alive."

"Well, that's who I meant. The Canadian. Uncle Buck."

"Too late."

"Name the actor who played Mr. French, the fat butler in Family Affair with Brian Keith and the two cute kids."

"Sebastian Cabot."

"Right. Who played the really, really fat detective in Cannon?"

"William Conrad. That's enough of Fat Man Trivial Pursuit. I get your point. William Conrad lived to be an old man, by the way. So did Sebastian Cabot."

"I want my quarter when we get back to your house."

They walked for half a block in silence.

"You get any more details from Jake about the two cops?"

"Just what I told you last night. He said he was taking Kitty to dinner in the Quarter after we talked."

"They dating again?"

"No. I'm pretty sure Jake would like to but apparently Kitty doesn't think it's a good idea. He doesn't tell us much."

"That's a shame. She's one good-looking woman."

"Smart, too."

"You know, it's like that e-mail I got a couple of years ago. This beautiful woman in a bikini, I mean gorgeous, and built like a brick shit house. Even at my age, like old man Fite says, she made little ole Tiny get hard as Chinese arithmetic. And that's hard."

"You going somewhere with this?"

"Just hold your horses. So, anyway, the caption under the picture said, 'No matter how good she looks, somebody, somewhere is tired of putting up with her shit'."

"Yeah, I saw that one. Let's pick up the pace a little."

Jimmy Gray tried to keep up. "Hey. I provide the entertainment here and you ain't even half-listening."

"No, I am half-listening. You left out the one about lips that looked like they could suck a tennis ball through a tail pipe. You need some new material."

"Made it so hard a cat couldn't scratch it."

"Calf rope."

"Jake tell you any more about that sawed-off dip shit Whitman?"

Willie Mitchell slowed to let Jimmy catch up.

"No. I asked him again if he was in contact with Dunne and he talked around it and changed the subject."

"No one ever gets a straight answer out of any of you lawyer-types," Jimmy said, "but sounds like Jake must be talking to him."

"Yep. Tell you something else. I've been doing some checking on Dunne. Remember when he had drinks at my house during the Zegarra trial last year? We looked at some pictures from my old basketball days. We'd both had a few pops."

"I remember."

"I'm going to send those pictures to a friend of mine at the State Police Crime Lab in Jackson. You've met Robbie Cedars before. If Dunne left some prints on those photos and Robbie can lift them somehow, I'm going to get him to run the prints through every state and federal database that the state police can access."

"You don't think Dunne's who he said he was?"

"I know this. I've tried to find Dunne through every contact I have at Quantico and D.C. and nobody's ever heard of him, or so they claim. Jake's not telling me everything he knows about Dunne and what happened that night on the reservoir when I almost died."

"How come he's keeping it to himself? That ain't like Jake."

"I don't know," Willie Mitchell said. "But I intend to find out."

Chapter Ten

Three hundred miles due south of Sunshine, two hours before Willie Mitchell and Jimmy Gray began their walking and talking, Brujo walked in the darkness of Chartres street and slipped into *La Casa de Mama Coba*. He grunted at Mantis, who was re-stocking shelves with the squatty candles made from the fat of ritually slaughtered pigs. Even the occasional tourists who browsed through the shop and tittered at the labels on the powders and potions could use an odd-looking candle.

The same tourists gawked at Mantis. He was 6'4" and gaunt, shaved head and sunken cheeks below prominent cheekbones. He never spoke to anyone except Mama Coba, which was fine with Brujo. Mantis always wore a black cassock with no adornment. His skin was light copper, and Mama Coba told Brujo that Mantis came to Miami from the Dominican Republic. He worked for her in her Miami shop, then moved with her to join Brujo in New Orleans. Mama Coba said they never discussed Mantis making the move with her—it was just understood. When she made preparations for the move, he helped her every step of the way. To Brujo's knowledge, Mantis had never driven a car. The drive from Miami to New Orleans was the first time Mantis had ridden in an automobile. He rarely left the shop or Mama Coba's side, but when he did, he was a startling sight, even by French Quarter standards. Staring straight ahead and walking fast, bent forward at the waist, he took long strides in the middle of the bumpy streets, his black robe flapping. His huge hands hung down to his knees and he waved his long, bony fingers behind him as he walked, as if paddling thorough water. Pedestrians and motorists stopped to let him pass and gawked, but he never acknowledged their existence.

When Brujo was introduced to Mantis in New Orleans, he knew immediately that Mantis was an old spirit, caught in modern times, uneasy in the world. Brujo had known others like Mantis, in Cuba and in Los Angeles. These spirits tolerated their life among today's humans, biding their time, waiting for their next embodiment. To Brujo, Mantis was a familiar—available to do Mama Coba's bidding—and absorb her wrath.

Brujo walked past Mantis into the chapel and closed the door. It was four-thirty in the morning, but he was not sleepy. Dealing with Green Eyes, Shadow, and his other men during the night at Los Cuervos' main house in the Ninth Ward had been disturbing. Brujo was not accustomed to dealing with Green Eyes or the other men of Los Cuervos—that was Big Demon's job. Brujo missed him. Big Demon was good with the men. He was one of them; Brujo was not.

Big Demon took care of enterprise details during the day while Brujo slept. But even if Brujo could have functioned during the day, he did not have the ability to pay attention to the mundane "business details" like scheduling shipping or collecting, cleaning, and boxing the guns. All that was Big Demon's responsibility. He directed the men. Brujo identified with the men of Los Cuervos no more than the stray dogs he saw in the Ninth Ward. If he could have run his operation without them he would have.

It was becoming clear to Brujo that without Big Demon, the business would fail. Since Big Demon's arrest at the wharf, things had begun to fall apart. Brujo stood at the altar and prayed, thinking about the night two weeks before when the cops took Big Demon.

That night, Brujo had finished with the supplicants in the chapel and Mama Coba had counted the money. She said it was their best night. He drove to the warehouse on the river that Big Demon had leased to collect and store the weapons they were accumulating to ship to Nicaragua. It was going to be a big transaction, with at least a hundred thousand dollar profit for Brujo and Big Demon—an almost ten-fold increase over the biggest profit they ever made in Houston. They were a good team—Brujo the strategist, Big Demon the tactician. Brujo connected with the network of gun smugglers around the Caribbean his grandfather Hidalgo and his father Santos had dealt with in the seventies and eighties. These deals were so much better than the nickel and dime transactions he and Big Demon started with in Houston—stealing weapons in burglaries and extorting gun dealers for inventory to sell to the Mexican drug cartels so they could shoot each other along the Mexican border with the United States.

Brujo cursed the two cops that took Big Demon from him that night at the wharf.

Brujo had driven to the warehouse at eleven that night to meet Big Demon. When he saw the NOPD cruiser parked outside the main door on Tchoupitoulas, he knew there was trouble. Brujo was unarmed, but tried to figure out a way he could help Big Demon. He parked on a side street and ran to the warehouse adjacent to theirs. It was in disrepair and not in use, like theirs before they leased it, and it shared a wooden dock with their warehouse. He crouched and ran in the darkness along the wooden dock without making a sound, then climbed a rusted iron ladder that ran from the dock up the back of the warehouse to a small office in the corner of the building thirty feet above the concrete floor. He crept into the office and looked out of the dirty windows at Big Demon and the two cops on the warehouse floor.

The tin building was empty except for the crates of guns stacked in one corner, ready to ship. Brujo opened the metal door to the office that led to steel steps down to the warehouse floor. He lay flat on his stomach to listen and watch for an opening to help his partner.

Big Demon faced the wall with his arms raised and legs spread. The large freight door of the warehouse was pushed all the way open, flooding the empty space with light from the headlights and strobes of the cop car.

"Search him," the muscular white cop yelled at the younger Hispanic cop. While the younger cop was checking Big Demon's pockets, Big Demon spun around and grabbed the young cop around the neck. The white cop screamed.

"Let him go or I'm going to kill you, asshole."

Big Demon was much stronger than the young cop. He held him around the neck with one arm, pressing the cop's back into Big Demon's chest, and went for the young cop's gun with his free hand. The white cop charged and smashed Big Demon on the side of his head with his automatic. Big Demon grabbed the white cop's gun hand and wrenched the gun free just as the young cop removed a knife from his belt and flipped it open.

Brujo jumped up and started out the office door to help his partner but two more NOPD squad cars pulled into the warehouse with strobes flashing. Brujo dropped back down on the office floor thirty feet above the action and watched, seething.

The young cop was still in Big Demon's grip, his back against Big Demon's chest. He stabbed blindly over his shoulder, and stuck the knife directly into Big Demon's left eye.

Big Demon did not scream, but he let the young cop go and dropped the white cop's gun. It was over. Big Demon reached up and pulled the knife out of his eye, dropped it, and placed his big left hand over what little remained of his eye. Blood squirted between his fingers and coursed down his cheek.

Four cops jumped out of the two cruisers with guns pointed at Big Demon. He raised his right arm but kept his left hand on his eye.

Brujo knew there was nothing he could do. He watched as two unmarked sedans pulled in behind the NOPD units. *Federals* stepped from the cars. One was a woman. Brujo stared at her. She was young and pretty, long brown hair and olive skin. Maybe Brazilian, he thought, or Puerto Rican. She pulled her gun, too, but it was not needed.

Big Demon lay face down on the concrete, blood flowing from his left eye. Brujo focused on the white cop and the younger cop who attacked Big Demon. He had seen them patrolling the area before.

He vowed he would see them again.

~ * ~

After re-living Big Demon's arrest, Brujo continued to stand immobile at the altar. His trances were becoming deeper, more frequent, and more important to him. Enhanced by the brown liquid he drank from the chalice, it seemed he had developed the ability to move at will from the real world to the world of his trances—a world he began to crave more and more. It was his own world, unavailable to anyone else. At times he wished he could stay in that world all the time. Except for Mama Coba, there was little that he enjoyed about the real world and the small, insignificant people in it.

Brujo re-entered his trance, and remembered the first man he saw murdered. His father Santos and Brujo had just arrived in L.A. from Miami late in the afternoon. From the downtown bus station they walked to the address cousin Jaime had given them. When they arrived at the apartment building on Virgil Street north of the 101, it was not what they had been led to expect from Jaime's letters and photographs. It was an old, run-down building. They walked to the second floor and stood outside Jaime's apartment. The door was ajar and loud music escaped into the hall.

Santos pushed open the door and walked in ahead of Brujo. Passed out on the couch, fat and shirtless, was cousin Jaime. There was a nasty hypodermic and heroin works on the plastic coffee table. On the floor against the wall was another disheveled, unconscious man.

Santos clapped his hands and nudged Jaime's belly with his shoe. Jaime sat up, dazed. He ran a pudgy hand through long, greasy hair.

"I don't have your money," he said.

"*Oye*, Jaime. It's me, Santos. *Santos Torres de Cuba.*"

Jaime tried to focus. Finally he recognized his cousin. "Welcome to L.A.," Jaime rasped. He gestured at the squalid surroundings. "You can stay with me until you get settled. Long as you want."

Santos did not ask about the beautiful women and fancy cars in the photographs. He and Brujo walked through the nasty kitchen and put their suitcases in the back bedroom, which was not as dirty as the rest of the place. Brujo made a face, wrinkling his nose. Santos shrugged.

"I know. Just for a few days," Santos said.

Thirty minutes later, Jaime walked into the back bedroom. He wore a shirt, had combed his hair, and looked somewhat alert.

"Santos," Jaime said. "I need a favor. I need you to run an errand with me. It will only take thirty minutes. You can see some of L.A."

"Brujo must come with me."

Jaime reacted to the name, studying the young boy for a moment. "Uh, sure," Jaime said. "No problem."

They drove east on Temple in Jaime's dark red Buick Regal, turned onto Coronado and stopped in front of an apartment building with a half-dozen *cholos* lounging on the stoop in loose-fitting khakis and undershirts. Before he opened his door, Jaime retrieved a revolver from under his seat and stuck it in his pants.

"For protection," Jaime said.

"Brujo, you stay here," Santos said to his son.

~ * ~

Brujo sat quietly in the back seat, watching the *cholos* for a while. He picked up a magazine from the floor and thumbed through it until he stopped at a full page photograph of a robed Madonna with a skeleton face. He stared at the empty black eye sockets and hideous sharp teeth. He read the caption: Santa Muerte and the Cult of Holy Death.

Brujo jumped when the apartment building door flew open and Jaime ran out, a crumpled paper bag in one hand and his revolver in the other. Santos followed close behind, running to the passenger side of the Regal. Jaime jumped in the driver's seat and stuck the gun in his pants.

Before Jaime could start the car, two men holding pistols raced from the building down the steps, causing the *cholos* to scatter. Jaime panicked, dropping the keys on the floor. Brujo watched Santos, standing outside the passenger door, in one lightning fast motion, stick his head and shoulders through the open passenger window and grab Jaime's revolver from his waist band. Santos stood outside the Regal, his two hands gripping the revolver, resting on the roof of the Buick.

When the two men got closer and raised their guns to shoot Jaime, Santos fired Jaime's pistol over the Regal, hitting each man. Santos jumped into the car. Jaime floored the accelerator and peeled off from the curb.

Jaime yelled and laughed, slapping his cousin Santos on the leg. Santos smiled and nodded, but Brujo could tell his father was angry.

"You were great," Jaime yelled. "What a team we are."

Santos picked up the paper bag. In the back of the Regal, Brujo sat up and peered over the seat. He saw Santos remove from the bag many small, glassine packets of white powder and folding money, mostly tens and twenties. Santos counted the cash while Jaime whooped and giggled like a kid. Santos divided the cash into two stacks.

"I'm keeping half of the money," Santos said, "about four hundred dollars. You keep the drugs and the other half of the money."

"Okay, cousin. Okay by me. You a good shot."

"I've spent a lot of time with guns."

When they returned to Jaime's apartment, Santos told Brujo to go upstairs and get their suitcases from Jaime's apartment. When Brujo returned to the sidewalk with their bags, he watched Santos shake Jaime's hand, noting the contrast in the two men. Santos was tall and slim, light-skinned; Jaime was short, fat, and dark. He looked Mexican, but Brujo knew he was Cuban like them.

"We will find a temporary place," Santos said.

"You should stay here, with me. It will be fun."

"We need a quieter home for Brujo," Santos said. "He is a studious boy."

"May I have the magazine from the back seat?" Brujo asked and retrieved the magazine with the Santa Muerte picture and article.

"Sure, *mi amigo*. Now Santos, you let me know where you are staying, soon as you get a place."

"I will, cousin," Santos said. He picked up his suitcase and gestured to Brujo. "Let's go."

Santos and Brujo walked hand-in-hand away from Coronado Street, west on Temple for so many blocks Brujo lost track. Brujo studied his father. He did his best to walk and carry himself like Santos. He tried to duplicate the look on his father's face, a look of confidence. Brujo was very proud to be his son.

~ * ~

That night they rented a bedroom on a side street off Temple from an ancient, wrinkled Mexican lady. The bathroom was in the hallway, but the house was clean, and the lady offered breakfast and dinner for both of them for a few extra dollars. Santos was very polite to her, as was Brujo. In their bedroom, there was a large picture of *La Virgen de Guadalupe,* her sweet visage in sharp contrast with *Santa Muerte.*

"I am glad we did not stay with Jaime," Brujo said. "He may be our cousin, but he is not smart. He lied to us in the letters."

"Mark my words, cousin Jaime is not long for this world. Those men he robbed today, the ones I shot, their associates will not let Jaime live. And if they don't kill him, the drugs will."

"Are we in danger?"

"No. Jaime does not know where we are and no one else in this town knows us. We will stay quiet for a while, use the time to learn the city, meet some people. I have a few names from friends of mine back in Miami. I will contact them soon. And tomorrow, we will find a pay phone and you should call Mama Coba."

"I would like that."

Brujo was very tired from the long trip and the excitement with Jaime. He climbed into the double bed and read about Santa Muerte in his magazine. In less than two minutes, he was asleep.

At four the next morning, Brujo awoke in the dark room. He reached over to Santos' side of the bed. It was empty. He jumped up and looked out the small window. He saw his father standing behind the house, and walked out to be with him.

Brujo walked carefully in the darkness toward his father, who stood on the edge of the yard, staring off into the orange lights in the distant hills and valleys.

"Be careful," Santos said quietly, "there is a drop off beyond me. Walk to my side and no further."

Brujo stood next to his father and looked into the dark abyss, a small canyon, adjacent to the old lady's back yard. Santos stared at the cars speeding by on the freeway, and so did Brujo.

"Where are they all going at this time of the morning?"

"They are living their lives. Some going to work, some going home from work. Some coming in from a night on the town. Some delivering fish or bread or milk to stores all over this city. Some just passing through the city on their way north or south."

"Some of them are good people," Brujo said. "And some of them are bad."

Santos lit two cigarettes, left one in his mouth and gave the other to Brujo. He put his arm on his son's shoulder and took a deep drag of the cigarette. Brujo sucked the cigarette smoke into his lungs and exhaled at the same time as his father.

"And how do we fit in, with the good or bad?" Santos asked.

"In neither," Brujo said. "We exist far above their world."

Chapter Eleven

Jake thought he heard something.

It was four-thirty in the morning, five hours after he walked Kitty back to her apartment in Marigny. He ate too much at Beaufort's and had been in the middle of a strange dream. Jake was at Ole Miss in law school. He was late for a critical final exam, and when he finally found the room where the test was being given, the door was locked. He peered through the reinforced glass panel at eye level and saw the tattooed man, Brujo, inside holding a gun on Mr. Lattimore, the old, stooped law professor who taught Jake ethics. Brujo spotted Jake. He released the professor and ran straight at Jake. Jake was frozen, unable to move, and watched through the glass panel with increasing terror as Brujo raced for the door. Jake reached for his Sig but it wasn't there. Brujo grabbed the door handle and jerked on it, somehow jostling Jake. Brujo pulled harder, bumping Jake again.

"*Jake,*" he thought he heard Brujo say through the door. "*Jake.*"

Jake jumped, threw the covers back. His feet hit the floor and he tried to stand. He couldn't. He felt a hand on his shoulder, holding him down. The globe light on the ceiling fan was on, blinding Jake.

"Calm down, Jake. It's me."

Jake was groggy; confused but relieved. He finally focused.

"Jesus, Dunne. You scared the crap out of me."

"Sorry. I tried to be gentle."

"You need to work on that. How'd you get in?"

Dunne shrugged and Jake knew it was a silly question. There were few conventional residential locks that could keep Dunne out. Jake's condo complex had a weak level of security on the Magazine Street entrance, but none at the underground parking ingress on Julia. Jake's condo door had an automatic lockset and a deadbolt, neither of which was much of an obstacle for Dunne.

"You need to teach me how to do that," Jake said.

"After your physical and firearms training. Let me take a look at your arm."

Jake turned to display his left arm. Dunne studied the long cut.

"Lupo needs to be more careful. I'll have someone talk to him."

"Wasn't his fault," Jake said. "Don't make a big deal out of it."

"Hurt pretty bad?"

"Yeah, but it's better than it was. What are you doing here?"

"Why don't you get dressed and I'll make some coffee. You had enough sleep?"

"I'm okay."

Dunne walked out of Jake's bedroom. Jake went into his bathroom, splashed water on his face and brushed his teeth. He put on some jeans and a tee shirt to join Dunne, who leaned against a cabinet in the kitchen, waiting for Jake's one-cup Keurig coffee brewer to finish.

"These things are cool," Dunne said, pointing to the machine.

"A lot easier and quicker. I usually take the cup with me on my way out the door."

Dunne lifted his mug from the brewer and took a sip. Jake removed Dunne's plastic coffee packet and inserted his own to brew.

"Leopold Whitman was in the office yesterday."

"So I heard," Dunne said. "He give you a hard time?"

"He was very unhappy with my attitude. Wanted to know the last time I had seen or spoken to you."

"Sorry you got put on the spot. You haven't done anything. It's me he's after."

"I didn't answer his questions, but he's not through with me. He's a smart, tenacious jackass. In his OIG position he can make it very uncomfortable for me, probably get me fired, if not indicted."

Dunne nodded. "I hated to see that little pissant get that appointment, but there wasn't anything I could do about it at the time. I think I can keep a little of the heat off you. I'll make a call today."

"Hope you can do some good." Jake took a sip of his coffee. "I'm really anxious to get some prosecutions going against the local gangs. Met my new supervisor yesterday at Whitman's interrogation."

"I checked Romano out. He's a stand-up guy. Good prosecutor, they say, not the typical Justice Department bureaucrat."

"He said he's met Daddy a couple of times."

"How's Willie Mitchell doing?"

"A lot better. Almost back to normal. You ought to call him."

"Wish I could. He doesn't know about your training...."

"No. He asks about the hit and run, and he's curious about you. I've avoided talking about it as much as I can, but he's not going to let up until he finds out the truth."

"He can't know what you're doing."

"I know." Jake took a sip of coffee.

"You still haven't told me why you're in New Orleans."

Dunne gestured to the small living room and sat on Jake's sofa.

"Brujo is why I'm in New Orleans. Soon as you called and told me that you were the passenger on the ride along when the two cops were killed, I made arrangements to lay over a couple of hours down here. You need to know who you're dealing with. So does Eustis. I e-mailed Eustis some files on him just a few hours before we talked that day."

"He told me. I know from the other night he's a cold-blooded killer. And crazy."

"He's more than that." Dunne looked at his watch. "I got to get to the airport. I've only got another thirty minutes on the ground here. I've got an ongoing operation in the woods up north that I have to tend to. It's moving into the ninth inning and I have to be there."

Jake watched Dunne sip his coffee. At six-two and about one-eighty, Dunne was the same height as Jake but ten pounds heavier. He was mid-forties, almost twenty years older than Jake, and clean cut, with a military bearing. A two-inch raised scar on his left jawbone was the only indication of the dangerous life Dunne lived.

Jake knew Dunne had given up any hope of a normal life in order to defend the United States and its citizens from terror and mayhem arising from within the country's own borders. Jake admired the hell out of him for what he was doing. Jake was bound and determined to help Dunne any way he could.

"Tell me everything you can about what happened on your ride along, then I'll tell you why Brujo has popped up on my radar screen."

"Okay. While you're at it, maybe you can tell me why he didn't kill me? He could have easily."

"I've been thinking about that. With what I know about Brujo, there's no way you should be alive."

Jake heard the soft buzz of Dunne's phone vibrating. Dunne held up his right index finger and pulled his phone from his pants pocket.

"Dunne," he said. Jake sipped his coffee while Dunne listened.

After a moment, Dunne said "I'll get him there." He folded his phone and stuck it back in his pocket.

"That was Eustis. They think they might have Brujo cornered."

"Where?"

"One of those abandoned homes on the eastern edge of the Ninth Ward. He thought you might want to be there when it goes down."

Jake jumped up.

"Hold on," Dunne said. "You got any gear?"

"Not here. Let's go anyway."

Dunne walked into Jake's narrow entrance hall and came back with a black duffel bag. He tossed it on the sofa and from its impact, Jake could tell it was heavy. Jake unzipped the bag and looked in.

"You can check it out later. Get dressed and I'll drop you off. I'll fill you in about Brujo on the way."

Jake rushed into his bedroom and came out two minutes later dressed in black from head to toe: combat pants and long-sleeved knit shirt, military boots, baseball-style cap, and his .40 caliber Sig Sauer P229 in a black holster on his side.

Dunne had emptied the contents of the duffel bag on the sofa. Jake stared at pistols, knives, grenades, and a pile of other gear.

"Just leave that stuff on the sofa. I've put everything you need for this gig in the duffel. Let's go. I parked on Magazine."

Jake glanced at his watch. Five o'clock. Still dark. He told Dunne no one would be stirring in the condo complex. They walked out the main entrance. Dunne sped on the surface streets toward I-10 and began to tell Jake the history of Ignacio Torres, a.k.a. Brujo.

Jake listened while examining the contents of the black duffel bag on his lap. He pulled out the twelve gauge Benelli shotgun with a pistol grip and loaded it with the tactical buckshot rounds Dunne had provided. Jake checked out the Kershaw folding knife, compact trauma kit, and heavy black body armor vest.

Racing up the ramp to head east on the elevated interstate, Dunne was talking fast. Jake interrupted.

"This isn't the best way to the Ninth Ward."

"That's not where we're going."

Jake thought a moment. "You're taking me to the FBI office on Leon Simon?"

"That's right."

"Why don't we just meet them in the Ninth Ward. It's a lot closer."

"You're a fed. Eustis says feds are in on this, but just in support mode. NOPD is primary. They're going in first and they would not want you showing up separately from the fed contingent."

"Why'd I bring all this gear?"

"You never know," Dunne said.

Jake smiled. Dunne was right. It was a good mantra. Jake was glad Dunne shared it with him months ago. You have to prepare for every possibility. You have to be ready, always aware of your circumstances. *You never know.*

"When I watched Brujo kill Byrne and Dominguez," Jake said, "it was like he was on a mission. It didn't seem like he was just killing them for pulling him over, or just to kill cops. He seemed really mad at those two guys in particular. I mean, yelling at the dead bodies, pacing around, doing some kind of prayer. And the way he looked at me in the back seat of the cruiser. It was very strange."

"Brujo is a highly unusual offender."

"So why are you investigating him? Why would the DOGs care?"

"Guns," Dunne said. "Lots of guns."

Jake said nothing.

"Let me tell you about this cat."

Dunne recounted what he knew of the history of Ignacio Torres beginning with his father Santo's rise to prominence in the L.A. gang world, resurrecting a moribund Chicano street gang known as *Calle Virgil Rifa*, named for Virgil Street, where the founders lived.

"A lot of this information comes from interrogations of the gang members by LAPD after Santos was killed in a raid. They said Santos joined the gang in the early eighties and began importing the highest quality cocaine and heroin from Mexico. He was smarter than the guys at the top, and reorganized their distribution channels. In 1983, Santos saw to it that *Calle Virgil Rifa* was the first Hispanic gang to market crack cocaine. White boys from Hancock Park, Brentwood, and Beverly hills with more money than sense found their way to Virgil Street for Santo's drugs. The money was pouring in, and in short order, Santos was running the gang. *Numero Uno*.

"Because he was Cuban, Santos figured he needed an angle to control the Mexicans working for him. Santos became known in gang circles for his bloody animal sacrifice rituals and witchcraft. He and Brujo had all the gangs spooked, even his own men."

"So that's where Brujo learned all this Santa Muerte and Santeria hocus pocus," Jake said. "From his father in L.A."

"I don't know," Dunne said, "but Brujo conducted weekly religious or black magic ceremonies, whatever it was, and the gang members were required to attend. They had animal sacrifices and drank the blood of goats or calves they killed. They said young Brujo's favorite ritual involved wringing the neck of a strong young chicken and watching the headless bird flap his wings and run around, then picking up the dead bird and squeezing drops of blood from the chicken's neck into his mouth. They said he would laugh, blood running out the sides of his mouth. And Brujo was only a teenager at this time. Santos kept his men scared with the Santa Muerte shit, and provided them the best weaponry available so that *Calle Virgil Rifa* became known not only for its high quality drugs but also for having the best guns on the street."

"And the Santa Muerte and animal sacrifice stuff," Jake said.

"Yeah. So LAPD started paying attention. About this time a crew of up-and-coming gang bangers east of Virgil Street began poaching, trying to take over some of Santos' streets. It was a bunch of teenagers, and Santos decided to make an example of them. He had the leader kidnapped, and took him to a room in the back of a cantina on Virgil Street. Santos stripped the kid and hung him upside down from a ceiling rafter, leaving him hanging for two days without food and water. Santos spread the word and made every member drop by the cantina to witness Santos take his revenge.

"At the end of the second day, with the seventeen-year-old pleading for mercy and promising never to trespass again, Santos shot the boy in the head with a dozen *Calle Virgil* members watching, then skinned the kid's face and left him hanging. Brujo mixed the boy's blood with whitewash and painted his own face and Santos' with it. Eyewitnesses swore that Brujo chanted while Santos skinned and dismembered the teenager."

"Holy shit," Jake said.

"They say Brujo was no more than fourteen or fifteen when he did all this with his father."

"Some of the members told LAPD that Brujo chanted around the dead seventeen-year-old in *Nahuatl*, the ancient, dead language of the Aztecs and Zapotecs."

"How would they know that?"

Dunne shrugged. "That's what they told LAPD. Anyway, by 1990 Santos was on top of the drug world in L.A., but he went the route of most of these assholes—he used so much of his own dope he went off the deep end"

"What did he do?"

"He claimed he had a vision about a rival gang leader. He sent one of his men in to meet and negotiate one-on-one, and the guy Santos sent not only killed the rival gang leader, he cut off his head and brought it back to Santos in a bag. LAPD found the head under Santos' bed when they raided *Calle Virgil Rifa* headquarters. Cops pumped fifteen rounds into Santos. That was the end of *Calle Virgil Rifa*."

"Man-oh-man," Jake said.

"And they could never prove it, but guess who the gang members told LAPD was the go-between who cut off the rival gang leader's head and brought it back to Santos."

"Brujo," Jake said.

"You got it."

Chapter Twelve

Dunne turned into the parking lot of the FBI office near Lake Ponchartrain and drove Jake as close to the building as he could.

"Good luck," Dunne said, shaking Jake's hand.

"I'll call you later and let you know...."

"No," Dunne said. "I'll be incommunicado for a while. Call you as soon as this operation up North is over. But Jake, don't be disappointed if Brujo's not where NOPD thinks he is. Lot of these raids fizzle out."

"I'm hoping for the best. Maybe he got sloppy."

"Maybe," Dunne said and sped away. Jake slipped on his body armor vest, wincing when he bent his left arm. Alone in the parking lot, holding the Benelli, Jake realized walking through the front door in full gear might not be a good idea. Darkness was giving way to dawn, but even in good light, the feds didn't know him, and would not assume he was on their team. He grabbed his justice department badge, ready to flash it.

As he walked toward the entrance, the front door burst open and Kitty flew out, dressed in black combat attire and body armor.

"What are you doing here?" she yelled.

"I'm here for the raid on Brujo in the Ninth Ward."

"No, you're not."

"Check with your supervisor. Captain Eustis called him."

"Stay right here," Kitty said. She ran inside. Five minutes later, she came out fuming. "Great," she said.

"What?"

"You're coming along all right, but you can't ride in the SUV."

"Why?"

"Policy."

"What policy?"

"Shit. I don't know. It's what my supervisor said. I've got to drive you in a separate vehicle. A crappy Ford sedan."

Jake shrugged. "Sorry."

"Stay here," she barked.

Kitty took off at a trot. Two shiny black SUVs with dark-tinted windows roared past Jake headed east. A few minutes later, a navy blue Crown Victoria that had seen better days raced around the side of the building and screeched to a stop next to Jake.

"Get in," she said through the open passenger window. "Hurry."

"Okay," Jake said. "Why don't you drive?"

She shot him a glance that said he was a smart ass.

Minutes later, Kitty was headed south on Franklin. She drove aggressively, passing slower traffic, trying to catch the black SUVs.

Jake looked out his window. In Jackson, when they dated, Kitty always drove her BMW E-26 convertible like she was late for a meeting. She never needed directions, either. Unlike any woman Jake had known, Kitty was a human GPS. She even knew north from south, east from west. She knew her way around New Orleans better than Jake.

"Don't get us killed."

"Did your boss say where y'all are meeting up with the NOPD SWAT team?"

"No. That's why we have to catch them."

"There they are," Jake said. Kitty closed quickly and followed the second SUV. She used the same techniques Jake learned at the camp Dunne sent him to in Texas—staying within a few feet of the vehicle in front of her in the caravan to make sure no vehicle could cut her off from the others. Kitty was right on the SUV's tail. The SUV windows were heavily tinted, and its profile was three feet above Kitty's sedan.

The FBI three-vehicle caravan turned into a Popeye's Fried Chicken parking lot near North Claiborne Avenue and waited. Ten minutes later, two NOPD black SUVs turned onto Franklin from North Claiborne and passed Popeye's, driving south on Franklin.

The three FBI vehicles left Popeye's parking lot and fell in behind the NOPD SUVs. The armada turned left off Franklin and onto St. Claude. With little distance between the vehicles, they moved slowly toward the eastern horizon, which grew brighter by the minute.

Jake slid lower in his seat to study the rust-encrusted drawbridge on St. Claude that crossed over the Inner Harbor Navigation Canal.

"Jeez," Jake said. "Like something out of the nineteenth century."

"You think they could have replaced these with the billions they wasted down here on Katrina relief," she said.

The NOPD vehicles slowed to a crawl on St. Claude, then came to a stop six blocks east of the drawbridge. A fully-armored SWAT officer left the first NOPD SUV and walked past the other NOPD vehicle. He stopped at the lead FBI vehicle. He talked to the FBI driver for a few minutes, then raised his left wrist and pointed to his watch. The officer walked back to the lead NOPD SUV and got in. The five vehicle caravan turned onto Flood Street, creeping south toward the river.

"Look at this," Jake said. "Unbelievable."

In the first few blocks off St. Claude, five years after Katrina's devastation, there were a dozen vacant lots. The homes had been bulldozed. There was no sign of any work on the empty lots—these homes would not be replaced.

There were a handful of frame homes on either side of the street that were vacant, but appeared to be salvageable with some work. Large, spray-painted red circles still graced the front walls, along with letters and numbers in the four quadrants created by a faded red "X" inside the circle. Jake did not know what the letters and numbers meant, though he knew the rescue workers used special codes to indicate the number of dead bodies inside some of the houses.

Jake saw other homes on the street that should have been bulldozed. The front yards were grown up in weeds; trees grew through porches and inside rusted automobile hulks in the front yards.

"No one lives on this block," Jake said. "And they never will again. It's a damn shame."

"Be a good place for a hideout," Kitty said. "Like a ghost town."

"I guess that's why Brujo's here."

The caravan stopped. The lead officer stepped from the first SUV and made a circle in the air with his index finger. NOPD and FBI SWAT teams poured from the SUVs. Each man quickly checked his semi-automatic carbine, and held it across his chest in a tactical carry method. The swarm of black-helmeted, armored men with a lot of fire power ran south toward a frame house in the next block, less than a hundred yards from the Mississippi River.

"Here we go," Jake said as Kitty and he exited the Ford sedan. "Time to boogie."

Jake wanted to be the first man through the door.

"We're just observers, Jake. Remember. Stay out of the way. NOPD SWAT is the lead, FBI SWAT is backup. We are here to watch. We only help if we're needed."

"Okay. Okay."

Jake's eyes remained glued on the small house. He and Kitty watched the NOPD team surround it. Jake began walking faster to catch up, then half-jogging as the lead SWAT officer stepped back to let the cop behind him smash the door in with a steel ram.

~ * ~

The lead NOPD officer entered the house with his carbine at his shoulder, his right cheek against the stock, ready to fire. He saw no one in the small front room. A half-dozen SWAT members were right behind him, ready to kill. The leader moved quickly into the empty kitchen, and through a swinging door into a sitting room.

A heavily tattooed Mexican in the sitting room stood and aimed an automatic pistol at the SWAT leader. The SWAT officer shot him in the chest and knocked him backwards onto the grimy red velour sofa.

The SWAT leader and the men behind him kept moving. They opened a door in the sitting room and entered the next room. There was no one in it, but the SWAT men stopped for a second to gawk. It was a shrine of some sort, with odd murals and writing on the walls and ceiling. Candles were everywhere, some burning dimly. There was a robed figure with a skeleton's face.

They moved into the last room in the house, a bedroom. It was already secure. NOPD SWAT officers entering from the other door had a Hispanic man, about twenty, face down on the bed, his hands behind his back, bound with a plastic zip tie. Huddled in the corner, trembling, was a pre-teen Hispanic girl wearing only a small, dirty tee shirt. Her knees were pulled up under her chin, her face buried in her folded arms.

~ * ~

When Jake heard the shot he ran toward the house.

"Stop," Kitty yelled after him.

He kept running until he entered the tiny front yard. Two FBI SWAT men stopped him just as the NOPD SWAT stepped onto the porch and announced: "All clear."

Jake relaxed. The action was over.

One of the FBI agents grabbed Jake's upper left arm. Pain shot through him and by instinct and training, Jake turned and trapped the agent's hand. Jake applied pressure like he was taught and the agent yelped in pain, going down on one knee.

Kitty grabbed Jake's right arm. Jake let the agent's hand go.

"Have you lost your mind, Jake?"

"Sorry," Jake told the agent and offered to help him up.

"Fuck you," the red-haired, crew cut agent said and walked away.

"He's with the U.S. Attorney's office," Kitty said loudly.

"What the shit's he doing here?" the second agent said.

Jake looked behind him in the street. Captain Bill Eustis had seen the whole thing.

Eustis walked into the yard next to Jake. "Let's have a look inside when it clears, Jake," the captain said.

They waited for a moment to let the SWAT teams exit the house. Kitty walked over to the red-haired agent who stopped Jake in the yard. Jake could tell he was still mad. Kitty was trying to smooth things over. As he stood with Eustis, Jake felt the hair on his neck bristle. He had a strange feeling.

Someone was watching him.

He turned away from the house and searched the street. His eyes stopped at a two story structure on the river at North Peters. Jake saw no one. But there were eyes on him. He was certain.

"Watch your step," Jake heard someone say. He turned to see three SWAT members escorting an Hispanic man in his late teens or very early twenties. His head was shaved; his body covered with tattoos.

"Stop here," one of the SWAT men said in the yard. They replaced the plastic zip tie with handcuffs.

Jake watched the man straighten up and stare at the two story building on the river. Jake spun around to study the building.

Brujo is on that roof. He's watching it all.

The handcuffed gangster turned his attention to Kitty, still standing with the two FBI agents. He winked and flicked his tongue at her. Jake stepped between Kitty and the gangster. Jake glared at the man in custody.

"Come on, Jake," Captain Eustis said from the front door of the house. "Let's go on in."

"Yes, sir," Jake said.

Jake waited for Kitty to join him. They walked onto the small porch. Jake searched the roof of the two story building on the river one last time, and entered the house.

He followed Eustis through the kitchen into the sitting room. Jake looked at the dead gang banger on the filthy red couch. He was early twenties, shaved head, tattooed to the max, and holding the chrome .357 automatic he never got to fire.

"Two to the chest," Captain Eustis said. He picked up the sofa cushion without disturbing the body. "Here you go," Eustis said.

There were two semi-automatic rifles, a shotgun, and another chrome .357 automatic in the sofa. Eustis lay the cushion on top of the weapons.

"You wanna find guns, always check the sofa. Stupid bastards always hide them in the sofa. Nine times out of ten."

Kitty walked through the door into the last room. Eustis pulled Jake to the side. "I saw the move you put on that FBI agent outside. Brought him to his knees. I know that agent. He's no lightweight."

"I didn't even think. He grabbed me where my arm was cut."

"The guy they took away in cuffs," Eustis said, "the Romeo with the ten-year-old girl friend, is Tito Garcia. 'Green Eyes' they call him. We missed Brujo, but we got the next best thing. They say Green Eyes is way up in the organization, right under Brujo and Big Demon."

"Come look at this," Kitty said from the other room.

Jake followed Eustis into the room and was stunned. The walls were covered with stylized graffiti. "Los Cuervos" was written ten different ways. There were crows drawn and painted, in flight and on wooden posts, so professionally done they looked real. Jake moved closer to Kitty.

"What planet are we on anyway?"

Two large eyes dominated the top of one wall. Jake would have recognized them anywhere. They were the eyes he saw on Tchoupitoulas—the eyes of the man who killed Dominguez and Byrne.

Jake was drawn to a robed figure in the corner. It was not a statue, but a frame in the shape of a woman, draped with a satin robe and head covering. It stood on a cheap end table, at least four feet tall. The woman was dressed like the Virgin Mary, with a glittery tiara, but with the face of death—a skeleton head with empty black eye sockets.

"Santa Muerte," Eustis said. "Saint Death. The patron saint of Mexican gangsters. They think she protects them. This shrine's where they worship her. Their church."

Eustis pointed to the sinister crow perched on Santa Muerte's shoulder. To Jake, the crow looked real, stuffed by a skilled taxidermist. The artist preserved the crow's penetrating eyes.

"Los Cuervos," Eustis said. "The Crows. Brujo's gang."

Kitty walked across the room. Jake whispered to Eustis. "You get all this info on Brujo from Dunne?"

Eustis nodded.

"Can you forward it to me?"

"Not to your office."

Jake pulled out a card and printed his personal e-mail address.

"Your eyes only," Eustis said.

Jake said okay, and continued to study the macabre display. In front of Santa Muerte, arrayed like offerings, were an unopened bottle of El Conde Azul Blanco, which Jake knew was a very expensive tequila, two shiny red apples, a partially burned Cohiba cigar, and a small stack of ten dollar bills.

Scattered around the room on every flat surface available, were hundreds of candles of every size and shape. Tiny flames flickered weakly from two dozen of the candles.

Jake walked a couple of steps and stood next to Kitty. He looked up at the piercing eyes on the wall and shuddered.

"What do you think about all this?" she asked.

Jake could not shake the feeling that Brujo was aware of everything that was going on.

"I think we need to be really careful. Both of us."

Chapter Thirteen

Jake stood next to Kitty behind one-way glass. Consistent with their rank and importance in their respective agencies, the two of them were in the last row of viewers behind three FBI supervisors and four NOPD detectives. Jake recognized the detectives from the briefing on Brujo the day before by Captain Eustis. From their vantage point, it was difficult for Jake and Kitty to get a sustained look at the defendant. They shifted positions frequently, depending on movement in the rows of the men in front of them.

On the other side of the glass, in the interrogation room, Tito "Green Eyes" Garcia sat shackled and silent across from Captain Eustis and Detective Pizzolato. Green Eyes said nothing. No matter what Eustis said or did, Green Eyes did not respond. Jake watched Eustis close his file folder. Pizzolato followed suit.

Jake stood on his tiptoes to study Green Eyes' tattoos in the fluorescent light of the NOPD interrogation room. No color, black and gray style—the way prisoners tattooed each other. Tito wore a sleeveless tee shirt, so all Jake could see were his arms, neck, and head. Even so, there were plenty of tattoos for Jake to decipher.

Green Eyes sported two vicious crows that began on his cheeks and curved around his eyes so that their sharp beaks met in the center of Tito's forehead. The skeletal head of Santa Muerte graced his left arm and Quetzalcoatl, the Aztec feathered serpent, covered his right. A gray and black rattlesnake slithered around Green Eyes' neck.

"Charming," Kitty whispered.

"This guy's never going to tell Eustis anything," Jake said quietly.

Two men in the first row turned to glare at Kitty and Jake. Jake gestured to Kitty to follow him to the back of the observation room.

"This thing's about to wrap," he whispered.

"I'm headed to my place to clean up, then I'm going to the office. You need a ride?"

"If you could drop me by my condo that would be great."

Ten minutes later Kitty was driving the dark blue FBI sedan on Tulane Avenue toward downtown.

"That was a bonehead move bringing that Special Agent to his knees at the house," she said. "He was really pissed."

"Sorry. He grabbed me right on my sore arm."

"He didn't know. You embarrassed him in front of all those cops."

"Think he's going to say something to cause me a problem?"

"I think I talked him out of it. His name's Larry Beauvais. For future reference, they don't want you or any other DOJ prosecutors going with them on raids. They don't like lawyers."

"Neither do I."

Kitty pulled over to the curb on Magazine and Jake grabbed the black duffel, making sure it was zipped so the Benelli was concealed.

"See you later," he said.

Jake closed the door and watched her drive off. He hustled through the common area up the stairs to his condo. As he neared the door, he saw a long cardboard tube lodged between the door knob and jamb.

Remembering his training, he looked at the cardboard thoroughly before he touched it. It was exactly what he thought it was—the rough cardboard from inside a roll of paper towels.

Jake touched only the edges of the cardboard. It had been sliced cleanly down one side. He opened the tube and inside, written in primitive child-like print in gritty charcoal were five words:

I know who you are.

Jake looked around. He dashed to the rail overlooking the central atrium. He flew down the steps two at a time to the first floor. Jake did not draw his Sig, but kept his right hand on it in the holster on his side. He stepped out into the common areas on the first floor and scanned every walkway and alcove. The place was deserted. He walked outside to the sidewalk on Magazine Street and looked north and south, then to the corner and searched east and west on Julia. Nothing.

Back inside, Jake placed the cardboard tube in a Ziploc freezer bag. He moved aside the guns, knives, and ammunition Dunne left for him on the sofa to clear a place to sit. He held up the Ziploc bag and studied the jagged, black scrawl for several minutes.

"Uh-oh," he said.

~ * ~

Brujo watched the FBI woman drive the dark blue FBI sedan away from the curb on Magazine. He pulled his Astros baseball cap lower on his forehead and cranked the tan 2004 Pontiac Grand Am. He saw her turn onto Camp Street north toward the Quarter and followed. There was no need to stay close; he knew where she lived on the other side of Esplanade. He thought about the first time he saw the woman. She was among the federal agents who joined the New Orleans *Policia* at the Tchoupitoulas warehouse right after the two rogue cops tried to kill Big Demon. They attacked Big Demon for no reason—they took his left eye.

Brujo pictured the black blood of the two dead cops pooling around their bodies. It was right and just to kill them. He owed it to Big Demon to pray the powerful incantation of Ekahau on their souls as they departed the unholy bodies of the two cops.

May their spirits wander in fear for eternity.

Brujo made the sign of the cross, and kissed the small image of Santa Muerte tattooed on the knuckle of his right index finger.

He saw the FBI woman the second time, the morning of the raid in the Ninth Ward, standing with The Other. The way they stood together and talked, the way The Other looked at the woman—Brujo knew they were connected. She was his woman. Their auras commingled. He was angry at himself for not sensing it when he saw her at the warehouse. He was certain he could have divined it had he not been so angry at Big Demon's attackers.

Brujo had warned The Other with the note he left at his door. He wanted him to understand what was coming. When he recognized him that night in the back seat of the dead cops' car on Tchoupitoulas, Brujo was actually relieved. He had long wondered when The Other would appear again, and in what form. Brujo followed The Other from the police station to his apartment the morning he slayed the demon cops.

Now was as good a time as any to begin the conversion of The Other. It was the only way to stop the pursuit. Killing the young man would not put an end to The Other. In order to stop him, Brujo had to show him the way of knowledge and power, the way Mama Coba showed Brujo from an early age.

Only then would the harassment end. The Other will become an ally instead of an enemy, perhaps take over Big Demon's duties until he's released.

Brujo knew how to start The Other's re-education process. But first, he had to get his attention.

We will begin with the consort.

Chapter Fourteen

Kitty was tired. The debriefing at FBI headquarters started at noon and lasted until way past quitting time. The bureaucrats wanted to know every detail of the raid in the Ninth Ward. There were scores of forms and reports to file.

"Everything but an environmental impact statement," Kitty said to a fellow agent. "Takes more time to do the paperwork than the actual raid." The photographs one of the FBI SWAT guys took of the shrine room were a big hit in the meeting. Comments about the shrine had begun to filter in from all over the country, especially from Houston and Los Angeles, after the digital photos were downloaded into the FBI nationwide computer system.

It was close to dark when Kitty left the office. She did something she rarely did in New Orleans. She pushed the button under the BMW dash to put the top down on her convertible. It was a warm night with no chance of rain. After rising at four and a grueling day, Kitty wanted to feel the wind in her hair on the way home. Before she pulled out of the parking lot, she placed her Glock in the narrow console between the seats to keep it handy.

Like Jake says: You never know.

She saw where Jake had called her cell several times since she dropped him off at his condo after the raid. She called him back when she had decent service and left him a voice mail that she was tired and going straight to bed, and would call him first thing in the morning to let him know how the debriefing went.

Kitty enjoyed working in New Orleans much more than her assignment in Jackson, where she met Jake. New Orleans was a bigger office, with more interesting investigations underway. Her involvement in the Brujo case had been exciting. She was the youngest agent and only woman on the raid, and it was fun describing in detail the Santa Muerte shrine on Flood Street to the desk bound agents at the office.

New Orleans was a cosmopolitan city, and her office personnel reflected it. Jackson had been much more provincial, the culture stilted. It was like they had never seen a female cop or FBI special agent in Jackson. She got to the point where if another person said *"yes ma'am"* to her she thought she would scream. Kitty felt she had clawed her way to where she was. She was no ingénue. She was a capable agent in the field, and demanded respect from those around her, not condescension, and certainly not lechery.

Mississippi had been good in one respect, though. She met Jake. Kitty was head over heels for him for a while. She loved being around him, and the sex was incredible—the best she ever had. But after she spent time with Jake's mother Susan in their home in Sunshine, Kitty knew she was not the kind of girl Susan and Willie Mitchell Banks wanted for their oldest son. Kitty was sure they wanted grandchildren sooner rather than later, and by Mississippi standards, Jake and Kitty were getting on in years.

She also knew Jake would want to marry someone who would please his parents, and she did not think she was that girl. The Banks were a close knit family, and Kitty was positive she would never fit in. She had no interest in learning which crystal stemware went where, or what to do with the half-dozen silver flatware pieces that Susan placed around her plate at the dinners at the Banks home in the heart of the Mississippi Delta.

Formal place settings for the four of us, Willie Mitchell, Susan, Jake, and me when I was there. It was second nature to Jake, all the rigmarole around the dinner table. Susan would have to teach me everything if I married Jake. Hell. What am I saying? I don't want to marry anybody. I would love to see Jake again, and not just as a friend, and would love to live with him, as long as he did not want me to have babies. Living in sin—Susan would not like that at all. I don't want children. Mother was clingy and subservient to the men who lived with us from time to time. It made me sick to my stomach to see her grovel and put up with what she did. It's why she's in that facility in Tacoma—it drove her insane. It's a miracle I didn't get raped by one of her white trash boyfriends. Thank God she only had me.

The warm evening air was drier than normal and Kitty loved the feel of the wind. When she stopped at one of the many red lights on Elysian Fields, she made a point to check out her surroundings. With the top down she knew she was vulnerable, but the Glock was a great equalizer. As she neared St. Claude, the last big intersection before Marigny, she began to think how good it was going to feel to crawl into her bed and go to sleep.

Kitty stopped on Dauphine before she pulled into her parking place to make sure there was no one lurking. It was dark, but she could see well enough to know it appeared safe. She parked and raised the top, securing it inside and rolling up the windows. She stuck the Glock in her purse and patted the BMW's dashboard and spoke to it.

"Thanks. That was fun." She loved her little car.

She did not know her neighbors, except for the woman pharmaceutical rep who rented the front half of her house. There were several that she recognized. Kitty waved to them and they smiled and waved back, but that was it. She told herself she needed to hang out in the neighborhood more, meet some people instead of working seven days a week.

Kitty locked her car door and walked on the narrow brick walkway toward her apartment entrance on the side of the house. She walked up the brick steps in the alcove and slipped her key in the door.

~ * ~

Panik and Smokey would never have found the place if Brujo had not showed them earlier in the day. They both had lived in New Orleans for several years, but still had trouble finding their way around.

Panik and Brujo were *Mexicanos* with different histories and backgrounds. They did firmly agree on one thing: Brujo was a sorcerer of incredible power. They believed he was a *diablero,* a shape-shifter who could move among people without being recognized. They were certain he had a direct link to Santa Muerte and her Cult of Death, and if they did not obey Brujo he could curse them and their families, a hex that could end in death.

Panik and Smokey, along with the other gang bangers in Los Cuervos, never referred to Ignacio Torres by his given name. They called him *Brujo*.

Gabriel "Panik" Marquez left Saltillo with his family when he was five. They crossed the Rio Grande and made their way to eastern Harris County, near the Houston Ship Channel. Carlos "Smokey" Delgado was a U.S. citizen, born in Logan Heights in San Diego County. He moved to Houston to work with Big Demon in the nineties.

After Katrina, Panik and Smokey moved to New Orleans to smuggle guns with Brujo. They did whatever Brujo or Big Demon said, including murder. Smokey was adept at "hot prowl" burglaries—robbing homes at night with people in them. Panik was an enforcer, though not nearly as big or tough as Big Demon. Both Panik and Smokey had killed people before, Panik in Houston and Smokey in San Diego. Neither of them had a problem with killing. They would do anything for Brujo.

They had ridden with Brujo through Faubourg Marigny in Smokey's two-door 1998 silver Honda Civic earlier in the day. He showed them where the consort lived. They dropped Brujo off at his Grand Am. He told them he would stake out the woman at her office and call them when she left.

When Brujo saw the woman lower the convertible top and leave work, he called Smokey and Panik. They were sitting in Smokey's Honda two blocks from Kitty's apartment.

"We will be ready, Brujo," Smokey said.

~ * ~

Kitty turned the key and pushed her apartment door open. When she reached for the light switch someone grabbed her hand, jerked her inside and tripped her. On the floor she lashed out, kicking in every direction she could. She stopped kicking when a fist smashed into her left eye and caused the back of her head to hit the hardwood floor with such force that she almost blacked out.

The pain around her eye and the back of her head dazed her. She tried to shake it off and get to her feet, but another fist slammed into her nose. Kitty felt the cartilage crunch and tasted blood in her mouth.

The darkness in her apartment seemed to intensify as Kitty again felt like she was going to pass out. Someone grabbed her shirt and jerked her to her feet, then planted a fist in her stomach. It seemed to penetrate all the way to her spine. It was the hardest body blow she ever felt. Kitty doubled over and her breath exploded out of her.

Kitty began to panic when she could not inhale. She never before had the breath knocked out of her, even in her four years of playing soccer at Washington State.

She tried to scream but with no air in her lungs, the sound she made was a shrill squeak, which did not last long. Fists crashed hard into her ribs, right and left side, then into her face. She lost count of how many times she was hit. She thought it might be over until a fist, or maybe two, hit her in the temple and forehead.

That was it—she was out.

~ * ~

The strong smell awakened Kitty. At first she thought it was marijuana, but decided it was something else. She never smelled anything like it before. Maybe some kind of incense.

Then the pain brought back her recollection of what just happened. She was groggy, but knew she was in bed. It felt like her bed. She tried to open her left eye, but couldn't. Must be swollen shut, she hoped. Kitty opened her right eye and concentrated hard to bring her vision into focus. The room was dimly lit, but she could tell she was in her own bedroom. She looked around.

Where did all these candles come from?

There were a couple of dozen lighted candles on her night stand, chest of drawers, and bookcase. As her head cleared, Kitty realized she was naked, spread-eagled, her arms and legs bound tightly to the bedposts. She struggled through the pain to see her right hand. What looked like a torn sheet was used to tie it to the post. She pulled against it, but it was very tight, and it hurt.

She tested her ankles and left arm, and they were tightly bound as well. They hurt, but nothing like her face, head, and ribs. Kitty had never felt pain like this.

The strangest looking man she had ever seen appeared at the foot of her bed. She shuddered when she recognized him.

Kitty knew her agony had just begun.

Two men stood on either side and behind Brujo. Both men had shaved heads, wore saggy jeans and no shirts. Their upper bodies and arms were covered with dark gray tattoos. She tried to figure out patterns or symbols, but the light was too dim and with only one eye working, the tattoos on their bodies ran together, creating an indistinguishable collage. On their faces, she recognized the sinister crow wings, just like the ones on the walls of the shrine in the Ninth Ward. The wings curled around their eyes and across their foreheads.

Brujo had no tattoos on his neck or face. Spanning across his bare chest, partially covered by five necklaces, Brujo had the crow wings of Los Cuervos, a cursive, flattened **m**, the two humps curving around Brujo's breasts and meeting at his sternum. One of his necklaces was laced with black crow feathers, another with pieces of leather. There were multicolored beads on the others. On his head he wore something asymmetrical and bright red. It flopped over to one side, like a beret.

He held a wooden stick with the Santa Muerte skull at top, complete with veil. The stick was painted in alternating stripes of red and green, as was most of Brujo's face. In the center of his forehead was a single white star in a red triangle. Brujo's nose did hook, like Jake said. *Vicious* was the only word she could think of to describe his penetrating eyes.

Brujo turned to one of the other men, who stood like altar boys. The bigger of the two men gave Brujo a clay bowl, out of which smoke curled. Brujo walked around to the side of Kitty's bed. He passed the bowl in a circle over her torso. The smoke descended on her—it was acrid and foul-smelling. He passed the bowl back to the altar boy.

Brujo held out his stick so that the Santa Muerte skull was only inches from Kitty's face. He began to chant, first quietly, then louder. He chanted as he moved around the bed, waving the stick over Kitty as he moved. When he stopped at the foot of her bed, he placed the skull end of the stick on her forehead, moving it down over her nose, mouth, then circling her breasts with it. He moved the skull from her sternum down her stomach, pausing it for a moment between her spread legs.

Kitty was so frightened she thought she would faint.

Brujo gave the stick to the smaller man, then made the backward sign of the cross. His eyes grew wider and he spoke quietly in a language Kitty had never heard. It wasn't Spanish. After two minutes of what Kitty guessed was some kind of perverted prayer, Brujo stopped and made the backward sign of the cross again. He walked out of her bedroom and the two men followed.

Excruciating pain shot through her body as she struggled against the cloth bindings. She hurt everywhere. She tried with her only working eye to look into the next room, but could not see the men. Kitty knew they were not through with her.

After five minutes of terror, the two altar boys came back. Brujo was not with them. The bigger man opened a knife and murmured to the smaller man. Kitty's one working eye was glued to the knife blade—it looked very sharp. In horror she watched the big man sit on the bed between her legs.

He began to slice her stomach. At the first cut, Kitty screamed. The smaller man stuffed something in her mouth. She thought it might be a face towel or a wash cloth.

The slicer continued to carve. She screamed in pain through the cloth in her mouth, and little sound came out. She knew no neighbors on the block could hear, and as usual, the woman pharmaceutical rep renting the front of the house was on the road.

Kitty knew she was on her own. She figured she was good as dead.

Kitty felt tears course down her cheek and behind her ears. Warm blood flowed from all the cuts on her stomach down each side, puddling under her backside. Blood from the cuts he made below her navel trickled down through her pubic hair and into the valleys between her legs and groin.

Just when Kitty thought she would die from the pain, the bigger altar boy stopped slicing. He stood with the smaller man at the foot of the bed, admiring his handiwork.

Through her slightly opened right eye, she watched the bigger man gesture to the smaller one. There was no doubt in its meaning.

"You first," was the message.

When she saw the smaller man begin to remove his pants, she closed her good eye. She didn't want to see any more. Kitty had no religious training and knew no formal prayers, but she began to pray to God in her own words, asking him to help her through this.

If they are going to kill me, please God let me die fast. If there's a heaven, God, please let me in. I've never hurt anyone on purpose. If you let me live through this, I promise I'll be a better person. Please help me.

When the smaller man moved his naked body onto her, the pressure on her ribs was so acutely painful, it took her breath away.

The bigger man slid a cloth of some kind under her neck and tied it so tightly at her throat she could not breathe. She tried to scream and the big man hit her face with his fist or something very hard.

Perhaps the divine intervention she invoked occurred, because Kitty lost consciousness—she didn't make another sound.

Chapter Fifteen

It was dark when Jake left his condo and drove to Audubon Park to run. He had not slept well, in spite of the sleep deficit carried over from the previous days. At five he got tired of tossing and turning. He put on his running gear.

This time of morning there were no cars on the asphalt road that wound through the park. There were a few walkers and bikers. By seven-thirty the exercising traffic would pick up significantly. Most of them lived uptown, around the park, or were students from Loyola or Tulane, whose campuses adjoined the park.

He rotated his left arm and shoulder. It was feeling much better. The inflammation around the cut had gone down and the pain diminished, thanks to the steady dose of Bayer. Jake picked up the pace when he crossed Magazine into the southernmost tip of the park, where the Zoo was located, along with Jake's favorite part of the park—the batture. He crossed the railroad tracks and ran up the incline to the batture, a flat expanse adjacent to the Mississippi River that the City of New Orleans built up and protected from the river with riprap to keep it from flooding. There were a few trees, but mostly wide open space for Frisbee games, kite flying, and picnicking in the Spring, before it became too hot outside to be anywhere but in the shade.

Jake looked out into the river as he ran along the concrete arc adjacent to the riprap. He saw a tanker riding low in the water, full of crude oil probably from the Persian Gulf or the coast of Brazil, moving upstream to one of the many refineries dotting the riverbank to Baton Rouge and above. Jake had never been on the batture when there wasn't river traffic—oil tankers, barges, and tugs. One time he saw a gigantic oil rig that had been constructed inland and floated down the river to be placed in service in the Gulf. He thought it too big to make it under the two bridges crossing the river downtown, but it must have because he never read anything about it.

He glanced at his watch. At the pace he was running, Jake figured he had put in six miles. He picked up speed and headed back to his 4Runner parked near the Audubon Park golf clubhouse.

Jake opened the door and grabbed his towel and cell phone. He checked to see if Kitty answered his text. She hadn't. He tossed the phone back on the seat and stretched his hamstrings as he wiped off sweat and cooled down.

She worked late last night. Probably sleeping in.

Jake drove out of the park and turned left toward downtown and his condo. He took Magazine, which he thought might be the narrowest major street in the United States. Cars parked at the curb on both sides, leaving barely enough room for a car headed uptown to safely pass a car driving downtown. Adding to the tight squeeze were the huge NOPSI busses that ran the length of the street, pulling out from bus stops into the travel lane with no concern for the vehicles traveling toward the bus or behind it.

When he turned left onto Camp he called Kitty. No answer. Jake left her another voice mail asking her to call him right away. For a moment he thought something might be wrong, but dismissed it as overreaction. If she planned to sleep in this morning, Jake knew from her past habits she would turn off her phone. He figured he would hear from her later in the morning, and put it out of his mind.

He showered, dressed quickly and drove to work. Like he did every morning, he ducked into Pudge's Po-Boy Shop on the short walk to the federal building. Pudge ran a thriving breakfast and lunch business in a tiny building on Camp Street at Lafayette Square. Every day at lunch lawyers in two thousand dollar business suits stood four deep waiting to yell an order at Pudge, who took every order himself, and delegated the preparation to the half-dozen employees that worked behind the counter. Jake had met them all, and each one was a child, nephew, or niece of Pudge. Unfortunately, they all looked like Pudge.

Pudge raised his hand quickly and pointed at Jake when he walked in this morning.

"Large coffee, black," Pudge said to the hefty twenty-something girl next to him. While she poured chicory coffee into the treated cardboard cup, Jake slid by the other customers, and squeezed between the counter and the wall, stopping next to Pudge, who was about sixty, a tad taller than 5'6" but well over two hundred pounds.

"Makin' a deposit?" Pudge asked.

Jake smiled and pushed open the swinging half-door to Pudge's office, a tiny space, not much bigger than a closet. Pudge kept his business records and his money in an ancient steel safe in the corner. There was room for little else in the office, but Pudge somehow managed to shoehorn in a narrow desk and oak chair.

Jake pulled a small metal box from under the desk. He opened it on the desk, reached behind him under his coat and removed his Sig. He placed it carefully on top of Pudge's .357 chrome-plated revolver, closed the box and slipped it back under the desk.

"Thanks, Pudge," Jake said on the way out. "See you later."

"I'll be here," Pudge said and yelled: "Next."

Jake walked toward the federal building. He was grateful to Pudge for letting him park his weapon in Pudge's office. He couldn't bring the gun into the U.S. Attorney's office without getting an okay high up the chain of command in DOJ. With the current administration in power in D.C., permission to carry in the U.S. Attorney's office was rarely granted.

Pudge's accommodating Jake wasn't due entirely to Jake's charm and winning personality. He inherited the relationship from his Daddy. Willie Mitchell had become friends with Pudge two decades before when he came frequently to the Fifth Circuit Court of Appeals in a building adjacent to Jake's current office to fight post-conviction habeas corpus claims filed by criminals he convicted in Yaloquena County. Once a defendant exhausted his state appeals in Jackson, he had the legal right to start over from scratch in the federal system, always alleging ineffective assistance of counsel, deprivation of some vague Fifth or Sixth amendment right to a fair trial, and a race-based allegation of violation of due process or equal protection of the Fourteenth Amendment, usually involving the racial makeup of the grand or petit jury. At first, the duplicate appeals irritated Willie Mitchell. Jake remembered as a kid his Daddy complaining about the system. Later, Willie Mitchell began to see it as an opportunity for Susan and him to make a quick getaway to New Orleans for a couple of days. Jimmy Gray owned a historic duplex in the back of the Quarter on Ursulines. Both sides were well-furnished, and Jimmy did not rent them out. He told Willie Mitchell and

Susan on their trips down that one side was the Gray's, and the other side the Banks'.

Jake stepped out of the elevator and swiped his access card. He winked and blew a kiss at the camera for Gertie. She buzzed him in.

"Morning, Gertie."

Gertie was all business. "Mr. Romano wants to see you right away. In his office."

Jake strode toward his boss's office. He rapped lightly on the door and entered. There were two men in suits in chairs in front of Mr. Romano's desk. They stood when Jake walked in.

"Meet these gentlemen," Romano said. "Larry Beauvais and John Proffit. They're with the FBI."

Jake smiled and shook Beauvais' hand first.

"I know agent Beauvais," Jake said.

He's the agent at the raid I put on his knees when he grabbed my arm, the guy Kitty said was very pissed.

"Sorry about yesterday, Agent Beauvais," Jake said. "It was just a reaction because I've got this bad cut on my arm where..."

"Right," Beauvais said. He tried to smile, but it came off as a sneer that Jake could have done without.

Nothing good can come of this.

Jake guessed that Beauvais was about five inches shorter than he, but twenty to thirty pounds heavier, with a red crew cut and fair skin. His partner Proffit looked like a skinny CPA.

"Pull up a chair, Jake," Romano said. "These guys have been assigned to investigate the matter that Mr. Whitman discussed in here the other day."

"Yes, sir," Jake said.

"They've driven in from the lakefront this morning to ask you some questions about David Dunne."

Beauvais flashed another smile at Jake. Jake decided he was glad he brought Beauvais to his knees in front of his federal peers.

"When's the last contact you had with Dunne?" Beauvais asked.

"Mr. Romano, I have to take the same position I took with Mr. Whitman about this. Until I am advised what my status is..."

"You don't have that right, Banks," Beauvais growled.

"Hold on, Mr. Beauvais," Romano said. "We're going to do this civilly or not at all. Jake told Mr. Whitman he wasn't answering any questions about Mr. Dunne."

"Actually, Mr. Romano, I didn't say that. I just didn't answer."

"And we're here to tell you this morning you don't have that luxury," Beauvais said. "Isn't that right, Mr. Romano?"

"Sorry, Jake. Word's come down from D.C. You either cooperate or you're suspended without pay, effectively immediately. I want you to know this isn't my call."

"All right," Jake said. "I understand."

Jake stood to shake Romano's hand. When Jake turned to leave, out of the corner of his eye he saw Beauvais stare at the slight bulge in the middle of Jake's back at belt level. Beauvais jumped up and reached under Jake's coat.

"Gun," Beauvais barked.

Jake spun and elbowed Beauvais in his right cheek bone, then extended his right leg and followed through, using Beauvais' momentum to flip the agent onto his back on the ugly burgundy carpet in Romano's office. Jake grabbed Beauvais' throat and squeezed.

"I don't have a gun on me," Jake said to Romano. He let go of the agent, stood and lifted his coat, revealing an empty leather holster. He turned to Beauvais. "This is the second time you've grabbed me. If there's a next time, you're going to get hurt."

Romano rushed around his desk to stand between them. Proffit kept his distance.

"You son of a bitch," Beauvais said. He rubbed his neck.

"That's enough," Romano said to the FBI agent. "You started it."

"Is there anything I need to do other than leave?" Jake asked his boss? "Any forms or anything I need to sign?"

"No. But wait for me in your office. Gather up any personal things you want to take and I'll be down in a minute to give you the protocol."

"Yes, sir," Jake said and left.

Jake went through his drawers quickly. He had spent so little time in his office in his eight months in New Orleans, there was little to identify it as his. When he shut the last drawer Romano walked in.

"Sit down, Jake."

Romano pulled up the only other chair in the office and sat across the desk from Jake. He stroked his thick black beard and rotated his thick neck as if trying to work out some kinks.

"I hate this," Romano said. "You're the kind of guy we need in the department. I don't know all the details about what's up with you and Whitman, but I know DOJ has too many jerks like Whitman. Political appointees or lifelong bureaucrats who've never tried a case or made a case against a bad guy their entire life. You know my hands are tied."

"I know there's nothing you can do. This die was cast last year. Whitman wants payback. I just appreciate your attitude."

Romano removed a business card from his pocket, wrote on the back and gave it to Jake. "That's my cell. You call me if I can do anything. I'll help any way I can."

Jake shook his boss's hand. "Thanks, Mr. Ro…"

"Pete," Romano said. "You call me Pete."

Jake walked out the exit line parallel to security on the ground floor. First time Jake had ever been canned or suspended from anything—and it felt very good.

"If they want me to talk about Dunne," Jake muttered to himself as he approached Pudge's PoBoys, "they better change their policy against waterboarding."

Pudge was still snowed under behind the counter, taking and giving orders, when Jake slid through and retrieved his gun from the office. Jake waved on his way out.

"Won't see you for a while, Pudge."

"Going undercover?" the fat man asked, laughing.

"Kind of."

Jake pulled out of the parking garage, took Poydras toward the river and turned left on Decatur, driving as fast as he safely could past the Café Du Monde and the French Market, which had not changed since the first time Jake walked through it holding Willie Mitchell's hand. Jake was six and Scott was two, Susan pushing Scott in a baby stroller past the fresh vegetables.

He zipped through the poorly marked maze between Decatur and Esplanade, and turned into Marigny. He stopped on Dauphine behind Kitty's BMW. Jake felt the cold hood of the BMW as he walked past it onto the brick sidewalk down the side of her house. He stopped at the alcove and walked up the brick steps.

Jake tapped on the door. He tapped again. He turned the knob and the door cracked opened. Something was wrong. Kitty never left her door unlocked, even when home.

Jake reached behind him and drew his Sig. He pushed open the door and moved inside without making a sound. He smelled something sharp, unpleasant—not sure what, but he had never smelled it before. With both hands on the Sig at shoulder level pointed to the ceiling, Jake looked quickly around the living room and kitchen. Nothing. He moved toward the bedroom door. It was slightly ajar, and Jake noticed very dim, flickering light coming from the crack in the door.

He made no sound. He pushed it open with the back on his hands. Jake took a quick glance inside and pulled his head back behind the limited protection of the wooden door.

Jake lowered his head. The image of the woman spread eagled on the bed, tied to the bedposts, legs and arms spread, was seared in his brain.

Please God, let her be alive.

Jake took a deep breath and dashed into the room onto the floor beside the bed. He rose to his knees and pointed the gun in every direction. He glanced under the bed then went into the bathroom.

No one was in the room but Kitty.

Jake stood next to the bed and stared down at Kitty, the woman he still loved. Her face was swollen almost twice its normal size. Her lower chest and stomach was caked in black, dried blood. He concentrated on her chest. It rose slightly, then fell.

Thank God. She's breathing.

Jake dialed 911. He explained to the dispatcher the need for an ambulance, NOPD, and the FBI.

He looked at her wrists and ankles, red and swollen around the tightly knotted cloth binding her to the bedposts. Her hands and feet were white, starved for blood.

Jake touched the binding on her right wrist but caught himself. His training kicked in. *Preserve the crime scene.* He tapped the camera app on his phone. After checking to make sure it worked, he walked into Kitty's bathroom and returned with three face towels. He placed them strategically on her body and looked at Kitty's image on his telephone.

Preserve the crime scene.

Jake grimaced and lowered the camera. He removed the three towels, completely exposing Kitty again, just as she was when he walked in her bedroom.

Jake took a dozen photos from different angles.

He closed the phone, retrieved a sheet from the bathroom and covered Kitty. Worried about her extremities, he pulled out his tiny, razor-sharp pocket knife and carefully cut the cloth bindings from her wrists and ankles, touching as little of the cloth as possible. He gently placed her arms by her side. For the crime scene technicians, Jake placed the bindings in four plastic baggies from the kitchen, placing each one at the corner of Kitty's bed where it was used.

Jake gently massaged each of Kitty's ankles and wrists to encourage blood flow. He stroked her hair gently and whispered.

"Hang on, baby."

Jake's throat seized up. He squeezed his eyes shut and suppressed his emotions. He took a deep breath.

"You're going to be fine, Kitty. I'll take care of you."

The EMTs burst through the apartment door and stopped in their tracks when they saw Jake standing over Kitty's naked body.

Jake held up his U.S. Attorney's badge. With his other hand, he waved them closer.

"Please help her," he choked. "Please."

One of the EMTs flipped the light switch. For the first time, Jake realized how dimly lit the room had been since he entered.

"Thanks," Jake said to the EMTs, both of whom stared above his head. Jake turned around to look at the wall above Kitty's bed.

Painted in blood were the letters L C and a crude outline of Santa Muerte, whose hollow eyes seemed to look down on Kitty, battered and sliced in her own bed.

Chapter Sixteen

Late that afternoon, Jake stood with Eustis and Pizzolato in the hallway outside Kitty's hospital room. Her FBI supervisor had come and gone, asking Jake to call him when she came to.

"Here comes the doc," Pizzolato said.

Jake positioned himself outside Kitty's closed door so that the doctor had to go through him to enter the room.

"Dr. Abbott," Jake said, "how'd the MRI and x-rays look?"

Dr. Horace Abbott, mid-fifties, salt-and-pepper brown hair and aviator-style glasses, stopped in front of Jake. He scanned the chart he carried, looking for information.

"Uh, Mr. Banks, right?"

"Yes, sir. Her only next of kin is her mother, and she's in a mental institution in Tacoma, Washington."

"Right. I see that in the notes." He cleared his throat. "Well, Ms Douglas is very fortunate. Her skull is not fractured, and though severely bruised, her orbital socket is intact. Her brain is swollen, but not badly enough for us to intervene. It will heal on its own. We'll continue with the regimen of pain and steroidal compounds to reduce the inflammation and swelling, and we'll closely monitor her. She will be in and out of consciousness, so if you try to question her don't put her under any pressure."

"Yes, sir."

"She's had a terrible shock to just about every system."

"What about her stomach. When I found her...."

"We debrided and cleaned the wounds and have treated them with antibiotic cream. Some of the cuts were deep enough that they had to be sutured." He studied the chart. "She had about four hundred stitches."

"Damn," Pizzolato said behind Dr. Abbott.

"We'll change the dressing every few hours, as needed. The stomach wounds are generally superficial, but they are extensive. She will have major scarring."

Dr. Abbott paused to check the hall and gestured for Eustis and Pizzolato to move closer.

"There's no evidence that penetration was by anything other than the rapist's genitals, so there's bruising and abrasions, but no tearing or damage to the vaginal vault or uterine wall, as far as we can tell. We've administered the appropriate post-rape pharmaceutical regimen to avoid pregnancy and STD transmission to the extent possible."

"Thank you, Dr. Abbott," Jake said. "Is it okay if I stay in there with her, if I don't bother her."

Dr. Abbott thought for a moment. "I guess that will be all right. Don't be alarmed if she loses consciousness. Her brain's had a severe injury and if she tries to communicate she probably will not make much sense."

"Yes, sir."

"And one other thing. The cuts on her stomach. It's not random slicing. There seems to be a pattern, or symbols. With the swelling and jagged nature of some of the wounds I can't make out what it is. It might be nothing, but it appears to be a design of sorts. I could be wrong."

Jake extended his hand to Dr. Abbott, who shook it and entered Kitty's room.

"Fuckin' freaks," Pizzolato said, "what they did to her."

"I'm going to stay here with Kitty," Jake said. "Around the clock. No need for you guys to stay."

"We're on this," Captain Eustis said. "FBI will want to help, too. I'm putting as many men on it as I can. Think we need security here?"

"No," Jake said. "I can handle it. I do need my laptop from my condo." Jake drew closer to Eustis. "It's got the data dump on Brujo our friend sent to you."

"I'll stay here while Pizzo runs you to your condo to get whatever else you need besides your laptop."

"Great," Jake said.

~ * ~

Willie Mitchell sat in the passenger seat working a crossword puzzle while Susan drove her silver Lexus south on I-55 past Middendorf's Restaurant at Pass Manchac. He looked up.

"We ought to stop there on the way back if we have time," he said.

"It's all fried food."

"But it's delicious. The thinnest fried catfish and the best soft-shell crab po-boy I've ever had. I'll get the sweet potato fries instead of the regular kind. And just light beer."

"What a sacrifice."

"I never get to eat fried food. I read it's okay every once in a while."

"Where did you read that?"

"Somewhere."

"Well, we'll see," Susan said.

"I'll buy." He put on a fake pout. "I remember when I was in the driver's seat."

"Those days are over, Sweetie Pie."

She winked at him. He reached over and patted her leg above the knee, then moved it slowly up her thigh as high as it would go.

"Don't distract the driver," she said.

He laughed and moved his hand. "Remember when we were first married and sometimes when we got on the interstate you would...."

"Hush," she said.

"If you don't stop at Middendorf's on the way back, I'm going to tell your bridge group about those early road trips."

"And I'll tell them about the time you came in from a weekend goose hunt in the Louisiana marshes with Jimmy Gray and were so drunk you woke up at two a.m. and thought you were in the bathroom and ruined the carpet in the corner of our bedroom."

"Oops. Touché."

At the highest point on the bridge across the slender pass between Lake Maurepas on the west and its much bigger sibling, Lake Ponchartrain on the east, Willie Mitchell looked to his right to watch the sun pick up speed as it plunged below the horizon. There were cabins on stilts along the waterway that paralleled I-55. He wondered how in the world they had survived Katrina on those skinny poles. Many camps on the edges of both lakes perished in the storm surge.

"I hope Kitty's going to be all right," Susan said.

"Jake said the doctor told him she would. She's going to have a lot of scarring."

"Physical and emotional. I can't imagine going through something like that."

"She's a strong girl," Willie Mitchell said. "I'm sure being in good shape like she is helped."

"Physically. I don't care what the doctor or Jake says. Kitty's going to need a lot of support to come back from this."

"And she doesn't really have anyone," Willie Mitchell said, "except Jake. I don't think he can be much of a caretaker."

"Takes after you-know-who," Susan said.

"What? When you had the stomach flu last year I went and got you some Gatorade."

"One time. You stayed away mostly, leaving everything to Ina."

"You told me to leave when I came in the room to check on you. I was just doing what I was told. Like now. You're in charge, and I'm just a little peon."

"Poor little pitiful you."

"It's true," he said, laughing. "You have most of the money. You do all the driving. You only keep me around to service your account as needed." He changed his voice to a higher pitch. "Come here, boy. Take those britches off. Let's see if that thing still works."

Susan laughed and slapped Willie Mitchell's leg. He picked up her hand and brought it to his lips. He kissed the back of her hand.

"Thank you for seeing me through all this," he said. "I love you."

Susan's eyes filled with tears. "I am so glad you're still here. I don't know what I would do without you. You're my heart and soul."

He watched a small tear escape and run down her cheek. He grabbed a Kleenex from the small box Susan kept in the console and dabbed her cheek, then gave her the tissue. He kissed her hand again.

They rode a while in silence. Willie Mitchell went over what Jake had told him on the phone late in the morning. He looked up from his crossword puzzle at Susan—he could tell she was thinking about Kitty and what they could do to help.

Willie Mitchell was thinking more about Brujo, and why the son-of-a-bitch had it in for Jake and Kitty.

~ * ~

Jake had been dozing in Kitty's room. He fell asleep reading the Brujo files on his laptop. The light tap on the door startled him and he jumped up out of the chair. He walked quickly and slid behind the door as it opened, his hand on his Sig. He glanced quickly around the door and saw his mother walk toward Kitty's bed.

"We come in peace," Willie Mitchell said, hands in the air.

Jake closed the door behind his parents. Standing next to the bed, Susan stared down at Kitty for a while before she turned and spoke to Jake. Her face was ashen.

"My God," Susan said. "Look what those animals did to her. Poor thing, has she been awake any today?"

"In and out mostly. She'll come to and mumble something, just random words, then conk back out. I'm not sure she recognizes me or where she is. Doctor Abbott says that's typical and she'll gradually be able to communicate in a day or so. Maybe longer."

Susan turned back to Kitty. She patted and rubbed Kitty's hand and spoke softly to her. Jake slid a chair over for his mother to sit next to Kitty. Willie Mitchell signaled to Jake to follow him into the hallway.

"They sure did a number on her," Willie Mitchell said.

"Bastards," Jake said. "We don't know how many of Brujo's people were involved. We don't really know what happened because Kitty hasn't been able to tell us anything yet."

"Ought to be plenty of DNA evidence."

"Yes. But unless they're already in the system somewhere, that's only going to help us after we make an arrest."

"This maniac Brujo, why'd he pick you and Kitty out of all the people at the FBI and NOPD trying to arrest him?"

"Maybe it's because I was there when he killed Dominguez and Byrne. That's the only thing I can think of."

Jake and Willie Mitchell moved closer to the wall to let an orderly push a gurney past them. Jake leaned against the wall.

"It might be crazy, but when Kitty and I were at the raid on his headquarters in the Ninth Ward, yesterday morning just before dawn, I had a feeling...." Jake's voice trailed off.

"What? Go on."

"Anyway, I just had a feeling he was watching me. Brujo was. Kitty and I were standing there waiting to go in after NOPD cleared it."

"Is that what your gut told you?" Willie Mitchell asked.

"It is."

"Then there's something to it more than likely."

"They attacked Kitty because she was with me. There's no other possible reason. I've been thinking about it all afternoon. She was one of dozens of agents and cops out there, but she was the only one talking to me almost the whole time. She was with me at NOPD watching Eustis question Green Eyes. Gave me a ride to my condo where Brujo left me that note."

"Who is Green Eyes?"

"One of Brujo's men they arrested at the raid."

"Why don't you talk to your new boss and see if he can get ATF or ICE or some other federal agencies to help the FBI on Brujo?"

"Got something to tell you, Daddy. I got suspended yesterday."

"For what?"

"Whitman was down from D.C. a few days ago...."

"You told me that."

"Well, he's put a couple of local FBI agents on it and they showed up this morning at the office and asked me the same questions."

"About Dunne?"

"Yes."

Willie Mitchell put his arm on Jake's left shoulder and squeezed. Jake winced.

"What's wrong with your arm?"

"It's nothing."

Willie Mitchell gently felt Jake's upper arm.

"You've got a bandage on it. What's that from?"

"Long story."

"We've got plenty of time, son. Let's go downstairs for some coffee and have a talk. I've got a lot of questions I've been wanting to ask you for a while now."

"I'm not leaving Kitty and Mom up here by themselves. We'll have to talk right here in the hallway."

"All right. Let's start with what happened the night I got hurt."

"I've told you."

"I know. But now I want the truth. That was no accidental hit and run. Whoever was driving that car wanted to kill me. They almost succeeded."

Jake pursed his lips.

"Did David Dunne have something to do with it?"

"He saved your life. And mine."

"I don't think that's possible."

"Why?"

"Because David Dunne is dead."

"No, he's not," Jake said.

"The guy we know from the El Moro fiasco as David Dunne, the guy who left his fingerprints on some old basketball pictures I showed him when he was at the house during the trial—according to federal records he's dead. Robbie Cedars at the State Police Crime Lab lifted the prints early this morning and ran them through a database of federal law enforcement and military that he can access kind of on the sly. He called me on my cell on the drive down this afternoon."

"And?"

"He said the prints off my photos match the prints on record of a David Dunne who worked at the Pentagon and was killed when American Flight 77 crashed into it on September 11, 2001. Someone took the fingerprints of the guy we know as David Dunne and substituted them for the real David Dunne's prints in the federal database. So if anyone check's our buddy's prints they match up with a dead guy's."

Jake said nothing.

"Jake, you've got to come clean with me. It would take someone at the highest level of government to do something like this."

"He's doing good work," Jake said. "That's all I'm saying."

"Listen to yourself, son. You've put your career on the line for him, and we don't even know who he is."

"I know enough."

"Well, I don't. You get in touch with Dunne. You tell him that he and I need to have a talk."

"It doesn't work like that."

"Starting now it does."

Chapter Seventeen

Willie Mitchell stared out the hospital window at the soupy fog that had descended on New Orleans since he and Susan arrived. He checked his phone. *Three a.m.* Willie Mitchell and Susan left Jake at the hospital at eight the previous evening and took their bags to Jimmy Gray's duplex on Ursulines, the west half of which Jimmy Gray said was reserved exclusively and permanently for Willie Mitchell and Susan.

Jimmy said he had "bought it right" years ago at the urging of his only sibling, Rodney Foreman Gray, an architect who lived in the Quarter. Rodney was two years younger than Jimmy, and left Sunshine in 1975 for Tulane's School of Architecture. He made New Orleans his home from then on, rarely returning to Sunshine. In 1983 Rodney bought a three-story brick and stucco home in the Quarter on St. Philip one block off Bourbon, and made its restoration a lifetime project. He ran his architectural practice on the first floor, and lived with his longtime companion, Winston, on the upper floors. Jimmy told Willie Mitchell that architectural historians in the city said Rodney's home on St. Philip's was the most perfectly restored home in the French Quarter.

Willie Mitchell thought about the Gray brothers. They were both smart and successful, but polar opposites. Jimmy was bigger than life, loud, and had no secrets. Rodney was reserved, private. He named Willie Mitchell executor of his will, though Willie Mitchell had only been in Rodney's home twice in the last two decades. Rodney told Jimmy that Willie Mitchell had more integrity than anyone he knew, and that's why he wanted him distributing his estate. It was a compliment that Willie Mitchell always treasured.

Rodney had been right about Jimmy's duplex. He convinced Jimmy to buy it in 1982. They restored it immediately. Jimmy always joked that the pot full of money Rodney made off Jimmy in the renovation was what Rodney used to buy his own mansion on St. Philip. In the next breath, Jimmy told Willie Mitchell that he turned down a Hollywood power couple who offered him 1.5 million dollars for the duplex, which was three times what he had in it. Jimmy said he would never sell or rent it out, that it would always be available to them, the west half for Willie Mitchell and Susan, the east half for Jimmy and Martha.

Willie Mitchell moved Jake's Sig from the floor to his lap. He felt its weight and balance, pointing at a sodium street light providing a gauzy orange glow outside in the dense fog. The fact that the pistol had no exterior safety kept him on edge, because Jake insisted that he keep a round in the chamber, ready to fire.

He was not sleepy. He caught four hours at the duplex while Jake remained at the hospital. Susan drove Willie Mitchell back to the hospital to take the early morning watch so Jake could get some sleep. Jake took his turn sleeping in the duplex because Susan did not want to drive through the Quarter and return to the duplex by herself.

Except for Kitty's occasional moan, the room was silent. Every twenty minutes or so, Willie Mitchell heard a nurse or aide walk by, their rubber soles squeaking on the polished tile. It seemed much quieter here than St. Christopher's Hospital in Jackson, where Willie Mitchell spent many nights recuperating after multiple surgeries.

Willie Mitchell grew stiff and uncomfortable in the chair. He stood up quietly, put the Sig in the seat, and opened the door to walk the stiffness off in the hallway. A long, white flower box that had been leaning against the door fell inside.

Probably from her fellow FBI agents.

He closed the door without making a sound and looked at the box. There was no card. He wasn't sure what to do. Kitty might not come to for another day or two, and if there were cut flowers in the box, they needed to be put in water. He slid the black ribbon off the box.

Odd color for get-well flowers.

Willie Mitchell opened the box and almost dropped it. Inside was a headless chicken, blood from its neck smeared all over the white interior. Next to the chicken, there were two black roses wrapped in tissue paper, part of which was stuck to the inside of the box with the dried blood from the chicken.

Willie Mitchell looked up and down the empty hallway. He placed the lid and black ribbon back on the box, silently retrieved the Sig from the chair in the room, and stood outside the door with the gun stuck in his pants, concealed under his shirt.

An overweight black nurse in her fifties turned a corner and walked toward him. She smiled as she drew closer and he smiled back.

"Excuse me, ma'am," he said, "did you just come on duty on this floor or have you been here a while?"

"Oh goodness," she said, "I've been here since ten last night down at the nurse's station. You and your son walked past me about an hour ago or so. How's our patient doing?"

"She's still out."

"She'll be better tomorrow."

"I hope so," he said. "Did you see whoever dropped off these flowers for her? They left them here outside the door."

"I didn't. But I'm not always at my station. I'm up and around checking on patients and the nurses I supervise on this shift."

"Okay," he said. "Thanks."

The nurse walked on past. Willie looked at his phone, deciding whether to call Jake or Eustis at NOPD. Jake had left him the number.

Three-fifteen. I'll wait until morning.

Willie Mitchell retrieved the chair from Kitty's room and parked it outside her door. He adjusted the gun in his waistline, placed the flower box and its disturbing contents on the floor, and waited.

After a few moments, Willie Mitchell dialed the number of the only person he knew outside his immediate family he could call at 3:15 in the morning and depend on him to do whatever was asked of him.

~ * ~

Six hours later, Jimmy Gray drove the black Cadillac hearse up on the sidewalk in front of the duplex. It was too long to fit into the parking lot around the corner where he kept a reserved parking place for three hundred dollars a month. He leaned his large body against the hearse and punched in Willie Mitchell on speed dial.

"You made it," Willie Mitchell said.

"Yep. People on the interstate make way for a hearse. We ought to buy one for road trips."

"It's going to take us a while to make all the arrangements here at the hospital. Jake and Susan are talking to the hospital administrator right now. We're waiting on the doctor to come in to make rounds."

"He ain't going to like it."

"I know. He'll get over it."

Jimmy Gray started laughing. "You should have heard old Brick Head cuss when I woke him up at three-thirty and told him I needed an ambulance or hearse."

"You must have made him an offer he couldn't refuse."

"The mortgage on his funeral home has a balloon payment due in a month and he's got to refinance. He's been whining that it ain't enough people dying and his P and L ain't going to look worth a shit. When he started in on how much trouble it was going to be to let me use the hearse I reminded him I carry his note. Then all he said was "I'll fill it up and get it right there. Where you want me to bring it?"

Willie Mitchell laughed. "It might take all day to get her out of here. You got anything to keep you busy?"

"I'll drive this big Caddy around the block to Rod's. He's got off street parking behind his house that's plenty enough room. I ain't seen him in a while. Be good to catch up."

"Tell him hello for me," Willie Mitchell said. "And don't tell him what we're up to."

"Anything else, boss man?"

"There is. Get your map out and check the route I want you to take back. I'll be riding shotgun."

"We ain't going up the interstate?"

"We're going west on I-10 and cross the river at Baton Rouge, then up I-49 to Alexandria, 165 to Monroe, then east on I-20 to Vicksburg then north on 61 home."

"Shit. That's eight or nine hours."

"That's about right. Good thing you got that fat ass to sit on."

"Hey, dick nose. At least I got an ass instead of the scrawny little bag of bones you got underneath your britches"

"I'll call you."

Jimmy Gray wedged his 312 pounds under the steering wheel and headed for St. Philip's street.

~ * ~

Willie Mitchell's prediction was exactly right. It did take most of the day. Dr. Abbott said it was impossible to move Kitty until he saw the dead chicken and black roses in the flower box and listened to Jake describe the shrine room in the house in the Ninth Ward. Willie Mitchell told the administrator that NOPD was unavailable so the hospital was going to have to provide around the clock security now that they had been put on notice of the danger to Kitty. He added the hospital would be liable if anything happened to her. After a moment of consideration and a quick call to the hospital's attorney, the administrator agreed that transporting Kitty might be best "considering all the circumstances."

Willie Mitchell drafted a release of liability and hold harmless agreement at a secretary's desk. He signed it, along with Jake and Susan in front of the hospital notary and two witnesses. He failed to mention the fact that the documents were of no legal effect at all, since none of them had a power of attorney from Kitty authorizing them to act on her behalf, nor were they kin.

Willie Mitchell called Dr. Nathan Clement, an internal medicine solo practitioner in Sunshine and close friend of Willie Mitchell and Jimmy, and explained the situation to him. Nathan said he would have a bedroom upstairs in Willie Mitchell's house ready by the time they returned, outfitted with a hospital bed, supplies and equipment so that Kitty could recuperate there instead of the Sunshine Hospital. Willie Mitchell put Nathan on the phone to talk to Dr. Abbott. After a few minutes of conversation, Dr. Abbott was satisfied that Kitty would be in good hands.

Dr. Abbott agreed to give Kitty enough pain medication to keep her sedated for most of the trip. Susan gathered copies of the charts and records from the administrator to give to Dr. Clement when they arrived in Sunshine.

At seven p.m., a nurse and two orderlies exited the elevator on the ground floor and pushed Kitty, swaddled on a gurney, to the hearse in the patient departure area behind the hospital. Jake walked next to the gurney, his eyes peeled for trouble. Jimmy Gray had the motor running and Willie Mitchell held open the back door while the nurse and orderlies collapsed the gurney and slid Kitty in the back. The nurse hopped in and re-started the IV. She made sure Kitty was strapped in and the gurney secure.

"I've got Kitty's purse," Susan said to Willie Mitchell and Jimmy. She hugged Jake and got into her Lexus.

"I'll keep you posted," Willie Mitchell said to Jake. He made sure the back door was closed tightly then sat in the passenger seat. Jimmy Gray pulled away from the hospital followed closely by Susan. Jake ran and started his 4Runner to follow them as far as the I-10 on ramp at Carrollton. Willie Mitchell had told Jake to hang back at least a block to make sure no one tailed them.

Jake pulled into a Fast Lane convenience store at the corner of Washington and watched the hearse and Lexus up the ramp. Traffic was intermittent. Jake watched the cars stopped at the traffic light at Washington, waiting to get up on the Carrollton ramp. None of the drivers or passengers looked like they belonged to Los Cuervos. He called Willie Mitchell as he turned right off Carrollton onto Tulane toward downtown. He told him he was heading to the condo to get some sleep.

"Watch your back, son," Willie Mitchell said. "Be careful."

~ * ~

"When you said you were riding shotgun, you really meant it," Jimmy Gray said.

Willie Mitchell grabbed the pistol grip of the twelve gauge Benelli next to him, the barrel pointed to the floor.

"I'm a man of my word," he said.

"I hope Jake's going to be okay at his condo without that shotgun."

"He said he's got plenty of firepower without it."

Willie Mitchell pointed to the bright green sign over I-10 a half-mile away. "Change of plans. Instead of going through Baton Rouge, take the Boutte exit to U.S. 90 through Houma and Morgan city to New Iberia and Lafayette, where we'll catch I-49 to Alexandria."

"Damn," Jimmy Gray said. "Ain't nobody following us."

"I want to make sure."

Willie Mitchell called Susan to tell her they would be heading southwest before they got to LaPlace and that she was to drive on home on I-55 through Jackson. He said Jimmy and he would be in Sunshine at three or four the next morning. Susan told Willie Mitchell she would coordinate with Dr. Clement and make sure the room was ready.

Jimmy took the I-310 exit off I-10 and drove southwest.

"I'm hungry. I don't guess we'll pass Mosca's, huh?"

"Not this trip."

"Best eating in New Orleans. Oysters Mosca, barbecued shrimp and little chicken legs in that butter and garlic sauce."

"It's in Jefferson Parish."

"But it's still in the metro area."

"Not much metro left around New Orleans."

"All right, smart ass. How's this: it's the best food in the world."

Willie Mitchell poked Jimmy's big stomach.

"High praise from the guru of gastronomy."

Jimmy flipped him the bird. Willie Mitchell turned to check on Kitty. She had moved very little since they left New Orleans, moaning once when Jimmy Gray changed lanes abruptly to avoid a dead nutria south of Des Allemands.

"Sorry, honey," he said over his shoulder to Kitty. "Don't want to get nutria guts all over Brick Head's Cadillac."

They crossed Bayou Lafourche then headed west on the four-lane that bypassed Houma, through Terrebonne Parish and over the high bridge between Berwick and Morgan City. Northwest of Berwick, the four-lane seemed to float through the marshland as it traversed the inky blackness of the swamps and marshes of St. Mary's and Iberia Parishes.

Willie Mitchell had driven this part of U.S. 90 before. He figured the pavement was at or below sea level. There was water on either side of the road, sometimes in the ditches, other times in cypress and willow swamps that came right up to the shoulder.

"Lots of dead meat on this road," Jimmy said as they passed an indeterminate wad of hair, blood, and flesh on the side of the highway. "That another nutria?"

"Nah," Willie Mitchell said. "I'm pretty sure that was a big possum. You know, I've seen alligators and good-sized moccasins dead on this road plenty of times."

"When did you drive this way?"

"A couple of times on golf trips, a few times on hunts."

"Where was I?"

"These trips were mostly district attorney get-togethers. Louisiana and Mississippi prosecutors and some regional feds spending grant money on meetings to coordinate inter-jurisdictional crime or prosecution problems. Bunch of bull shit stuff of no use to anyone, just a chance to get out of the office and waste some federal money."

"Didn't we come down here fishing one time?"

"Yeah. You and I drove this way to Avery Island one time to a fishing rodeo you got us hooked up with through some banker."

"I don't remember too much of that trip."

"You were drunk most of the time. That's the trip you did the pole dancing in that Cajun bar and pulled the pole out of its brackets. You fell flat on your back. The pole and part of the ceiling fell on top of you."

"I remember hearing about that."

"It's a miracle you're alive."

"That makes two of us, gimp."

Chapter Eighteen

Jake moved the heavy dresser, jamming it against the condo door. The locks on the door and the dresser would not keep someone out if they were determined to get in, but moving the dresser would make so much noise he hoped it would wake him from the deepest sleep.

That's the plan, anyway.

He checked his Sig and put it in the belt holster in the middle of his lower back. Jake tied his red knit tie from Land's End and wore his all-purpose dark blue, light wool blazer to hide the weapon.

He re-read the text he received from Willie Mitchell earlier. *Made Sunshine at 4. Kitty did fine. Doc Clement waiting for us at house. Checked her out. Said vital signs ok. Needs rest. Call U later. WM*

Jake opened his door, careful to look in every direction before he walked out. The condo posed a serious security problem. One way in and out; easy access to the common areas with little effort; locks easily picked; condo door a flimsy barrier. He thought about taking Jimmy Gray up on his offer to stay at the duplex until Brujo was behind bars. At least it had reinforced doors and a back exit through the courtyard patio, even though Jake would have to scale an antebellum brick wall covered with fig vine.

Jake sent Dunne a text the previous evening when he returned to his condo from escorting the hearse and Susan's Lexus to the Carrollton ramp. He told Dunne what happened to Kitty at her apartment and in the hospital, and that he had been suspended. Dunne had not responded. Jake tried calling twice this morning, but still had not heard.

He drove the 4Runner to NOPD headquarters and called Eustis and Pizzolato when he got close. By the time he parked, they were waiting for him in the main lobby.

"Let's go see Mr. Salazar," Eustis said when Jake walked in. On the walk over, Jake filled them in on Kitty's condition and her speedy discharge from the hospital.

"We're going to need to talk to her," Pizzolato said.

"Willie Mitchell and I thought keeping her alive was the most important thing. It might be days before she can talk."

"We know who we're after," Eustis said. "It was the right call to move her. We sure as hell couldn't guarantee her safety. To get the feds to protect her, we'd have to give up some control to them. I don't want to do that."

"Me either," Jake said.

Jake had read several articles on the internet about the Orleans Parish Prison complex in preparation for taking the Assistant U.S. Attorney job in New Orleans. Kitty told him when he first arrived in New Orleans the OPP housed only a handful of federal pre-trial detainees and no post-conviction federal defendants. Still, Jake felt he needed to know all about the state and local detention facilities in the city. He toured the OPP his second month in New Orleans, in between trips to training camps arranged by Dunne.

Orleans Parish Prison was a huge system, housing around 2700 pre-trial detainees and 800 state prisoners already found guilty by a jury or by plea agreement before a judge. Jake remembered Kitty saying that the few federal pre-trial detainees were held at OPP or Jefferson Parish Jail under an intergovernmental agreement between the sheriffs and the U.S. Marshal's office. She said there were usually less than a dozen federal prisoners at OPP at any time.

OPP sprawled over many blocks near the Criminal District Court at Tulane and Broad. The Orleans Parish Sheriff had more than a thousand employees dedicated to housing and guarding the prisoners. Though the city had lost thirty per cent of its population since Katrina, New Orleans's prison population had not declined, causing the city's per capita percentage of inmates to rise considerably. Jake read some publications that referred to New Orleans as the "the incarceration capital of the world."

Jake felt ill at ease when he was processed with Eustis and Pizzolato. They turned in their phones and weapons, and walked through the heavy steel bars into the prison interview area of the prison. The facility was old, and the refurbishing done after Katrina had done little to allay the claustrophobic atmosphere. The place gave Jake the creeps.

The three of them sat at the gray metal table in the small interrogation room, waiting for the prisoner.

"He's being held here on state or federal charges?" Jake asked.

"Both. We're holding him on the assault on Byrne and Dominguez at the warehouse when the guns were seized. ATF and FBI have a hold on him for the weapons trafficking. Even after he attacked our guys at the warehouse, we might have considered turning him over to the feds because Byrne and Dominguez weren't hurt that badly. But after Brujo killed Byrne and Dominguez the other night, we upgraded the charges against Big Demon to attempted murder of both cops in hopes we might get some information on his boss. Your people are okay with it."

"My former people," Jake said.

"I talked to Romano. He thinks you're getting the short end of the stick. Said if it were up to him...."

"Here he comes," Pizzolato said.

Two big deputies walked in with Big Demon heavily shackled. They escorted him to the table, sat him down, and locked his shackles to the thick steel grommet in the floor under the table.

"You can wait outside the door," Eustis said.

"No, sir," the biggest deputy said. "The sheriff said we have to stay in the room at all times with this prisoner."

"All right," Eustis said.

The deputies stood against the wall behind Big Demon.

"Good morning, Mr. Salazar," Eustis said. "Good to see you again." He gestured to Pizzolato. "You remember Detective Pizzolato?" He turned to Jake. "And this is Assistant U.S. Attorney Jake Banks."

Big Demon had no reaction. Jake was not surprised. Big Demon was well-named, Jake thought. About six-one, two seventy-five or so, Jake estimated. But he didn't appear fat, just solid. Jake glanced at his huge tattooed arms and his neck, the size of a telephone pole. His skin was dark, coppery.

"How's your eye?" Eustis asked.

Big Demon did not move a muscle. He stared through Eustis as if he weren't there. Big Demon's left eye was gone. There was no patch, just red, raw skin that had been sutured together over the orbital rim.

"You ought to axe 'em to get you a new one," Pizzolato said. "At least stick a marble or something in the hole." The fat detective grinned at Big Demon, but Big Demon acted as though he were alone in the room, neither seeing nor hearing the three men across from him. Captain Eustis kept at it.

"Our information is that if anyone knew where we could find your boss it would be you. They say you and Brujo are like brothers. You know where he is?"

No response from the other side of the table. Only one eye, staring straight ahead.

"We reviewed the evidence," Eustis said, "and upgraded the charges against you to attempted murder on both of the policemen you attacked at your warehouse on Tchoupitoulas. Under state law, that means you could get at least twenty-five years on each charge. I would personally testify at every parole board hearing to make sure you didn't get released early."

There was no indication from Big Demon that he heard Eustis.

"What's the matter with you," Pizzolato said, raising his voice. "You don't understand English? They ought to call you Big Dumbass."

"You know Shadow is dead," Eustis said. "We killed him at your headquarters on Flood Street in the Ninth Ward. And we arrested Green Eyes. He's in secure lockdown in here. He'll talk eventually. Seems like you would want to give us the information to get some consideration in your case. You don't, Green Eyes will get the deal."

Big Demon stared straight through the three men. There was no expression on his face, no reaction.

"Where's Brujo?" Jake asked.

Big Demon turned his eye to Jake and stared for a moment.

"Do you know where he is?" Jake asked.

Big Demon grinned at Jake. He spoke slightly accented English in a slow, deep voice. "How do you know he is not with us now, right here?"

"I guess he's under the fuckin' table, huh?" Pizzolato said.

"Brujo is everywhere," Big Demon said. "No jail can hold Brujo or any man who believes in him. Santa Muerte watches over us, and Brujo shows us the way. Brujo and Santa Muerte free us from bondage."

Big Demon lifted his left hand from between his knees and placed it on the table before him. It was not handcuffed.

The two deputies reacted quickly. The bigger one grabbed Big Demon's left wrist and pushed it back under the table. Jake heard a click, and the deputy stood up.

"Sorry about that," the taller deputy said.

Big Demon grinned from ear to ear.

Captain Eustis signaled that they were through with him. The deputies released Big Demon's shackles from the grommet, stood him up and helped him shuffle out the room.

Captain Eustis leaned back in his chair, looked at Jake, and shrugged.

~ * ~

Brujo left his men at the makeshift headquarters in one of the few remaining buildings in what had been the Erato Street Project. Abandoned since Katrina, most of the buildings had been bulldozed. The meeting had not gone well. The men wanted money; they had expenses.

Brujo was sick of dealing with them. The leadership vacuum left by Big Demon's arrest was growing more pronounced. Brujo had given Felipe $25,000 cash to deliver to the lawyer for the retainer he demanded to represent Big Demon. The lawyer was supposed to be good. He said there was a possibility he could get Big Demon out on bail because of the brutality of the cops during the arrest, putting out his eye. The two cops that destroyed his eye, the lawyer said, were dead, so they couldn't testify about what happened. It's Big Demon's word against nobody, the lawyer said, because Big Demon was on the floor bleeding from his punctured eye when the other cops and feds arrived.

Brujo was not going to put out any more of his cash to the men right now, no matter how much they whined. In contrast, when Felipe found out from the lawyer how much the bail bond would be, Brujo vowed to put out as much money as it took to get Big Demon out, no matter the cost. Brujo had his priorities.

Felipe dropped Brujo off on the corner of Rampart and Esplanade at two a.m. It was as close as Brujo wanted him or any Los Cuervos member to Mama Coba's. They did not need to know about her.

Brujo walked on Esplanade toward the river. The boulevard was dark. There were no pedestrians and only an occasional vehicle. He wore a long-sleeved, collared cotton shirt to hide his tattoos, soft chinos, and sandals. It was warm and humid; his shaved head and face glistened with a thin sheen of sweat.

Brujo's walk was a distinctive lope—he moved up and down like a carousel horse as he walked at a steady pace toward the Mississippi. Near Decatur, a car slowed next to him. Brujo moved his left hand under his cotton shirt and gripped the automatic pistol he carried with him whenever he left Mama Coba's. He kept his hand on the pistol and glared at the black man in the passenger seat sizing him up.

Just come on out, amigo. I'd love to introduce myself.

The black man turned to the driver. The car made a u-turn at the next cross street and drove away from the river on Esplanade. Both the driver and the passenger stared at Brujo as they passed him on the other side of the boulevard.

Another time, prietos, another time.

Brujo continued, crossing the railroad track and sliding through an opening between a reinforced concrete stanchion and the seawall. He was downriver from the end of the wide promenade that ran from the aquarium at the foot of Canal Street to the old mint. He moved easily on the riprap toward the water, stepping from stone to stone, until he reached his usual spot. No one could see him in the darkness.

Brujo sat on a broad stone and removed his shirt and sandals. He slid the cord of his slender leather wineskin over his head and removed the stopper. He raised the wineskin and squeezed. A stream of the bitter brown Chinese tea that Mama Coba kept in stock for him rushed into his mouth. He held the tea in his mouth for a moment, moving it around, swallowing it after it warmed to body temperature.

He took another long drink of the tea, sloshing it around his gums and tongue to increase the absorption, letting its temperature rise. He raised the wineskin and drank twice more. Brujo placed the wineskin on his shirt and sandals, then removed his pants.

He sat on the stone, listening to the river. He began to pray, then chant, so quietly only the river could hear.

~ * ~

An hour later, Brujo stood naked on the rocks, his hands folded in prayer. He had not eaten in twenty-four hours. The Chinese tea abated his hunger.

He opened his eyes. There below him, almost in the water, was the white coyote he had expected to see. The coyote seemed to glow, and his cobalt blue eyes were fixed on Brujo. They stared at each other through the blackness.

There was a flash of light above the coyote, and a huge crow flapped its wings, descending toward the coyote. The coyote never moved when the crow landed on his back.

The crow hopped off the coyote and perched on the jagged riprap. The crow raised its beak to the black sky and screeched.

Brujo sang to the coyote and crow. He sang the songs Mama Coba sang to him as a baby. The coyote and crow swayed to the music and laughed with Brujo.

Behind the coyote and the crow a tanker floated above the water, riding high and light after offloading its cargo upstream. Brujo was in awe of the tanker, its size and grace. Just beyond them, the tanker eased back into the water and continued its journey to the Gulf of Mexico. Brujo turned his attention back to his friends, who were watching something behind him.

Brujo turned and saw a malnourished stray dog on the rocks behind him. He moved quickly, removing his knife from the front pocket of the chinos then grabbing the emaciated dog by the scruff of its neck.

Brujo sliced the frightened dog's throat, and hurled its body into the river over the coyote and crow, who laughed and sang to Brujo as the dog's blood rained down onto them.

The coyote turned and walked across the river; the crow flew off toward the two massive steel bridges that spanned the river downtown. As the crow disappeared into the black sky, Brujo saw the face of the young *gringo,* The Other, appear over the lighted bridges.

He watched The Other hover above the bridge for a moment. He dressed and walked up the riprap toward home. It was time to go.

The mescaline he mixed in his chapel with the brown Chinese tea would be in his body and mind for many hours. The thought of it made him smile. He looked forward to the dreams he knew would have. He hoped to see his father Santos, and his man Big Demon. He would also see Mama Coba in his dreams. He always did. And The Other. Brujo had plans for him. Perhaps he would share those with him soon.

Chapter Nineteen

Big Demon woke up in his cell at five a.m. worried about Brujo. He sat on the side of his jail cot and rubbed his left eye socket. It was itching something fierce. He was careful not to re-open the wound.

He was alone in his windowless cell. After Brujo killed the two policemen on Tchoupitoulas they moved Big Demon to solitary confinement in the most secure section of OPP. Big Demon guessed that they connected him with Brujo from their history together in Houston and Los Angeles. The questions the detectives asked him the previous day confirmed they knew Brujo and he worked together.

Big Demon stood next to his cot and stretched, then kneeled on the concrete floor in the center of the small room. With open palms and outstretched arms, he prayed to the Earth Goddess Oshun and to Santa Muerte, imploring them to protect Brujo. In Big Demon's heart, he believed Brujo was the principal *orisha* on earth, manifesting the most power of all the earthly saints. After several minutes of prayer, Big Demon sat down on his bunk. He thought about the first time he met Brujo.

It was 1991 in California State Prison, Solano, in Vacaville, California, midway between San Francisco and Sacramento. Francis Salazar was doing two easy years on possession of cocaine with intent, and enjoying the bay area weather, which was cooler than his home turf of Hawaiian Gardens in Los Angeles County, where he was born. The facility was medium security, and small by California standards.

His cellmate was released on parole, and when the guards escorted his new celly in, Big Demon knew immediately Brujo was no ordinary gangster from Los Angeles.

At first, Brujo kept to himself. The fact that he stayed awake most of the night bothered Big Demon initially, but he grew accustomed to his new celly's strange hours. He was quiet—that was the important thing. After couple of weeks, Big Demon asked him where he was from.

"I ain't never seen tattoos like you got," Big Demon said.

"Cuba," Brujo said. "Came to Miami on a boat when I was nine. Lived there a few years. Moved to L.A. with my father about eight years ago. Lived on Virgil Street."

Big Demon raised an eyebrow. "Your *padre* the one hung that kid up upside down for poaching, shot him through the head and skinned him?"

"*Muchacho* deserved it. My father did it to warn others."

"Damn. He's famous. What's he doing now?"

"He was murdered," Brujo said. "LAPD."

"Figures," Big Demon said. "I think I heard about that."

"Why do they call you Big Demon?"

"Because I'm big, and they say when I get mad I look like the devil. You want to see?"

"No. I have no fear of the devil. The devil should fear me."

"That's cool," Big Demon said.

Brujo went on to tell Big Demon that after LAPD murdered Santos in his own house, they took Brujo into custody and threw him in an asylum. "Just like in Cuba," Brujo said. He explained how he jumped on a crazy man in the asylum and was arrested for attempted murder.

"I didn't try to kill him," Brujo said. "I could have if I wanted to. I just wanted to punish him for the way he looked at me."

Brujo's public defender plead him down to an aggravated assault, his first felony, and they sent him to Vacaville to do his three years. Big Demon told Brujo he'd be out a lot sooner than that, and took his new celly under his wing in the yard.

Almost twenty, Brujo was six feet tall and wiry. In Vacaville, under Big Demon's supervision, he developed a "prison body," ripped and lean with muscle. He added to his collection of tattoos. The prison tattoo artist wrote BRUJO across the top of his back in Old English. He already wore the Cuban flag in gray on his right shoulder and SANTOS TORRES in cursive on the left side, both below the collar line. Along his left bicep was a large, gray tattoo of the hollow-eyed skeletal Santa Muerte. Above his heart he wore MAMA COBA in black, encased in a gray heart.

Big Demon remembered the bizarre incident that made Brujo the talk of Vacaville. A white inmate nobody liked named Ross Mancuso developed an obsession with an Hispanic female guard. He wrote her love letters and professed his love to her face-to-face whenever he had the opportunity. He was written up twice for exposing himself to her.

Everyone in the prison, inmates and guards alike, was disgusted by Mancuso's behavior. None of the white inmates would have anything to do with him. Mancuso was on his own, unprotected. Brujo waited for the perfect opportunity. It came sooner than expected. Mancuso rushed the woman guard in a corner of the yard that everyone knew was a blind spot in camera coverage. Brujo spied Mancuso trying to force himself on the guard. Brujo sprang into action. He sprinted and dove head first into Mancuso, knocking him off the female guard. Brujo sat astride Mancuso's chest, pummeling him with his fists, pounding his face into a bloody mess.

The woman blew her guard whistle and other guards and inmates rushed to help Brujo. Before they could pull Brujo off the unconscious Mancuso, Brujo bared his teeth and bit a large chunk of skin and muscle out of Mancuso's chest. Instead of spitting it out, Brujo raised his arms to the sky and chewed the bloody hunk of meat, then swallowed it. The inmates backed away. When the guards pulled Brujo to his feet and away from Mancuso, Brujo began to speak in an exotic language. The inmates later agreed they had never heard this language, that it was not mere talking in tongues. It sounded more, they said, like another language. Big Demon was there. He never heard anything like it.

Blood poured from Mancuso's chest as the guards rushed him to the infirmary. The inmates who gathered around the scene barely made way for Mancuso to be carried off. For Brujo, they parted and gave him a wide berth. They gaped at Brujo as he walked through them, chanting and spitting Mancuso's blood.

Brujo gave the administration a statement, the content of which spread like wildfire through the population. Brujo said he had a vision while praying that Mancuso was going to attack the woman guard. He told the transcriber that he knew Mancuso was haunted and possessed by an evil spirit he called The Other, and he tore the hole in his chest to give The Other a way out of Mancuso's body. Brujo said when he passed Mancuso in the yard one day before the incident, he felt the presence of the evil spirit in Mancuso, and decided to exorcise it when he could. Brujo asked the prison administrators to go easy on Mancuso because the evil spirit caused him to attack the woman. With it cast out of him, Brujo explained that Mancuso would not offend again.

In spite of Brujo's strange and violent behavior, the guards did not want him punished because he rescued the female guard. The inmates were scared of Brujo from that point on, many believing that he possessed mystical powers. Big Demon had witnessed the entire episode, and after he heard his celly speaking and chanting as he was taken away, Big Demon was absolutely certain that Brujo was a sorcerer. Big Demon wanted to learn the source of Brujo's power.

From that day forward, Big Demon became Brujo's student. He listened as Brujo explained how he grew up learning the secrets of Santeria, and in Los Angeles, he discovered the power of Santa Muerte. He said the two belief systems merged organically inside him, and greatly increased his powers. Big Demon spent hours listening to Brujo, and came to believe in Brujo's power to cast spells and predict the future. Big Demon was raised Catholic, but had fallen away many years before, leaving a vacuum in his spiritual world. Brujo's teachings filled the void.

Big Demon continued to revel in the memories of his days in Vacaville with Brujo, when his cell door opened. An older black OPP guard yelled out as if Big Demon were deaf.

"Salazar. Your lawyer's here."

Chapter Twenty

Kitty awoke in the guest bedroom upstairs in the Banks home twenty-eight hours after she arrived in Sunshine. She had no idea where she was. The last thing she remembered was something around her neck choking her. She had no recollection of anything since.

She opened her right eye. Outside light poured through the tall windows on the wall to her right. Her left eye would not open. Kitty focused on the antique chest between the tall windows and the wallpaper above it. She recognized them.

I'm at Jake's house. The guest bedroom. How did I get here?

When strain of keeping her right eye open became too much, she closed it. She remembered in an instant what happened to her in her apartment on Marigny, but put it out of her mind. Instead, she focused on her physical condition.

With eyes closed, she pushed the cover down just below her waist. She raised her dominant right hand, keeping her elbow resting on the mattress. Her wrist hurt. She remembered the cloth strips tying her wrists to the bedposts. Ankles, too. Her arms and legs spread.

Oh, God. Oh, God. Oh, God.

A sob erupted from deep within her, but she suppressed it.

We're not having that. None of that. No crying like a little girl. Act like the Special Agent of the Federal Bureau of Investigation that you are.

She continued the inventory. Kitty reached under the covers and felt herself. She was sore there, but not as badly as she expected. No wounds or injury she could feel. No bandages, no sutures.

Kitty moved her right hand up, but not far. Between the top of her *mons pubis* and her navel she felt a bandage and tape. She raised her left hand and felt the IV tube against her left arm. Being careful with it, she moved her left hand to her stomach and explored with both hands the extent of the bandage and tape across her mid-section.

She felt her breasts for injuries or stitches and was relieved to find none. The thick bandage ended under her breasts and went no further than the midline of each side.

Now the face.

She lifted her hands to touch her face. When she did, excruciating pain from her ribs shot through her and almost made her scream. When it subsided, she felt the bandage over her left eye and nose. Her scalp felt sore in several places, but was not bandaged.

She heard a light knock and sturdy creak of an old door hinge. Kitty pulled the cover up to her neck. The door was to her left, so she turned her head and opened her right eye. Her neck and head ached from the slight movement.

Susan Banks stood next to the bed and smiled. Kitty thought Susan looked like an angel. She was, compared to the last humans Kitty had seen. Susan placed her hand on Kitty's.

"How are you, Kitty?"

Kitty tried to talk but couldn't get words to form. Her mouth was incredibly dry and her throat hoarse.

"Not so hot," she whispered.

Susan poured a small glass of water from the Waterford ewer on the nightstand. She placed it carefully to Kitty's lips. Kitty took slow, small sips. Water never tasted so good.

"Thanks," she said, her voice stronger.

"Dr. Clement asked me to call him as soon as you woke up."

"Who is he?"

"He's a longtime friend of ours, a local internal medicine physician. He tended to you when you first got here."

"When was that?"

"Yesterday morning, about four o'clock."

"How long have I been out?"

"It's been a little over four days since you were attacked. But the doctor in New Orleans said the good news is no brain injury. You've got knots and bumps and bruises around your head and face."

"My eye?"

"The doctor in New Orleans had to put a few stitches along the brow line and on the lid, but your eye itself has no damage, thank God."

Kitty closed her right eye. She was tired.

"I'm going to call Dr. Clement."

Kitty nodded slightly and fell asleep.

~ * ~

Later in the morning, Kitty watched Dr. Clement remove the IV needle from her arm and roll the stand away. He had raised the hospital bed thirty degrees from horizontal to make her more comfortable during the examination.

He removed the patch from her wounded left eye. She could open it slightly, just enough for him to shine a light to look at her pupil. He held a ballpoint in front of her face and asked her to follow it with her eyes as he moved it from side to side.

"The ophthalmologist in New Orleans said your eye would be fine when the swelling went down. I don't see anything to make me question his conclusion. Your left eye is moving normally and the pupil reacts to light properly. Amazing how resilient such a soft organ can be."

He studied the sutures around the orbital socket.

"Unless you really insist, I'm not going to re-bandage your eye. Leaving it open will make it heal faster."

"Good," she said. "What about my nose?"

"They set it at the hospital. I'll take the bandage off tomorrow and check it out. It was broken."

"I remember when it happened."

Tears filled her eyes. Dr. Clement gave her a Kleenex. She dabbed each eye softly and thanked him. He was a short man, maybe 5'6", and bald, but trim and athletic-looking. About Willie Mitchell's age, she guessed. He had a kind voice, and a gentle bedside manner.

"Now," he said. "Your ribs are going to be sore a long time. If you've ever had a broken or cracked rib you already know."

"I haven't."

"There's really nothing we can do, treatment wise. You can move around as much as you want, depending on how much pain you can tolerate. About a month or so you should be back to normal.

"What about the rape?"

"Your reproductive system was thoroughly checked out at the hospital. There's a report in your chart I can share with you if you want. You were given appropriate preventive medications, and there was no internal damage, or external for that matter."

"My stomach. I know I was cut with a knife."

"Your mid-section is severely sliced and cut. The report estimates about four hundred stitches. I changed the bandages yesterday morning when you arrived. That's the most significant permanent physical damage you suffered in the attack. Everything else will heal back to normal, but you're going to have significant scarring."

"I guess I was lucky. I thought they were going to kill me."

"But you've suffered a severe trauma, and not just physical. I've contacted a clinical psychologist, a woman, to come see you as soon as you're up to it. You need to talk about what happened."

"I don't need her," Kitty said. "I know I was raped by those men. I know what happened. I know it wasn't my fault. I fought them as hard as I could. I just need to get back on my feet and get back to work."

"Well, do me a favor and meet with her one time. Just humor me."

"One time. But not now."

"All right. I'll talk to Susan and coordinate it with her. And I'll be back to check on you tomorrow."

Dr. Clement gathered his equipment into his bag and started out.

"Thank you, Dr. Clement."

"My pleasure, young lady. Willie Mitchell and Susan told me all about you when you and Jake were dating. It's a pleasure to finally meet you. Sorry it's under these difficult circumstances." He closed the door behind him.

I'm sure they did tell you plenty.

Kitty did a slow burn remembering what she disliked about Mississippi in general and Sunshine in particular. She bet Dr. Clement got an ear full when Jake and she broke up.

Everybody wants to know my business. Where are you from? What do your folks do? Why did you break up with Jake? Are you seeing anyone? What's it like being a woman in the FBI. Now they'll be wanting to know how I'm feeling after all this. What was it like being raped and beaten? Am I getting better?

"If you have to know, I'm doing just fine," I'll tell them. "Just fine."

~ * ~

Martha Gray rolled her eyes.

"I've been doing research online," her 312 pound husband Jimmy Gray said. "I have the body type that's going to be fat, no matter what. Now Martha, she's an ectomorph. Slender, small bones, petite—and beautiful...."

"If you think flattery will get you somewhere with Martha," Willie Mitchell said, "I think you're underestimating her intelligence."

"No," Martha said. "He's not. I'm very open to flattery of any kind and I'm not nearly as smart as I used to be. Go ahead and complete that thought, honey. Petite and beautiful is where you left off."

"See," Jimmy said to Willie Mitchell, shaking a drumstick bone at him. "Martha knows. I'm an endomorph. I'm heavy, lots of subcutaneous fat. Daddy was an endomorph. The men in our family all have big bones. Even if I lost a hundred pounds and exercised a lot more than I'm doing now, I wouldn't look like you."

"I think we can all agree there's no danger of that," Martha said.

Susan laughed. She stood and picked up her plate and Willie Mitchell's. Martha did the same with hers, but Jimmy Gray had not finished his third helping of baked chicken. They took the plates through the swinging wooden door into the Banks' kitchen

"I wouldn't call the casual strolls you take with me three days a week exercise," Willie Mitchell said.

"It is strenuous for an endomorph. I looked up the recommended workout for people built like me."

"And?"

"I think I'm overdoing it. I read this one guy who said he believes that we all have only so many breaths in our lives. A finite number, different for each of us. He says when you take your last breath, you're done for, no matter what kind of shape you're in. You've read about joggers and athletes dropping dead, people who were skinny and exercised all the time. They used up all their breaths. Remember Jim Fixx and Pistol Pete."

"Jim Fixx died of genetic coronary artery disease, major blockages. He probably extended his life a decade by jogging and losing weight. His father died of the same thing at forty-three. Pete Maravich had a congenital aortic defect."

"My point exactly. My doctor son Jimmy Jr. says my arteries are remarkably clear, and my cholesterol is low. He said my Daddy's blood work showed the same thing. My fat daddy outlived your skinny one. And Dr. Nathan Clement said Daddy endowed me with an excellent aorta, among other things."

Susan and Martha pushed open the swinging door and rejoined their husbands at the dining room table.

"Jimmy says he thinks he's been working out too much," Willie Mitchell said to Martha. "And having too much sex."

"I don't know about the exercise, but I can do something about the other thing," Martha said.

"I didn't say that, sweetheart. Ole gimpy here is trying to cause trouble between you and me." He winked at Martha. "I think our love life is wonderful."

"When is Jake getting in?" Martha asked.

"Any minute," Susan said. "He called a little bit ago."

"Does Kitty know he's coming?" Jimmy asked.

"No," Susan said. "She's been sleeping since Nathan finished examining her this morning. I've checked on her several times and she hasn't moved."

"Captain Eustis called the feds and told her supervisor about the threat," Willie Mitchell said. "He told them concerned relatives were seeing to her recovery away from New Orleans. Eustis told them if they needed to get in touch with her they could go through him. He told them the doctor said it would be many months before she was up and around, and he would keep them informed."

"Good for him," Jimmy said.

"Is that what Nathan said?" Martha asked.

"No," Susan said. "He said it would be a few weeks. Maybe a month. Nathan said it depends on her. He told me this morning when Kitty feels up to it he wants a counselor to see her."

"She's going to need it for sure," Martha said. "Bless her heart."

"They need to catch those bastards and kill them," Jimmy Gray said. "No trial, no arrest, no nothing. Just shoot them."

"Yep," Willie Mitchell said. "This country might be coming to that."

"That would be a good thing," Jimmy Gray said. "Lawyers have ruined our way of life, destroyed our freedom. Common sense is out the window. Most every legal principle has been extended to its absurdity. *Reductio ad absurdum.*"

"That's not quite appropriate, the Euclidean mathematical term," Willie Mitchell said, "but I agree with what you're trying to say. So many things in the criminal law and procedure have been extended in ways that render an absurd result that the original law never intended. And our country is the worse for it."

Jimmy looked at the two women and pointed at Willie Mitchell. "Exactly. What he said."

~ * ~

Ten minutes from home, Jake entered the long straight stretch that led to Sunshine. He remembered as a child recognizing this final leg of the journey home, seeing the Sunshine water tower, the joy he felt as a little boy returning to their big house. But there was no joy entering Sunshine this night. He was worried sick about Kitty.

Jake parked in the gravel drive in front of the house and walked in. Susan and Willie Mitchell, Jimmy and Martha Gray all stood up from the dining room table to greet him.

Jake tossed a small canvas overnight bag on the floor. Susan bounced up and hugged him.

"Have you had supper?" she asked.

"No, and I'm really hungry. But I want to see Kitty first."

"Let me go look in on her," Susan said. "She's been asleep most of the day and I think we ought to let her rest."

"I'd like to see her now, Mama."

"Let me check first."

Susan walked out quickly. Willie Mitchell and Jimmy shook hands with Jake and Martha hugged him.

"Have a seat, son," Willie Mitchell said.

"No, thanks. I've been on my behind for almost six hours. I got caught in traffic trying to get out of New Orleans. I'd just as soon stand."

"Any news on Brujo?" Jimmy Gray asked.

"No. He flies under everyone's radar. He's like a ghost."

"Might have to smoke him out through his men," Willie Mitchell said. "Eustis has two of them in jail."

"Big Demon and Green Eyes aren't going to say anything to anyone. And Eustis called me this afternoon while I was on the road to tell me Big Demon's hired Sam Weill to represent him."

"Crap," Jimmy Gray said. "How'd he get the money to hire Slam Dunk Sammy? He's the one got the governor over there off on those election fraud charges. My brother Rodney says he's the best criminal defense attorney in Louisiana."

"There's a lot of money in selling guns illegally," Jake said. "The little stash they seized the day they arrested Big Demon was worth a half a million, the ATF people said. Brujo and Big Demon started small in the gun trade but in their New Orleans operation, they began shipping guns all over the Caribbean. They were also picking up shipments from foreign suppliers in a friendly port like Cuba or Maracaibo and delivering them to buyers in South and Central America."

"Where'd you get that information?" Willie Mitchell asked.

"Captain Eustis."

"And where'd he get it from?"

"I guess the feds, ATF or FBI probably."

Susan walked back into the dining room. "She's awake," she said. "But she said she didn't want to see you just yet."

"I'm going up."

"Jake," Susan said. "She's been through a lot."

"I'm the one found her tied up, remember?" Jake said. "She can't look any worse now than she did then."

Standing with his parents and the Grays, Jake realized for the first time how differently they looked at him now. He had known Jimmy and Martha Gray all his life. They were his Godparents. Their son Beau, who died five years earlier in a hunting accident, spent the night at the Banks home with Scott every other week. Their oldest son Jimmy Jr., the doctor, was one of Jake's heroes growing up, a star athlete. The families did everything together. His own folks had never acted the same toward him since he saved Willie Mitchell's life—twice. It was a turning point. With Jake out on his own, in control of his own life, he was doing things with Dunne he could not tell them about. It was the first time he had ever kept anything from Willie Mitchell and Susan. He was doing things they could not know about.

It seemed Willie Mitchell and Susan were more than grateful to him. They deferred to him. It was an odd feeling. Rolls had been reversed.

Everything is different now. Nothing will ever be the same..

Jake walked toward the stairs. Susan started to follow Jake but Willie Mitchell touched her arm. He gestured; let Jake go.

~ * ~

Jake opened the door quietly and entered the guest bedroom. The small lamp on the bedside table threw off a dim, yellow-brown light, which Jake thought made the bedroom feel Victorian. Kitty's head rested on the pillow facing the big windows.

"You awake?" he whispered.

"No," she said.

"Then you're talking in your sleep."

He walked around the bed and pulled up a cane-bottomed straight-backed chair and sat down close to her. He stroked her hair gently, bent over and kissed her forehead. She turned from her side onto her back.

"Can you figure out how to raise the bed some?"

Jake found the controls and raised it. "How's that."

"A little more," she said.

He moved closer and studied the sutures and swelling over her left eye. "You look much better than when I saw you last."

"Thank you," she said and started to cry. "And thank you for checking on me. I would have died."

He grabbed a Kleenex and daubed the tears on her cheeks.

"I'm going to find them," he said.

"Don't get yourself hurt."

"They'll be the ones getting hurt."

"An Assistant U.S. Attorney is just supposed to prosecute. You're not supposed to investigate and arrest."

"I've taken care of that problem," he said. "I've been suspended without pay until further notice."

"Sorry," she said. "Your old boss, I guess."

"Yep. Whitman strikes again. He's got a couple of guys from your office investigating me. Proffit and Beauvais."

"Oh, no. Beauvais is a first class jerk. He's the one you took down at the raid."

"No kidding. Even though you asked him to cut me some slack, I think he's still a little upset with me."

Kitty took a deep breath and winced.

"Ribs?" he asked.

She exhaled slowly and nodded.

"I did that one time in flag football when I was an undergraduate. They stay sore a good while."

She looked up at Jake, her left eye only a slit. She began to cry.

"A lot of good all my training did," she sobbed. "I'm a fool for thinking I could ever be a match for a man. Those men were so much stronger than me."

"How many of them were there?"

"Two that hurt me. Then there was Brujo."

"He was there?" Jake asked. "You sure?"

"I'm sure. He did some kind of ritual, burned something."

"That's what I smelled when I first got there. Did he...?"

"I don't know. The two others were cutting me up and then they choked me out and I guess I passed out before they...raped me."

She sobbed again, and winced from the pain in her chest.

"Can I get you anything?"

"Some water."

Jake poured from the Waterford ewer into the small glass. He put it to her lips but she pushed his hand away. The effort made her wince.

"I can do it."

She drank from the glass and gave it back to him.

"Dr. Clement is a really good doctor," Jake said.

"He told me my left eye was going to be okay. And all this swelling and bruising around my face would go down in a few days, maybe a week. He said the ribs would take the longest to heal." She paused for a moment. "They put 400 stitches in my stomach."

Jake nodded.

"You saw it at my apartment," she said. "I haven't seen my stomach yet. What does it look like?"

"They cut you pretty bad."

"How's your arm?" she asked.

Jake felt his left arm below the shoulder and rotated it. "It's a whole lot better. The scab is going away and it's not so sore anymore." He thought how small his cut was compared to the slicing Kitty suffered.

"I imagine those cuts are painful."

"Oh," she said, "the pain in my ribs is so bad I haven't had time to think about the cuts."

"The doctor in New Orleans said they can fix you up good as new with plastic surgery."

~ 138 ~

"That's a lie," she said. "I may just live with the scars as a reminder of how weak and pathetic I am."

"You're not weak. Stop saying things like that."

"Why did they bring me here?"

"We all thought it was safer up here, away from Brujo and his men. And Susan said she could take care of you better here at home."

"There's something you're not telling me."

"They sent you a flower box in the hospital. Inside was a headless chicken and two black roses."

She raised her voice as best she could. "Why are they doing this to me? What did I do to them?"

Jake shrugged. He didn't want to tell her it was because Brujo had seen her with him several times.

"As soon as I can," Kitty said, "I'm going back to New Orleans, get back to work."

"It's going to be a while."

"What day is it? I need to call my supervisor."

"It's Saturday night," Jake said. "And I don't think that's a good idea. We're supposed to talk to Eustis and he'll talk to the feds."

"Who decided that?"

"It's a security thing. We don't want anyone to know you're here."

"You should have left me in New Orleans."

"And who would take care of you?"

"I can take care of myself."

"You can't right now. And you don't have anyone else."

Tears filled her eyes.

"I don't need anyone else," she said. "I can take care of myself."

Jake was surprised at the anger in her voice.

"Is there someone you want me to call?" he asked. "Would it do any good to call your mother?"

Tears streamed down her cheeks as she shook her head slowly from side to side. "No."

"And no other family, cousins or…friends?"

"No."

For the first time, Jake realized how isolated and alone she really was. He had his parents, his brother, the Grays and hundreds of people in Sunshine, and many hundreds of friends and acquaintances from Ole Miss that would help him out if he got into a jam. Kitty had no one. She grew up in a city of strangers, and Jake knew she didn't keep up with anyone from Washington State. She didn't know anyone in New Orleans. In the eight months since moving there from Jackson, she had worked long hours, including weekends, trying to climb the ladder. She was all business. No social life at all. No girl friends. The FBI was all she wanted. A deep sadness overcame Jake as he watched her lying there crying, her eyes closed.

I'm all she's got. And she doesn't really want me.

Chapter Twenty-One

Big Demon sat in the bleak jail conference room across from Sam Weill. Though the lawyer protested, the deputies shackled Big Demon to the table, and checked twice to make sure his hands and feet were tightly secured before they left the room.

Sam Weill was a small man. Very short with an average build, he had a deeply receding hairline with reddish-brown hair in tight curls. His beard was neatly trimmed, the same color except for a smattering of gray around his chin. The manic, nervous energy he exuded was in sharp contrast to Big Demon, who moved slowly and only when necessary.

"So the two cops attacked you for no reason in the warehouse? Right? Isn't that right."

It took Big Demon several questions before he caught on. The lawyer was providing the narrative for the next day's bail hearing. He was telling Big Demon how he needed to testify, but preserving some sort of deniability. Smart.

Big Demon was impressed with Sam Weill. First, it was Sunday. How many lawyers came to central lockup on Sunday to prepare a client for a hearing? Big Demon did not know, but he imagined the answer was very few.

Second, Sam Weill already knew everything about the arrest and charges. He never asked Big Demon about what happened or whether he was guilty. He wasted no time, jumping right into training Big Demon how to play it the next day.

"You see, Mr. Salazar, there are no witnesses to what transpired between you, Byrne, and Dominguez. Only three people know the facts, and you're the only one alive. So the D.A. has no evidence to rebut what you say. You get it?"

Big Demon nodded when the lawyer laid it out. Brujo was smart—he knew how to take care of his main man. Brujo eliminated the two witnesses. He made sure they could not testify.

"So, you're walking down Tchoupitoulas and they stop you in front of this warehouse, and take you in there to question you. You're not sure what all is in the warehouse. You do maintenance work and clean the place like a custodian. A janitor. Right? You understand what I'm saying?"

"I understand and speak English very well, Mr. Weill."

"All right, but you got a Mexican accent. So if the assistant D.A. asks you a question that you need some time to think about, you ask him to repeat the question, slower this time. You got it?"

"Yes."

"And we've already gone over the fight. They jumped on you and tried to beat you and you fought them off in self-defense but the young one stabbed you in the eye with his knife. You got it? We need to go over that again?"

"Not necessary."

"I know you're a citizen and I have your record from California. You were never arrested in Texas? Don't lie to me. Tell me if you were."

"Never. Only in California. Only did time once."

"That's where you met Brujo. Before we get to talking about him, I want to ask you about the damage those cops did to your eye. It's worth a lot of money."

Sam Weill leaned forward and gestured for Big Demon to do the same. Big Demon wasn't sure why they were doing it, but whatever the lawyer Sam Weill said, Big Demon was doing.

"I've got this lawyer I partner with on personal injury cases. I don't do any plaintiff's work, but I send all the cases I run across to him, give him all the information, and we split the fee, fifty-fifty. Your case is a lead pipe cinch against the NOPD. Two cops with guns, and you unarmed, and they come out of the deal with no significant injury and you lose an eye. The lawyer's fee on a case like this is forty per cent, whether we try it or settle, fifty if it goes on appeal. But your fifty or sixty per cent is still going to be a big wad of *dinero*. These juries around here, they hate the NOPD. They're people that have been hassled and oppressed by the local cops all their lives. You know what I mean?"

"Yes." Big Demon knew the lawyer was saying the jurors were almost all black, like the population in OPP, like the New Orleans population, and much like Houston. Big Demon knew from experience in L.A., Houston, and now New Orleans, that lawyer Sam Weill was saying big city black jurors were almost certain to rule against the NOPD in a claim for damages, or in a criminal prosecution.

Big Demon liked living in Houston. He and Brujo were there selling guns to the Mexican cartels in 2005 when so many New Orleans people were evacuated to the city. But Brujo and Big Demon began moving their Los Cuervos men and their operations to New Orleans shortly after the city dried out. Big Demon's Hispanic *compadres* who still lived in Houston said Hurricane Katrina was Houston's Mariel boatlift. They said the *gringos* who run Houston claimed they did not know how many black New Orleanians fled Katrina for shelter in Houston, but they said over a hundred thousand of them stayed on permanently. His *compadres* said the immigrants were poor and many were violent.

It was something Brujo had already told Big Demon. The wholesale removal of New Orleans gang bangers to Houston was one of the reasons Brujo moved their operations to New Orleans. He saw the opportunity. And Big Demon knew from the success they had in shipping guns from the Port of New Orleans to all points south that Brujo was right.

The lawyer went on and on about suing NOPD for a lot of money. It was difficult for Big Demon to sign the form to hire Sam Weill's lawyer friend because of the shackles. Sam Weill held the paper low enough in Big Demon's lap for him to sign the attorney contract, so he did, even though he had no interest in such a claim. He would sign anything the lawyer wanted him to sign. It was amusing to Big Demon to think about being on a witness stand in a case against NOPD for money for putting out his eye. When the NOPD defense lawyer asked him what he did for a living, what would Big Demon say? When the NOPD lawyer asked him to give his education and employment history, what would Big Demon say?

I was a drug dealer in Los Angeles and spent two years in prison where I met Ignacio Torres, Brujo to me, a powerful sorcerer who combined the forces of Santeria and Santa Muerte; a high priest who can do amazing things. Brujo and I paroled out of Vacaville in 1992 and have been in the gun selling business ever since. At first we started small in L.A., stealing guns in burglaries and selling everything locally to drug gang bangers for big profits. But keeping enough guns in stock was hard and high risk, because no matter how careful you are, there's a chance of arrest every time. Brujo convinced me we'd never be players in L.A., and he was right. In 1997 we moved to Houston, where we improved our business model. We bought weapons from burglars instead of doing the break-ins ourselves. But we really made a difference in our supply lines by using straw men for the first time, and blackmailing dealers. Our biggest purchases were through gringos who were gun dealers and had a weakness for beautiful young Chicanas. We would send one in posing as a customer, wearing a very tight, short skirt and a low cut blouse. She would start pleasing him, if you know what I mean, and we would take pictures in cheap motels. These were married men. Then me and Brujo would call on the gun dealer and show him the pictures, and he would sell us guns to keep us quiet. Not to us, but to a person we sent him with a clean record, a citizen, you know. One dealer, Randy something or other, he got so hot for this one little chick, he sold our straw men AKs, 9mm Rugers, shotguns, and all the ammo we could carry out. He was a devout Christian, by the way, and ended up shooting himself in the head with one of his own guns, all over that little piece of ass. But the best thing we did in Houston was in distribution—we did not sell guns on the street. We sold them directly to the drug cartels just across the border. We bribed the Mexican border guards. Their government paid them almost nothing, and nobody cared in those days what we brought into Mexico. The border was tight coming into the U.S., but not going into Mexico. One of our men in Los Cuervos, his name was Panik Marquez, had an uncle who crossed the border every day, buying used washing machines in the U.S. and repairing them in Mexico. All the guards knew him, gringos and Mexicanos. He would stuff the money in the bottom of the washing machine and we would get our cash when he crossed the Rio Grande at Matamoros. He did this, took all the risk, for peanuts. By the way, Houston is where we really cranked up Los Cuervos because of the money we made off the cartels. They would pay us sometimes ten times what we paid for the guns. This was big money for us at the time. The cartels had lots of cash, and did not care what they had to pay for the weapons. They bought all we had.

We were rich, or so we thought. Then one night in Houston, Brujo and I saw this show on television, 60 Minutes, about all the weapons, not just small arms but military weapons, howitzers and RPGs, pouring out of the little countries that were part of Russia, you know, like Ukraine and the others, I don't know the other names. Brujo said his dead father Santos and his dead grandfather Hidalgo had contacts all over the Caribbean for guns. Brujo said he could get Mama Coba to make the introductions, she knew all these people, and then we could buy them from dealers in these Russian countries and ship them to Cuba or Venezuela where they hated the U.S. We would pick up the guns with our own ships and crews that we would lease; old boats that were cheap.

The Hurricane of 2005 happened, and Brujo said it was time. We moved all of Los Cuervos, our men, our money, our operation to the port of New Orleans. Brujo moved his Mama Coba and that freak who works for her to New Orleans, but kept information about Mama Coba a secret, not only from the world, but from all the men of Los Cuervos, except me. We have sold a lot of weapons to the Mexican cartels and to needy buyers in Central and South America since the early months of 2006. It took us a while to get everything set up right in New Orleans. But since then, we have made a lot of money.

Sir? How much? Millions. Many millions.

Where is it? Brujo keeps it hidden. He gives me all the money I ask for. I say I want a hundred thousand. He gives it to me, no questions asked. Brujo gives me whatever I want. He treats me like a brother.

"You with me?" Sam Weill asked. "Hey!"

"*Lo siento,* Mr. Weill," Big Demon said. "I am sorry." Big Demon focused on what Sam Weill was saying.

"Okay. No problem. Don't give this lawsuit against NOPD for destroying your eye another thought. Right now, all that's important is the bail hearing tomorrow morning. You've told me everything about the fight and we've gone over it and you know exactly how you're going to testify, right?"

"Yes. I've got it."

"See you tomorrow morning," Sam Weill said and banged on the door for the deputies. He hustled out without another word.

~ * ~

Big Demon sat in his cell. The meeting with Sam Weill brought back memories of the early days in L.A. after Vacaville. Big Demon and Brujo had been released in the fall of 1992, two months apart. The seeds of their partnership were planted in the prison in many late night talks in the cell. Big Demon remembered watching in April of that year the Rodney King riots in Los Angeles on television with Brujo and thirty other inmates in the common area. When Big Demon and Brujo returned to their cell, they talked about what they saw.

"What do you think about the riots?" Brujo asked.

"The people are angry."

"*Los prietos,* the blacks."

"Yes."

"Why would they burn their own neighborhoods? The stores where they buy their food and clothing."

"I guess LAPD lets them burn their own areas."

"To keep them from invading the white areas north of them. It still makes no sense to me."

"No," Big Demon said. "It does not."

"What are your plans when you get out this year?"

Big Demon shrugged.

"Are you going back to doing what you were doing before?" Big Demon said he did not know. "You'll wind up back here if you do."

"What will you do?"

"I will never deal in the drug trade again. Drugs killed my father.

"There's much money in the drug business," Big Demon said.

"You'll never get to the top in the drug business unless you sell your soul to the South Americans. They will never trust me because I was born in Cuba. They fear me because I know the secrets of Santeria and Santa Muerte."

"So what will you do, Brujo?"

"Have I ever told you how my grandfather made a living in Cuba?"

Chapter Twenty-Two

Jake hit the LaPlace exit at two a.m. Monday and slowed down to seventy when he entered I-10 and drove eastward, the final leg into New Orleans. He knew the Louisiana state police swarmed this fifteen mile segment of I-10 close to New Orleans, even this time of the morning.

Kitty was in a better mood Sunday. Dr. Clement spent an hour with her in the morning. Susan asked him when they could expect Kitty to be up and around. He told the family that her activity would be limited only by pain, and Kitty could do whatever she felt like doing. Dr. Clement said she could eat, drink, try to stand, whatever she wanted to do. It was up to her.

When Jake talked to her late in the morning, she asked him to help her sit up on the side of the bed. When she bent at the waist in an attempt to sit up, she cried from the pain. Jake told her when he had cracked or broken ribs in college, it was less painful to get out of bed by turning over on his stomach in bed, then swinging his legs out and letting his feet hit the floor. He said then he would use his arms to push off the bed onto his feet.

Kitty tried it Jake's way. She stood up on the first attempt, but the effort made her woozy. Jake put his arm around her to steady her. Kitty stood for two minutes, with Jake's help.

"That's enough," she said.

Jake had lunch with Kitty in her room. She asked him to come back to help her try to walk after her nap. Jake returned with Susan, and the two of them helped Kitty walk to the bathroom and back to bed. Kitty said her head and eye felt much better, and that Dr. Clement said the yellowing of the bruises on the edges meant they were healing.

"He let me look at my stomach this morning when he changed the bandage," Kitty said. "You should see it."

"It's going to heal just fine," Susan said. "And with plastic surgery these days they can remove a lot of the scars."

"I'm not having plastic surgery," Kitty said. "I'm keeping every one of my scars as a reminder of what those pigs did to me. It will never happen again."

Jake did not blame Kitty for being angry, but he agreed with Dr. Clement. She needed to talk to a counselor right away. With Jake back in New Orleans, he hoped Susan and Willie Mitchell could talk Kitty into it. Knowing how strong-willed she was, he wasn't sure they could.

With no traffic on the interstate at two-fifteen on a Monday morning, Jake passed Veterans Boulevard and Causeway in a flash, then the giant mausoleums in the cemetery next to the New Orleans Country Club. He sped down the Poydras exit and waited at Claiborne for the light to turn. Within ten minutes he entered the underground parking at his condominium complex. Bone tired, he knew he would fall asleep as soon as he hit the bed. Before he stepped out of the 4Runner, he set the alarm on his phone for eight to make sure he would make Big Demon's bail hearing at Criminal District Court at nine.

Jake did not know what it was, but something made him check his rear view mirror before he stepped out of the car.

Brujo stood directly behind the 4Runner.

Jake felt the adrenaline rush through him and worked to control his breathing. His right hand trembled as he grabbed his Sig off the seat and checked the rear view mirror.

Brujo was gone.

Jake checked the side mirrors. He looked in every direction. There was no sign of Brujo. Jake opened the door. With two hands he aimed the Sig in every direction.

Nothing.

Am I losing my mind?

He grabbed his canvas overnight bag from the back seat, and backed slowly toward the steps. He was on full alert, pointing the gun where he looked, waiting for Brujo to appear.

Nothing.

Jake opened the door to the steps, checked inside quickly, then again looked in every direction in the parking garage.

He bounded up the stairs two at a time, raced across the concrete landing at the main floor then ran up the steps to his floor. Jake threw the door open and waited. Nothing. He walked quickly to his apartment, backing up the last twenty feet with his gun pointed and ready to fire. He stood at his door and checked out every possible source of attack while he removed his key. Jake glanced down long enough to slip the key in the lock while still pointing his gun, ready for Brujo to rush him.

He unlocked the door and opened it, took one final look around and dashed into his apartment locking it securely and pushing the chest of drawers against the door. Jake leaned against the dresser and exhaled. He was sweating profusely.

Jake smelled something. His senses went on high alert again. It was a foreign smell. Nothing in the condo smelled like this. He walked with both hands on his Sig, first into the kitchen, then into the living room. *Jesus.* He stared at the wall above his television and counted the dimly burning candles placed around the room. *Ten.* He held the pistol in front of him and pushed his bedroom door open with his foot. He checked the closet, the bathroom, then went back over every inch of the condo. *Nothing.*

Jake rushed back into his bedroom and opened the closet. The black duffel bag Dunne brought him was on the floor. He unzipped it and did a quick inventory. Everything seemed to be there. Jake thought for a second and checked the contents again.

Except the grenades.

Jake grabbed a face towel from the bathroom and sat down hard on his sofa. He wiped the sweat from his face, and dried his Sig, slick with sweat from both hands. He studied the wall above his television.

The same eyes Jake saw in the shrine room in the Ninth Ward house were now painted on his wall. Sinister, piercing eyes, Brujo's eyes. In blood red paint, a stylized L and C. *Los Cuervos.* The flying crows.

Painted on his flat screen television was the evil visage of Santa Muerte, her hollow eyes and skeletal grin in glossy black.

The son of a bitch.

He grabbed a bottle of water from the refrigerator, picked up his overnight bag and tossed it into the bedroom.

Jake heard a thump from his entrance hall. He pointed his gun toward the chest of drawers and walked slowly. There was nothing in the hall. He checked the peephole in his front door. *Nothing.* He chalked it up to jittery nerves.

THUMP.

It wasn't his imagination. Something hit the door again. Something heavy. He checked the peephole, but saw nothing outside his door. Jake took a deep breath and cracked open the door. On the welcome mat was a bronze statue of a cougar, the front paw raised, ready to swipe. Jake recognized it immediately. It was Kitty's award from Washington State, honoring her as most valuable player on the women's soccer team her senior year. The last time he saw it was in Kitty's Marigny apartment while he waited for her to dress for their dinner at Café Beaufort's.

Jake walked out of his condo, gun in front of him. He saw no one. He walked toward the common area of the condominium. When he passed the brick and stucco wall, he saw Brujo in the common area on the main floor below Jake.

Jake stood at the steel rails and looked down on Brujo, twenty feet away. He was barefoot, shirtless, and wild-eyed. Brujo's hands were raised above his head as if surrendering. Jake pointed the Sig at Brujo's head. Brujo moved his hands so Jake could see he had nothing in them, then turned around so Jake could see he had nothing in the back pockets or stuck in the waist of his ragged chinos. When he made the turn to face Jake again, Brujo patted his front pockets.

Jake continued to aim his pistol at Brujo's face. Brujo raised his hands in surrender again.

"Get on the ground," Jake growled.

Brujo tilted his head as if he did not understand.

"I would like to talk," Brujo said.

"Lie flat on your face and put your hands behind your back. Then we'll talk."

Brujo kept his hands over his head.

"We have been down this road before," Brujo said. "The time has come for us to work together."

Jake moved down the rail toward the stairs. Brujo turned his back to Jake and took a small step.

"Stop right there. Don't make me shoot you."

I can't shoot him like this. What would Dunne do?

Jake heard something behind him. He turned for just a second. It was his condo neighbor, a fast-talking real-estate broker in his early thirties, walking toward Jake in his tee shirt and underwear, rubbing sleep from his eyes. He had to stop him.

"Stay right there, Robert."

"What's going on, Jake?" Robert asked.

Jake turned back to Brujo. He was gone. Jake knew he would be.

Damn. I should have shot him. Dunne would have.

Chapter Twenty-Three

Sitting at the prosecution table with Assistant District Attorney Walton Donaldson a little before nine, waiting for Judge Zelda Williams to open court, Willie Mitchell found it hard to concentrate. The text from Jake that woke him at three this morning about Brujo in the parking garage was more than disturbing—Willie Mitchell was afraid for his son's life. With what he had been through in the last year, Willie Mitchell was acutely aware that life was fragile. The difference between being alive and dead was sometimes a matter of inches or minutes.

Dead before you know it.

Willie Mitchell did not wake Susan when the text came. He wanted some time to think about the best way to tell her. He walked downstairs and called Jake. Jake answered every question Willie Mitchell asked, but cautioned his Daddy against telling Susan. She would insist on getting in her car and driving to New Orleans immediately, gathering up Jake in her arms, and bringing him to Sunshine. Willie Mitchell couldn't say that was a bad idea. Jake would have none of it. Even though his suspension from the U.S. Attorney's office put him in legal limbo, Jake was determined to stay and fight.

Willie Mitchell said he could not keep the information from Susan. She had to know. Jake told Willie Mitchell it was his decision. Jake said he had to get off the phone, he needed a few hours sleep before the Big Demon bail hearing at nine. Willie Mitchell made Jake promise to fill Captain Eustis in on what happened, and ask him about NOPD offering him some protection. Maybe change locations, move into Jimmy Gray's duplex. Jake said he would talk to Eustis, but Willie Mitchell wasn't convinced Jake would follow through.

He's going to downplay the threat. At his age he thinks he's invincible. So did I. But I never had the guts Jake has.

Willie Mitchell put the incident in the least threatening light possible when he told Susan over coffee. He told her Jake was going to talk to Captain Eustis and get some help, maybe stay in a different location, get NOPD protection. Willie Mitchell assured Susan now that Jake and the cops knew Brujo was definitely after Jake, they would take the steps necessary to make sure he was safe at all times. Susan was distraught and wanted Jake home. Willie Mitchell agreed, but said Jake was a grown man and this was his decision.

Willie Mitchell had not gone back to sleep after the text, and was yawning when the fat, semi-retired bailiff *du jour* opened the side door to the courtroom and instructed everyone in the packed courtroom to stand. He waddled in ahead of the Deputy Circuit Clerk Eddie Bordelon, a transplanted Cajun from Acadia Parish who single-handedly kept the justice system working efficiently in Yaloquena County. Eddie was small, bald, and wore rimless glasses. Today Eddie was acting as Judge Williams' Minute Clerk for the preliminary hearing, the sole matter scheduled for the day.

Judge Zelda Williams followed Eddie into the courtroom. She walked up the riser and stood behind her bench. The judge grabbed the gavel, banged it twice.

"Come to order, please."

The low murmur that spread through the crowded court as she ascended the bench disappeared. Zelda Williams was fifty-seven, dignified but forceful on the bench. Her skin was dark brown, her dark hair beginning to gray. She was thin, had a son doing a medical residency in at the University of Mississippi medical center in Jackson, and a paralegal daughter in a silk-stocking firm in Manhattan. Her husband retired from teaching in the Yaloquena school system and tended to their forty-acre farm in the county.

Zelda Williams was Willie Mitchell's favorite judge, and in his view, the best judge on the Yaloquena County bench in the twenty-three years Willie Mitchell had been District Attorney. They were professional friends, mutual admirers, but Zelda did not always rule in his favor. She made her decisions based on the law and the facts she found. Willie Mitchell wouldn't have it any other way.

"Is the State ready to proceed?" Judge Williams asked.

Willie Mitchell stood. "We are, your honor. Assistant District Attorney Walton Donaldson is second chair for the State this morning."

Judge Williams acknowledged Walton with a nod. He was thirty, dark-haired and handsome, the father of twins. His wife Gayle and Susan were good friends. Willie Mitchell was proud of Walton's growth as a lawyer. Under Willie Mitchell's tutelage, Walton had become a first-rate litigator. They worked together every day, and Willie Mitchell knew Walton was more than capable of handling this preliminary hearing without Willie Mitchell's help. But this case had political implications, and though he hated to admit it, Willie Mitchell was a politician. He held an elective office. And because the defendant was Bobby Sanders, Willie Mitchell was handling it himself.

Willie Mitchell's plan as Walton matured was to turn over most of the jury trials and all of the non-felony prosecutions to Walton. The injuries Willie Mitchell suffered eight months ago had accelerated the plan's implementation dramatically.

"Ms Bernstein," Judge Williams said.

"Eleanor Bernstein for the defendant Bobby Sanders, your honor."

Willie Mitchell admired Eleanor's navy blue pin-striped business suit and matching heels. She was the Yaloquena Public Defender and always dressed sharply for court. Willie Mitchell knew how much she made as the indigent defender, and was always impressed she could dress so well on such meager pay. She was forty and single, attractive, darker than Judge Williams; never a hair out of place.

The defendant Bobby Sanders was not indigent. Willie Mitchell knew he was paying Eleanor, and he hoped she was charging the smart ass an arm and a leg. Bobby was *the* up-and-coming black preacher in Sunshine, and was no fan of Willie Mitchell. Willie Mitchell disliked Bobby Sanders as much as anyone he knew. They had several run-ins in the past couple of years and Bobby had sworn to Willie Mitchell that he was going to get someone to run against Willie Mitchell and beat him like a drum.

"Yaloquena County is eighty per cent African-American, Mr. District Attorney," Bobby Sanders told him after one of their confrontations, "and your days are numbered."

The charge against Bobby Sanders was theft by fraud. Judge Williams had signed the arrest warrant based on the sworn affidavit of Reverend Paul Gray, pastor of Ebeneezer Primitive Baptist Church. Pastor Gray's congregation met on the third Sunday of every month in its white frame church near Sadie's Bend, a small unincorporated community in the southern part of Yaloquena County. The salient allegations were that Reverend Bobby Sanders had members of his Full

Gospel Non-Denominational House of the Lord in Sunshine raid the church at Sadie's Bend and steal the brass collection plates, the altar cloths, and the oil paintings of Jesus On the Cross and The Last Supper.

Willie Mitchell and Judge Williams discussed the issues in chambers with Eleanor Bernstein. They all knew the underlying problem was not theft, but the continued deterioration of Pastor Gray's membership, a substantial number of whom had pleaded with Reverend Sanders to allow their church to merge into his. Pastor Gray had a handful of loyal followers, all over seventy, who would have none of it.

Though the crux of the case was not a real theft, the judge suggested the theft charge and the hearing to give everyone their day in court, let them air their grievances and be heard. Bobby Sanders did not mind being charged, he knew he had not stolen anything and welcomed the forum of a packed courtroom to display his eloquence under fire.

Willie Mitchell and Zelda had been through many of these church fights in the past, and agreed that once the parties were able to testify and point fingers, the animus would eventually dissipate.

Walton was incredulous when Willie Mitchell explained it to him.

"That's because you've never been through one of these," Willie Mitchell said. "Just watch and learn."

Willie Mitchell called the first witness, Mrs. Lawanda Perkins, wife of Elmore Perkins, the head deacon of Ebeneezer Primitive. Before she took her seat, Eddie Bordelon asked her to raise her right hand and be sworn. "Do you swear or affirm...," Eddie started.

"I will not swear," Mrs Perkins said. "I will affirm."

The short Cajun nodded and started over. "Do you affirm...."

Mrs. Perkins affirmed the oath and took the witness stand. She was a large woman, and took a moment to settle in between the arms of the witness chair. Willie Mitchell started with a few background questions, but moved quickly to the heart of the case because everyone in the courtroom was familiar with the back story. Mrs. Perkins testified that Reverend Bobby Sanders had directed the conspiracy and theft by telling members of the Ebeneezer Primitive congregation to bring him the items in question.

"Do you know the names of the persons who actually entered the church house and removed the items we discussed?"

"I most certainly do."

"Are those persons in the courtroom today?"

"They sure are."

"Could you name them and point them out to the court at this time?" Willie Mitchell asked.

"The ring leader was Mrs. Doris Price," she said.

Willie Mitchell noticed Deputy Clerk Eddie Bordelon trying to keep up with his notes while Mrs. Perkins went on with the names. Eddie would look at the witness, then down at his note pad and write furiously. The courtroom light over Eddie's desk caught the Clerk's rimless glasses at just the right angle so that the glare from the lenses struck Willie Mitchell, on and off.

By the time Willie Mitchell realized what was happening, it was too late. The process had started. He felt himself reach the neurological plateau from which there was no turning back. Willie Mitchell entered the nothingness he had come to know since he left the hospital.

The state achieved, I float alone in the void. No color, no substance, no sound, no thoughts. An empty black hole, I am no more.

Just before he zoned out, Willie Mitchell saw out of the corner of his eye Mrs. Doris Price leap over the courtroom rail and rush the witness. Mrs. Perkins tried to stand up but was wedged tightly in the chair. The deacon's wife grabbed a hand full of Mrs. Perkins' hair and pulled hard. Instead of a hank of hair, Mrs. Price ended up with *all* of Mrs. Perkins hair. Mrs. Price held the shiny black wig high for everyone to see. Mrs. Perkins shrieked and tried to cover her nylon wig cap with her hands. The courtroom erupted.

Sitting in his chair, eyes opened and fixed, Willie Mitchell might have observed or heard some of what happened. There was no way to tell, because nothing registered, nothing at all.

~ * ~

Walton and Willie Mitchell sat in the D.A.'s private office with the door closed.

"I wish I could have seen it," Willie Mitchell said.

"It was unbelievable," Walton said. "There were women swinging purses and old men throwing punches that missed by a mile."

"How long did it last?"

"About ten minutes or so. Judge Williams hit the panic button under her desk and about seven or eight deputies were there in no time. They separated the congregations and Judge Williams dismissed the charges and told them all to leave and don't come back."

"Good for her. How long was I out?"

"Probably another five minutes. I saw you go into the seizure, so I guess all in all about fifteen minutes before you came back to the world of the living."

"Man-oh-man," Willie Mitchell said. "That's why they call them *absence* seizures."

"Yeah, Willie Mitchell. You were gone. Way gone."

Chapter Twenty-Four

Jake, Captain Eustis, and Pizzolato sat in the courtroom in Criminal District Court. Big Demon's bail hearing was supposed to start at nine, but as usual, Judge Gamba Issa was late. Big Demon had been escorted in by two deputies earlier. He sat at the defense table, fully shackled. The deputies remained in the courtroom, stationed against the wall not far from Big Demon.

Jake was surprised to see so few people in the courtroom until he learned from the bailiff that Judge Issa had pushed everything else on his docket to eleven to make the enhanced security measures for Big Demon easier for the sheriff's office to manage. The NOPD patrolmen who arrived at the warehouse after Byrne and Dominguez had finally subdued him were there and ready to testify, along with all of the federal agents who arrived after the NOPD cops, except for Kitty.

The Hispanic female Assistant District Attorney walked into the courtroom through the door to the judge's chambers behind the bench followed by Sam Weill, Big Demon's attorney. She was short and attractive, but appeared to Jake to be right out of law school. She was giggling at something the slightly taller Sam Weill said to her coming out of the door. Weill was smiling and jovial.

"Aw fuck," Pizzolato whispered. "Look at this shit."

"Doesn't mean anything," Jake said quietly.

Eustis was checking his texts when the bailiff walked in ahead of Judge Issa. The three men and everyone else in the courtroom stood while the judge ascended the steps to the bench.

It was the first time Jake had seen Judge Issa, *nee* Cedric Walker, who legally changed his name during his first term on the Criminal Court bench to Gamba Issa, which Eustis told Jake loosely translated to "Messiah Warrior" in the African dialect Judge Issa had chosen to adopt. He wore a multi-colored dashiki-type robe, which surprised Jake. He always assumed there was a dress code of some kind limiting what Louisiana district judges could wear on the bench.

"Miss Juarez," the judge said. "Before we start the testimony, would you state for the record the State's position on bail."

"Your Honor," she said, "the State asks that the defendant be remanded to OPP and the custody of the sheriff pending trial, that no bail be granted. The defendant is a flight risk and is associated with an individual who is suspected in the death of two police officers a little over a week ago."

Jake was not impressed with Ms Juarez's brief presentation. She did not sound confident or forceful, nor did her body language indicate she was convinced of the merits of her position.

"Mr. Weill," Judge Issa said. "State your case."

Sam Weill stood next to Big Demon, who sat motionless. "Your honor," Weill started, "the State's position is wholly without merit. We start from the premise at this hearing that the only purpose of bail is to assure the defendant's presence at subsequent proceedings. Mr. Salazar is presumed to be innocent at this stage of the prosecution, and the State has no evidence to support either proposition that it asserts. First, they are asserting some type of guilt by association with this unnamed person, which this court knows is impermissible. My client has been incarcerated for several weeks, isolated in the most secure part of OPP. It's impossible to connect him with the tragic death of the two officers—he was in jail at the time. Moreover, as to the second argument, that he is a flight risk, my client has been convicted of only one offense, over eighteen years ago in California when he was no more than a teenager, Judge Issa. He learned the error of his ways, and has not been arrested since. I have subpoenaed the records from California to prove that Mr. Salazar appeared at every stage of the proceedings in L.A. County."

"We have not been provided with that transcript," Ms Juarez said.

"I have not received it yet, but I plan to put on testimony to that effect and will supplement the same with the documentation as soon as I receive it, which should be shortly."

Jake almost laughed. The idea of even getting eighteen-year-old records from L.A. County was ludicrous, and Sam Weill was promising their prompt delivery to the court.

"Additionally, your honor," Weill said, "the defense will prove that the NOPD officers who made the arrest used so much unwarranted force against my client that they put out his eye. My client will testify that as soon as they identified themselves as NOPD officers, he submitted to the arrest and did not resist in any fashion. Yet, these rogue officers took away not only the vision in his left eye—his left eye is gone. They stuck a knife in my client's eye, Judge Issa!" Weill paused for a moment and continued in a quiet voice. "The NOPD's own records of the event reflect that the two officers were uninjured."

Jake watched Judge Issa while Sam Weill made his argument. The judge began to shake his head when Weill spoke of the knife taking out Big Demon's left eye. By the time Weill sat down, it was obvious from Judge Issa's tone that he was not happy with NOPD.

"Call your first witness, Ms Juarez" Judge Issa growled.

"I call officer...."

"Objection," Weill said. "The State has not a single witness who was present before and during the arrest of my client. All these witnesses in the court room arrived at the scene after the arresting officers had my client on the floor, blood pouring from his left eye where they stabbed him."

"Is that correct, Ms Juarez?"

"Yes, your honor."

"Then what is the relevance of their testimony. We know the defendant was arrested. What more can they add?"

Ms Juarez thought for a moment.

"Ms Juarez?"

Weill jumped in the gap. "Your honor, my client intends to file a civil suit against NOPD for the loss of his eye and has already retained counsel. He intends to stay in this city to help prepare his case for damages and wrongful arrest. He's not going anywhere."

"But your honor, there were guns seized..."

"Guns they cannot link to my client, Judge Issa."

"Ms Juarez," the judge said, "is there really any need for testimony? Mr. Weill has presented a strong case for bail."

Jake wanted to scream.

Weill hasn't presented anything. He's just talking, making allegations. Make him prove what he's saying. Make him call witnesses.

"The State asks for remand without bail."

"I know that, Ms Juarez. What can you prove this morning?"

After thirty seconds of thoughtful silence from Ms Juarez, Judge Issa banged his gavel.

"Bail is hereby set at $50,000. This court is adjourned."

Judge Issa left the bench in a rush. Ms Juarez turned to the law enforcement witnesses and shrugged. Sam Weill whispered something to Big Demon before the deputies came to his side to escort him back to his cell. As he turned to leave, Big Demon looked at Jake and grinned.

"Piss poor lawyer the D.A. sent," Pizzolato said after the courtroom cleared. "Pathetic."

"We need to investigate and follow anyone who shows up to get him out. This might be a chance to find Brujo."

"Already covered," Eustis said. "I've got men all over it. If Big Demon makes bail we're tailing him, too. Twenty-four hour surveillance. I went ahead and set it all up, cleared the overtime, because I figured we didn't have a chance in front of Issa. He doesn't like us, and doesn't care who knows it."

Jake started to leave, but Eustis stopped him. "Before you take another step," the captain said, "let's talk about how we're going to keep you safe from Brujo."

Chapter Twenty-Five

While Jake watched Judge Issa grant Big Demon bail in New Orleans and Willie Mitchell missed the fight of the century in the Sunshine courtroom, David Dunne leaned back in a rickety wooden chair on the front porch of a cabin in Maine. He was cold, and bored to tears.

The cabin was deep in the woods off I-95 five miles north of Smyrna Mills, about fifteen miles from the border separating Maine from New Brunswick. He was in his sixth day at the cabin, arriving in Bangor shortly after noon in the Cessna Citation, the same day he dropped Jake off at the FBI headquarters on the New Orleans lakefront. He drove due north on I-95 to Smyrna Mills that afternoon in the gray Ford Explorer waiting for him outside the general aviation terminal in Bangor. The Explorer was packed with the equipment and supplies they needed for the operation. The rest of the DOGs had already arrived at the cabin late that morning, waiting for Dunne, their commanding officer.

As soon as Dunne arrived, the four of them conducted a thorough inventory of the Explorer contents. The next morning, they test fired then broke down and cleaned all of the weapons, making sure every piece of equipment was in good working order. Dunne was expecting instructions from Big Dog the second day at the cabin. He heard from him all right, but it was just to report that there had been a delay in acquiring details from the informant on Aleem's movements and more precise logistics. The informant was in the neighborhood, holed up in a twenty-year-old Winnebago in an RV park on Baskahegan Lake about ninety minutes southeast of Smyrna Mills. Dunne told Big Dog if the informant didn't come through with the information right away, Dunne was going to send Bulldog and Hound to forcibly extract him and invite him to spend some quality time with the four of them in the cabin. It would be like a party, Dunne told Big Dog. He was sure the informant would have a swell time.

For a man like David Dunne, accustomed to being on the move, six days felt like a lifetime. The operation was not supposed to take this long. Dunne knew from experience delay increased the number of things that could go wrong.

Dunne rubbed the multi-day growth on his cheeks and chin, eventually making his way to the two-inch scar on his left jaw line where no beard grew. The scar was courtesy of a roadside IED in Baghdad in 1992. Dunne rubbed it for luck during intense moments on the job.

He wondered how things were going in New Orleans. Brujo was a formidable, unpredictable criminal, and Dunne felt bad about leaving Jake. Dunne would have enjoyed working with Jake and NOPD to bring down Brujo. Maybe they had already captured him by now. With no communication except over the encrypted Globalstar satphone, and that strictly limited to NORTHSTAR details and directives, it seemed to Dunne he had been in these woods forever.

Doing nothing meant too much time to contemplate. During slack times, Dunne invariably looked back on his life. Both marriages ended badly. His first marriage was the worst decision he ever made; the second was the best. It ended tragically with the death of Maggie Evanston, the only person in the world he could say he truly loved. Dunne tried to keep his examination of his personal life to a minimum because it depressed him. Reliving his service history, on the other hand, was much more fulfilling. Parts of it made him very proud. His work history for the United States read like a compendium of modern conflicts—one way or another, he was involved in most of them. His best work in the eighties was in Central America. The nineties were a globe trotting blur: Desert Storm, Bosnia and Herzegovina, Rwanda, Kosovo, Djibouti, Tajikistan, Mogadishu, Afghanistan, Lebanon, Cambodia, even the Chiapas uprising in Mexico—Dunne had a hand in all of them.

But since September 11, 2001, his focus was the U.S. Dunne was the first operative General Evanston brought into the program. It was hard for Dunne to believe he had been working for Evanston for a decade. He went abroad now on very few occasions, and only to investigate terrorists and criminals planning lethal operations inside the United States.

Working with Jake had made him wonder what it would be like to have a son or daughter that he could be proud of. He wished he had time to spend with Willie Mitchell Banks. In another life they would have been good friends. Dunne envied Willie Mitchell—a beautiful wife who loved him, two smart and accomplished sons.

He leaned forward. The front legs of his chair banged onto the wooden porch floor. He stood and stretched, zipped his OD green parka up to his neck, and removed a small pocket knife from the front pocket of his well-worn jeans. The blade on the knife was razor sharp. Dunne began to shave wooden strips from the porch column so thin they were almost opaque. After he tired of that, he carved a fairly respectable Santa Muerte on the column, boring out the black, empty eye sockets and making a depression to effect the sunken cheeks.

One of Dunne's men, Jeff Redding, pushed open the screen door and joined his C.O. on the porch. At forty-two, five years younger than Dunne, Redding was an inch taller but twenty pounds lighter. As with the other members of the team, Dunne never referred to Redding by his name. Redding's code-name was Doberman.

The team manager, General John Evanston, sequestered deep in the bowels of Homeland Security, always called his men by their full code-names. Since David Dunne was not his real name, General Evanston and the three men Dunne commanded always called him "Dunne."

The other two DOGs were Hound and Bulldog.

General Evanston was Big Dog, and no one currently at Homeland Security knew who Big Dog was or what he did. Evanston had been there since 2001. In the first few months after nine-eleven, he assembled and commanded a large force, hundreds of special ops and technical specialists to operate covertly within the United States. The mission was to protect the homeland. In the early days, with express orders from the White House and D.O.D., they did exactly that, no matter the circumstances. Shortly after the change of administration in January of 2009, DOGs was abruptly terminated by the White House. General Evanston had a different agenda, however. He figured a way to secure his own funding and continued to operate out of the same office in Homeland Security. He dealt with no one else in the agency—not a single other government employee. He transitioned to covert ops, and from 2009 on, Big Dog's Domestic Operations Group (DOGs) flew unnoticed under government radar. It consisted only of Evanston and his best four men, all of whom were in on Operation NORTHSTAR.

"Nice to see you up," Dunne said. "Hope you got enough sleep."

"Not yet."

Doberman stretched and yawned. Doberman reminded Dunne of a young Steven Seagal, without the ponytail. He was lean, and wore his black hair slicked back. His face was hard, lupine—making his code name Doberman particularly apt, in Dunne's view.

"You snipers can wait around forever for something to go down, can't you?" Dunne asked.

"I admit it's difficult sleeping sixteen hours a day, but I'm doing my best. I went through years of training to develop the skill."

"I haven't heard from Bull or Hound."

"I expect we will soon enough. Getting about that time."

"As soon as they get back, we're all taking a drive down south to check out some of the sights. Lovely natural beauty around here."

"Don't you mean s-i-t-e, like a camp site, where they have old RVs?"

"That's correct."

"I figured we would. About time we got to work."

"I was going to send Bull and Hound alone, but I'm aching for something to do. I think we all should go."

"Okay by me."

"If Mohammed won't come to the mountain."

"My thoughts exactly," Doberman said. "We'll go to Mohammed."

Doberman stepped off the porch and started through the woods.

"Where are you going?" Dunne asked.

"Just stretching my legs. I'd like to get a little exercise before I start in on my next nap."

"Well, don't be gone too long," Dunne said. "I want you back here in fifteen minutes so we can get busy again sitting on our ass."

"Yes, sir," Doberman said. "That I can do."

Chapter Twenty-Six

Brujo's men assembled at two a.m. at an abandoned grain elevator on the river two blocks inside St. Bernard Parish between Marais and Villere Streets. It was the last multi-story grain silo on the east side of the river, the others having been demolished as the grain export industry moved out of the city for cheaper real estate upriver.

The elevator consisted of three four-story concrete silos connected to a concrete office structure that resembled a World War II bunker. The elevator complex had not been used for grain storage in over a decade, but had not been demolished because the owners did not want to pay the tremendous cost of the asbestos abatement necessary to obtain a permit from the EPA to legally tear it down. The stalemate between the owners and the EPA had effectively taken the once valuable riverside property out of commerce, and rendered it perfect for Los Cuervos.

Big Demon had scouted the location several months before he was arrested. It was an alternative gathering spot for Los Cuervos when Big Demon wanted absolute privacy and isolation. They met in one of the concrete silos, accessing it from the office structure. When Big Demon closed off the door to the office, no light escaped from the silo. The interior of the silo was musty and dank. Brujo's men were spooked the first time they met there, but Big Demon convinced them they were more secure there than anywhere else, even their houses in what was left of the Ninth Ward.

Brujo had given the instructions to Felipe to notify the men of the meeting. All of the members of Los Cuervos had followed Brujo to New Orleans from Houston, except one. When they gathered without Brujo, Spanish was the only language spoken. Brujo insisted on English when he attended. All the men were at the silo at two o'clock, but Brujo was late. After fifteen minutes in the silo, the men began to grumble.

The loudest complainant was Mario Vargas, the one member of Los Cuervos who joined the gang in New Orleans. Mario was born in Puerto Rico and immigrated to New Orleans in 1980 when he was five years old. His skin was very black, and appeared more African-American than

Hispanic. Mario met Big Demon in a bodega in the Irish Channel shortly after Katrina. Mario was just what Big Demon was looking for—a New Orleanian who blended in with the locals, spoke Spanish as a first language, and knew his way around the city. Mario was a valuable addition to Los Cuervos in the early years, but in the past year, had become disgruntled with Brujo and Big Demon. He was the first member to complain openly in meetings. The issue was money. Big Demon would not distribute to Mario what he thought his services were worth. Though strictly against Los Cuervos' rules, Mario had been secretly supplementing his income by selling drugs in his old neighborhood. After Big Demon's arrest, Mario's complaining and drug-selling increased significantly.

Brujo was thirty minutes late, and the men were not happy. Without Big Demon there to supervise, Mario's complaints about money incited and emboldened other members, who joined in the chorus of discontent about their pay. Panik and Smokey tried to quiet the men, but the men continued. At two-thirty, Felipe left the silo.

Ten minutes later, Brujo appeared in the dim candlelight of the silo. He walked in behind Felipe, who carried a large, shiny silver shopping bag by its silver rope handle. The men in the silo grew silent. Brujo stood before them, shirtless and barefoot. Instead of chinos, he wore a red codpiece. On his head was a red Toltec ceremonial jaguar headdress.

Felipe placed the shopping bag on the dusty concrete floor in front of Brujo, who stood silently over it for five minutes, his eyes closed and hands folded in prayer. His men were transfixed.

Brujo opened the shopping bag and removed a trussed up white alligator. His men gasped. The gator was young, but big enough to be scary. Brujo unwrapped the tape that bound the tail and legs under the gator's belly. The gator's jaws remained bound with gray duct tape. The gator struggled, squirming to break free. Brujo kept one hand around the gator's neck; with the other he grasped the tail. The white gator was strong, but no match for Brujo. His powerful grip kept the gator under control. Every muscle in Brujo's lean body flexed and rippled; the gator bent and strained with all its might, swiping its front claws at its captor.

Brujo placed the white gator on the floor on its back. He kept his right hand clamped around the neck. He let the tail go and with his left hand stroked the gator's stomach, chanting. At first, the gator swung its tail, trying to hit Brujo. The gator tried to roll, but couldn't. Brujo continued to rub the stomach and chant. The gator grew calm. Brujo continued to stroke the belly, and the gator became immobile. The tension in the gator's muscular tail and neck grew slack. After a minute, Brujo continued to rub the stomach as he unwrapped the duct tape from the young gator's powerful jaws. The men backed away and watched, their eyes wide.

The gator was no longer restrained, but it remained motionless, its jaws closed. The only contact Brujo maintained was his hand on the gator's stomach, moving back and forth gently, rubbing the rough skin.

Brujo gestured for Felipe to come forward. Felipe stood as Brujo lifted the gator off the floor and placed it gently in Felipe's arms. Felipe stood motionless, arms outstretched, holding the gator. Brujo passed his hand over the gator and prayed. After a moment, Brujo took the gator from Felipe and held it out to the men, inviting others to come forward. Panik moved first, taking the gator from Brujo and holding it in outstretched arms for Brujo. Brujo blessed Panik and the gator.

Before he took the gator from Panik, Brujo gestured for Mario to come forward. He directed the rest of the men to line up behind Mario. Brujo gave the gator to Mario, who extended his arms and held the gator, waiting for Brujo's prayer. Brujo glanced at Felipe, who stood behind Mario. Felipe reached into the silver shopping bag, removed a machete. He held the blade, pointing the wooden handle to Brujo.

Brujo grabbed the machete and moved quickly in the dimly lighted silo, spinning on one leg and swinging the sharp blade through the neck of Mario Vargas, whose head toppled off his shoulders, bouncing on the concrete floor in front of the remaining members of Los Cuervos.

For a moment, arterial blood shot from Mario's neck like a fountain until Mario's torso stumbled forward onto the concrete. Blood continued to gush with each pulse, until Mario's heart stopped. The gator awakened from its stupor when it spilled from Mario's arms. It started moving slowly, then picked up speed and scampered away from the men.

Brujo bent down and let his palm fill with blood from Mario's neck. He grinned at his men and slurped the blood from his hand like a dog. Wiping his bloody hand across his chest, Brujo left an uneven red trail on top of his gray tattoos.

Brujo instructed Felipe to bring him the shopping bag. When Brujo reached into it the men backed away, afraid of what he would pull out this time. They stopped when Brujo held high a thick stack of one hundred dollar bills. He gave the money to Felipe.

"Fifty thousand American dollars for the lawyer," Brujo told the men, "to pay the bail to free Big Demon from the jail."

Brujo gestured for Panik and Smokey to come forward. He counted out fifty one-hundred dollar bills for each of them and for Felipe. He gestured for the rest to line up. Brujo gave them each four thousand dollars.

"Now," Brujo said, "does anyone else want to discuss their money while we are here?" Dead silence. "Then let us pray."

Chapter Twenty-Seven

Big Demon walked out of OPP at eight p.m. the next night. He walked east on Tulane Avenue toward the river in the vanishing daylight. There was no need to check behind his back or in any other direction for the police. Big Demon knew he was being followed by NOPD. They wanted Brujo, and following Big Demon would be the easiest way to find him.

In his first four blocks walking east on Tulane Avenue, past the intersections of Dorgenois, Rocheblave, Tonti, and Miro, he paid attention to the shuttered buildings, denuded concrete slabs, and grown over vacant lots. Big Demon had plenty of time to read about the city while in OPP. One AP story said New Orleans had 44,000 dilapidated structures, giving the city a higher percentage of distressed property than any city in the United States except Detroit. Big Demon had never been to Detroit, but reasoned that if it looked worse than New Orleans, it had to be pretty bad. His part of L.A. County, around Hawaiian Gardens, was run down, as were many of the sections of Houston he worked with Brujo and Los Cuervos.

But they were nothing like this.

He passed the deserted, crumbling Dixie Brewery between Rocheblave and Tonti, then made the sign of the cross as he passed in front of St. Joseph's church, which seemed to Big Demon to be still in use, even though the entire city block across Tulane Avenue from St. Joseph's had been razed.

He continued to walk toward the river—under I-10, across the wide and confusing intersections at Loyola and South Rampart where Tulane Avenue disappeared into Common. He walked on to the foot of Canal Street and waited for the ferry. He had come up with a plan.

Big Demon rode the free ferry across the river to Algiers on the West Bank, but did not disembark. He rode the ferry back to the city side of the river. It was full dark now.

As the ferry approached the landing, running upriver against the current, Big Demon moved discretely to the stern, then jumped off the ferry into the black water as close to the pier as he could. He knew this part of the river well. He and

Brujo had walked the riprap on the left descending bank many times, north from Canal Street.

Big Demon heard shouting from the dock and the ferry. He had upset the police. He drifted with the swift current, staying close to the rocky bank, and in a couple of minutes passed the St. Louis Cathedral and the French Market. Big Demon was a strong swimmer and had no fear. He came ashore on the big rocks at Brujo's favorite place to sit and watch the river. He squeezed through a gap in the seawall, next to a concrete stanchion north of the end of the pedestrian promenade, crossed the railroad tracks and walked steadily toward Chartres Street.

Big Demon knew Brujo's ministering to his supplicants would end soon. He sat on the sidewalk and pretended to beg like a homeless person, keeping an eye on the front door of *La Casa de Mama Coba*. Big Demon was the only member of Los Cuervos who knew where Brujo lived. Brujo had insisted on it when they moved their operations from Houston to New Orleans. Big Demon now saw how wise it was for Brujo to insulate himself from the men. Not one of them could give him up to the police. Only Big Demon knew about *La Casa de Mama Coba* and he would die before giving Brujo to the police.

When Big Demon saw Mantis escort the final patrons out and lock the door behind them, Big Demon walked across Chartres and knocked on the door. Mantis bent over and looked through the glass in the door. He opened it quickly for Big Demon, then closed and locked the door. He released the Roman shade to cover the glass in the door. Big Demon could not tell If Mantis noticed his missing eye. As usual, the strange man said nothing to Big Demon.

Big Demon walked quickly through the shop but stopped when Mama Coba saw him. She approached Big Demon slowly, studying the skin covering his left socket. When she reached him, she touched the skin around his missing eye. Mama Coba removed a jar of salve from a shelf, opened it, and rubbed some of it gently on the skin on and around the left eye socket. She pulled a feathered amulet from a display case and placed it around Big Demon's neck. She pulled him toward her and kissed each cheek. Mama Coba gestured toward the chapel.

Big Demon quietly rapped on the door.

When Brujo opened the door and saw Big Demon, he stood still for a moment, then shouted. He pulled Big Demon inside and hugged him. He sat Big Demon down on a bench in front of the altar, then stood behind the polished limestone holy table. He lit two ceremonial candles and incense, and began to chant.

Big Demon felt proud and grateful to be in Brujo's presence again.

~ * ~

Jake woke up a little before six a.m. in the Banks family side of Jimmy Gray's duplex on Ursulines. It was familiar territory. He had stayed there many times with his parents on trips to New Orleans. Since his own condo's primitive security was obviously no match for Brujo, the Ursulines street duplex seemed the best alternative lodging, at least on a temporary basis.

He had slept very little, worried about Kitty and thinking how bad the day before had been, starting in the wee hours with Jake dropping the ball in the parking garage. He tossed and turned in the night, replaying the confrontation with Brujo over and over.

I should have shot him. I should have killed him. Dunne would have killed him. I should have killed the crazy son-of-a-bitch. Dammit. Dammit. What could Brujo possibly want to talk to me about? What did he mean "we've been down this road before." Just like on Tchoupitoulas when he acted like he knew me from somewhere. Makes no sense.

Jake hoped Big Demon was still in OPP. Eustis was right about Judge Issa. They never really had a chance in the bail hearing. Jake wished that Los Cuervos wouldn't be able to come up with the money. But like Pizzolato said after the ruling, if they had enough money to hire Sam Weill, they probably could make bail. The last time Jake checked on Big Demon was around five p.m. He was still in central lockup.

Susan's call in the afternoon was unsettling. It was the first time Willie Mitchell had a seizure in the courtroom. She said he wasn't upset about anything but missing the free-for-all and learning that no one had cold-cocked the Reverend Bobby Sanders. Susan, on the other hand, was very worried. Jake could tell from her voice.

And still no word from Dunne. No telling where he was.

Jake walked to the kitchen and turned on the monitor for the outside security cameras. Jimmy had them installed after the incredible outbreak of violence in the city during Katrina. Because the front door of each duplex opened right onto the sidewalk, it made plenty of sense to check the monitor before venturing out.

You never know.

On the screen Jake watched one officer wake the other in the NOPD cruiser parked on the sidewalk outside the duplex. He felt sorry for them. What crappy duty, babysitting a defrocked Assistant U.S. Attorney from ten until six in the morning. Jake told Eustis it wasn't necessary, but the captain insisted. The patrol car blocked Jake's 4Runner from leaving the garage. Each side of the duplex had a one-car parking garage on the front of the building with automatic doors, so that Jimmy or Martha, or the Banks family, could engage the remote while on the street, drive into the garage and close the door behind the vehicle, all without getting out of the car. Jimmy Gray insisted on adding the garages during the renovation, and gradually overcame his brother's objections. Jake had to admit Jimmy had foresight. The garage bays with automatic doors for each side was an excellent security measure.

Jake watched the monitor. The policemen were driving away from the duplex. His cell phone rang.

"Big Demon's out," Captain Eustis said. "Left OPP about eight o'clock last night."

"Who posted the bail?"

"Sam Weill. That's not the bad news."

"They lost him?"

"Yep. He jumped off the Canal Street ferry into the river. It was dark; my men couldn't see much."

"Damn."

"Sorry," Eustis said. "One of those things."

"Your two officers watching me just drove off."

"We're continuing your guard duty every night until we get Brujo."

"Any other ideas on getting a line on Los Cuervos?"

"No. They're like a bunch of ghosts. You hear from our buddy?"

"Nope. Still no word."

"He'll call when he can."

Jake was about to jump out of his skin. He had to do something to ease the stress. He put on his running stuff, checked the sidewalk and street on the monitor, opened the front door and took off jogging. He ran west on Ursulines to Rampart and took a right to Esplanade. Jake ran faster than usual—fueled by a combination of nervous energy and the need to sweat out the stress he had accumulated.

Big Demon on the loose. Crap. Thanks for nothing, NOPD.

He turned right on Chartres to cut back through the Quarter to Jackson Square, where he would cross the tracks and get up on the Moonwalk to head south and west along the river to Audubon Park. It would be a long run, but he needed it.

In the second block of Chartres off Esplanade he passed a really tall, thin man with a shaved head, dressed in a black cassock, sweeping the sidewalk in front of a store. The block consisted of one run down specialty store after another, mostly catering to tourists.

Jake had never seen the man before, but then he rarely jogged in the French Quarter, and never on Chartres.

Jake usually greeted every person he passed while running, either with a nod or a "good morning." He said hello to the skinny man with the long, bony fingers wrapped around the broom handle. The tall, thin man in the cassock continued to sweep. He did not acknowledge the young runner.

~ * ~

Jake walked with Pizzolato at one p.m. into the meeting room at NOPD. Captain Eustis had scheduled a meeting with the detectives working the double homicide of Byrne and Dominguez. Every detective in the room was unhappy.

"All right, men," Eustis said as soon as he entered. "Just wanted to make sure we're all on the same page, information-wise. No good news to report. You all know Big Demon Salazar shook the surveillance by jumping in the Mississippi last night. We've got boats in the river, and we've got every available patrolman on the lookout. No luck yet.

"Jake Banks here, you guys know him from the last meeting, he had a confrontation with Brujo in Jake's parking garage about two-thirty in the morning the day before yesterday. I've filled most of you in on that.

"Why didn't you shoot him?" The question was quietly and seriously asked. It came from somewhere in the back of the room.

"I should have," Jake said.

"There was a civilian at the scene," Eustis said. "Jake did the right thing. We've got to do a better job canvassing the Irish Channel and the other Hispanic neighborhoods. Put more pressure on your informants."

"These guys ain't like a regular gang, Captain," a black detective in his late thirties said. "They don't have a territory, they don't sell drugs or have hookers out on the street."

"We know they're all Hispanic males, heavily tattooed," Eustis said. "They're in the Latino neighborhoods somewhere."

"Nobody I deal with has any information on them," a salt-and-pepper mustachioed Hispanic officer in his fifties said. "They don't traffic their guns locally, and they don't talk. It's like they're really controlled. And this Brujo. It's like he don't exist at all."

"Big Demon says he's real," Eustis said. "He said he's everywhere."

The detectives chuckled.

"I'm serious," Eustis said. "Big Demon said no jail can hold Brujo."

"He ain't never been in the OPP," the black detective said. "We can keep his ass locked down tight as a drum in there, at least until some candy ass judge lets him out."

"What about Green Eyes?" the only Asian detective asked. "He still not talking?"

"Not a word," Eustis said.

"Ought to be some way to put pressure on him," the detective added.

Eustis shrugged.

"All right, men," he said. "Keep at it."

Chapter Twenty-Eight

Kitty walked down the stairs slowly. It was her sixth day in Sunshine and she was ready to get some fresh air. She wore a pair of Susan's old gray Champion sweatpants with the white drawstring in front. The sweats had been washed "a thousand times" according to Susan, and were beyond soft. 100% cotton, with a knobby interior, the sweats felt so good to Kitty she asked if she could take them back to New Orleans with her.

Susan laughed and said "sure, but I wouldn't recommend going outside your apartment in them. They're at least fifteen years old."

The red cotton Ole Miss hoodie Kitty wore was Jake's, but all her other clothes and undergarments were hand-me-downs from Susan, including the rubber-soled fuzzy pink slippers she wore for her first trip outside. Kitty chose the hoodie so she could pull the hood over her head and cover the bruises on her face, neck, and head.

"Well, good morning," Susan said, looking up at Kitty from the base of the stairs. "Are you sure you feel up to this?"

"The physical therapist said I can do anything that I want, as long as I can stand the pain. I don't know how long I can keep moving, but I'm feeling okay right now."

"If you'll wait just a second," Susan said, "I'll put on my walking gear and join you. That okay with you?"

"I think that's probably a good idea," Kitty said. "How about if I wait out on the front porch?"

Susan walked beside her and pulled open the front door. Kitty moved deliberately out onto the porch to the rail between the columns.

"Do you want to sit in the rocker while I get dressed?"

"I'd rather stand."

"Okay, but steady yourself against the rail."

Susan hurried inside. Within minutes she was back. They walked down the front porch steps onto the brick sidewalk, then the pea gravel circular driveway. Kitty stopped and removed the red hood. She took a deep breath. It was a relatively crisp morning for Sunshine, seventy-three degrees but low humidity. It would be hot by noon.

"The skin around your eyes looks so much better," Susan said.

"I put on a little makeup," Kitty said.

They walked on the pea gravel to the concrete sidewalk paralleling the street. Kitty pulled the hood back on.

"I don't want to scare anyone."

"A lot of people have been asking about you," Susan said. "They all said to wish you a speedy recovery."

"I don't want to see anybody."

"They know that. They're just concerned, that's all."

"How did they even know I was here?"

"A few old men in the neighborhood who wake up at four every morning saw the hearse and the commotion when you arrived. They were worried something happened to me or Willie Mitchell. Sunshine's a small town, and people find out just about everything."

"Nosy."

"Maybe, but I like to think it's concern. I know you're not used to everyone wanting to know what's going on in your life."

"It's one of the reasons I left Jackson," Kitty said. "Everyone pries down here. It rubs me the wrong way."

"Have you talked to Jake this morning?" Susan asked.

"We talked last night. He's really frustrated with NOPD. They blew the tail on Big Demon and he's out, now, no telling where. They had a meeting yesterday and there's been almost no progress finding Brujo, much less the guys that assaulted me. I tried to describe them as best I could, but their faces are kind of a blur. Maybe when my head clears up I'll do better job of remembering what they looked like. They were two Hispanic-looking males with tattoos. I know Brujo was with them at first, I recognized him from the photo Captain Eustis had."

"It will all come back to you." Susan took a deep breath. "I'm so worried about Jake down there, that evil man stalking him. I wish Jake would come home."

"You probably don't know this, but your son's a pretty tough guy."

"I never have thought of him like that."

"He's been through a lot of training. He's a good shot with his gun, too. If someone tries to mess with Jake they're in for it." She paused. "If he had been with me at my apartment he would have disabled both of those worthless, evil men."

Susan shuddered. "For some reason, that doesn't make me feel one bit better. I wish he would just be a regular lawyer."

"Because you're his mother. Mother's worry."

"You'll find out one day," Susan said.

"I'm not so sure of that."

"Would you like me to call the hospital in Tacoma and check on your mother?"

The question seemed to jar Kitty.

"There's no reason to."

"I just can't believe there's not something they can do for her."

"There's not." They walked a few more paces. "Jake told about Willie Mitchell having a seizure in the courtroom."

Susan pulled a Kleenex from the pocket of her Nike running shorts. She dabbed her eyes and blew her nose. More tears fell.

"I wish we could get back to having just a normal life. Jake is being stalked by a madman. Willie Mitchell's still not all the way well from the hit and run. And now you, what you've been through."

The two women walked in silence while Susan gathered herself. She placed the Kleenex back into her pocket and smiled at Kitty.

"Sorry. Let's get back to your situation. Is your office getting involved in the search for the men who hurt you?"

"Jake says they're still sitting on the sidelines. They told Captain Eustis they were letting NOPD proceed with the case as a state matter for now. They're waiting for word from the Justice Department whether they can pursue a federal investigation on my case since they abstained from charging Big Demon for gun smuggling, deferring to NOPD to prosecute him on the assault on the two policemen that Brujo eventually murdered."

"I'm not a lawyer," Susan said. "But that doesn't make any sense to me. They all ought to be after these people. NOPD, FBI, ATF, and anybody else they can throw into the mix."

"That's way too logical. If you were a government lawyer, you'd be focused on tiptoeing around these jurisdictional issues rather than concentrating on catching the bad guys. And I think Whitman might have something to do with it."

"But he has time to go after Jake for not answering questions about David Dunne."

"That's personal, Susan. Whitman's got his stinger out because of what happened in Jackson."

"It just sounds so petty and vindictive."

"Welcome to the federal system," Kitty said. "You'd be surprised at the number of decisions made on personal and political grounds. I've only been an agent for a year, but I've seen it often enough."

Kitty stopped twenty feet from an intersection. "I think we better turn around and go back," she said.

"You shouldn't overdo it your first day out. I'm really impressed you could get this far."

"I've got to get back in the saddle, got to get my strength back. I want to be there in New Orleans when they bring those bastards in."

They walked slower back to the house. Susan helped steady Kitty up the front porch steps and led her to the big wooden rocking chair.

"This rocker won't be too hard on your ribs?" Susan asked.

"If it is I won't rock. It hurts the most when I change positions."

Susan stood by to assist, but Kitty eased herself into the rocker without help. She grimaced when bending her knees and waist to sit made her ribs and entire torso ache.

"I'm going in to get us some lemonade," Susan said. She turned to go inside but stopped when Ina walked onto the porch with two ice-filled glasses and a pitcher of light yellow liquid on a serving tray.

"Thought you could use this," Ina said.

"Thank you, Ina," Susan said and moved a wicker stand between the two wooden rockers. Ina placed the tray on the stand and poured the glasses. She gave the first one to Kitty.

Kitty studied Ina's hands. They were calloused, weathered but strong, the dark brown skin on the back of her hands fading with age.

"Would you like to join us?" Susan asked Ina.

"Got too much to do. Got ironing stacked up from last week."

Ina looked at Kitty's face. "Those bruises look better."

"Thanks," Kitty said. "I think so."

Ina was silent, not moving. After a moment she walked around the rockers so that she stood in front of Kitty. It was awkward until she pointed an index finger crooked with arthritis at Kitty.

"You know it happened to me when I was a young girl. Couldn't been no more than thirteen."

"You never told me," Susan said.

"No need to. I put it out of my mind. He was about sixteen, one of Mr. Prather's best workers. None of us went to school back then past sixth or seventh grade. He caught me behind the big house hanging out wash on the clothesline. Everybody was off somewhere. He knew what he was doing. Twice as strong as me, a big buck. I wasn't no bigger than a minute back then. He dragged me into one of the tractor sheds. I fought some, but gave up pretty quick. Weren't no use fightin'. I figured I'd get hurt less just lettin' him have his way."

When Susan saw big tears rolling down Kitty's cheeks, Susan started crying again. Ina's eyes were dry, her voice strong.

"Did they arrest him?" Susan said.

"Like I said, he was one of Mr. Prather's best hands, and it was my word against his, and I weren't nothing but a little house maid."

"So they didn't do anything to him?" Susan asked.

"I didn't tell no one. But I waited late one night and slipped into the tenant house where he and some other single men stayed. I knew which bed he slept in. I stuck a butcher knife against his throat. I had stropped it 'til it was so sharp I had to be extra careful with it. I held it against his throat real hard and he started bleeding. His eyes was big as baseballs. I told him I would have a knife this sharp with me from now on, and if he ever tried something like that with me again I was going to cut him the way they cut those young bulls on the place, make him a steer so he don't bother nobody no more."

"Did he leave you alone after that?" Susan asked.

"Sho' did. Kept his distance. Sometimes when I saw him I'd pull my knife out and jug it at him, show him how I'd cut him."

Kitty dried her eyes with a napkin from the lemonade tray.

"Now you get over this business, young lady. Just put it out your mind. It's been happening since men and women been on this earth. If you let it bother you then they win. It's like they take you all over again. You get yourself well and get on with your life. Forget about it."

Ina nodded firmly and walked inside.

"What Ina did," Kitty said to Susan, "that's what I'm going to do. I said I'd talk to that counselor once for Dr. Clement. I saw her yesterday, so I kept my word. That's enough."

"I think you should see her again."

"I know you do. So does Dr. Clement. But I'm not. I'm just going to put it behind me, forget it ever happened."

Susan stood to go inside. "Martha Gray is joining us for lunch. I'm going in to set the table. Do you feel strong enough to help?"

"Is it a formal setting?" Kitty asked.

"Yes."

Kitty got up slowly from the rocker after setting her lemonade glass on the tray. She walked to Susan and hugged her.

"Was it that obvious when I first started dating Jake," Kitty said, "that I didn't know which fork or spoon to use when I sat at your dinner table?"

Susan pursed her lips.

Kitty hugged her again. "Yes, I would like to learn. The crystal, too. I've got to start acting like a grownup. I ought to know how to set a table. I don't know exactly why, but ever since that first dinner in the dining room, I've secretly wanted to ask you to teach me, but I guess I was too proud. I never told Jake."

"Wonderful," Susan said, grabbing Kitty's hand. "It's really easy."

~ * ~

Late that afternoon, Jake tossed a white shell into the Mississippi River from the river bank a hundred feet north of the brick and concrete promenade along the river east of the French Quarter. The police officers tailing Big Demon told Captain Eustis and Pizzolato that Big Demon probably drowned. They all knew how hard it was to swim in the current, and no one had seen Big Demon crawl out of the river.

Jake had no doubt Big Demon was still alive. Jake rode the Canal Street Ferry to Algiers, then back to Canal Street twice. Based on where the officers said the ferry was when Big Demon jumped, Jake figured that Big Demon swam to the rip rap and pulled himself out of the river with ease. Jake had seen Big Demon up close. He knew how strong he was, and how determined.

Jake walked up the levee and across the tracks to his 4Runner illegally parked near the French Market. It was difficult to park anywhere in the Quarter that wasn't illegal. His boss Peter Romano followed protocol and required Jake to turn in his badge and laminated Justice Department identification card when he suspended him. Romano had not asked for the U.S. ATTORNEY OFFICIAL BUSINESS sign Jake kept in his 4Runner, probably because Romano didn't know about it. Jake had printed in small letters in parentheses on the bottom of the sign "On Suspension" just in case his continued use of the sign ruffled the feathers of someone in local law enforcement or in the Justice Department. Jake believed in full disclosure.

Your Honor, it says right there on the sign in plain English: "On Suspension." I submit to the court this proves I didn't mislead anyone.

Jake left the sign on the dashboard by the steering wheel in an effort to influence whichever French Quarter Parking Police officer happened by the 4Runner in one of their ubiquitous scooter cars.

"Yes," Jake hissed when he saw the windshield—no ticket.

Jake turned right on Decatur then left on Ursulines, crossing Chartres Street less than a block from *La Casa de Mama Coba*. It was almost seven and he wanted to get a few hours sleep before he began his patrol. Two nights of the NOPD cops babysitting him on the duplex sidewalk was enough. Jake and Eustis had words over it, but Jake insisted Eustis discontinue the protection. Eustis told Jake he was calling Dunne that afternoon to have Dunne order Jake to accept the surveillance. Apparently Dunne was still on his mission, and incommunicado, because Eustis had not called Jake back. Jake would know for sure at ten o'clock if the cops showed.

Jake fell asleep much quicker than he expected and slept until midnight. When his cell phone alarm went off, he showered and dressed, and hurried to check the monitor to see if the outside camera showed an NOPD cruiser. There was no squad car on the sidewalk, so Jake opened the door off the kitchen that led to the one car garage, started his 4Runner, engaged the automatic door, and backed out slowly onto Ursulines Street.

He planned on driving from midnight until dawn through the streets and areas of New Orleans he suspected Brujo and Los Cuervos might frequent. Jake knew it was probably a stupid idea, that the NOPD already had its patrol units on the lookout for Los Cuervos, and the NOPD cops knew the city a lot better than he did.

But Jake was the only person who had seen Brujo and lived, besides Kitty, and was one of a small number of people who had seen Big Demon up close.

He knew he might drive all night and see no one of interest. He spoke enough Spanish to put him in danger, not enough to understand something a witness or gangster might tell him. He knew for a fact the NOPD detectives, including Eustis and Pizzolato, would think it was a stupid thing to do. He patted his Sig resting on the passenger seat.

It may be stupid, but I'm doing it—every night until I find him.

Chapter Twenty-Nine

"How's our man doing in there?" David Dunne asked Doberman.

"Pretty docile," Doberman said. He sat down on a crude wooden bench across from Dunne on the front porch. Doberman's dark beard was filling in after ten days without shaving. So was Dunne's.

Dunne glanced at Doberman. With his black hair slicked back and his dark beard, Dunne thought Doberman was looking more like his canine namesake.

"I agree with Hound," Dunne said. "I think your beard makes you look more like Steven Seagal in *Hard to Kill*, when he came out of that two-year coma and got revenge on the guy who killed his wife."

"What's Bull got against Seagal, anyway? Who gives a shit if Bull thinks Chuck Norris can whip Seagal's ass. And how would we ever find out who's the toughest?"

A dirty tan Tahoe drove into view on the narrow dirt road to the cabin. Two men exited when it stopped ten feet from the porch. One was 5'9" and stocky at 200 pounds with a blond crew cut that had grown too tall. The other was three inches taller and weighed 165 pounds, with black, wavy hair—Hispanic in appearance. They unloaded paper grocery bags from the back of the SUV.

"About time," Doberman said. "Mohammed's cell phone is just about out of juice. Give me the keys so I can charge it up."

"Why not use the Explorer to charge it?" the stocky blond asked.

"Because the charger is in the Tahoe," Doberman said.

"You should have gotten it out before we left," the stocky man said, his ice-blue eyes flashing. "Oh, but that would have required you to wake up before eleven."

"Now, girls," Dunne said.

"And Dunne and I want to know what's your problem with Seagal?"

"Whoa," Dunne said, "leave me out of this."

"Nothing," Bruce Batovsky, code-named Bulldog, said to Doberman. Bulldog was by far the strongest of the DOGs, with a blond crew cut badly in need of a trim. "But I'm telling you Chuck Norris would beat Seagal like a yard dog in any kind of matchup. Chuck is tough. Seagal is a pussy."

"And you base this conclusion on what?" Doberman asked.

"Watching them in their movies. You can tell by the way they fight and move around."

Doberman turned to Carlos Tomas. Carlos was code-named Hound, born in Miami to parents who emigrated from El Salvador. He was the quietest and most pleasant of the DOGs. A powerful long-distance swimmer, Hound was trained in the Pararescue forces in his days in the United States Air Force.

"Tell him Hound."

"They fight in different disciplines," Hound said with a smile. "It's like comparing George Foreman's skills with Randy Couture's. Foreman's a boxer; Couture's mixed martial arts. Apples and Oranges."

"Coward," Doberman said to Hound.

"But Chuck Norris definitely has the best beard."

"He dyes it, dumbass," Doberman said.

"And you don't think Seagal uses Just For Men?" Bull asked.

"Let's eat," Dunne said. "Enough of this crap."

Bull moved both grocery bags to his left arm and popped Doberman on the upper arm with his huge right fist. Doberman exaggerated a stagger, coming back toward Bull with fists raised knuckles out and moving in circles like pistons *a la* John L. Sullivan.

All four DOGs put up the groceries inside, returned to the front porch and tore into the sandwiches Bull and Hound purchased from the deli section of the Smyrna Mills grocery store. Dunne brought one of the sandwiches to Abdul Nasser in the cabin's back bedroom. Abdul was the informant the DOGs extracted from the RV park south of the cabin when Abdul began to drag his feet providing the information the team needed to intercept Aleem and disrupt his planned terrorist attack. Abdul's feet were shackled together and tethered to the heavy iron bedpost.

"Thank you," Abdul said to Dunne when he gave him the sandwich and a Pepsi. "If you let me out of here I promise I will not try to escape."

"You think about what we want to hear from you on your buddy Aleem, and I'll think about letting you out of this room," Dunne said. "Do you really want to help kill hundreds of innocent people?"

Dunne rejoined the others on the porch and finished the last half of his sandwich with Doberman, Bull, and Hound.

"Abdul wants yard privileges," Dunne said.

"Who cares what he wants," Doberman said.

"If he gives us the information, I don't have a problem with it," Hound said. "We're going to need him to talk to Aleem soon."

"Sooner the better," Bull said patting the top of his blond crew cut. "I stay out here any longer I'll be six feet tall."

"Fat chance, Shorty," Doberman said and poked Bull in the stomach. Bull made a big fist and shook it at Doberman.

"Why don't we bring Mohammed out here on the porch and let him enjoy this camaraderie," Hound said. "Our friendly give and take on the world and our lighthearted banter should engage his imagination."

"Abdul," Dunne said.

"They're all Mohammed to me," Hound said.

Doberman raised his MP5 submachine gun. "This'll engage his ass."

"I vote with Mr. Seagal over here," Bull said, pointing his thumb at Doberman.

Dunne took the last bite of his sandwich, and drained his Coke.

"I'll bring him out," Dunne said. "See what happens."

"I'll do it," Doberman said and opened the door. "It's my responsibility. I'll leave his ankles shackled."

"Man," Bull said, "I'll be glad to get back to electricity."

In a few minutes Abdul Nasser shuffled through the front door ahead of Doberman. Doberman nudged him with the submachine gun toward the bench. Hound and Bull stood to allow Abdul to sit on the bench by himself. Doberman walked to the Tahoe and plugged in Abdul's cell phone.

"You get enough to eat, Abdul?" Dunne asked.

"Plenty," Abdul said.

Abdul spoke with a slight Arab accent, had light brown skin and close-cropped curly hair.

"Amazing there's such good reception out here in the sticks," Doberman said as he ran his free hand through his slick-backed hair then his dark beard, cupping his hand around his chin.

"There are cell towers all along I-95," Abdul said.

"How long have you lived in that RV park?" Hound asked.

"A few months."

Hound followed up. "You moved up here to coordinate with Aleem?"

Abdul nodded.

There was silence on the porch for a moment.

"Don't take this the wrong way, Abdul," Dunne said, "but you don't seem like the kind of person who would blow up people for no good reason, people who have nothing to do with your cause."

Abdul was sheepish. "That's why I started trying to get the attention of the FBI and Homeland Security. I've known Aleem all my life; our fathers are on the faculty at Tufts. We went to summer school at Al Amasan school in Hartford together after our junior year in high school."

"That's a Muslim school?" Bull asked.

"Yes. And when he got back from London and contacted me about helping him, he said he had a "project" to start a new business in Canada, in the Atlantic Provinces. By the time I realized what the "project" really involved, he threatened me if I backed out. Said he would turn me in and I would be deported to Libya."

"But you're a U.S. citizen," Dunne said. "You can't be deported."

"I know that now. Anyway, the people I talked to in the government never called me back. Until Mr. Johnson, your boss, called me I didn't know what I was going to do."

Dunne gave the other DOGs a subtle wink.

Abdul's talking about Big Dog.

"So why'd you quit helping us?" Doberman asked. "Why did we have to come get you out of that run down RV park?"

"I was scared. Aleem would kill me if he found out."

"He won't find out," Dunne said. "Mr. Johnson has checked out Aleem and has told us to take him alive, not to hurt him. Mr. Johnson says Aleem has been mislead by some radicals, and wants us to bring Aleem in so he can be deprogrammed and become a productive citizen again. By helping us save lives in New Brunswick or wherever in the Atlantic Provinces he's planning to hit, you're helping Aleem.

If somebody else in the government gets hold of Aleem before we do, Aleem's headed to the next world. Know what I mean?"

Abdul thought for a minute.

"I believe I can trust you to do what you say. Aleem is a good person. He has just fallen in with some bad people."

"Tell us how it's going to go down," Dunne said. "We'll take care of Aleem. We'll bring him in safely. Besides, Mr. Johnson is going to want to debrief him. Aleem is bound to have a lot of information on the higher-ups that have brainwashed him. That's who Mr. Johnson is interested in. Aleem is just a tool these people are using. They don't care about him."

"Do you have a map of New Brunswick and Nova Scotia?"

Dunne gestured to Hound, who went into the cabin and came out in fifteen seconds unfolding a map. Hound spread the map on the floor of the porch in front of Abdul.

"There are four targets," Abdul said, pointing to one after the other. "Moncton, St. John, New Glascow, and Truro."

"Two of those are ports," Dunne said. "Any reason for that?"

"I don't think so. They each have small shopping districts where it is easy to find over a hundred people gathered together at the same time."

"You're sure of this?" Dunne asked.

"Positive."

"Aleem can't get enough explosives across the border, even a low security station like Houlton," Doberman said.

"He doesn't need to," Abdul said. "The explosives are already on the Canadian side. His contact in Canada is providing them at the meeting place in Fredericton. The two men with Aleem will join the contact in Canada who has one associate with him. Aleem will not be crossing the border. Four backpacks will explode simultaneously at the locations."

"Suicide bombers?" Dunne asked.

"No. They will leave the backpacks in the crowded area. They will be on synchronized timers."

"Why do they need you?" Bull asked. "What role are you supposed to play in this massacre?"

"Just communications, so that Aleem and the Canadians never talk to each other directly. They call me on my pre-paid phone and I pass the information along."

"You haven't had a call since we picked you up," Doberman said. "I've had the phone. I know."

"There has been no need," Abdul said. "Everything is set."

"When is D-Day?" Hound asked.

Adbul was puzzled.

"The day the bombings will take place?" Dunne said.

"Soon," Abdul said. "The day after tomorrow; in the late afternoon."

"That's Saturday," Doberman said. "Big shopping day, even in the frozen north."

"When does Aleem take his men to the border?" Dunne asked.

"Early Saturday morning. He will leave them with the car at the Houlton crossing. I will pick him up at a coffee shop on the American side. The two bombers will cross into New Brunswick without him."

"And they'll meet the contact in Fredericton early Saturday morning," Dunne said. "The explosives in the backpacks will be primed and ready, the timers set. How do they get to the targets?"

"Four separate cars, all legal and licensed," Abdul said.

"When's your next call?" Doberman asked.

"Tomorrow. Friday at noon. Then there will be calls for me to coordinate Saturday morning beginning at four a.m."

Abdul seemed disconsolate. Dunne patted him on the shoulder.

"You've saved a lot of lives, Abdul. You've helped yourself and you've saved Aleem's life. You've done him a real service."

Abdul managed a weak smile.

"We'll all be with you when the calls come in," Dunne said. "We'll be with you every step of the way. You're not going to have to carry this burden by yourself."

Dunne shook Abdul's hand and pulled him up off the bench. He drew Abdul close and hugged him in a fatherly way.

"One day Aleem and his family will thank you," Dunne said.

Chapter Thirty

Jake engaged the electronic garage door as he slowed on Ursulines near the duplex. He pulled in and waited for the door to close, concentrating on his rear view mirrors to make sure no one slipped into the garage while the door was up. Only when he was certain he was alone inside did he unlock the door and get out of the 4Runner.

Inside, Jake cleared every room before he sat on a barstool at the island in the kitchen. He was frustrated. Eustis and Pizzolato were right. Driving through Hispanic neighborhoods from midnight until dawn was turning out to be a complete waste of time. He stuck out like a sore thumb with his *gringo* face and his yuppie 4Runner. He thought about the pee-wee lookout, Juanito, whose walkie talkie phone Byrne and Dominguez confiscated minutes before they died. Los Cuervos probably knew he was in each neighborhood before Jake did.

But then NOPD was doing no better. Jake was shocked at the dearth of information they had on Hispanic gang activity in New Orleans; and in the lack of enthusiasm he sensed in NOPD and in the feds operating in the city. Until Byrne and Dominguez were murdered and Kitty attacked, it had not seemed to Jake that anyone in New Orleans law enforcement was interested in Los Cuervos or the other gangs, Hispanic or black, operating in the city. The bumper sticker he saw at three a.m. this morning on Melpomene Street was apt: N'AWLINS: THE CITY THAT FORGOT TO CARE.

Almost all of the history NOPD had on Brujo and his gang came from David Dunne. Had Dunne not sent the data to Captain Eustis the morning the cops were killed, Jake would not have had Brujo's photograph to pick out of the lineup. NOPD would really have been in the dark about Brujo, because no one in the entire city had apparently ever seen the bloodthirsty Cuban "priest," and no one knew what he was up to. Brujo and Big Demon were moving thousands of guns into Mexico and sending God knows how much military-type weaponry to every country in the Caribbean basin that hates the United States, and until David Dunne gets involved, no one had a clue.

Which reminds me....

Jake felt a surge of energy and opened his laptop on the kitchen island. He pulled up the file Eustis forwarded to him about Ignacio Torres, a.k.a., Brujo. Jake's plan was to start from the beginning, combing through all the data to see if there was something he had overlooked, something that might provide a clue to where Brujo might be.

~ * ~

Four blocks away, Mantis sat on a tiny stool, no more than a foot off the floor. His sharp elbows rested on his bended knees, almost at eye level. Mantis' black cassock stretched between his legs, and resting in the cassock was a pile of United States currency.

Mantis was counting it.

Mama Coba walked down the narrow steps from her living quarters into her shop. She stood over Mantis while he wrapped a rubber band around a stack of hundred dollar bills. Mama Coba glanced into the mini-basement Mantis had constructed years earlier, as soon as they bought the building on Chartres. Access to it was by a trapdoor, which had been a heavy wooden closet door upstairs in Mama Coba's apartment that Mantis had appropriated to use as the trapdoor to the secret compartment under the floor.

The mini-basement was no bigger than a double closet, and had only one purpose: to store the millions of dollars Brujo had made selling guns in his New Orleans operation.

"Are you almost through?" Mama Coba asked him.

Mantis nodded.

"Have you written down the totals like I asked?"

Mantis gave her a small, spiral bound notebook. She looked at the entries for a moment and gave it back to Mantis.

"Good," she said. "This is the total even after I gave my sweet *brujito* the money for Big Demon's bail and the payments to his men this past Monday?"

Mantis nodded.

"Excellent," she said.

Mantis stacked the currency in a metal strongbox and backed down the ladder he built from two-by-fours. He stepped onto the brick floor he had laid with his own hands in the mini-basement and stacked the strongbox on top of others already there. He turned on the yellow Eveready utility lantern he kept on a steel hook he had screwed into the side of the ladder and surveyed the mini-basement.

"Let me see," Mama Coba said. She was on all fours looking down on Mantis, stooped over in their secret vault. He shone the light in every direction so she could see every metal box.

"All right," she said.

She pointed to the hallway leading to Brujo's chapel.

"*Mi hijo* and Big Demon haven't gone anywhere, have they?"

Mantis shook his head, then turned off the big flashlight and climbed up the ladder. Mama Coba stood up, wincing and rubbing her old knees. Mantis closed and locked the trap door, then neatly spread the hemp area rug one of Brujo's congregants had woven for Mama Coba. It was dyed a lovely terra cotta and more than big enough to cover the trap door. Mantis moved the coffee table and chairs onto the rug, a seating area for customers and followers, a place to sit while waiting for Brujo's healing touch.

~ * ~

In Sunshine, Kitty walked down the steps with more confidence. This would be her third morning walk with Susan, and she was feeling so much stronger. As on the other days, Susan was waiting at the base of the stairs.

"You must be psychic," Kitty said.

"Not hardly. This is an old house, and I hear you when you walk around upstairs. How are we feeling today?"

"A lot better. For the first time, I think I'm seeing light at the end of the tunnel. My head has stopped hurting, except right around my eye. And that's not as sharp a pain as it was."

"Your ribs?"

"They still hurt, but it doesn't take my breath away like it did."

"Let's get going, then," Susan said.

They walked out onto the porch just as Willie Mitchell and Jimmy Gray arrived at the base of the concrete steps in their workout gear. Willie Mitchell had finished his four-mile run and then the fifteen minute walk with Jimmy Gray, who wore his gigantic red nylon shorts and a sweaty gray tee-shirt.

"Look who's up and at'em," Willie Mitchell said.

"She's doing so much better," Susan said.

"Young folks heal so much faster than us geezers," Jimmy said.

"Utes," Willie Mitchell said.

Jimmy Gray snapped his fingers. "My Cousin Vinny," he said. "Joe Pesci and Marisa Tomei."

"Who played the judge?"

"Wait a minute," Jimmy said. "Herman Munster."

"Real name," Willie Mitchell said.

"Fred Gwynne," Kitty said.

"You owe me two bits," Willie Mitchell said to Jimmy Gray.

"Bull. I'da gotten that. I knew it." He pointed to Kitty. "The question is, how'd you know it?"

"We used to watch the Munsters in college," Kitty said, "in the freshman dorm late at night."

"We're going for a walk," Susan said. "You boys want to join us?"

"What a quartet," Willie Mitchell said, "the lame, the halt...,"

"Don't say it," Jimmy Gray said.

"...the fat."

"I asked you not to say it."

Kitty and Susan giggled.

"I already put in my mileage," Jimmy Gray said.

"Blockage," Willie Mitchell said. "Eight blocks does not make up even a half-mile, so mileage is not the right word. Blockage is more accurate."

"Good thing these ladies are present," Jimmy said to Willie Mitchell. "The tongue lashing you would have received...."

The four of them started walking.

"I just talked to Jake," Kitty said. "He said he thinks he's on to something about Brujo's background that might be useful."

"What?" Willie Mitchell asked.

"He didn't tell me, said he had to talk to Captain Eustis first and then he was going to call you."

"I'm going to call him," Willie Mitchell said, turning around and walking back to the house.

"Wait for me," Jimmy Gray said, waddling after his best buddy.

~ * ~

Jake checked Ursulines Street on the monitor before grabbing the keys and leaving. He had called Dunne and left another message, but did not expect to hear back any time soon.

Dunne picked a really bad time to disappear on me.

Poring over the data file about Brujo, Jake discovered that everything Dunne and his sources had accumulated started in Los Angeles—the early days of Brujo and his father Santos selling drugs and running *Calle Virgil Rifa*. The file seemed to indicate that Brujo's father Santos taught him the Santeria and Santa Muerte mysticism they used to control his gang and strike fear into their rivals in the Los Angeles drug industry.

But Santos Torres was Cuban, so how did he get to Los Angeles? How did he become a United States citizen?

Jake had followed links buried in the data to corroborate the U.S. citizenship of both Santos and Brujo, but he hit a brick wall trying to dig further for birth records and information on Brujo's early years. All the information about Santos and Brujo began in Los Angeles in the early nineties.

Where did Brujo come from? Where was he born?

Jake was sure he was on to something. There had to be a reason there was no access to information on Brujo's birth. Whatever or whoever concealed the birth records did it for a reason. Jake could not access the federal or state databases. He knew Dunne could, but he was MIA. Jake decided to start with Captain Eustis, who might have to get the FBI or ATF involved to dig further.

Jake started the 4Runner and opened the garage door. He started backing out, but there was a car in the middle of Ursulines, blocking his way. Jake blew his horn, but the car would not move.

"Dammit," Jake said and jumped out of his car. He ducked under the garage door and walked to the dark blue Mercury Marquis sedan.

The driver lowered his window.

"Good morning," FBI Special Agent Larry Beauvais said to Jake.

"I'm in a hurry," Jake said, trying to be pleasant to the red-haired crew cut jerk he had already bested twice in physical confrontations, one accidental, one on purpose. "Can you move out of the way?"

"Sure," Beauvais said, "but first, hear me out."

Jake waited.

"You are under arrest for obstruction of a federal investigation," Beauvais said with a grin.

"Bull shit," Jake said. "I don't have time for your crap."

"You have the right to remain silent," Beauvais said.

Chapter Thirty-One

"You know, Beauvais," Jake said in the back seat of the Mercury Marquis, "with your combination of stupidity and arrogance, you should shoot right to the top of the federal bureaucracy."

"If you're so smart," Beauvais said, "how come you're the one handcuffed in the back seat of an official FBI vehicle on your way to be booked into the Orleans Parish Prison, and I'm the one driving?"

"Because you're so ignorant you don't realize you're involved in a totally illegal arrest that's going to cause you significant problems."

"Yeah, yeah," Beauvais said. "Justice Department says different."

"What about you Proffit?" Jake asked Beauvais' partner in the passenger seat. "You sure you want to let your partner get you in the middle of something that's going to blow up in your face? Maybe affect your GS level and ultimately your pension?"

Jake could sense Proffit's discomfort. He had a bookkeeper's demeanor, and was rattled. He wasn't sure about all this.

"We're almost at your new home," Beauvais said. "Tell all this to the jailers. They probably never heard someone say they were innocent."

Jake was glad the ride was over. Beauvais overrode Proffit's suggestion that they handcuff Jake with his hands in front. Jake's hands were cuffed behind his back, causing him to lean forward in the back seat and keep his head down.

"Here we are," Beauvais said as he parked in front of OPP.

"You know, Beauvais," Jake said, "what goes around."

"Ooohhh," Beauvais said. "I'm shaking."

"You ought to be."

Proffit opened the back door and Jake swung his feet out to stand. Beauvais grabbed Jake's left arm and jerked him out of the car. Jake winced. His left arm was almost fully healed, and had not bothered him for days until Beauvais' rough handling.

Beauvais kept his grip on Jake's arm, pulling him forward then pushing him roughly as they walked up the stairs.

"Careful," Proffit said, his voice quivering.

Beauvais glared at his partner and pushed Jake through the main door to the intake and processing wing of the prison.

~ * ~

Jake sat on the bench in the crowded holding cell, as far in the corner as he could. His goal was to be as innocuous as possible, to blend into the grimy walls. It had been a while since he slept, but he vowed to stay awake—he had to for his own safety.

As Jake knew it would be, processing him into OPP was a nightmare. He was a federal detainee, and there were a limited number of cells in the federal wing of the prison. It was, after all, only supposed to hold city and state prisoners. OPP held some federal pre-trial defendants solely as an accommodation to federal law enforcement. If the Sheriff of Orleans Parish refused to hold federal detainees, FBI, DEA, and ATF arrestees would have to be transported to the nearest federal facility, Oakdale, Louisiana, which was designed to hold only federal defendants who had been convicted or plead guilty.

Like the intake officer told Beauvais at the front desk when the officer was trying to figure out what to do with Jake, "This is just one more inter-governmental cluster-fuck." Jake smiled when the officer said it; Jake knew the soft-spoken, older African-American deputy sheriff handling the intake had seen more than his share.

Beauvais was belligerent with the officer, insisting that Jake be thrown in with the other offenders arrested by NOPD the previous night and early this morning.

"You don't want to throw this young man in with the shit birds and dope heads in the drunk tank, do you Agent Beauvais? That ain't right."

Beauvais was persistent, and the intake officer relented. Jake thanked the officer for his concern, and assured him he would be all right, as long as he could make a telephone call.

"No calls," Beauvais barked.

"Hold on now, Special Agent Larry Beauvais of the Federal Bureau of Investigation," the officer said, pronouncing each syllable slowly and distinctly, "you're in my backyard now. You turning him over to me, so we playing by my rules now.

He can make all the calls he wants, to whoever he wants, within reason."

Beauvais rubbed his red crew cut and grimaced like a spoiled brat.

"Come on, Larry," his partner Special Agent John Proffit said, finally showing some spine. "We've done what we were told. We brought him here, now let's leave."

They left, and Jake made his call. The deputy was apologetic.

"I'm sorry to have to do this, young man, but I ain't got any other place to put you. I'll tell the watch deputies to stay close to the cell."

Jake shook the officer's hand. "No sweat," Jake said. "Thanks."

~ * ~

It had been a long time since Jimmy Gray had seen Willie Mitchell so worked up. A long time. Willie Mitchell's intensity was something to behold. Anyone around him could sense it, no matter how defective their intuitive abilities.

Jimmy was there at the Banks home at the end of the walk when Willie Mitchell answered the call from Jake. Willie Mitchell's first response was anger, but Jimmy Gray watched his pal quickly convert that negative energy into the effort to rescue his son from a grave injustice.

Willie Mitchell dispatched Jimmy to take Willie Mitchell's truck and find Susan and Kitty. He located them four blocks away, and gave them a ride home, filling them in as he drove. Willie Mitchell got busy on the phone, calling U.S. Attorney Joe Joe Barnes. He didn't know Barnes personally, but Willie Mitchell knew a lot of prosecutors and politicians in Louisiana and Mississippi who did know him. Barnes had the reputation of being more of a politician than a prosecuting attorney, which Willie Mitchell felt was something in Jake's favor. Willie Mitchell had heard more than one Louisiana lawyer or political figure say Joe Joe was a man "you could talk to," which was Louisiana code for a man comfortable with the give and take of compromise and accommodation—a man with whom "you could work something out." Willie Mitchell knew what they meant.

A man with no principles except one: expediency.

Jimmy Gray walked in with Susan and Kitty just as the receptionist told Willie Mitchell that Joe Joe Barnes was not in. Willie Mitchell gestured for them to wait until he finished the call.

They heard Willie Mitchell stress to the receptionist how important this call was. He asked her to find the U.S. Attorney and have him call Willie Mitchell's cell as soon as possible.

"Is this Jake Banks' father?" the receptionist asked when Willie Mitchell gave her his name and cell number, spelling the last name.

"It is," Willie Mitchell said. "And Jake is in Orleans Parish Prison, under arrest pursuant to a federal warrant, as we speak."

Tears filled Susan's eyes as she listened to her husband. Kitty scowled and clinched her fists in anger.

"Oh, my God," the receptionist said. "My name is Gertrude Wilson. I know Jake. He's a fine young man. I can't imagine what is going on."

"Do you know Leopold Whitman, now with OIG?"

"Yes. He was in here two weeks ago, but I don't think Mr. Barnes has spoken to him recently."

"What about Jake's supervisor?"

"Mr. Romano. He's in court this morning."

"Could you do this for me Ms. Wilson? Would you notify Mr. Romano as soon as possible, and try to find Mr. Barnes and let him know what's going on. I'll be down in your office today. What time do you close to the public?"

"Four-thirty," she said.

"I'm leaving in a few minutes. I'll get there by then, somehow."

Jimmy Gray stood in the library, Susan and Kitty sat close to him. All three were spellbound, hanging on Willie Mitchell's every word.

"I've got to get cleaned up and dressed," Willie Mitchell said. "I'm driving down there right now."

"Wrong," Jimmy said. "We, as in you and me, are going to New Orleans, and we ain't driving. I already called the pilots. My Lear's available and we're flying down there. They'll have the jet on the tarmac, warmed up and ready to fly as soon as we get to the airport."

Jimmy Gray shared the ownership of a Learjet 60 with three customers of Sunshine Bank, an oil man, a fast-food magnate, and a planter, all in north Mississippi. They kept it in a hangar in Greenville at the Mid-Delta Regional Airport. Jimmy's part of the cost, all in, including a full-time professional pilot and co-pilot, principal and interest, fuel, maintenance, insurance and every other conceivable expense, ran him about $350,000 per year, every nickel of which he ran through the Sunshine Bank as a legitimate business expense. Almost all of his travel on the jet, which he meticulously documented in an electronic log on the Sony laptop that he synchronized with the Lear's computer system, was bank-related. Jimmy and the three owners began sharing planes a decade earlier, and had graduated from twin engine turboprop planes of increasing size to jets, culminating in the six-seater Learjet 60, by far their most powerful and expensive airplane. The $350K entitled Jimmy to 65 hours of flying time per year, thirty minutes of which he was going to burn late this morning flying Willie Mitchell and him to Lakefront Airport in New Orleans.

"I'm going," Susan said.

"Me, too," Kitty said.

Willie Mitchell looked down at his feet. He didn't want to say it, and was glad when Jimmy Gray did it for him.

"Now, Kitty," Jimmy said, "in your condition you have no business getting out of this house for more than thirty minutes at a time much less fly to New Orleans. If we get bounced around with turbulence it's going to hurt those ribs of yours so bad you'll cry. I ain't no doctor, but even though we're only going to be flying at about fifteen thousand feet or so, I'm pretty sure that's not good for your head, with all the injuries your brain and eye have been through."

"And Susan," Jimmy continued, "I know you want to be down there by Jake's side, but Ina cain't take care of Kitty; she's too old. Somebody has to be here around the clock."

"I'll call you every hour," Willie Mitchell said. "We're going to be hustling all over town and I can guarantee you it's going to be a roller-coaster. I'd just feel better if you were here taking care of Kitty."

Jimmy could tell that both women knew Jimmy and Willie Mitchell were absolutely right.

"Okay," Willie Mitchell said. "I'm going to shower. Jimmy, you take my truck and get home and clean up. And put on a dark suit and come back and get me."

"A suit? Why?"

"Take my word for it. People take someone in a suit a lot more seriously than someone in a golf shirt. We're going to need all the credibility we can muster."

Chapter Thirty-Two

Willie Mitchell and Jimmy Gray climbed the retractable stairs into the Learjet 60 at Mid-Delta Regional. Willie Mitchell buckled up in the soft leather seat while Jimmy stuck his head in the cockpit and spoke briefly to his pilots. He gave Willie Mitchell a thumbs-up then raised the armrest on his seat, extended the seat belt as far as it would go, and belted himself in. He engaged his Sony laptop and synched it to the jet's computer as the jet taxied to the end of the 8,000 foot runway.

"Clear sailing," Jimmy told Willie Mitchell. "No weather to speak of. Flight plan has us at 15,000 feet on the way down."

The jet turned sharply and stopped. The engines roared and the pilot took his foot off the brakes. The Lear sprang forward and in fifteen seconds was airborne.

"Wheels up," Jimmy said and typed data into the Sony. "I've got an Escalade waiting at Lakefront for us," he said to Willie Mitchell over the jet engine noise. "One of the new versions, redesigned."

Willie Mitchell, deep in concentration, ignored the takeoff and initial banking, which he normally enjoyed viewing out of his window. He was busy playing out possible scenarios. There were so many intangibles. He reached into his soft black leather briefcase and pulled out his Federal Code of Criminal Procedure. He read every one of the articles on pre-trial procedures, including the major notes under each provision giving the history of the section and the changes it made to prior law.

Thirty minutes after "wheels up," the Learjet 60 touched down at Lakefront Airport on the shore of Lake Ponchartrain in New Orleans.

"Beats driving," Willie Mitchell said to Jimmy. "I appreciate your doing this."

Jimmy Gray extended his beefy right paw to his best friend in the world. "There's nothing I'd rather be doing, podnuh. Nothing on this earth. You and me are going to get Jake out of this bind."

A big lump jumped into Willie Mitchell's throat as he shook Jimmy's big hand. His eyes grew watery and he tried to speak, but nothing came out. Willie Mitchell took a deep breath as Jimmy Gray continued to grip his friend's hand, then took his big left hand and patted the back of Willie Mitchell's. "No sweat, skinny."

Jimmy Gray made a phone call while his pilots taxied to the General Aviation terminal. Through the small window Willie Mitchell watched a bright red Escalade drive onto the tarmac through the automatic chain-link gate.

They stepped off the jet and into the Escalade. Jimmy Gray took the wheel. "I'll drive," he told Willie Mitchell turning onto Downman and heading south to I-10. "Tell me how we're going to pull this thing off."

~ * ~

As the Escalade entered the I-10 on ramp, a fist with "p-a-i-n" tattooed on four fingers smashed into Jake's left jaw.

Jake woke up on the bench in the holding cell to a bolt of pain shooting through his head. Before he could react, another fist hit him in his right cheekbone, though not as hard.

Jake was awake now. He rolled to his left to avoid another fist to the face and came up in a fighting stance, his weight balanced, facing two nasty-looking white men, one with long, greasy hair and the other with a shaved head.

Jake ducked a punch from the shaved head. At the same time Jake moved in close to hit him hard in the adam's apple. The shaved head grabbed his throat and gasped for air.

Greasy hair lunged for Jake's face. Jake sidestepped him and used greasy's momentum to slam his dirty face against the wall. Jake grabbed him by the back of his greasy head, kicked his feet out from under him and popped his forehead onto the concrete—twice. That was it for greasy hair. Shaved head backed away from Jake, his eyes wide, one hand at his throat and the other palm out. "No more," shaved head rasped.

A half-hearted round of applause broke out in the holding cell. Jake stood in the middle, turning around, assessing the remaining danger. At least half of the fifteen miscreants in the cell slept through the fight.

Jake was mad at himself for dozing off. He had been awake for a long time, but that was no excuse. He knew the importance of staying alert in the holding cell. Dunne had suggested Jake go through some sleep and sensory deprivation drills at a small encampment in Arkansas, but the session was an entire week. With Whitman showing up out of the blue and interrogating him about Dunne, then the suspension, Jake had run out of time.

"Nice going," a young black man in the cell said. A few other brothers murmured their approval.

Two burly black jailers opened the cell door.

"You all right?" one of them asked Jake.

"I'm okay."

The jailers half-dragged greasy hair out of the cell behind shaved head, still holding his throat as he walked out.

"You want to see a doctor?" the one of the jailers asked Jake.

"No, but I'd like to wash my hands." Jake pointed to greasy hair. "I had to grab that one by the hair."

"We can do that," the jailer said. "You sure better wash those hands. We got some industrial strength disinfectant you ought to use."

Jake cleaned up in the jailers' bathroom and returned to his spot on the bench in the cell.

The young black man in the cell who congratulated Jake earlier spoke quietly. "Real happy you ran they ass off," he said. "Those filthy crackers stunk something awful."

"Glad to be of service," Jake said.

~ * ~

Jimmy Gray pulled into a vacant spot on the fourth floor of the five-story concrete parking garage on Magazine Street south of the federal building. He grabbed the aluminum case on the floor behind him and opened it in his lap. Resting in the cutout in the foam interior was a titanium gold Desert Eagle .50 caliber automatic with a six-inch barrel.

"I wish you had never seen *Snatch,*" Willie Mitchell said.

"I should have got the ten-inch barrel like Bullet Tooth Tony. Now, that was a gun."

"You can't take that cannon inside the federal building."

"I know. You think it's okay to leave it in here?"

"We don't have any choice," Willie Mitchell said.

Willie Mitchell opened the soft black leather briefcase and removed his 1911 Springfield .45 caliber automatic in a well-worn brown leather holster and his .38 caliber Chief's Special chrome-plated revolver. He tried to slide them under the passenger seat but couldn't. He stepped out of the Escalade and placed the two weapons under the floor mat.

"I hate that about new cars. You can't put anything under the front seats because of all the motors and computer stuff under there."

"Yeah," Jimmy Gray said, still in the driver's seat with the aluminum case in his lap. "What about this?"

"Do like I'm doing," Willie Mitchell said.

Jimmy placed the floor mat on top of the case on the floor. He closed his door and peered inside to check it out.

"It ain't perfect, but…"

"It'll have to do," Willie Mitchell said. "Let's go."

Halfway to the elevator, Jimmy Gray exaggerated his normal waddle and simulated zipping his pants.

"Leave the gun. Take the cannoli."

"Peter Clemenza," Willie Mitchell said, "after whizzing on the Long Island Expressway. They had just shot the driver who called in sick the day Sollozzo tried to kill the Godfather."

"Shit, that was too easy."

"Yep," Willie Mitchell said.

They walked the two blocks to the federal building on Poydras and passed through security on the first floor for the public access portions of the building. They cleared another security station and rode the elevator, exiting into the empty foyer outside the U.S. Attorney's office. Willie Mitchell pushed the buzzer and looked into the camera.

"District Attorney Willie Mitchell Banks from Yaloquena County, Mississippi," he said, "and my associate Jimmy Gray."

He pushed the door open when it buzzed and walked up to Gertrude Wilson's reception desk.

"Hello, Mr. Banks," she said.

"Ms. Wilson," he said. "This is Jimmy Gray."

"Pleased to meet you, ma'am."

"Let me ring Mr. Romano," she said. "He's expecting you."

E. Peter Romano walked out to the reception area and shook hands with Willie Mitchell and Jimmy, then led them down the hallway to his office. He wore a heavily starched white oxford cloth shirt and a rep tie under his thick black beard. Romano left his door open. He sat and stuck two fingers inside his collar, stretching it away from his thick neck.

"I want you to know, Willie Mitchell," Romano said, "that I don't agree with what's being done with Jake."

"I assumed you didn't," Willie Mitchell said. "No decent prosecutor would. Leopold Whitman is driving this bus."

"That's correct," Romano said. "And I don't have the authority to intervene and back him down. OIG works outside the normal lines of authority. I have to do what I'm told."

"Where's Mr. Barnes?" Jimmy Gray asked.

"He's not in."

"I thought the New Orleans Country Club was closed on Mondays," Willie Mitchell said.

"It is. But his group drives over to the coast on Monday mornings. They play that Tom Fazio course at Beau Rivage."

"Fallen Oaks," Jimmy Gray said. "I guess being U.S. Attorney's a pretty tough gig."

Romano cleared his throat. "What can I do for you?"

Willie Mitchell suppressed his anger. "Well, first things first. Do you know where Jake is?"

"He's at OPP. Probably in one of the federal detainee rooms."

"You're half right. He's at OPP. But he's in the drunk tank with about a dozen or so criminals NOPD picked up last night or this morning."

"That can't be right," Romano said. He picked up his phone. "Ms Wilson, get the Orleans Parish Prison please, the federal liaison. Find out Jake's status and buzz me back."

"I'd like for you to bring him before the magistrate this afternoon," Willie Mitchell said.

"I'll have to check with OIG to see how they want us to handle this."

Willie Mitchell leaned forward.

"Is there anyone in this building that knows something about when DOJ was planning to give Jake a Section 3142 appearance?"

Romano was embarrassed. He stood and closed his door.

"Nobody in this office, including Mr. Barnes and me, knew anything about this. The order went directly from OIG in D.C. to the FBI office on the Lakefront. I didn't know Jake had been arrested this morning until I got back here from court and Ms. Wilson told me you had called."

"Well," Willie Mitchell said. "You know about it now. And I'm telling you Jake is in the general criminal population in the holding cell."

Romano's phone light blinked. He picked up and listened. Willie Mitchell watched displeasure spread through Romano's demeanor.

"Get Leopold Whitman for me," Romano said. "Immediately." He slammed the phone down. "Dammit to hell."

"Is there a magistrate available this afternoon?" Willie Mitchell asked. "Because if there's not, I would like you to advise whichever federal judge is available that Jake is entitled to an immediate hearing."

"Let me check with the Clerk of Court's scheduling officer," Romano said and left the office, closing the door.

"My tax dollars at work," Jimmy Gray said. "Ain't this some shit?"

"When I was a young lawyer, DOJ was the most efficient agency of the government. Now, it's five times the number of lawyers and probably ten times the bureaucrats, and they can't find their butts with either hand. They lose every big case they try, and politics drives every decision. It's a damned shame what's happened to it."

"Just like every other federal agency and office. If they had to make a profit they'd be bankrupt."

Romano's phone buzzed. Jimmy Gray closed the office door and stood behind the desk. He punched the speakerphone button and gestured for Willie Mitchell to get close to the speaker. Jimmy tried to sound like Romano.

"Hello."

"This is Leopold Whitman."

"Uh, Mr. Whitman. Thank you, sir, for calling. There's someone here that wants to talk to you."

"Who is that?"

"This is Willie Mitchell Banks, Whitman. How are you today?"

There was silence from the phone.

"Leopold," Willie Mitchell said. "You still there?"

"Yes. What can I do for you?"

"I'm going to do my best to keep this civil," Willie Mitchell said. "Are you aware that Jake is being held in general population at Orleans Parish Prison as we speak?"

"I am not. I was informed of the arrest, but I don't get involved in the details of pre-trial detention."

"I've requested an immediate bail disposition," Willie Mitchell said.

"That's your right, certainly. Arrange it with Romano there."

"He's not in here," Willie Mitchell said.

"Did he leave during this conversation?"

"Uh, no sir, Mr. Whitman. That was me answered the phone. Jimmy Gray from Sunshine. Mr. Romano left a few minutes ago to check somebody's schedule. I answered because I gave my bank this number and thought the call might be for me. You remember I met you in Sunshine during that trial you and Willie Mitchell had. Kind of a big guy. Not really fat but big-boned. Remember?"

"Have Romano call me," Whitman said.

"I will for sure," Willie Mitchell said, "but before you hang up, Whitman, I want to tell you something. You've had my son Jake suspended from his job, and now arrested on a bogus charge, all for your own petty, personal reasons. You will look back on this as the worst decision of your entire career. You've not only taken on Jake, you've taken on me. I will work non-stop until I make this right for Jake. There will be consequences for you that you will not like."

"Are you quite through with your threats?" Whitman asked.

"I believe so," Willie Mitchell said, "Jimmy?"

"No, I'm good," Jimmy Gray said. "Good talking, Leopold. If you run into my good friend Senator Skeeter Sumrall, tell him Jimmy says hey."

There was a loud click.

Willie Mitchell lightly punched Jimmy's large bicep. "Big-boned."

"That's what my mother said. About me and Daddy."

The door opened and Romano entered.

"The magistrate is available this afternoon. I explained everything to him and he sent for the U.S. Marshal to bring Jake over. Sorry it took so long, but I waited until I got a confirmation from the magistrate's clerk that he would have a Section 3142 hearing at four."

"Mr. Whitman wants you to call him," Jimmy Gray said.

Romano was puzzled. "Whitman called?"

"I answered because I thought it might be for me."

Willie Mitchell retrieved a yellow legal pad from his briefcase and prepared to write. "What's the magistrate's name?"

"Elmo Wainwright," Romano said. "Nice fellow. He's only been magistrate for a couple of years."

Willie Mitchell wanted to make the sign of the cross.

Thank you, Jesus. Thank you.

Chapter Thirty-Three

Willie Mitchell sat on the first row of the gallery in one of the smaller courtrooms on the first floor of the U.S. District Courthouse. He pored over his Code of Federal Criminal Procedure. Jimmy Gray sat next to him, reading the Wall Street Journal he bought from the blind vendor behind the counter of the small commissary not far from the main security checkpoint.

The side door opened and two U.S. Marshals led Jake, still handcuffed, into the courtroom. Willie Mitchell stood at the rail. He wanted to hug his son but he knew no personal contact was allowed. The Marshals brought Jake within three feet. It was close enough to talk, but the Marshals stayed between Jake and Willie Mitchell.

"Sorry," the older Marshal said to Willie Mitchell.

"No problem." He studied Jake for a moment. "What happened to your jaw? Why is it red?"

"It's nothing," Jake said. "Couple of the guys in the cell wanted to dance. It was a very brief encounter; no big deal."

"Otherwise, are you all right?"

"Fine," Jake said. "I'm not as upset as I thought I might be."

"Well, I am," Willie Mitchell said.

"Thanks for coming down, Mr. Jimmy," Jake said.

"From now on," Jimmy Gray said, holding his meaty fist toward Jake, "you drop that Mr. or I'm going to put a red mark on your other cheek. You got that?"

Jake laughed. So did the Marshals. The back door opened and Peter Romano walked in, trailed by a woman so young Willie Mitchell figured she had to be an intern or a law clerk. Romano put his file on the U.S. Attorney's table and walked over.

"You can take those cuffs off," Romano said to the Marshals.

"Not until the judge tells us," one said.

"It's okay," Jake said.

"Sorry about all this Jake," Romano said.

"I know it's not your doing."

"Nobody upstairs knew about the FBI arresting you this morning or putting you in jeopardy in that cell at OPP."

"I know," Jake said. "It's OIG. Whitman."

A door behind the bench opened and black-robed U.S. Magistrate Elmo Wainwright walked into court. He was a tall, bald African-American, and was followed by a deputy clerk, who took his seat at a small desk close to the judge's bench.

"Good afternoon, gentlemen," the magistrate said in a deep baritone, looking around the courtroom. "And lady. Would one of you gentlemen kindly remove the restraints from Mr. Banks."

Both Marshals stepped to Jake and unlocked his handcuffs.

"Now," the magistrate said, "Mr. Romano?"

"Yes, sir, Your Honor. This is a Section 3142 hearing. The defendant is Jacob Pinckney Banks, and he is charged..."

"I've read the charges and supporting affidavits," Magistrate Wainwright said. "What is the government's pleasure?"

"We'd ask for a substantial bail, Your Honor."

Magistrate Wainwright looked hard at Romano.

"Really, Mr. Romano?" the magistrate asked.

Romano spread his hands, palms up, and rolled his eyes.

"And this request is being made by OIG, I take it? You are here at the direction of OIG, not Mr. Barnes. Is that correct?"

"Yes, your honor."

"Do you have anything to offer in the way of evidence to establish that Mr. Banks' is a danger to the community or a flight risk?

"No, Your Honor, other than the affidavits previously submitted."

"Mr. Jacob P. Banks, are you represented by counsel?"

"I'm representing myself, Your Honor."

"And your position?"

"I would ask for immediate recognizance release. If the court wishes, I will be sworn in and testify that I'm not going anywhere and that I'm not a threat to the general public."

"What about to Mr. Whitman at OIG?" Magistrate Wainwright said.

"Sir?" Jake said.

"Are you a threat to Mr. Whitman?"

Before Jake could fret over his answer, the Magistrate started laughing. So did Willie Mitchell.

Willie Mitchell recalled the many boring ArkLaMiss Tri-State Prosecutors' Commission meetings he and Elmo Wainwright suffered through together in Monroe, Vicksburg, and Pine Bluff. Elmo was the elected District Attorney for three of the poorest parishes in Louisiana: East Carroll, Madison, and Tensas. Part of the Louisiana Delta, the demographics of the three parishes mirrored those of the Mississippi Delta. Jobs were scarce; public schools disastrous; and teen pregnancies and poverty-driven crime rampant. Willie Mitchell and Elmo spent their lunch and coffee breaks in the federally-funded, day-long commission meetings comparing horror stories about their jobs and their jurisdictions. When Elmo was offered the magistrate's position in the Eastern District of Louisiana, he grabbed it, and Willie Mitchell did not blame him. They had not seen each other since the last commission meeting, but had spoken on the phone many times, trying unsuccessfully to get together for a golf game somewhere between Sunshine and Elmo's home in Tallulah.

Magistrate Wainwright had not seen fit to bring up his relationship with the father of the defendant, and neither did Willie Mitchell. It was not technically a ground for recusal, and this was only a bail hearing, so Willie Mitchell knew no one was going to complain—especially since Romano and Whitman had no clue. Since Whitman was playing dirty, Willie Mitchell saw no reason to take the high road.

Fighting fire with fire, you bastards.

"I see no need to hold Mr. Banks, nor to require the posting of bail. Recognizance is sufficient."

"Your Honor," Romano said.

"Hold on. I will order Mr. Banks to remain in his residence from six p.m. every night to six p.m. every morning. And I further order Mr. Banks to restrict his movements to Orleans Parish during the pendency of these proceedings. Mr. Banks, if you have a need to travel outside New Orleans for urgent business or personal matters, notify the U.S. Marshall's office and they will run it by me. Do you need any clarification of these orders?"

"No, Your Honor. I understand. One point of clarification. Because of a security problem at my condominium on Magazine street, I am currently staying in a duplex in the French Quarter owned by a friend of my family."

Jake gestured to Jimmy Gray on the front row.

"Very well. Please state for the record and the U.S. Marshals the address of your current residence."

"889 Ursulines Street," Jake said.

Willie Mitchell saw one of the Marshals walk to the back of the courtroom and talk to the young Hispanic couple that Willie Mitchell had seen enter in the middle of the hearing and sit in the last row. He watched the Marshal tell the couple something. They left, thanking him and smiling. The Marshal spoke briefly to the only other spectators, Captain Eustis and Detective Pizzolato. Willie Mitchell had seen them come in as well. He had a bone to pick with the NOPD.

"Anything else?" the magistrate asked.

Romano and Jake shook their heads no.

"Then court is adjourned. And Mr. Banks, you might consider hiring counsel prior to the next stage of these proceedings. You know what they say about a lawyer who represents himself."

"Yes, Your Honor. Thank you."

Magistrate Wainwright looked directly at Willie Mitchell for a moment, but gave no hint of recognition. Willie Mitchell gave him a barely perceptible nod, and the magistrate walked down the stairs and through the door behind his bench.

Jake walked back to the rail and hugged his father and Jimmy Gray.

"Thanks for coming to the rescue," Jake said.

"We've got a lot to talk about," Willie Mitchell said.

"Thanks for using your jet, Jimmy," Jake said.

Jimmy patted Jake on the arm as Willie Mitchell turned to the Marshal who had spoken to Eustis, Pizzolato and the Hispanic couple before they left the courtroom.

"Who was that young couple in the back?"

"I knew they were looking for the immigration hearing room," the marshal said. "It's the next courtroom down. Happens all the time."

"Let's get out of here," Jake said to his father and Jimmy.

"I'm craving some raw oysters," Jimmy Gray said. "Let's go have a beer and get four or five dozen shucked to hold us until supper."

"First I want to hear what Captain Eustis has to say about all this," Willie Mitchell said. "Where the hell have they been?"

~ * ~

Jimmy Gray was working on his second dozen on the half-shell at Felix's on Iberville Street, one block off Canal in the Quarter. Willie Mitchell was very familiar with Jimmy's oyster-eating routine, which Willie Mitchell first labeled "The Dance of the Dead Oysters" on a road trip to N.O. during their college years at Ole Miss.

First, Jimmy mixed ketchup and fresh horseradish in a small bowl. He added Worcestershire sauce but didn't stir it in, allowing the black liquid to puddle on top of the ketchup and horseradish mixture in the bowl. Over each of the raw oysters lying in its half-shell, he sprinkled a generous amount of Tabasco sauce. Jimmy then skewered the oyster with the small oyster fork that looked even tinier in Jimmy's meaty right hand, and submerged it in the bowl. He struggled to keep as much ketchup and horseradish sauce on it as possible, and moved his big head forward to engulf his helpless, naked prey. Jimmy kept the oyster and sauce in his mouth for only a second or two, barely chewing before doing a mini-thrust backward with his head, starting the slimy, raw sea creature down his gullet to its Waterloo.

Willie Mitchell caught Jake staring at Jimmy's routine.

"'The Dance of the Dead Oysters' is something to behold, don't you think, Jake?"

"I've seen it before," Jake said, "but it's been a while."

"A thing of beauty is a joy forever," Willie Mitchell said.

"Keats," Jimmy said, spraying a small cracker crumb into the center of the table when he spoke. "Ode on a Grecian Urine."

Willie Mitchell placed his palm over his mug of Tin Roof draft beer. "Right on Keats, bad joke on the poem. You owe me a quarter."

"Crap," Jimmy said, spewing another bit of cracker.

"You might want to consider going into contamination prevention mode," Willie Mitchell said to Jake. "There's a lot of collateral damage during the Dance. One stray bit of ejecta can ruin a beer."

Jake placed his palm over his beer mug. "Good idea," he said.

"Why'd we come to Felix's instead of Acme?" Jake asked.

Jimmy raised his index finger and took a big gulp of his Tin Roof draft to wash down the remains of the dead mollusks.

"Nobody goes to Acme anymore," Jimmy Gray said. "It's too crowded."

Jake laughed; Willie Mitchell chuckled.

"Yogi Berra," Willie Mitchell said.

The waitress brought their fried seafood po-boys and removed the big round trays littered with dozens of saltine wrappers scattered among dark gray, empty oyster shells with their luminescent nacre lining.

"Captain Eustis sure is a disappointment," Willie Mitchell said.

Jimmy Gray smeared thick tartar sauce on one side of the buttered French bread, then dipped the corner of the big sandwich in the bowl with the remaining ketchup and horseradish sauce, made spicier now by the runoff of Tabasco and oyster juice from the "Dance of the Dead Oysters."

"Don't blame him," Jake said. "He's been a lot of help. He insisted on security for me every night at the duplex until I asked him to stop."

"Looks like the only people you need protection from is the feds," Jimmy said. "That prick Whitman."

"Eustis had no choice," Jake said. "His boss told him to quit cooperating with me. Whitman put pressure on NOPD to keep me out of the loop on the Brujo investigation. Eustis didn't know I had been arrested until after I was released to the marshals."

"That makes no sense," Jimmy said.

"It's all about power," Willie Mitchell said, "and pressure. He's making it tough on Jake to get at Dunne."

"Speaking of which…," Jimmy said.

"I called him a few minutes ago," Jake said. "Left a voice mail. It's never taken him this long to get back to me."

Jake yawned. "I'm beat."

Jimmy signaled the waitress for the check.

"Let's get you to the duplex so you can sleep," Willie Mitchell said.

"I am tired. I didn't get back to the duplex until almost daylight this morning. Then I spent some time on my laptop studying the data Eustis sent me. I thought I figured out something that might help us get more information on him when Beauvais showed up. But I had time to think about it in jail, and I'm not so sure any more."

"What is it?" Willie Mitchell asked.

"I'll tell you tomorrow. I want to go over the files again in the morning when I'm fresh."

Jimmy Gray glanced at the bill and gave his credit card to the waitress.

"You know," Jimmy said, "when you're standing on the green lining up a putt, your first read is right nine times out of ten."

They settled up and Jimmy drove the red Escalade to Ursulines. He pointed the remote at the garage door on his side and drove in. The three men gathered outside the duplex on the sidewalk. It was almost dark, and they were all tired, and full.

"I'm going to stay on my side," Jimmy said, "unless you need me for something. I could use some sleep myself."

"Nah," Willie Mitchell said. "Jake and I will be fine over here. I'm going to stay downstairs, probably sleep on the couch, keep an eye on things while Jake catches up on his rest. We'll get a fresh start in the morning. I want to talk to Eustis and see what NOPD's doing to catch Brujo. Give Skeeter a call tomorrow morning and let him know what's going on. See if he knows anyone at Justice we can talk to."

"I'll try Dunne again in the morning," Jake said. "Good night, Jimmy, and thanks again for everything."

"Sure thing, kid."

~ * ~

Thirty minutes after midnight, Willie Mitchell sat on a barstool at the kitchen island working Friday's New York Times crossword, the most difficult puzzle for him to solve. He could finish if he gave it enough time, but it took many hours, even days sometimes. The clues were devious, the answers arcane. He glanced at the monitor every few minutes to check the street and sidewalk outside. Vehicular traffic was heavy and steady, to be expected on a Friday night in the Quarter. The number of pedestrians dwindled the later it got. It was easy for Willie Mitchell to tell the difference in the gait of those walking to a party or bar and those walking home later in the evening after partying. A good number of the late walkers were unsteady on their feet. Willie Mitchell had seen only one college kid vomit in the gutter, not bad for a Friday night. He and Susan had seen a lot worse things on the monitor during their stays in the duplex.

Willie Mitchell's left leg began to ache. He left the puzzle on the counter and lay on the couch in an effort to allay the pain, positioning himself so he could still see the monitor. Willie Mitchell placed the 1911 Springfield automatic in its holster on the coffee table next to the couch.

Fifteen minutes later, he dozed off.

At two-thirty a.m., Willie Mitchell awoke with a start. He heard something. He looked at his watch, then up at the monitor. There were two men working to get in the front door.

On the wall next to the monitor, the red light on the silent alarm began to flash. Willie Mitchell tried to avoid looking at the blinking red light, but it was too late. He felt himself entering his private world of nothingness.

Had he been in control of his faculties, in a few seconds Willie Mitchell would have seen Brujo and Big Demon standing over him, both holding automatic pistols, curious about Willie Mitchell's open eyes and thousand yard stare.

Willie Mitchell would have seen them move quietly up the stairs; and he would have heard the scuffle in Jake's room and the dull thud when Big Demon brought his heavy automatic down on Jake's skull.

Willie Mitchell would have seen Big Demon walking down the stairs, carrying Jake's limp body over his shoulder, following Brujo. Willie Mitchell would have seen Big Demon's eye staring down at him still stretched out on the sofa, and he would have seen the backs of Brujo and Big Demon on the monitor as they walked on the dark sidewalk and placed Jake in the huge trunk of the 1996 Lincoln Town Car that two Los Cuervos members appropriated that afternoon from a carport in a quiet neighborhood in Kenner near New Orleans International Airport.

Minutes later, when Willie Mitchell rejoined the world, he looked at the monitor. There was no one on the street. Willie Mitchell was careful to avoid looking at the red alarm light. He heard the noise of a car driving on Ursulines. It was unusually loud. He grabbed his .45 automatic and left the couch.

He stopped in the hallway. The front door was wide open.
Damn. Damn. Damn. Damn.

Willie Mitchell slammed the door and raced up the stairs into Jake's room. The bed was empty. He flipped on the light. There was a streak of blood on Jake's pillow—a large, wet streak.

Chapter Thirty-Four

Aleem Davi drove his light blue Volvo station wagon on I-95 north toward the border crossing at Houlton. He was forty miles past East Millinocket and was expecting to see the sign for Smyrna Mills any minute.

He was glad it was finally daylight. Aleem disliked driving in the sticks in the dark, especially in Maine. He had made this trip several times in the past two months, making sure everything was in order for today's event. He was not crossing into New Brunswick at Houlton today. The two men with him were. Aleem was turning around and heading back to Boston as soon as he dropped them off on the U.S. side. They would pick up the vehicle awaiting them in New Brunswick and drive to Fredericton.

Maine was too rural, too uncivilized for Aleem. At least this time of year there was no snow or ice. He had encountered a moose in his travel lane ten miles outside East Millinocket on the last trip. A moose! Praise be to Allah that his birthplace, Boston, had no wild animals running around loose on the roads.

His family was Pashtu. His parents immigrated to Boston in 1970 seeking a better life. They had succeeded, his father rising steadily on the University faculty until he was chairman of the economics department. Aleem was a young boy when his father was honored by the Pakistani community in Boston for achieving such a lofty position.

His parents found a better life, or so they thought. To Aleem, they had lost their way. Their reform version of Islam was repugnant to him. He had finished at the top of his high school class, but being valedictorian where the other students were lazy and immoral did not seem like much of an accomplishment to Aleem.

Aleem thought about the best years of his young life—the six years he lived in Oxford, England after graduating from Tufts. It was there he learned the true ways of Islam and shed the western influences his parents ingrained in him. The imam in Oxford was divinely inspired by Allah and his only true prophet on earth, Mohammed. The imam not only showed him the way to divine inspiration, he allowed munitions and bomb-making experts from Afghanistan and

Pakistan to teach Aleem and others in the mosque about bombs.

The three years he had been back in Boston proved to Aleem that America's corruption was too pervasive to cure without violent means. Aleem believed in the inevitability of the universal caliphate. The death and destruction he was about to visit on the four little towns would go a long way toward expediting the conversion of the Americas to Islam.

Aleem saw the sign for Smyrna Mills. According to plan, he placed the call to his friend Abdul.

~ * ~

Dunne sat in the driver's seat of the muddy, tan Tahoe. Doberman rode shotgun, and Hound was in the back behind Doberman. They left the cabin hours before in the pre-dawn darkness. David Dunne had never been anywhere as dark as their cabin headquarters. He would be glad to get back to electricity.

Dunne answered the dummy cell phone with pre-paid minutes. It was Bull. Dunne listened for a moment then closed it.

"Bombs away," Dunne said.

He drove closer to I-95 to get a better view of the roadway. He kept the motor running. Just like the practice runs, there were no cars on the highway. None.

"Blue Volvo station wagon ought to be in sight any minute," Dunne said. "Check your weapons."

"There it is," Hound said from the back seat.

Dunne timed it so that he pulled out onto the highway after the Volvo passed. He didn't want Aleem seeing him leave the lookout post. Dunne stepped on the accelerator, gradually getting closer to the Volvo.

Dunne checked the highway ahead and behind, then activated the left-turn blinker, lowered Doberman's and Hound's windows, and pulled into the left lane to go around the Volvo.

Dunne felt his heart thumping. He had completed scores of operations, not many this easy, but still managed to get worked up each time. Dunne knew a touch of adrenaline and nerves was good—it helped him operate at peak efficiency.

Aleem was not much of an operative. It appeared to Dunne that Aleem was not aware of danger until the tan Tahoe was right beside the Volvo. Doberman shot once, the bullet entering Aleem's left temple and exiting the right, along with a large amount of blood and brain tissue.

Hound blasted the Volvo as it drifted across the shoulder and into the pasture next to the highway. The Volvo slowed gradually, finally stopping in dark green grass as high as the door handles.

Dunne kept the Tahoe on the Volvo's tail. When it stopped, Dunne observed the two passengers frantically moving inside. Doberman and Hound jumped out of the Tahoe, guns at shoulder level, pointed at the two occupants. One of Aleem's men dove out of the front passenger side window. Doberman shot him twice. Either bullet would have killed him. Hound looked into the back seat. Aleem's second man's eyes were shut tight—he was praying. Hound slowly squeezed the trigger. The back seat passenger's prayers were over.

Dunne exited the Tahoe and opened the driver's door. He verified Aleem's identity. With most of the right side of Aleem's head gone, there was no need for another shot.

Doberman put another round in the head of the passenger who dove out of the window. He dragged the body behind the Volvo.

"Can you pop open the back?" Doberman asked Dunne.

Hound put another bullet in the bomber wannabe in the back seat, this one through the heart.

Hound walked behind the Volvo and helped Doberman load the corpse of the jumper. Dunne sat in the Tahoe, waiting. Hound pushed Aleem into the Volvo's passenger seat. Doberman closed the doors, making sure all limbs were inside, then returned to the Tahoe.

Dunne backed up until it was safe to turn around. So did Hound. They caravanned south, as planned. Dunne followed closely behind the Volvo for the three mile drive to the dump site they scouted two days earlier.

~ * ~

Dunne took a deep breath.

"Man, this air is fresh."

"Yeah," Doberman said.

They admired the gorgeous lake, the sun burning off the rest of the morning mist, and watched the last bubble of oxygen escape from the Volvo as its roof finally went underwater. The water was pure, and clear. They watched the well-built, safe-for-humans blue wagon sink toward the bottom, until it finally reached the depth where they could no longer see the Volvo.

"Beautiful day," Doberman said, stretching.

"Thank you," Dunne said, "and what a beautiful lake to sink a Volvo in." He looked up at the vivid blue sky, the coniferous evergreen-lined lake. "This place, this lake, kind of reminds me of Bosnia."

"Yeah," Doberman said, "but without the dead bodies."

Hound joined them.

"What have you been doing?" Doberman asked. "You know necrophilia is against the law, even out in these woods."

"Double-checking everything," Hound said, "making sure the bodies have no i.d. of any kind on them, removing their clothes so the bears have an easier time eating them."

"Lots of carnivores in these woods," Dunne said. "There will be no meat left on the bodies this time tomorrow, and the bones will be scattered from here to kingdom come."

"I think sinking the Volvo into the deepest part of this pristine lake does less environmental damage than burning it," Hound said.

"That was my concern, too," Doberman sneered.

"Much less likely to be noticed like this," Dunne said. "Let's ride."

They piled in the Tahoe, Dunne driving and Doberman in the back. They drove toward the cabin north of Smyrna Mills on the narrow, remote state road.

"I can't wait to get back to the world," Hound said.

"We might have some legal problems," Doberman said. "We just violated the restraining order Aleem's father got from the judge in Boston to keep federal law enforcement agencies away from Aleem."

"What?" Hound asked Dunne. "Is that right?"

"Partially. Doberman is right that Aleem's father sued the federal government to enjoin any of its representatives from harassing him, surveillance, phone taps."

"You are shitting me," Hound said.

"Nope. Ballsy, wasn't it? And the leftie federal district judge that the liberal senators from Massachusetts got appointed granted the injunction. It's true. But, Doberman is incorrect in saying we violated the restraining order."

"We got pretty close to him," Hound said.

"But," Dunne said. "We are not technically federal employees."

"I stand corrected," Doberman said. He turned to Hound. "When you do get back to the real world, what do you have planned?"

Hound shrugged. "Get some decent food and a *cerveza* or two." Hound turned to Dunne. "I guess I see the logic in the four small towns in Canada," Hound said. "It says everyone is at risk, no matter where they live."

"It's the smart move," Dunne said. "It sends a message that no place is safe from *jihad*. We concentrate on defending New York, L.A., D.C., Chicago—big targets with concentrated populations. Aleem hits these little bitty towns and the terrorists tell every citizen in North America that he or she is just as likely to die from a bomb as the people in the big cities. Four remote communities in Canada, a country that prides itself on being more tolerant of everyone, including atheists or Muslims, than the U.S."

"No one can escape *jihad*," Hound said. "Puts everyone in fear."

Dunne knew Doberman, Hound, and Bull better than they knew themselves. The four of them spent a tremendous amount of time together, sometimes in places just as remote as the Maine cabin they had hunkered down in the past eleven days.

He knew Hound and Bull had always lived simply in their off time. Nothing flashy to draw anyone's attention. Doberman was a high roller once, living in the fast lane, spending more money than he made, which was a hell of a lot. Big Dog had talked to Dunne twice about Doberman's lifestyle, the need to slow him down, keep him under the radar. It turned out Dunne didn't have to talk to him. Doberman calmed down on his own. Something happened, an awakening of sorts, that changed Doberman. The next time they were alone, Dunne planned on asking Doberman what happened.

No matter his character and off duty life, Dunne did not want to lose Doberman, by far his best sniper. His accuracy was uncanny. Moreover, Dunne had never seen a man so cool carrying out his missions. During an operation, Doberman was absolutely reliable, a true professional. But

Dunne also knew Doberman was a stone-cold killer. Taking out Aleem behind the wheel of his Volvo—Dunne knew Doberman never gave it another thought. Blowing an exit hole in the right side of Aleem's head the size of a softball stirred no more emotion in Doberman than the paper targets they periodically practiced on at training camps.

Hound and Bull had some of that in them, so did Dunne. You couldn't do the job if you didn't. But Hound and Bull felt human emotions. Dunne wasn't sure Doberman did.

Dunne stopped the Tahoe at the cabin, parking as close to the front as he could. Bull was waiting for them on the front porch.

"Go okay?" Bull asked.

"Exactly as planned," Dunne said. "Aleem is with his seventy-two virgins in the great beyond."

"I wonder if he can still get in," Hound said, "if their version of St. Peter knows about the Chinese hookers and rum cocktails Aleem enjoyed so much in Boston's Chinatown?"

"Got some bad news," Bull said. "Big Dog called on the satphone."

"Aw, shit," Doberman said.

Bull gestured for them to follow him away from the cabin.

"Abdul's secure in the back," Bull said. "He doesn't know about any of this. Big Dog said our Canadian counterparts ran into some trouble with their government. Their version of Homeland Security got wind of something in the works from online chatter surveillance, and they're bearing down on everyone with an operational history for their military services. Our two Canadian guys have to lie low. No way they can get to Fredericton."

"What does Big Dog want us to do?" Dunne asked.

"Big Dog wants you to call him right now," Bull said.

Ten minutes later, Dunne closed the satphone.

"Here's the deal," Dunne said. "We've got to go into Fredericton. We've got to meet Aleem's contacts."

"What do you mean, 'we'?" Doberman asked.

"With your dark beard and hair, you can pass muster as an Arab-American. Hound certainly can. I can't." Dunne turned to Bull. "You are too lily white to go in."

"Bull," Dunne said, "you stay here with Abdul. Doberman, Hound and I are crossing into Canada. Doberman and Hound are doing the meet and greet."

"How are we getting weapons across the border?" Doberman asked.

"Not a problem because Big Dog says no weapons. None. Zero. We'll have to improvise when we get there."

Dunne continued. "Bull, you get inside and get Abdul to call the Canadians and tell them Aleem's men are running a little late, but not to worry. They'll meet up at the coffee shop as planned, just a little later. Tell Abdul to sell it like it's no big deal."

"What if he asks about Aleem and the cause for delay?"

"Tell him Aleem is with Mr. Johnson's men already, and they've started to de-program him. And Bull, I'm positive from briefings that the two terrorists in New Brunswick with the explosives have never met the two men Aleem was sending in. But run in there and double check with Abdul, just to make sure. Tell him Mr. Johnson is de-programming them, too."

Bull took off in a trot to the cabin.

"Sorry about this, men," Dunne said. "But the good news is Operation NORTHSTAR will end today, just a little later and farther north. Let's hit the road."

As Dunne drove past the cabin toward the overgrown lane, Bull stepped onto the porch and gave him a thumbs up. Dunne returned it and plunged the Tahoe through the overhanging foliage onto the primitive road running from the cabin to the paved highway.

Dunne turned to Hound and Doberman.

"When you two meet the bombers at the cafe in Fredericton, I want you to put on an Oscar-worthy show. Make me proud."

Chapter Thirty-Five

Willie Mitchell paced in Jimmy's side of the duplex while on the other side of the common wall, NOPD crime scene analysts worked Jake's bedroom and the downstairs.

"They're wasting time and money," Jimmy said. "We know who broke in and took him."

"They've got to work the evidence," Willie Mitchell said. "I'm sure the bastards walked right past me, but I have no recollection of seeing anything. First thing I was aware of was the street noise from the front door being wide open. Hell of a time for a seizure."

There was a knock on the door and Captain Eustis walked in. Willie Mitchell glanced out at the early morning light on Ursulines. Instead of the optimism dawn usually brought, he felt nothing but guilt and shame. Although she was considerate on the phone, when he admitted to Susan that the people who took their son walked right past him on the couch, there was a long silence on the other end, a silence that grabbed Willie Mitchell right in the stomach.

With his current disabilities, Willie Mitchell felt extremely inadequate. He wasn't much of a protector for Jake—or anyone.

"We've got every available hand looking for Jake," Eustis said.

Willie Mitchell ground his right fist into his left palm. "I don't know why they didn't kill me, or at least take my gun." He pointed to his 1911 Springfield on the table near the kitchen.

"They don't need any more guns," Eustis said. "They got plenty."

"Dunne still hasn't called back?" Jimmy asked Willie Mitchell.

"I've left five messages."

Willie Mitchell reached in his pants pocket and pulled out a cell phone. "Captain, just so you know, I took this cell phone off Jake's night stand. I figured out which number was Dunne's, and I started calling him about three-thirty this morning."

"No problem," Eustis said. "He'll call back when he can."

"It's obvious they came specifically for Jake," Jimmy Gray said.

"Just like Brujo showing up at Jake's condo, and what they did to Kitty," Eustis said. "Brujo's focused on Jake for some reason."

"We need to learn why," Willie Mitchell said. "If we can figure out what Brujo has against Jake, maybe it'll help us find them."

"I been looking at some notes Jake made on some wadded up scratch paper I found in the trash can on the other side," Jimmy said. He turned to Eustis. "Jake told us at Felix's he was going through the file you sent him on our boy Brujo right before the feds picked him up yesterday morning."

"You put the notes back in the can, didn't you?" Eustis asked.

Jimmy shrugged. He reached into his pocket and pulled out a crinkled yellow sheet of paper.

"It's all in his handwriting. It ain't evidence. Anyway, Jake said he was going to go over the file again this morning. "

"He should have told us what it was," Willie Mitchell said.

"I think he did the next best thing leaving these notes," Jimmy said. "Look at this."

Jimmy put his fat finger at a word that was underlined three times with a little star beside it.

"Marielito," Willie Mitchell said.

Jimmy smiled. "Brujo's supposed to be Cuban, ain't he?"

~ * ~

Susan sped south on I-55 as fast as she felt comfortable driving. She didn't care if a trooper stopped her for speeding.

"Do you need to stop for anything?" she asked Kitty.

"No. I'm okay."

"Are you in any pain?"

"Not bad." Kitty reached for her bag on the floor and grunted.

"As long as I don't bend," Kitty said. "Can you get my bag?"

Susan checked the highway in front of her, and extended her arm to retrieve Kitty's purse.

"Heavy," Susan said.

Kitty dug through it and removed her .40 caliber Glock. She ejected the magazine, pulled back the slide to check the chambered bullet, and popped the magazine back in. She held the gun with two hands in front of her, aiming at some target out the front windshield.

"Uh, Kitty," Susan said.

"Sorry. Just checking to see how much it hurts to hold it out like I was shooting at someone."

"Does it?"

"Sure does."

"I've been around guns all my life, but they still make me nervous."

"I never held a gun until I was in college. Some guy I went out with a couple of times took me to a shooting range."

"Interesting venue for a date."

"It was fun. The first time I really talked to Jake was at the shooting range in Jackson."

"Really?"

"Well, I talked to him once before when I was doing an inventory of some drug money we were seizing, but that didn't count."

"Did you like him at first?"

"I thought he was good-looking. But I wasn't too nice because I thought he was just hitting on me like everyone else I ran into."

"You get that a lot I'm sure."

"But Jake was so nice. I was really a bitch."

Susan winced.

"You shouldn't say that about yourself."

"It's true. The whole time we were dating Jake was nicer to me than any man has ever been."

Susan glanced at Kitty and saw tears well in her eyes. Susan grabbed a Kleenex from the crumpled square container wedged between the console and the seat and gave it to Kitty.

"God, I pray Jake's all right," Susan said, grabbing another Kleenex and dabbing her eyes.

"He's got to be, Susan." Kitty sniffed. "If he hadn't come by to check on me at my apartment I would have died."

"Forgive my nosy question but can I ask why you and Jake broke up last year?"

"It's okay. The answer is so ridiculous. I just thought I had to be independent. I convinced myself I couldn't be tied down to a man if I wanted to move up in the agency faster than any woman in history. How stupid is that?"

"I don't think it's so dumb. It's important to be independent. I admire your ambition."

"I didn't expect you to say that."

"Why not?"

"I don't know," Kitty said.

"Because I'm a housewife who never worked at a real job? Because I've been dependent on Willie Mitchell?"

"I didn't mean it like that," Kitty said.

"When we first got married, I didn't want to stay home. I wanted to get a good job and have my own money. But then Jake was born, then Scott. And you know what?"

"What?" Kitty asked.

"I didn't want to do anything but stay home and take care of my babies. I didn't want to be away from them."

"That is something I hope I get to experience."

Susan was surprised. "Really?"

"Nothing like almost dying to make you reassess what you want to do with your life."

"Don't give up your goals," Susan said. "Maybe you can do both."

"It's nice you have your financial independence now, with your natural gas wells and everything."

"Thanks to my father. This might sound strange, but all the money pouring in from the wells has not made me one bit happier. We had no financial worries before. Willie Mitchell's always been a good businessman. Before I leased my 100 acres to Chesapeake, Willie Mitchell studied the lease proposal and insisted on changing some things that have really made a difference, in terms of what I get from each well. He did it for my sister, too. And that's when I wasn't around. The three years I went awol."

Susan clicked on the cruise control to increase her speed when she passed the southernmost McComb exit. She checked her odometer and watch. Less than two hours to New Orleans.

"You know," Kitty said. "It wasn't his fault he had a seizure."

"I know it."

"Blame it on those s.o.b.'s that tried to kill him and Jake last year."

Susan nodded. She grabbed another Kleenex and blew her nose.

"I can't wait to talk to Jake again," Kitty said. "I was so stupid."

"If you were with him right now, what will you tell him?"

Kitty took a deep breath. Her eyes filled with tears again.

Susan knew at that moment she wasn't the only woman in the car speeding to New Orleans to help save the man she loved.

~ * ~

Jake sat naked on a small stool. He slowly regained consciousness. Eyes closed, it took him a while to become fully aware. With his first cogent thought, he focused on the throbbing pain in his skull. Jake tried to determine where it originated.

He attempted to raise his right hand to feel but instantly realized his hands were bound somehow behind his back. He moved his fingers against the binding. It was a rope, a rough rope, made of hemp or sisal, the kind he played with as a child.

Better than handcuffs or plastic.

Jake struggled against the rope for a moment. It seemed to make the rope tighter.

Enough of that. Back to the head.

He concentrated and decided the pain was coming from his hairline above the left forehead. Jake remembered his training and began to inhale deeply, and exhale blowing short breaths. He focused on the breathing, away from the pain. Needing a focal point, Jake tried to open his eyes for the first time. They opened, but everything seemed blurry, and dark, too. He blinked several times and his vision cleared. It was impossible to tell what time of day it was. There were candles arrayed in an arc in front of him, fifteen feet away.

The first thing Jake saw was a small albino alligator walking slowly across his field of vision, inside the candles in front of him, moving from right to left. He had seen one before, an adult one, at a snake farm on a family trip to South Louisiana when he was seven years old. The slow-moving gator's jaws clamped around a large bone.

Maybe it's not real. An albino alligator?

As he watched the alligator take its time, Jake noticed an overwhelming stench. It was foul, the smell of a rotting carcass. There was no dead animal in his field of vision, but

Jake did notice the gray legs of an aluminum stool under him, his own bare legs, then his groin, which was missing his pubic hair. Everything else appeared intact—at least for now.

Jake's bound hands forced his head forward and down. He bent further to check out the floor but his head jerked back. Pain exploded from the top of his forehead. When the throbbing subsided, he realized there was rope around his neck, tied to something behind him. Careful of reaching the end of his leash, he studied his legs, arms, and torso—every part of his body he could see in the dim light.

He had no hair. Someone had shaved his body, and from the nicks and cuts, the abrasions and dried drips of blood, they were none too careful in the process. Like strawberries on his legs and elbows he remembered from sliding in baseball, the abrasions stung, but nothing like his head.

Jake did fast breathing for a few minutes, using a ragged black spot on the concrete floor as his focal point. The pain was still there, but not as insistent.

He inventoried his bodily systems and parts as best he could. His eyes were working okay, but there was so little light in the building it was hard to be certain. Breathing was steady, regular. He cleared his throat.

"Hello," he croaked.

It was the best he could manage with a throat that felt parched, so dry it was sore.

Jesus, am I thirsty. And where the hell am I?

The floor was concrete, the building massive. His bound arms restricted how far above him he could look. With some effort, Jake peered into the darkness above him. Squinting, he could not make out a ceiling. The cylindrical walls disappeared into a gray fog two or three stories up.

A concrete cylinder. What is this place? How long have I been here?

Jake knew who brought him to this place. Only one person had stalked him; only one person was whacked out enough to shave all the hair off his body—Brujo. Jake was grateful Brujo had not tattooed him.

Now that I think about it, Brujo's body might be shaved. All the tattoos make it hard to tell.

"Oh, shit," Jake muttered.

He heard something close, like a door. It was heavy. Jake squinted and in the distance, walking toward him, were two men, one large, one average size. The dark, dusty haze between them made it hard for Jake to identify them, but he knew who was coming.

Big Demon and Brujo. Got to be.

Sure enough, when they got to within twenty feet, there they were. The giant Big Demon, looking like a Cyclops with his left eye gone. And Brujo, resplendent in a bright red ceremonial headdress, naked except for a small, leather codpiece. They stopped five feet in front of Jake, fists on hips, legs spread.

"Howdy, boys," Jake rasped.

Big Demon lifted the cord of a slim leather wineskin over his head and pulled out the stopper. He extended the wineskin to Jake.

Do I dare? Man-oh-man I'm thirsty. Probably poison.

Brujo turned to Big Demon and opened his mouth. Big Demon started a stream at Brujo's mouth and moved the wineskin back slowly until it was three feet away. Big Demon moved closer gradually and stopped at Brujo's lips.

Big Demon raised the wineskin to Jake.

It didn't kill Brujo.

Jake leaned back as far as his arms would allow, and opened his mouth. Big Demon started the stream.

The taste was bitter, but wet. Jake had to have it. He swallowed awkwardly, trying not to lose any of the liquid when he gulped. Big Demon kept the stream going until Jake raised his eyebrows to signal he had enough for now.

Jake took a deep breath.

Be nice. Be humble.

"*Muchas gracias*. What is that?"

"Tea," Big Demon said.

The two men walked away, disappearing into the dark through the dusty mist.

Chapter Thirty-Six

In Fredericton, Hound walked with Doberman along the Saint John River to the Atlantic Café. It was six blocks from the mud and dirt encrusted Tahoe to the rendezvous.

It was a rare operation for the DOGs. It was outside the United States; they were unarmed; and it was totally unscripted. Unlike the earlier encounter with Aleem and his two partners in the Volvo, this venture into Canada was *ad hoc*, save for the parameters Dunne laid out on the drive up.

"Find the explosives," was one. "No witnesses," was another. "Improvise and innovate," was the last.

Hound and Doberman were on their own. Bull was at the cabin near Smyrna Mills with the hapless Abdul, Dunne a quarter of a mile away in the Tahoe. Hound glanced at Doberman. As usual, it was nothing more to Doberman than a walk in the park.

"Muslims in New Brunswick and Nova Scotia," Doberman said. "Who the fuck would have thought that?"

"I think there's a couple of thousand in the Atlantic Provinces."

"Sounds like a Saturday Night Live skit to me." Doberman picked up a rock off the sidewalk and threw it into the river. "How wide you think this river is, Hound?"

"I don't know. Maybe 800 meters? I could swim it easily."

"Shrink your balls. That water's got to be freezing."

"I'm not using them now."

Doberman laughed. Typical. Hound was reticent, fretting, going over the operation, thinking about contingencies, replaying Dunne's pre-game talk. Doberman was loose as a goose, nattering on about whatever popped into his head. Hound envied Doberman. He knew Doberman's confidence was partly a by-product of his operational skills and abilities. Outside of Dunne, Doberman was the best operative Hound had ever seen. He was fearless and smart, and had uncanny instincts under fire. No matter Doberman's personal failings, and Hound knew they all had them, Hound wanted Doberman in on every operation that involved a confrontation. Bull was valuable, too, and Dunne was the best, the glue that held them together. But Doberman was something to see in action.

Hound pushed the café door open. They stood inside the entrance for a moment, scanning the packed room. Hound made the two men right away.

"You got'em?" Hound asked.

"Yep."

"Didn't think it would be this crowded," Hound said.

"People up here got nothing else to do. I liked packed."

Doberman was right. It was easier to be part of the landscape in a crowded restaurant. They dodged waitresses with heavy trays and walked to the last booth.

"These seats taken?" Doberman asked the two men.

One was heavy, the other lean, both clean shaven and neatly dressed. They looked more like preppy college kids than terrorists. Living in Canada had apparently paled their complexions, but Hound could tell they were definitely Middle-Eastern.

Doberman's question appeared to startle the two. Their eyes were wide. The thin one gestured for Doberman and Hound to have a seat.

"Assalaamu Alaykum," the thin one said.

Doberman leaned closer to the thin Arab. "You think that's a good idea, greeting us like that in this place, with all these people here? And you two sitting on the same side of the booth, staring at the front door?"

The two men were nervous already, and Doberman's aggressive criticism pushed them further to the edge. Hound held up his hands, palms out, then patted Doberman on the arm.

"Hold on, now," Hound said. "Let's all just calm down. The reason we're all here is more important than anything else." He turned to Doberman. "Cool it."

Doberman leaned back against the padded booth. Hound had already created a workable profile of the two. He knew Doberman had sized them up as well. It was easy.

Rank amateurs. Way in over their heads. Nervous as the first day of school. Don't overdo it, Doberman.

"Is Aleem coming?" the heavy man asked.

"Is that a trick question?" Doberman asked.

Hound intervened. "We're following the plan, exactly as Aleem laid it out. You know he's too valuable to be here; he's got bigger things to tend to. Besides, with the fed surveillance it's too dangerous for him to come through a border checkpoint."

"But there is an injunction against the American government," the thin man said. "They cannot harrass him."

"You think those bastards in D.C. pay attention to a restraining order?" Doberman asked. "They'd kill Aleem if they could."

"Let's talk about today, where you want us to go," Hound said. "I know we've got many kilometers ahead of us."

The skinny Arab pulled a map from his lap and spread it on the table. Doberman grabbed it and stashed it under the table just as the waitress appeared.

"Get you gentlemen anything?" she asked.

"Two black coffees," Doberman said and patted Hound's arm. "And make one decaf for my brother here, *s'il vous plait.*"

Hound talked softly and politely to the men across from him. "Not a good idea to bring out a map in a public place. People remember that."

"Maybe we ought to just leave," Doberman said to Hound. "This is the big leagues, and I got a bad feeling about our partners here."

Skinny man leaned forward. He was in charge.

"Wait. Please do not. I know we are not experienced like you, but we are devoted to the cause. Everything is ready, just as we planned with Aleem. The four packages are ready. We have cars with Canadian papers for you, fueled and ready to go."

"Everybody has a first time," Hound told Doberman, then paused and looked into thin man's eyes. "Where are the devices?"

"At our house," thin man said, "with the cars. Follow us."

"You've got to wait for us to get back here," Hound said. "We parked six or seven blocks from here."

"I supposed you parked in the café parking lot," Doberman said.

The men were sheepish. "Our house is only five kilometers from here. We are ready, believe me. You will see."

"Lay off," Hound said to Doberman. "We're doing this."

Doberman exhaled. "We'll be back in ten minutes. You rookies see if you can pull out of the parking lot without hitting something."

"Wait for us by the river," Hound said.

~ * ~

Hound drove the Tahoe past the café parking lot and followed the blue Ford Escort on the main thoroughfare through town.

"Laurel and Hardy have not a clue," Doberman said, looking straight ahead at the Escort. "This is too easy."

"It's the easy plays that go bad," Dunne said, his voice muffled by the drab green canvas tarp that covered him on the back seat floor. "Complacency can get you killed."

"They're turning into a subdivision," Hound said.

In a few minutes the Escort stopped in the unpaved driveway of a two-story wooden house that had seen better days. Hound liked the location of the house. It was isolated, at least fifty yards from the street. There were trees and overgrown shrubs lining the property, shielding the house from view. Several cars were parked behind the house.

Hound made sure he left the Tahoe beside the house where no one could see inside. He and Doberman followed the men up the front steps.

"You did well choosing this house," Hound said. "Lots of privacy."

"Thank you," the skinny man said, regaining some face.

They walked through a central hallway, into a musty smelling dining room. The table was large. Hound was sure the barren table was the Laurel and Hardy's planning site. In the corner on the floor were four backpacks, each accompanied by a map and a small stack of papers.

"Each one of these devices is ready. The timer has already been set. There's nothing to do but deliver them to the sites. To activate...."

"Are we sure they will work?" Doberman asked.

"I assure you," the overweight Arab said, "they work. We have tested dummy devices over and over. They are reliable."

"I don't want to get blown up driving to these godforsaken places," Doberman said, ever the bad cop.

"Okay," Hound said. "Now we can look at the map."

The thin man spread the map on the table.

"You two have the shortest drives. Moncton and Saint John. You will have time to bring the cars back here, get into your SUV and return to Maine before the explosions occur."

He pointed to the towns on the map. Hound looked over his shoulder. Doberman hung back, checking out the backpacks. He picked up a map off the floor next to a backpack and unfolded it on the table.

"We can read a road map," Doberman said. "We need to talk about where the sites are in the cities."

Before the thin Arab could respond, Doberman pointed to a framed photograph of a pretty, dark-haired girl on the wall.

"Who is this hot-looking chick?" Doberman asked.

"My sister," the heavy man said. "Do not speak of her in that manner."

"Sorry," Doberman said. "She's cute, though."

The thin Arab unfolded a small tourist map of Moncton. Hound looked over his shoulder as he pointed to a plaza. The heavier man leaned against the table, focusing on the map. Hound noticed Doberman easing away from the table.

Hound and Doberman pounced at the same time. With a quick, powerful twist, Hound broke the thin Arab's neck. He collapsed on the floor, dead. The heavier man pawed at Doberman's arms, trying to break the choke hold. After thirty seconds, the red-faced Arab passed out, and in another thirty seconds, he was dead. Doberman let go and the fat man fell on top of his partner. Hound checked for a pulse.

"Both dead."

Doberman was winded. "Son of a bitch had a big neck."

Hound jumped at the sound of a glass pitcher crashing to the wooden floor in the doorway. He caught a glimpse of woman who dropped it before she bolted. It was the woman in the photograph, fat boy's sister.

"Shit," Doberman said. He took out after her.

"I'll look upstairs," Hound yelled as he bounded up the stairs.

Doberman checked the downstairs rooms. He called out to Hound. "Where's the back door?"

The front door slammed. Hound flew down the stairs. Doberman threw the door open and both of them raced onto the porch.

They stopped. Dunne walked slowly up the stairs, carrying the sister's limp body in his arms.

"She gone?" Doberman asked.

Dunne shook his head.

Doberman took the girl from Dunne.

"Dunne's law," Doberman said. "He who helps a terrorist is a terrorist."

Doberman walked inside. In less than a minute, Doberman returned to Hound and Dunne on the porch.

"She's gone now," Doberman said.

It had to be done. Hound and Dunne knew that. They just didn't want to do it. Doberman didn't mind.

~ * ~

Dunne drove the gray Explorer south in the darkness on I-95 toward Bangor. It was almost midnight. He was in decompression mode.

The day was intense. The early morning operation was well-planned, smoothly executed. Dunne took satisfaction in knowing that Aleem and his two pals would no longer be a threat to innocent people.

The late morning operation in Fredericton was almost a disaster. Laurel and Hardy and the young woman did not look like hardened terrorists, but had Dunne and his men not intervened, they would have planted those explosives and killed hundreds of Canadians. It was the kind of terrorist strategy that Dunne feared—soft targets, mass murder perpetrated by young people with no prior involvement in *jihad*. The Fredericton cell was almost impervious to intelligence. Had Aleem's father not sued the government, Big Dog General Evanston would never have begun to surveil Aleem, and never gotten wind of the plot.

What a war.

The U.S. Justice Department, Homeland Security, and every other federal law enforcement agency felt obliged to abide by restraining orders and injunctions imposed on them by naïve federal judges. The U.S. played by the "rules." The *jihadists* did not. They were at war. They said so. Apparently the President and executive branch did not believe them.

The four DOGs spent two hours at the cabin that afternoon after returning from Fredericton. They de-briefed and discussed what they could have done differently—what went right and what went wrong. Bull disposed of Abdul as soon as Dunne, Hound, and Doberman arrived at the cabin. Hound prepared the body for the carnivores. Everyone knew Abdul had to die. He broke Dunne's law. That was the discipline.

Dunne told Bull how they had defused the four backpack bombs and set off the explosives in remote, deep woods between Fredericton and the border. Dunne did not know as much about explosives as Bull, but he had learned a lot from him through the years. Dunne told the men Big Dog, per the DOG protocol, would transfer money into their encoded accounts in two days.

They said their goodbyes until the next operation. There was no celebration, no joy. There was only satisfaction in accomplishing a vital mission to save lives and protect civilians—a mission the U.S. Government refused to do under its current leadership.

Dunne's cell phone on the seat came to life.

Finally. Good of Big Dog to reactivate it after twelve days silent.

He checked his messages. He didn't expect any personal calls—he had no personal life. There would be no calls from Big Dog. Before he left the cabin, they had talked at length on the satphone. Dunne was glad to get rid of that bulky thing.

Dunne pulled onto the shoulder. He couldn't believe what he was seeing. Twenty calls from Jake over the last twelve days, five this morning. He punched the return call button and waited.

"Dunne?" the voice said.

"This Willie Mitchell?"

"Yes. Brujo got Jake. We need your help."

Chapter Thirty-Seven

Jimmy Gray's jet touched down in Miami at ten a.m., an hour and fifteen minutes after wheels up at New Orleans Lakefront. Jimmy looked out his window as his pilot taxied to the general aviation terminal. There were few people stirring and little activity. Even for a Sunday the place looked deserted.

Outside the gate Jimmy saw a small, older man waving at him. He was thin, with leathery brown skin. It had to be Fredo.

Jimmy had called Skeeter Sumrall Saturday afternoon and started the ball rolling. Jimmy said he wanted a list of the Marielito émigrés who stayed in the U.S. after the boatlift. The Senator told Jimmy that he would call his friend, Florida Senator Mark Rodriguez. Skeeter said Senator Rodriguez was the darling of the Cuban ex-pats in South Florida because of his consistent opposition to opening lines of communication and trade with Castro's Cuba. Rodriguez wanted the ban on travel and doing business with Cuba expanded and strictly enforced.

An hour after Jimmy's first call to Senator Sumrall, one of Senator Rodriguez's aides called Jimmy and asked for details of Jimmy's plans. The aide went into a detailed explanation of why the citizenship records of the Marielitos were classified, primarily for security and privacy concerns, and protection of their rights as new citizens.

"I don't care about all that bull shit," Jimmy Gray told the aide. "I need to find out some information about a person who supposedly came over in the boatlift, and who has kidnapped and may be planning to murder my Godchild, a young man I love and admire."

"There is a person in Miami," the aide said, "who will have all the information you need. His name is Fredo Vasquez. I'll call him right now and ask him to call you. Give me your number."

Fredo called Jimmy's cell an hour later. Jimmy launched his usual charm offensive, peppering his comments with his pidgin Spanish. By the end of the thirty minute conversation, Jimmy Gray and Fredo Vasquez were big buddies. Fredo insisted on picking Jimmy up at the airport Sunday morning.

Jimmy walked through the passenger gate into the terminal. Fredo greeted him with a big hug and a buss on each cheek.

"Sure is good to see you, partner," Jimmy said, tapping Fredo lightly on his flat stomach. "You looking fit. I guess that's from chasing all the pretty señoritas around down here."

Fredo laughed. "That's about all I can do at my age," he said with a heavy Cuban accent. "My wife knows I'm harmless."

By the time they reached Little Havana in Fredo's older model Nissan Maxima, Fredo had explained how his parents and he fled Cuba in 1958 to save his father from execution by Ché's death squads. Fredo returned to his homeland at sixteen in the Bay of Pigs invasion, miraculously surviving and escaping to the safety of the Cuban exile community in Miami. Fredo told Jimmy from that point on, he dedicated his life to liberating Cuba.

"How'd you get to be the expert on the Marielitos?"

"President Carter opened the doors to America for those who wanted freedom from political oppression. Fidel sent some of those people, but also many criminals, lunatics, and spies. I felt it was important to my community to account for all those people who came in and stayed in America, partly out of a concern for our safety. We were sure at the time that Castro sent in some assassins, how many we didn't know, to kill those of us trying to overthrow his regime."

Fredo parked in front of his small stucco home. He introduced his wife Carmen to Jimmy. She smiled, brought them two cups of very strong coffee, and disappeared into the back.

Fredo led Jimmy to a room that Fredo used as his office. There were large maps of Cuba covering the walls and at least a dozen filing cabinets.

Jimmy was sweating. "Pretty warm down here," he said.

Fredo turned on the window unit and sat behind his desk. "I'm sorry, he said. The heat does not bother Carmen or me. I never had air conditioning in Cuba."

Fredo opened a large book with a T stenciled on the front cover. He began turning the pages.

"I looked at all the Torres in this book last night after we talked. We have many people with that name. There are three

Santos. You said he had a son named Ignacio. Maybe there is an error. I found a Santos Torres who entered the U.S. with a brother named Ignacio, aged nine."

Jimmy quickly did the math. "That would be about right. He was twelve or thirteen when they surfaced in L.A."

"I remember these people," Fredo said. "The mother opened a Santeria shop on 54th Street, not far from here. She and the boy lived above the shop. The older one, Santos, ran with the *yeyo* crowd."

"I've read a little about Santeria. What's *yeyo* mean?"

"Cocaine. Would you like to see the building where her shop was?"

"Sure," Jimmy said. "Anything else you remember about these people? Particularly the boy, Ignacio."

Fredo thought for a minute. "Like you say, Santos and the boy moved away after a couple of years. That was almost thirty years ago. I know of no one who would know anything about the boy Ignacio. The mother ran the store until five or six years ago. *La Casa de Mama Coba* was what she called it."

"That was her name?"

"Everyone in Little Havana called her Mama Coba, and her customers thought she had special powers." He paused for a minute. "I remember she had a very strange man who worked for her in the store, lived there, too. He was tall, very thin. Dressed like a monk all the time. You know, wore a black robe like a priest."

Fredo showed Jimmy the two-story building where Mama Coba ran her store. He gave Jimmy a twenty minute tour of Little Havana, and drove him back to the airport.

Jimmy reached into his pocket and pulled out a tightly wrapped stack of fifty $100 bills. He gave it to Fredo and thanked him.

"For your Mariel Boatlift Museum," Jimmy said. "And to buy Mrs. Carmen a pretty new dress."

Walking through the terminal Jimmy went over what little he had learned from Fredo. He could not for the life of him reconstruct why he thought it was such a good idea to fly to Miami to try to find out something about Brujo when he was nine or ten years old.

"Big waste of jet fuel was all this was," he muttered to himself.

Jimmy stood outside the terminal, far enough from the roar of his Learjet to call Willie Mitchell and give him the bad news—ace detective Jimmy Gray had learned nothing and was on his way back to New Orleans.

~ * ~

Jake was so out of it, he had no idea how long the giant albino alligator in front of him had been there. The first time Jake saw the gator sauntering past, a bone protruding from his mouth, the alligator was small. Somehow, it had grown exponentially. It was now huge, and inside the gigantic gator, under its opaque white skin, a softball-sized emerald pulsated, giving the gator an intermittent green glow.

The alligator turned its huge head to stare at Jake—it looked sinister, hungry. Jake prayed it would not attack. It glared at Jake for a while, and in slow, ponderous motion, it walked away and disappeared into the darkness.

Thank God.

Within twenty minutes after the "tea" serving, Jake became frightened out of his wits by the sights and sounds around him. Sitting alone in the flickering, weak candle light, fear and paranoia gripped him. He saw snakes slither toward him and disappear under his aluminum stool; he watched a kaleidoscope of colors and shapes flash like lightning near the top of the concrete cylinder; he felt insects and invisible vermin crawl over his naked body; and he swore he felt the tendons and muscles in his arms and shoulders begin to tear apart, to unravel from within, so that if his hands were ever unbound, his arms would dangle uselessly at his sides, limp and powerless, flapping when he stood up from the stool to run away.

At some level, Jake knew he was hallucinating from the "tea." Even so, he was scared to death.

I wonder what time it is?

Jake had no idea how long he had been sitting on the stool in the dark, cavernous building, arms tied behind him, leaning forward at the waist to reduce the pressure on his biceps and shoulders. No light from the outside leaked into the concrete cylinder, making it impossible for Jake to know if it was day or night. The "tea" displaced all sense of time and space. He had been bound in the same position long enough that his arms had grown numb and he could no longer feel his hands.

Brujo appeared in front of him, resplendent in the red jaguar headdress. Jake sensed movement behind him. His arms dropped to his sides, useless and tingling.

Big Demon must have cut the rope. I hope this is real.

Jake tried to join his hands but his arms would not move. He hoped it was the lack of blood flow and not nerve damage. He winced at the needles spreading through both arms. His mental state enhanced every ache and pain; the needles seemed real.

Big Demon joined Brujo and gestured for Jake to stand. Jake forced himself up using only his legs. The effort caused both calves to knot up in severe cramps. Jake almost fell over. He stabilized on wobbly legs, opening and closing his fists. He felt a hint of strength returning with the blood flowing through his arms.

Big Demon moved closer to Jake and held out a small piece of red material with strings.

Holy shit. A codpiece.

Big Demon grunted for Jake to put it on. Jake's hands and fingers were clumsy and unresponsive, but he managed to figure out how to wear it. It did feel better than being totally exposed.

Jake had been so focused on his arms and the two murderers in front of him he had set aside thoughts of his raging thirst. His mouth was drier than ever, his throat parched and sore. He eyed the wineskin around Big Demon's neck.

Dying of thirst versus hallucinations.

Big Demon sent a stream of liquid from the wineskin to Brujo, then turned and offered it to Jake. He did not want to drink it, but his aching thirst overcame the fear of more visions.

Jake opened his mouth.

After Big Demon emptied the wineskin quenching Jake's thirst, he opened a switchblade knife from his pocket. Big Demon pointed the blade toward Jake. Even in the dim light, Jake could tell it was razor sharp.

Big Demon moved to Jake's left and grabbed his left bicep. Jake reacted instinctively, trying to pull away, but Big Demon was incredibly strong. Jake wanted to fight the giant, but his arms just wouldn't work.

Go ahead, dammit. Just be quick about it.

With a swipe of the blade, Big Demon reopened the two-week old slice that Sergeant Lupo inflicted on Jake in Virginia. The pain made Jake's knees weak—he almost passed out.

When Big Demon began cutting a new place on Jake's left arm, Jake jerked free from Big Demon's grasp and tried to run, but he his legs cramped again. The lengthy bondage had done some damage.

Jake felt something very hard strike the back of his head. He was out cold when he fell hard on the concrete.

Big Demon knelt beside Jake and resumed carving.

~ * ~

General Evanston's resourcefulness never ceased to amaze Dunne. Within an hour after Dunne talked to Willie Mitchell, Big Dog had located an off-the-books military flight leaving a SAC base near Bangor that had been "officially" mothballed. It was scheduled to take off for Eglin Air Force Base just east of Pensacola, Florida at two a.m. He warned the flight would be long and uncomfortable in the old C-130 Hercules, but it would get Dunne close to New Orleans sooner than any of the commercial flights available in New England in the wee hours of a Sunday morning.

Big Dog gave Dunne the name of the contact on the C-130 and told Dunne where to leave the Explorer. Dunne made the flight with time to spare. The steady drone of the four turboprops put Dunne to sleep for four of the five hours of flight to Eglin, where Dunne caught a cab to the Pensacola Regional Airport to wait on Jimmy Gray's Learjet 60.

Dunne worked online until after noon when Jimmy Gray's jet landed in Pensacola to pick up Dunne. They were on the tarmac at the general aviation terminal long enough to drop the stairs and pick up Dunne and his duffel bag. After waiting ten minutes for a takeoff slot from the tower, Jimmy Gray and Dunne were airborne for the twenty-minute flight to New Orleans Lakefront.

Jimmy Gray talked as fast as his Yaloquena County drawl allowed him, but the jet touched down before Jimmy could fill Dunne in on everything that had happened since Dunne dropped Jake off at the FBI office for the early morning raid on the headquarters of Los Cuervos on Flood Street in the Ninth Ward.

By the time Jimmy pulled the red Escalade into the parking garage on his side of the duplex on Ursulines it was mid-afternoon, and Jimmy Gray had told Dunne everything he knew.

"Time to get to work," Dunne said.

Chapter Thirty-Eight

Dunne concentrated on his laptop at the kitchen island in Jimmy Gray's duplex, mining the Brujo data. He walked outside and made calls in the courtyard for ten minutes. Susan and Kitty sat at the breakfast table with Jimmy Gray. Willie Mitchell paced. Every minute or so one of them looked outside to check on Dunne. Everything stopped when he walked inside.

"Nothing," Dunne said. "Nobody knows anything. Eustis will be here in a few minutes."

Dunne removed his phone charger from his heavy black duffel bag on the floor in the corner. He picked up the duffel and moved it closer to a wall plug, resting his charging phone on top. The black bag made a metallic clunk when he placed it on the slate floor.

Kitty stood up, grimacing and holding her side. "There must be something we can do," she said. "How can Brujo and his men be invisible?"

"What about the one in jail, the one arrested with the young girl?" Susan asked. "Can't we get someone to make him talk?"

"Eustis says Green Eyes has a lawyer," Willie Mitchell said. "Sam Weill. The same one representing Big Demon."

"So what?" Susan asked.

"Once the defendant gets a lawyer, law enforcement can't question him anymore unless the lawyer is present. Eustis told me that Sam Weill has notified by letter the NOPD and Orleans Parish D.A.'s office that no one is to have any contact with Green Eyes without his permission and his presence. Then he says in the last sentence he's not giving anyone permission under any circumstances."

"That's a stupid rule," Susan said. "It puts the defense attorney in control."

"That's the law," Willie Mitchell said.

"If you want to guess what the law is on an issue like that," Jimmy Gray said, "just think about the most common sense answer." The big banker paused for a few seconds. "When you get that answer, you can be sure that that ain't the law. Then figure out what's the opposite of common sense, and that's usually the law."

"Your trip to Miami didn't turn up anything on Brujo that might help us?" Susan asked.

Jimmy Gray laughed. "Nothing. I did get a nice tour of Little Havana. My guide Fredo took me by the Santeria store Brujo's mama ran in Miami. Brujo lived above the store while he was there. But he was only nine or ten and that was thirty years ago. Nobody remembers anything that far back."

"It wasn't a waste of time in my book," Dunne said. "Got me a fast ride from Pensacola here."

Jimmy Gray walked toward the French door to look at his courtyard. After a few quiet moments, out of the blue, while staring outside, Jimmy Gray said aloud in his best Spanish accent:

"La Casa de Mama Coba."

"What did you say?" Kitty asked.

"La Casa de Mama Coba," Jimmy said. "Sound like I was born in Latin American, don't I?"

"Have you been there?" Kitty asked. "To the store?"

"This morning, like I said. Fredo drove me by there. I didn't go in."

"There's one here," Kitty said. "On Chartres."

"One what?" Willie Mitchell asked.

"It's a store. It's called *La Casa de Mama Coba.* Just like Mr. Jimmy said. It's only a few blocks from here. I've jogged past it a lot of times. I always wondered what they sold there."

"Let's check it out," Jimmy Gray said.

"Hold on," Willie Mitchell said. "We've got an expert here." He turned to Dunne. "Tell us what to do."

"First thing is recon," Dunne said. "We need information and the lay of the land. I'll call Eustis and see if they have any intel on the place. And we'll need someone to go in the store and look around." He glanced at his watch. "It's almost five. And it's Sunday. They're probably not open."

"They might be," Kitty said. "A lot of these French Quarter shops stay open on Sunday for the tourists who wander through the Quarter."

"We need someone who could pass for a typical tourist," Dunne said.

Everyone in the room, almost at the same time, turned to look at Jimmy Gray.

"I'm your huckleberry," he said.

~ * ~

Jimmy Gray and Susan walked south on Chartres from Esplanade. Susan wore her hair up, sandals and white jeans, and a lime green cotton top with a scoop neck. Jimmy's khaki walking shorts exposed his massive calves, supported by Saucony running shoes and white golf socks that stopped at his ankle. He wore a bright gold golf shirt with a purple LSU tiger roaring on his left chest, and topped off the ensemble with a gold golf hat with the Country Club of Louisiana logo and trim in purple.

Susan peered through the windows of the stores they passed. Jimmy glanced briefly through each storefront, and leaned on a parked car, positioning himself to eyeball the pretty girls passing by. He paid close attention to Susan to avoid getting caught ogling when Susan turned to move on to the next store.

It was a lazy Sunday afternoon for the typical middle-aged tourist couple. She was pretty, in good shape, and stylish. He was overweight, bored, and apparently color blind. They were browsing and killing time. There were scores of other couples like them in the Quarter doing the very same thing.

Jimmy walked past the entrance of *La Casa de Mama Coba*. Susan stopped at the window and looked in. Two stores south of Mama Coba's, Jimmy realized he was by himself. He turned and joined Susan.

"What's this place?" he asked.

"It looks interesting. Let's go in."

She walked in ahead of him. Before the door closed behind him, Jimmy Gray said in a loud voice, "It's Miller time, honey. I'm ready for a beer."

"In a minute," she said.

She walked past the gaunt man at the counter and began picking up the odd smelling offerings and reading labels. Jimmy stopped at the counter and looked up at Mantis.

"You the tallest priest I've ever seen," Jimmy said. "What kind of store is this anyway?"

Mantis gave Jimmy a sheet describing the store.

"Santeria, huh? I've read some about that."

Jimmy joined Susan. She moved her reading glasses from her head to her nose and read the tiny print on the label of a dark blue bottle.

"These are potions, honey," she said. "They have one here for your back and knees. You want to try it?"

Jimmy took the bottle from Susan and looked at the price.

"No thanks. They got any love potion number nine?"

Jimmy laughed out loud at his hilarious comment. Susan paid him no attention and Mantis stared down at the counter.

"He don't talk much," Jimmy said to Susan in a loud whisper. "Maybe he ought to go to a Dale Carnegie seminar."

Susan shushed him.

"Let's go," he said.

Susan walked to the counter. She held the blue bottle.

"Can I ask you about this product?"

Mantis gestured and moved around the counter. He walked across the store to the stairs leading to the second floor. He rapped loudly on the wooden wall with his large, bony knuckles.

In less than a minute, an Hispanic woman in a long latticed cotton skirt and a white-on-white crinkled cotton wrap blouse appeared from upstairs, her head wrapped in a bright aqua sateen cloth, tied in the back. Her face was free of blemishes and bore very few wrinkles. She was attractive with an aristocratic mien.

"May I help you?" she said. "I am Mama Coba."

Jimmy Gray removed his gold golf cap.

"Pleased to meet you, ma'am," Jimmy said.

"You have some wonderful items in your store," Susan said, holding the blue bottle. "I was curious about this one. Where do you get your products?"

Mama Coba seemed puzzled.

"I'm sorry," Susan said, extending her hand. "I'm Susan Gray, and this is my husband Jimmy. I have a shop in North Mississippi and I'm always looking for unusual things. I also design websites for boutiques."

"Many of these things we sell are of religious significance. You know of Santeria, the religion found in parts of the Caribbean?"

"I know about it," Jimmy blurted. "There was a court case in Florida a few years back said you could kill animals as part of your religious rituals and it wasn't against the law." Jimmy was proud of himself. "I got a brother's a lawyer."

Mama Coba addressed Susan as if Jimmy were not in the room. "Unless you have Santeria communicants in your area, I doubt your customers would have any interest in what we sell here. I will be glad to give you a flyer...."

Jimmy held up the sheet Mantis had given him. "I got it already."

"Very well, then," Mama Coba said and made a move toward the stairs, "if there's nothing else."

"You live upstairs?" Jimmy asked loudly.

Mama Coba was startled. "Yes."

Jimmy pointed to Mantis. "This here your husband?"

Susan glanced at Mantis, who was not happy with Jimmy Gray's line of inquiry. He walked from behind the counter toward Jimmy.

"What's back there?" Jimmy said, pointing to the chapel.

Susan swatted his arm.

"Storage," Mama Coba said. She turned and walked up the stairs.

Mantis stood over Jimmy and Susan, staring. He tipped his head toward the door.

"Let's go, Jimmy," Susan said. She turned to Mantis. "Thank you."

Walking out the door, Jimmy was loud.

"Not very friendly, are they?"

Chapter Thirty-Nine

Jake woke up with a start. His left arm and chest hurt so badly he wanted to cry. Whatever Big Demon was pouring into his mouth had Jake scared and paranoid, and exacerbated the pain from the cuts.

No more tea. I'd rather die of thirst. I need my wits about me.

He was no longer on the stool. While he was out, Big Demon and Brujo tied him to thick wooden beams joined in the shape of a crucifix. He was on his back, bound with rope to the cross that lay on the concrete. Jake stared toward the top of the concrete cylinder. They had secured his head with something that was tight across his forehead. It wasn't rope; he thought it may be a cloth of some kind. He could not look left or right, up or down—he could only stare straight into the murky apex of the cylinder.

Being knocked unconscious again had one beneficial effect. The hallucinogen seemed to be wearing off.

But, Jesus, what dreams.

He tried to reconstruct the bizarre olio of vignettes that danced through his brain while he was out. Jake could remember very little, just snippets of scenes from Sunshine, Ole Miss, Dunne's training camps. The one recurring theme was Willie Mitchell's death. Jake saw different versions of his father's corpse. At times the corpse talked and moved as if still alive. Jake shuddered.

Jake was surprised when Brujo appeared in Jake's view, standing over him, studying Jake like a lab specimen.

"Good morning," Jake said. "I'd like another room, please."

Brujo left Jake's field of vision and returned holding a mirror. He moved two candles from the perimeter closer to Jake, placing one on each side. Brujo held the mirror over Jake's torso.

Aw, shit.

On Jake's chest, carved into the skin, was the Los Cuervos symbol, the flying crow wings. They stretched across his pectorals. Above the wings was an eye, Brujo's eye. It was the same eye on the wall of the shrine in the Ninth Ward and in Jake's condo. But this eye wasn't painted—it was carved. Dried blood, Jake's blood, streaked his torso.

"My compliments to the artist," Jake said.

Brujo ignored Jake. He moved the mirror over Jake's left side to his arm. The last thing Jake remembered was Brujo slicing open the old wound.

Jake was somewhat relieved when he saw that Brujo had turned the single vertical cut into an L. Inside the L was a smaller C. Los Cuervos.

Could have been a lot worse.

Brujo removed the mirror and disappeared from Jake's view. Jake heard Brujo moving near him, but could not see him. Jake smelled something burning. It was a strange odor.

Swinging back and forth over his face was a small thurifer, like the ones Jake saw at the Immaculate Conception Catholic Church in Sunshine when he was a child. He and Scott accompanied Willie Mitchell to Mass from time to time. Scott complained the smell of incense made him sick; Jake liked the smell.

Jake heard the thurifer clank when Brujo set it on the concrete. Brujo's hand moved over Jake's face. Brujo anointed Jake's forehead, lips, and the chest over his heart with something.

Hope these aren't last rites.

Brujo began to chant, circling Jake. Jake couldn't see him, but he could hear Brujo moving around him, and could hear his feet slide on the concrete every few steps. Then there was silence.

Brujo loomed over Jake's face. For the first time, he spoke.

"Thus begins the exorcism of The Other from your body. Do not be afraid of me. I will not harm you. You must beware of The Other. In his fight to remain in your body, he may sacrifice your physical being. It is The Other that may quench your life to save his."

Jake closed his eyes for a moment and prayed.

~ * ~

Mrs. Serio had enough of the late night comings and goings on her street. Her city councilman, Maurice Trosclair, promised her he would have the St. Bernard Parish Sheriff look into it. The Sheriff called Mrs. Serio. He gave her the number of the deputies on duty at night for her precinct, and told her to call the number the next time people disturb her on their way to the old grain elevator. The elevator was off limits to the public anyway, according to orders from the DEQ and the EPA.

So when she saw the big Lincoln drive past her house this night, she called the deputies. She couldn't sleep because of heartburn from supper, mirlitons stuffed with shrimp and crabmeat, so she thought this was a good night to put an end to the traffic coming and going to the elevator at all hours.

~ * ~

The deputies drove their patrol car slowly past Mrs. Serio's house. As they neared the grain elevator, they cut off their headlights. It was pitch black dark on the street. Many of the houses had been unoccupied since Katrina. Vandals had defaced the properties, burning two of them on Mrs. Serio's street.

Darrell Beaudoin was the young deputy driving. His partner was Wade Brewton, just a few years older than Darrell.

They rolled silently into the parking area for the grain elevator and stepped quietly from the cruiser. Both Darrell and Wade approached the silo with their guns drawn. They each carried a flashlight but kept them dark. Both men grew up in St. Bernard Parish and knew the area around the grain elevator. They were on familiar ground, and looked forward to confronting the freaks disturbing Mrs. Serio.

Darrell shone his light into the big Lincoln Town Car, but cut it off when Wade told him someone was coming. They crouched in the darkness behind the Lincoln as a large man approached.

"He's big," Darrell whispered to Wade.

They waited until Big Demon was ten feet from the Lincoln. They jumped from behind the car and shone their lights in his face.

Big Demon's one eye opened wide.

"Don't move," Wade said. "Raise your hands."

Big Demon moved. And instead of raising his hands, he went for his waist. Darrell and Wade opened fire immediately, shooting Big Demon twice each. Big Demon fell backward onto the asphalt.

Darrell and Wade walked cautiously toward the man, keeping their guns and flashlights on him.

There were four holes in Big Demon's chest, enough lead to stop the big man. Darrell knelt beside the man and checked for a pulse.

"Dead," Darrell said.

"He have a gun?" Wade asked.

Darrell removed an automatic from Big Demon's belt line.

"Yep."

"Thank God."

"He ain't got but one eye," Darrell said.

"Let's call it in," Wade said.

"Hold on," Darrell said. "You hear something?"

They crouched by Big Demon, doused their lights and listened.

"I guess it wasn't anything," Darrell said.

Darrell and Wade didn't hear it, but Hell was on its way.

~ * ~

Brujo quickly disappeared from Jake's view when the shots outside the grain elevator were fired. He raced to the exit through the concrete office structure then into the darkness surrounding the elevator.

Brujo's speed was incredible. He ran barefoot in the darkness toward the Lincoln carrying his favorite pump shotgun. He didn't need a flashlight. Brujo had lived in darkness so long his eyes were like a cat's.

When Darrell and Wade finally realized they were in jeopardy, it was too late. Brujo shot Darrell first, then Wade.

With both of them on their backs, bleeding and groaning, Brujo checked Big Demon. He said a prayer for Big Demon's spirit and pumped two rounds of twelve-gauge buckshot into the prone body of Darrell, then Wade.

~ * ~

Inside the silo, Jake heard the shotgun blasts. It had to be Brujo's twelve-gauge. Jake remembered the sound from Brujo's murder of Dominguez and Byrne. Jake struggled to move his head, and tested the ropes securing his hands and legs. It was no use—he couldn't move.

Jake heard Brujo's bare feet padding on the concrete nearby.

"What happened?" Jake asked. "Who'd you kill this time?"

Brujo's face appeared, six inches from Jake's. Brujo's eyes were different from when he performed the exorcism. They were distant, unfocused. Something bad happened.

"They killed Big Demon?"

Brujo took a deep breath. "Just his human form. He will return."

Brujo began working on Jake's bindings. He cut the rope around Jake's feet, then the cloth holding Jake's head.

"We must leave this place," Brujo said.

"To go where?"

"You will see."

"Why don't you go on without me. I'll just hang out here."

"I need you now that Big Demon is no longer with me."

"For what?"

"To take care of things. Like he did."

"What things?"

"I will explain. We must first exorcise The Other."

"Tell me who he is and I'll get rid of him myself."

"He is in you. But he is not you. I have confronted him many times before. Once in Los Angeles. The last time in a prison."

"What did you do to him in L.A.?"

"I cut off the head of the body he was possessing and brought it to my father."

Shit. I'm toast. Keep him talking. Go along with his plan.

"I'll go with you. Why don't you untie my hands?"

"Not as long as you are The Other."

"I swear I won't try anything."

Brujo untied Jake's right hand from the wooden beam, but kept the rope tight around his wrist. He jerked the rope on Jake's hand, pulling it across his body and tying it to the left hand, causing Jake tremendous pain. Brujo pulled on the rope, causing Jake to sit up. Atop the wooden beams, hands tied in front, Jake felt light-headed and weak from the pain and loss of blood. Brujo jerked the rope again.

"Wait," Jake yelled.

He rolled to the side and knelt for a moment. He struggled and put his left foot on the concrete, then his right. He was off the floor, but bent at the waist forty-five degrees, in agony.

The biggest cuts on his chest and arm began bleeding again.

Brujo pushed Jake, and led him by the rope into the darkness of the silo. Brujo walked fast. With one hand he tugged on Jake's rope; with the other he carried the twelve-gauge pump. Jake could not keep up. When Jake faltered, Brujo pulled harder on the rope.

"Hold on," Jake said. "I'm doing the best I can. Where are we going?"

Brujo didn't respond, and walked Jake outside to the Lincoln. Brujo opened the back door and smashed the fine-grained Black Walnut stock of the shotgun against the side of Jake's head.

Jake crumpled and Brujo shoved him into the back seat. Brujo jumped into the driver's seat and started the Lincoln. He made sure the heavy Lincoln rolled over the bodies of Darrell and Wade on the way out of the parking area to his chapel on Chartres Street.

Chapter Forty

Dunne was frustrated by the lack of cover on Chartres Street. He was by himself. There was no need to put the others in jeopardy, and involving them in the surveillance would have increased the chances of discovery. With only one way in and out, Dunne did not need their help. Willie Mitchell and the others agreed to stay in the duplex while Dunne staked out Mama Coba's. Because Chartres was narrow, and every building shared a common wall with the next, there was no place to hide near the store.

He finally settled on a rooftop two buildings south toward Canal and across Chartres from Mama Coba's. It wasn't ideal, but it was the only place he could keep an eye on the front door without being seen. The building he was on was for sale and seemed unoccupied. When Dunne scaled the fire escape behind the building he peered through a dirty window into the second floor rooms and saw no furniture.

Dunne lay on his stomach on the roof staring at Mama Coba's through night vision binoculars, the smallest ones Bushnell made. In Velcroed pockets or holsters, he had a .45 caliber Sig Sauer automatic, a .357 Colt revolver, two knives, and zip cuffs. His assault rifle rested on the roof next to him, ready to fire.

It was three a.m. in the French Quarter, so every few minutes pedestrians walked by. The majority of the walkers were talking loud, laughing and reliving the night. Others walked fast and close to the buildings, no doubt hurrying home and hoping to avoid trouble.

Dunne was tired, but staying awake was no problem. He had plenty of rest in Maine, in fact, too much. It made him lethargic. With the reservoir of sleep he had stored in the north woods, Dunne could go for days without sleeping.

He rested his arms for a moment, setting the glasses on the roof and sitting up, doing a few stretches to stay loose. Dunne lay back down on his stomach and stared south toward the lights of Canal Street for a moment. There was still a steady stream of vehicular traffic on the main downtown street.

Dunne turned to look north and saw a man walk around the corner of Governor Nicholls onto Chartres. Dunne picked up his binoculars.

Through the glasses he saw the man. Though the image was green and the movement jerky, Dunne had no doubt it was Brujo—and he had another man slung over his shoulder.

Dunne watched Brujo cover the short distance from the corner of Governor Nicholls to Mama Coba's storefront. Brujo stayed in the shadows and was through the door a few seconds after turning the corner.

Dunne remained on the roof, staring at the door. He catalogued the details he remembered. Brujo's head was shaved, his body covered with tattoos. At first Dunne thought he was nude until he saw the codpiece. Brujo wore nothing else, and was barefoot.

The man over his shoulder was limp, and naked. His arms hung uselessly down Brujo's back, swinging and swaying as Brujo walked.

Dunne never saw the face, but he was certain it was Jake. He was the right build and size for Jake, and through the glasses, when Brujo turned around before unlocking the door, Dunne saw the vicious cut on Jake's left arm.

Dunne kept watch for Big Demon, expecting him to join Brujo.

Maybe Big Demon's already in there.

Dunne called the duplex. Willie Mitchell answered.

"I need you to drive over here and park on Chartres where you can see the storefront," Dunne said.

"What's going on?"

"Brujo just walked in the front door with Jake over his shoulder."

Dunne anticipated the next question.

"There was nothing I could do. I'm on the roof across the street. I couldn't shoot without putting Jake's life in danger. I need you to cover the front door while I get off this building."

"I'll be right there."

"Willie Mitchell," Dunne said. "Bring your Springfield."

~ * ~

"You don't think we ought to wait for Eustis?" Jimmy Gray asked.

"No," Dunne said. "We've got to go in now. DOJ has NOPD walking on eggshells since the brutality and corruption complaints arising out of Katrina. Even with exigent circumstances, Eustis will have to get a warrant. Besides, a SWAT team's too much clutter, too many people. They're liable to get Jake with friendly fire."

"David's right," Kitty said. "And there's only one way in and one way out. A loud frontal assault is not the way to go."

Jimmy Gray pulled out his platinum gold Desert Eagle fifty caliber automatic pistol. "Let's go," he said.

Dunne eyed Jimmy's giant pistol.

"You know how to use that?"

"Don't worry about me. This ain't my first rodeo."

Susan looked at Jimmy.

"What?" she said.

Jimmy shrugged. "Well, it is my first human rodeo."

"Just be careful," Dunne said. "We'll be in close quarters and that thing will knock down a wall."

"Kitty, you and Susan stay here," Dunne said. "The three of us can handle this. As far as we know there's only Mama Coba and the tall man in the cassock, if he spends the night there."

"I think he does," Susan said. "He was very protective of the lady."

"Let's mount up," Jimmy said.

Dunne stopped Jimmy. "Let me call Willie Mitchell."

~ * ~

Willie Mitchell sat in the red Escalade one block south of Mama Coba's. The giant SUV seemed even bigger in the close confines of Chartres Street. Parking at the curb was legal, but it shouldn't have been. The driver's side of the Escalade protruded so far into the travel lane that passing vehicles hugged the left curb to get by. On the plus side, Willie Mitchell had an unobstructed view of Mama Coba's.

Dunne told him to sit tight until he called.

Thank God for Dunne. Jake said Dunne saved us both at the reservoir. I would have drowned, and Jake would have been shot to death. Jake said both of us would have been dead for sure. For Jake's sake, Dunne has to pull off another miracle. He's got to come through, to clean up the mess I made letting Jake get taken from the duplex right under my nose.

Willie Mitchell slammed his open palms into the leather-covered steering wheel.

"Dammit," he said.

Willie Mitchell picked up the Springfield and for the fifth time since he started the watch, made sure a bullet was chambered.

This time it's not going to be so easy for Señor Brujo.

Willie Mitchell's cell phone vibrated.

~ * ~

Kitty walked slowly, back and forth, in the duplex. She did not like to wait, and she hated being on the sidelines. She knew Dunne was right, that she couldn't go into Mama Coba's in her condition. She would be a liability.

Kitty glanced at Susan on the couch. Her eyes were closed, but Kitty knew she wasn't sleeping. Every minute or so Susan's lips moved.

She's praying. Maybe I should be praying, too.

She tried for a few minutes, but since she had prayed only three times before in her entire life, it didn't go so well. She was better at contemplating shooting Brujo and his altar boys between the legs, then between the eyes, in that order.

Kitty glanced at her watch.

Four-fifty a.m.

Kitty resumed her slow motion pacing. She had enough.

"Come on," Kitty said to Susan. "Let's go."

"Go where?"

"To Chartres Street."

"Dunne said stay here."

"He's not our boss. Come on."

"What do you think we can do over there?"

"Maybe nothing. But I can't stay here."

"You can't go in that store."

"I know. Not planning on it."

"Then what?" Susan asked.

"I don't know. I just want to be there."

Susan got up from the couch.

"It's my car and I'm driving. But I'm not taking you over there to get you hurt worse than you already are. You have to promise me you'll stay in the car."

"I promise."

Susan grabbed her keys and purse. "Okay. Let's go."

Kitty opened her purse, removed her forty caliber Glock 23, and chambered a round.

"What do you plan on doing with that?" Susan asked.

"You never know," Kitty said. "Let's roll."

~ * ~

It had been the longest two hours of Jake's life. He regained consciousness in the store, looking upside down, passing shelves covered with bottles, burlap and cellophane bags. His brain was fuzzy. He blinked several times, trying to remove the cobwebs from his eyes and his head.

Brujo entered a narrow corridor. Jake saw an empty cot against the wall. Brujo stopped. Jake heard a key enter and unlock a door. Brujo carried him inside, closed the door and turned the deadbolt.

Brujo dumped Jake on a cold, hard surface. When he realized he was being unloaded onto something, Jake turned his shoulder to absorb the shock of hitting it. He didn't know how many more blows to the head he could take.

Jake watched Brujo return to the door and engage another lock, then lower a steel bar in place. The door and jamb appeared to be metal.

Brujo turned his full attention to Jake.

"You are awake," Brujo said. "We will begin."

It took a significant effort and it hurt, but Jake swung his legs off the table and sat up, pushing off the polished surface he thought was marble. It was the first time around Brujo that Jake's hands and feet were not bound.

"You said once we need to talk," Jake said. "How about now?"

Brujo stood three feet from the altar.

"Very well."

Jake looked down and adjusted his codpiece to cover himself.

"This table is cold and hard. May I get off this thing?"

"No." Brujo paused. "It is an altar."

"An altar for what?"

"It's where I pray. It is where I minister to my followers."

"Where is this building? I saw we walked through a store."

"It is not important."

"You need to let me go," Jake said. "I'm an Assistant United States Attorney and if you kill me my government will never stop until they get you."

"I hope you do not die. I need you."

"I don't want to work for you," Jake said.

"When I destroy The Other you will. You will be grateful."

Jake was about to say he was leaving when Brujo threw a fine, brown powder in Jake's face. Jake was blinded and could not breathe for a moment. When he finally inhaled, his nose and throat burned from the powder, which had the fine consistency of gumbo filé.

Jake took a blind swing in the direction of Brujo, catching nothing but air. The momentum carried him off the altar onto the floor. He stood up and groped for Brujo—Jake still could not see.

Jake felt a powerful grip around his wrist. Another hand grabbed Jake's other wrist. His hands were pulled behind him. Jake struggled and twisted, but was unable to break free. When Brujo let him go, Jake's arms were tied behind his back once again.

"Shit," Jake yelled, turning around. "You asshole. Why don't you fight me man to man. You afraid of me?"

Jake's eyes stopped burning and through his watery left eye he was able to see Brujo.

Brujo was clad only in his codpiece. Instead of the jaguar headdress, Brujo wore a red bandanna across his forehead, tied in the back. Jake watched him sprinkle powder from a leather pouch onto the back of his wrist and inhale it.

Jake surveyed the room in which he stood. It was about twenty feet by thirty. The raised altar Jake had been dumped on dominated one end. In front of the altar was a *pres dieu* wide enough to accommodate several kneeling worshippers. On the other end was a small bed and an enclosure built out into the room, which Jake surmised was a bathroom.

"Untie me," Jake said to Brujo, who circled Jake slowly, mumbling words Jake could not understand. It wasn't English or Spanish.

Brujo sneered at Jake and grabbed a sword from the wall. It had a curved blade that wasn't metal. Jake studied it. It looked old. The hilt was made of wood, the blade glassy and sharp as a scalpel.

Obsidian. Man-oh-man.

"Submit to the holy saints," Brujo said.

Jake bowed his head. "All right."

As if I have a choice.

Brujo gestured and Jake walked toward the altar. Brujo pushed him to the *pres dieu.* Jake knelt down, his hands tied behind him.

Brujo stood behind the altar and prayed. Jake shifted his weight from one knee to the other on the uncomfortable kneeler. He looked at the incredibly sharp obsidian blade on the altar.

This is not going to end well.

~ * ~

Dunne crouched at Mama Coba's front door, working the lock with a slender steel pick. It was five a.m. and dark.

Dunne and Jimmy Gray stood behind him. After a minute, he turned the knob and lightly pushed the door open.

Dunne went in first. He stopped just inside, leaving barely enough room for Willie Mitchell and Jimmy, who carried Dunne's black duffel bag and placed it out of the way, on the floor inside the store.

Dunne turned on his tiny LED flashlight and quickly surveyed the store. He gestured for Willie Mitchell and Jimmy to stay put while he checked every aisle. He saw an empty cot in a corridor leading to the back of the building. Dunne returned to the front door.

"I'm going to the steps to see what I can," Dunne said. "Do you know what's in the back past that cot in the hallway?" he asked.

"The old lady said storage," Jimmy said.

Dunne nodded and eased toward the steps. He was halfway there when the lights came on.

Chapter Forty-One

Dunne froze ten feet from Mantis, who stood on the steps staring, a large machete in his right hand. Dunne aimed his Sig at Mantis. Willie Mitchell and Jimmy Gray spread out to different aisles, moving closer to Mantis. Willie Mitchell had his Springfield and Jimmy his Desert Eagle.

Dunne gestured with his Sig for Mantis to move down the steps. Mantis did not move.

Jimmy Gray walked slowly closer, moving across a rug on the wooden floor. When he stepped near the edge of the rug, the floor sagged under his 312 pounds.

"Whoa," Jimmy said out loud.

Mantis glared at him.

Jimmy went down on one knee and moved the rug, revealing a door in the floor.

"Well, looky looky. Wonder what they hiding down here?"

Mantis flew down the stairs in a rage, shrieking like a banshee, the long fingers of his right hand wrapped around the machete, raised high to strike at Jimmy.

In a nimble and athletic move for a 312 pounder, Jimmy stepped to the side and tripped Mantis, while crashing the full weight of the fifty caliber titanium gold Desert Eagle automatic with a six-inch barrel against Mantis's bald skull. The machete skittered across the floor.

"Nicely done," Willie Mitchell said as he and Dunne arrived at the same time.

Dunne grabbed Mantis by the feet and dragged him past the rug.

"Long drink of water, ain't he," Jimmy said as Mantis's body slid past him.

Willie Mitchell removed the rug and opened the trap door. Dunne shone his LED flashlight in the hole, revealing the dozens of steel lockboxes. Willie Mitchell eased himself into the mini-basement and opened the lockbox closest to him. Jimmy Gray whistled at the money.

"No wonder. Tall boy didn't want us getting at his pot of gold."

"What is the meaning of this," Mama Coba said at the base of the stairs behind them. "Who are you people? Are you robbers?"

Willie Mitchell stepped forward. "My name is Willie Mitchell Banks, ma'am. And your son Ignacio has my son Jake captive somewhere in this building."

Jimmy Gray backed away and pointed his Desert Eagle at Mantis, who was trying to stand up.

"You stay down there for now," Jimmy said and drew back the pistol to hit Mantis again. Mantis sat on the floor, glaring at Jimmy.

"That's not true," Mama Coba said. She looked at Mantis. His look indicated he didn't know.

"Is there anyone besides you two in this building?" Dunne asked.

"No," she said.

"That's a lie," Dunne said. "I saw your son Brujo walk in the front door carrying another man on his shoulder."

"I did not see him come in," she said.

"What about Big Demon?" Dunne asked. "Is he here?"

"I don't think so. What do you want?" she asked.

"My son," Willie Mitchell said. "Unharmed."

"Can you help us with that?" Dunne asked.

"My son may be in his chapel," she said, pointing to the back of the building. "He is a priest."

"Can you talk to him for us?" Dunne asked.

"I will try. If I can get your son for you, will you leave my son alone?"

"About the best we can do for you is promise that we won't kill him," Dunne said. "We have to turn him over to the authorities. He's a cop killer. If they find him, I can promise you they won't take him alive."

"Let me talk to him," she said.

~ * ~

Jake watched Brujo at the altar praying. He had not moved a muscle in fifteen minutes. Jake's knees were killing him. There were candles burning on the altar and around Jake's *pres dieu*. Brujo had burned a variety of powders and dried plants in a full-sized thurifer. He stepped down from the riser and circled Jake, moving the thurifer on its chain back and forth, bathing Jake in the acrid smoke. The silver container sat now on the altar next to the obsidian blade, still smoking.

Jake thought he heard something outside the steel door, but he must have been mistaken because Brujo never moved.

Brujo turned his back to Jake and opened a cabinet on the wall, removing a gold chalice and a plastic container. He poured the brown liquid from the container into the chalice, held it over the altar and chanted, then drank it.

Tea.

Brujo set the chalice down and began to pray aloud, holding his arms out with his palms open to heaven. There were no words that Jake could recognize.

After ten minutes, there was a rap on the door. Jake glanced at the door but Brujo ignored it. Thirty seconds later, more rapping, this time more insistent.

Brujo left the altar and stood at the door, listening. Jake heard someone, but could not understand what was said. Brujo hesitated, then opened the door.

An older woman entered. Tall and dignified, she bowed slightly to Brujo and cupped his cheek in her hand.

Has to be Mama Coba. What's she doing in New Orleans?

They spoke in a language unknown to Jake. She did most of the talking. Brujo answered in two or three word responses. After a while, she held the back of his hand to her lips and kissed it over and over.

She's crying.

Mama Coba opened the door and left. Brujo double locked it behind her, and dropped the steel bar into place.

Brujo returned to the altar and resumed praying.

~ * ~

The woman does not understand. The Other must be destroyed while in the body of this human being. There is no other way. To do as she asks is worse than death. In a prison again, I will face the evil spirits I did before, but without Big Demon. The Other will torment me there and my soul will never be at peace. If I cannot drive The Other out of the bag of meat and bones before me, it will be of no use to me. It will be a threat to my ministry. If I fail, I will destroy this body and leave it for the buzzards and maggots. The Other will be back to torment me, but it will be later, perhaps at a better time, perhaps when I find the soul of Big Demon in another body, at another place and time.

I will try once more.

Brujo stepped down from the altar and circled Jake, swinging the thurifer. He returned it to the altar and picked up the obsidian blade. He circled Jake, waving the blade overhead, chanting at the top of his lungs. Brujo's eyes were wide, unblinking. He grabbed Jake's chin with his left hand, and raised the sword in his right.

Be gone devil. Be gone devil.

Brujo closed his eyes and prayed with all his might. He prayed that when he opened them and looked into the boy's eyes, The Other would be gone. Brujo prayed harder.

~ * ~

Jimmy Gray jabbed Mantis in the ribs with the Desert Eagle and coaxed him into the mini-basement under the trap door. Willie Mitchell had checked it and there was no way out. Mama Coba went in gracefully, with Mantis helping her down. Jimmy closed and turned the deadbolt to lock the trap door. He hustled his big frame over to the corridor leading to the back room.

Dunne had retrieved small squares of C-4 from his duffel and shaped a charge at each corner of the steel door. Each one was armed but the last. He stuck the electronic detonator in the final charge and retreated out of the corridor to stand with Willie Mitchell and Jimmy.

With the flip of a switch, the four wads of C-4 exploded, blowing the steel door off its frame and into the chapel.

Dunne was first through the smoke. Brujo was starting down with the obsidian blade when Dunne shot him. The force of the bullet knocked Brujo off balance, but not down. Dunne looked quickly around the room. Big Demon wasn't there.

Brujo stared at Dunne.

Willie Mitchell and Jimmy stopped behind Dunne, guns drawn and pointed at Brujo.

"It's over," Dunne said. "Put that down or I'll kill you."

Brujo mumbled a prayer and raised the blade again.

Dunne shot him in the shoulder and the blade fell onto the floor, shattering into hundreds of shards and scalpel-sharp pieces.

Willie Mitchell hurried to pull Jake off the *pres dieu* to get him away from Brujo. Jimmy stepped between Brujo and Willie Mitchell, and aimed his giant pistol at Brujo's head.

"Get Jake out," Dunne bellowed.

Willie Mitchell hustled Jake out the corridor and into the store. He pulled out his pocket knife and cut the rope binding Jake's hands.

Willie Mitchell turned Jake around and hugged him hard. Jake hugged his Daddy back, harder.

"I'm sorry, son, for letting you down at the duplex."

Willie Mitchell's eyes filled with tears.

"You just made up for it."

~ * ~

Jake stood in the store with a sheet wrapped around him. Willie Mitchell draped his arm around his son.

Dunne pushed Brujo ahead of him.

"Two slugs in the son-of-a-bitch and he's still standing," Jimmy said walking behind Dunne.

Dunne had secured Brujo's hands behind him in the chapel with zip cuffs. Brujo walked with his head down, defeated.

Dunne stopped next to Jake to shake his hand.

Brujo came to life and bolted for the door, his hands cuffed behind him. Dunne followed quickly, the Sig pointed at Brujo's back.

With an incredibly forceful leap, Brujo crashed through the Roman shade and glass panes of the front door, landing on his feet on the sidewalk.

Dunne hustled behind him. Brujo raced down the sidewalk and into Chartres south toward Canal.

"Call Eustis," Dunne yelled over his shoulder.

~ * ~

Kitty stood outside the Lexus, her Glock 23 aimed at Brujo racing toward her in the middle of Chartres Street, Dunne in pursuit but far behind.

She rested the Glock on the top of the car, holding it with two hands and taking careful aim.

When Brujo was fifteen feet from her, she shot twice, both bullets striking him in the left chest at his heart.

Brujo tumbled forward, head over heels, and came to rest on the asphalt in the center of Chartres.

Kitty watched Dunne kneel at Brujo's side and check his neck for a pulse. He felt for thirty seconds, looked up at Kitty and shook his head, quickly ripped open a Velcroed pocket and removed his tactical knife. He cut the zip cuffs off Brujo.

Dunne stood and saluted Kitty.

"Nice shooting," he said.

Dunne took off, the zip cuffs in hand, and ran back to Mama Coba's. He ran in, grabbed his black duffel, and grabbed Jimmy Gray by the arm. He hustled Jimmy down to the red Escalade a block south, threw the duffel in the passenger seat and jumped in with it.

Jimmy cranked the engine and roared north up the narrow street, stopping in front of Mama Coba's.

Dunne lowered his window. He shook Jake's hand, then Willie Mitchell's.

"I gotta go," Dunne said. "I'll call you guys later on Jake's phone."

Jimmy gunned the engine.

"Where to?" he asked Dunne.

~ * ~

Kitty ran as fast as her broken ribs would allow and jumped into Jake's arms. His sheet fell off as he hugged her.

Susan was close behind. She smothered Willie Mitchell's face with kisses, then hugged Jake, laughing and crying at the same time.

The four of them, three fully clothed and Jake in his codpiece and nothing else, stood in the middle of Esplanade, a half-block from Brujo's dead body, and watched the red Escalade turn right on Esplanade and disappear.

Behind them, turning off Canal, a half-dozen NOPD cruisers raced toward them, sirens blasting and lights flashing.

Willie Mitchell picked up the sheet from the asphalt and wrapped it around Kitty and Jake, hugging both of them as hard as he could.

Chapter Forty-Two

A month later, David Dunne stood outside the front door of an elegant town house in Georgetown. He rang the door bell and pulled his Domino's baseball-style cap further down over his forehead.

While he waited, he turned to admire the lovely view of the Potomac and Key Bridge.

Swell digs.

The door opened.

"Large pepperoni, extra cheese," Dunne said.

"I didn't order any pizza," OIG Director Leopold Whitman said and started to close the door.

Dunne stepped forward and stopped the door with his foot. He reached into the chest pocket of his Domino's shirt, and pulled out a piece of paper.

"Leopold Whitman, 202-899-8799?"

"That's my name and number, but I didn't order a pizza."

"Well, I've got to leave this here and collect, company policy."

Dunne opened the pizza box, pulled out his Sig Sauer automatic and pushed his way in. Backing up into the front sitting room, Whitman fell over an ottoman onto an antique Herize covering the oak parquet wooden floor. He tried to get up, but Dunne put his foot on Whitman's puny chest.

"You're fine there," Dunne said, removing his cap. "Remember me?"

Whitman's eyes grew wide. "Dunne."

"That's right, Leopold. We've got a few things to discuss."

"Let me up," Leopold asked.

"Nope. First, I know you ordered a black judicial robe two weeks ago and it was delivered three days ago. Where is it?"

Whitman didn't answer. Dunne put more weight on his foot.

"I can't breathe," Whitman said.

"Quit whining. Tell me where the robe is and I'll let up."

"There," Whitman said, pointing to the hall closet.

Dunne walked to the closet and took out the robe, keeping his Sig on Whitman. He jerked the black robe off its hangar and threw it on Whitman on the floor.

"Put it on," Dunne barked.

Whitman stood up and threw the black robe over his head, stuck his arms through the billowy sleeves and zipped up the front.

"You're not a judge," Dunne said. "Why do you need a judge's robe?"

"I have to judge moot court finals at Georgetown Law School next week."

"You're lying. You're not judging anything. You put the robe on and parade around your fancy town house, admiring yourself in the mirror, thinking what a brilliant federal judge you're going to be."

"I do not."

Dunne reached into his Domino's shirt pocket and pulled out a photograph of Whitman standing in front of a full length mirror in his town house, admiring himself in the black robe. He gave it to Whitman.

"Where did you get this?" Whitman asked.

"I've got a video of you admiring yourself in different poses in the robe. I can make it go viral on YouTube, or maybe I'll just post it on the DOJ web site, but I wanted to talk to you first."

"May I sit down?" Whitman asked.

"Go right ahead."

Whitman sat on his sofa in his robe and looked up at Dunne.

"What do you want?"

"A few things. First, I want you to know I killed the guy in Jackson you're so concerned about. He needed killing and I worked alone; nobody else knew."

Whitman said "I thought it was you."

"The second thing, you can conduct the most thorough investigation in the history of mankind and you will never find me or anything about me. Take my word for it. And if you try to find me or anything about me, I will know you're looking for me and I will come back to D.C. and find you and put you out of your misery. You got that? That's a guarantee."

"I understand," Whitman said.

"Last thing, you're going to reinstate Jake Banks, rescind his suspension, make sure he gets his back pay, restore him to full status as an AUSA. You will never investigate him again, and he will drop off of your radar permanently. I don't want you checking on him, his status with DOJ. In fact, I never want to hear about your mentioning his name again. Understand?"

Whitman nodded.

"I'm telling you this for your own good. If Jake's name even crosses your lips I will know about it. I will find you and I might not kill you, but I will make sure you'll never be a federal judge or a judge of any kind. I don't really have to take you out. I can infect your computer and phone with lots of encoded child porn. You won't know it's there until the investigators seize your computer or phone and show the pictures to you. That's easy to do, by the way."

Dunne let everything sink in. He watched Whitman adjust his wire-rimmed glasses and scratch his closely trimmed reddish brown beard.

"We clear?" Dunne asked. "You understand?"

"Yes."

"By the way, I can make you or break you career-wise. If you act right, and do everything I just asked, I'll leave you alone. I won't intervene if you get nominated for a federal judgeship. If you get it, I will keep an eye on you, make sure you're doing right."

Whitman was interested in that.

"How could I reach you if that...."

"You can't," Dunne said. "But I can reach you. You mind your p's and q's, and you'll never see me again. You mess up, I'll be back."

Dunne walked to the door.

"You can keep the pizza box."

~ * ~

Fifteen minutes later, Dunne drove at a leisurely pace, admiring the beauty along Rock Creek Parkway. He phoned Jake.

"Hello," Kitty said.

"This is a surprise," Dunne said. "Where's Jake?"

"He's out jogging with Willie Mitchell. He asked me to answer his phone."

"You guys are in Sunshine?"

"Right. Ever since the day we saw Jimmy drive you out of the Quarter in that red Escalade."

"So, how are you?"

"Almost back to normal. Starting to work out, get back in shape."

"And Jake?"

"He's all well. He took it easy for a couple of weeks but he's blowing and going again, working out, getting stronger."

"Good. So how are you liking small town life?"

"You know, I used to hate coming up here. But I like it okay now. It's kind of grown on me. People have been so nice."

"You and Jake patched things up? Or is that being too nosy?"

She laughed. "It's okay. We're an item again. We've got matching scars. I've got more but his are bigger."

Dunne laughed.

"Well, tell Jake I've got good news for him. I'll call him back later."

"Okay," she said. "And David, thanks for saving his life again."

"Nothing to it, Kitty. Jake's my boy. Gotta take care of him. Talk to you later."

~ * ~

At sunset the same day, Kitty lounged by herself on the couch in the sun parlor at the Banks house. She was channel surfing, but her mind was elsewhere. Jake was excited to talk to Dunne in the afternoon, and had gotten a call late in the day from his supervisor in New Orleans, Peter Romano, telling Jake he was reinstated and asking him to come back to the office as soon as he felt healthy enough to do the work.

Kitty thought about her conversation with Dunne that morning.

She had lied to him. When he asked her how she was, she said she was almost back to normal. She wasn't.

Kitty's periods had been regular as clockwork since she got off the pill after moving to New Orleans from Jackson. But, counting today, she was thirty-three days late.

Kitty had been celibate in New Orleans, concentrating on her career, working long hours. Jake was the only man she had gone out with, and those dates and dinners were platonic.

Her only sexual contact in the last ten months was the night in her apartment, when Brujo's two altar boys beat and raped her.

She made a mental note to call Dr. Clement in the morning.

Jake walked into the sun porch wearing a tee shirt, baggy shorts, and a big smile, listening to his iPod. He paused his music, sat down and put his arm around her. He kissed her cheek.

"I love you," Jake said.

"Me, too," she said.

"Me too what?" Jake said. "You have to say it."

"I love you," she said, looking down at her hands.

"That's much better. Can I ask you something?"

"Sure."

Jake turned on his iPod, stood up and started dancing, twirling and juking, the music taking over.

"Who are you listening to?" Kitty yelled.

"Cee Lo Green. He's a bad boy."

She tugged on his baggy shorts. "What's your question?

He opened his eyes, spread his arms wide and danced. "Don't you think I look better in a red codpiece?"

Kitty laughed, pulled him back to the couch, and planted a big kiss right on his lips. She pushed him back and this time, looked directly into his eyes.

"You look good in anything," she said.

Photography by: T.G. McCary

Author Biography

Michael Henry graduated from Tulane University and University of Virginia Law School. He practiced civil and criminal law, including 16 years as a prosecutor, 12 of those as an elected District Attorney.

Henry currently resides and writes in Natchez, Mississippi.

Photography by: T.G. McCary

Author Biography

William Henry graduated from of the University of Mississippi in 2002. He worked in the entertainment industry and law enforcement before beginning his writing career. He currently lives and writes in Natchez, MS with his father Michael Henry.